SHORTY HARRIS

OR

The Price of Gold

LITERATURE OF THE AMERICAN WEST

William Kittredge, General Editor

Other Books by William W. Bevis

NONFICTION

BORNEO LOG
The Struggle for Sarawak's Forests
(Seattle, 1995)

TEN TOUGH TRIPS
Montana Writers and the West
(Seattle, 1990)

MIND OF WINTER
Wallace Stevens, Meditation, and Literature
(Pittsburgh, 1988)

SHORTY HARRIS

OR

The Price of Gold

A NOVEL

BY

WILLIAM W. BEVIS

UNIVERSITY OF OKLAHOMA PRESS: NORMAN

Although this book is based on a real person and includes extensive research in mining history, it is a work of fiction. Names, characters, places, and incidents are either the product of the author's imagination or are used fictitiously, and any resemblance to actual events, locales, or persons, living or dead, is entirely coincidental.

Library of Congress Cataloging-in-Publication Data

Bevis, William, W., 1941–
    Shorty Harris, or, The price of gold : a novel / by William W.
Bevis.
      p.   cm.
    ISBN 0–8061–3124–1 (alk. paper)
    1. Harris, Shorty, 1857–1934—Fiction. I. Title. II. Title:
Shorty Harris. III. Title: Price of gold.
PS3552.E867S54   1999
813'.54—dc21   98–49761
                                         CIP

Shorty Harris, or The Price of Gold is Volume 3 in the Literature of the American West series.

The paper in this book meets the guidelines for permanence and durability of the Committee on Production Guidelines for Book Longevity of the Council on Library Resources, Inc.∞

1 2 3 4 5 6 7 8 9 10

To my daughters,
Sarah and Karen Bevis

CONTENTS

CONTENTS

ACKNOWLEDGMENTS

Although it is loosely based on the real Shorty Harris, this book is fiction. Very little is known about the real Shorty's early life, and his stories about himself often conflict with each other as well as with known fact. Furthermore, those stories, although told in a wonderful voice, make Shorty sound like Gabby Hayes: a colorful western character. Along with most historians, I have always felt an essential dignity in Shorty's self description—"a single blanket jackass prospector"—which stories of colorful western characters fail to capture. How to get at that part of the man?

I have expanded Shorty's early childhood and background in Providence, and the early history of Panamint City, and I have given a family to this orphan. His later life in the desert stays closer to known facts.

Just about everyone in Missoula helped me with this book, beginning way back when: Bryan Di Salvatore, Steve Krauzer, Bob Hausmann, Earl Ganz, Jocelyn Siler, Juliette Crump, Leonard Robinson, and Patricia Goedicke. And special thanks to Bill Kittridge. I also appreciate a succession of chairs and deans at the University of Montana, from Merrel Clubb through Henry Harrington, Bruce Bigley, and Dean Flightner, who have tolerated and encouraged creative work by an academic professor. The symbiosis of writing and criticism in Missoula, from H. G. Merriam in the twenties to the present, is a fine tradition.

I am indebted to the historians and tale tellers of the Death Valley region, from Bourke Lee, Neill Wilson and Dane Coolidge in the thirties (Coolidge's photograph of Shorty is on the cover) to

Richard Lingenfelter's excellent new history, *Death Valley and the Amargosa*. All of the geology quotations in the gold chapters are from John F. Walker's eloquent *Elementary Geology Applied to Prospecting* (Department of Mines, Victoria B.C., Canada, 1935) and are used by permission. Many thanks for last minute help from Blair Davenport and Ruth Shandor at the National Park library and the bookstore in Death Valley, and to Robert McCracken for his fine performance monologue, "Short Man," based on Shorty's published interviews.

Finally, thanks to Dick and Viv, Lu, Lee, and Gib, for old times in Death Valley and the Panamints.

SHORTY HARRIS

OR

The Price of Gold

Prologue

I know the interview by heart.

"Shorty? . . . (wheeze) . . . Sure. That's what they all come here for . . . (wheeze) . . . The perfect knowledge of Shorty Harris . . ."

The plastic wheels of the old Webcor tape recorder go around, even and slow, the little motor makes a steady hum, the words go by; but in the background I can hear the rise and fall of the wind. The sound of the wind, not the words, takes me back.

He opened the door a crack, looked me in the eye, stuck out a meaty hand and pulled me in. The wind moaned and whistled through the cabin even though the lapped board walls—glowing with that impossibly healthy pine brown color that comes only to wood long dead and weathered—were paneled inside with raw rectangles of plywood dotted by nails and nail holes. The bare wood was greasy with shadows of fingers and palms beside the desk and around the bed, smudges not made, I guessed by the set of his mouth, with the help of a woman. The wind sifted into the battered white enameled medicine cabinet and laid dust on the rock specimens. He picked one out and blew the powder off. Big Red, they called him. He stood with arms folded across his chest, pink fingers wrapped around the rock, red face, red hair crew cut, two hundred and fifty pounds, red arms stretching his T-shirt, slick khaki pants filthy around the pockets, cowboy boots; he stood quietly, wheezing—how could he have asthma there?—and so young, surely under thirty—he would have been no more than ten years old when Shorty died.

"Perfect knowledge." I saw the pellet gun on the desk, and above the sink where the plywood wall was soft and dark and rotten with water stains, I saw the pellet holes. A right-handed man leaning back in the chair, feet on the desk, could draw a level bead across his left breast to the wall. An unchipped porcelain handle and a mirror to keep him honest. So there he sat alone in his two-room cabin that was once the jail, the old cell room crammed with prospecting tools, not fifty yards from the adobe hut where Shorty had lived his last twenty years; there he sat, not yet thirty, one of the five people living in Ballarat in 1949, shooting carefully at his wall above the sink and below the mirror while the wind of Ballarat moaned and whistled and etched his single window finely and evenly with sand so that he could not see out and no one could see in, sand drawn across the glass like a curtain to complete his privacy, at least until the pellets should penetrate the lapped boards and open a wound to the outside through which the wind, in return, would worm and work and finally bring the whole thing down to the dust it had always breathed, a conclusion so obvious and inevitable that it must have been what he desired, though the small caliber of the pellets bespoke a desert patience.

Without a word, glancing over his shoulder he walked to the back of the cell room, raised a fat arm and pointed to a tiny pack saddle on the wall. "Shorty's," he said.

Later, he took me to an older man who as a boy had known Shorty's mother, and who introduced me to Yarborough Johnson in Lathrop Wells, once a friend of Jim Dayton. These were some of my sources—as they say—for the life of Shorty Harris. These, and Shorty's daughter, Abigail, and history, and legend, and myself.

◆ ◆ ◆

4

Bury me beside Jim Dayton in the valley we loved. Above me write, "Here lies Shorty Harris, a single blanket jackass prospector." 1934

That's his grave, at the bottom of Death Valley. Nearby, four or five mesquites grow from the alkaline sand and cracked mud. As you face the stone marker that has replaced the old wooden headboard, the salt flat stretches ahead to the Funeral Range. Two graves, side by side. The other one says, "Jim Dayton. Perished 1898."

Death Valley is popular now, since the reliable automobile, the National Park, the Sunbelt boom, the movie *Zabriski Point*, air conditioning. The valley they loved, however, was not in vogue between Shorty's birth in 1849 and his death in 1934. Standing there in the off-season when the traffic is gone and the salt flat begins to dance with heat and the humming in your head grows louder and just for a moment your mind flashes to the last reading on your gas gauge, you may start to feel the fear. Then the desert grave, bones on bones, bones wedged in the ribs of earth, comes alive.

> It's not what he done. There was lots like him. It's what he loved.
>
> —GEORGE, IN TONOPAH, 1978

You have to stand right there, a little scared and thirsty, to read it: "in the valley we loved."

Desert graves: high up on the east slope of Owens Lake, there used to be a rude cross of wagon boards stuck in the pebbles and sand: "1868." Beside it was a smaller cross of greasewood sticks and wire. Across the Great Basin—the huge, arid bowl that is Nevada—nameless graves and abandoned shacks stick up like dried flowers, fragile and dead. Tommy, the Shoshone, said that the Giant of Silence, half ice, half fire, took three steps on earth—

north pole, Death Valley, south pole—and left for his grave between the stars. Coyote says the whole earth is a green fool rushing into the desert of space.

> We buried him standing up, you know. Well not quite. On a slant, like this. It was too goddamn hot to dig.
>
> —YARBOROUGH JOHNSON

> They never buried him at all. Ask Stump Mallis. He tried to dig him up.
>
> —PETE WEATHERALL

> Great man? I dunno. He sure as hell didn't start that way.
>
> —STUMP MALLIS

"The man could smell gold," Big Red said. A lot of people I met said that, but I knew Shorty. He could not smell gold. He did not even know what gold was, and anyway, when he finally knew—or knew he didn't know—it was gone.

I spent six days with Shorty, his last six days, when I was very young and he was very, very old. The man who loved Death Valley is dead. How he came to that condition—the dead part is easy—is our story, the only story. My story, too. But that comes later.

PART 1

Panamint City, July 4, 1872

All things are full of labor;
man cannot utter it; the eye is not
satisfied with seeing, nor the ear
filled with hearing.

—ECCLESIASTES

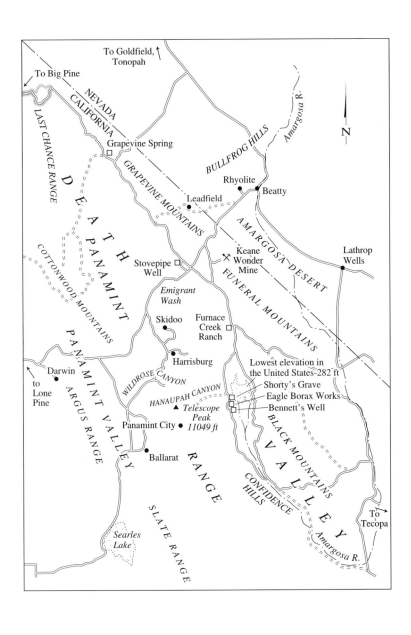

CHAPTER 1

Morning, July 4, 1872

But Shorty needed more. The faint dawn light on May's arm
descended in smooth round curves from her shoulder to her hand
dangling off the edge of the bed. He looked up and out, past the
timbered trestles, the tailings and the slag, past the town, to the
same dawn light on the bare hills descending in the same round
curves from the barren Panamint crest. He needed something
farther than that, too, something like what he had felt when they
were first in love, not the passion itself but the feeling of having
come to the other side, finally, to a place where he could rest.

"If I can just get through this day," he thought. What he did not
know was that this would be his last day in Panamint City. In
eighteen hours he would be gone.

"Shorty?" May turned over. "What's wrong?"

"Nothing new." He looked out the window. "Hicks wants
money." It was not exactly a lie.

"A lot of money?"

"Yes."

May settled back down in the bed and watched him closely.

"I'll make it," Shorty said.

She laughed. "June said you give willpower a bad name."

"Your sister has a tongue." June. June. He pulled on his boots
and got up, bent by unseen weight. One big strike could turn

things around. It really could. He had come to hate the whole town
for the thought.

May sighed and spoke gently. "This is the day your father died,
isn't it?"

He looked at her. "Tomorrow," he said. "July 5. And he didn't
die. He killed himself." Then Shorty loosened, walked over,
touched her hair, kissed her on the top of the head and held her
ears in his hands. "I don't know," he said quietly. "Maybe we
should go back East."

"You've had all those advantages, Shorty. I can't talk books.
What would I do there? What would you do? At least you can do
whatever you want here."

Where is here, he thought, looking out the window at the ore
dumps and mineshafts. And doing what? Wanting what? He let go
of her ears. She was right, of course. She hadn't had his advantages,
and the East could be rough on an uneducated half-breed, and she
wasn't smart like her sister, and none of that was her fault. He had
chosen.

"I know you miss those things, Shorty. The Ladies Auxiliary is
planning to bring the Virginia City Philharmonic, if they have one."

He walked out. It hadn't been worth it for two years. He peeked
through the door into Abigail's room. The colorless dawn glow
touched the mirror and the brass bed rails. Abigail cried. Shorty
crept in and picked her up in the blanket. She put her head on his
shoulder and went back to sleep. He pulled back the quilt, laid her
down, and drew the covers up.

Downstairs he lit the kerosene lamp and made a fire in the kitchen
range. Then he opened the door to the pantry and the light fell on
his father's saddlebags, on the leather pocket where his father had
kept his diary, the diary Shorty had taken out every night for the
past two weeks to read over and over again the opening page:

"What," said he, "makes the difference between man and all the
rest of the animal creation? Every beast that strays beside me

has the same corporal necessities with myself; he is hungry and crops the grass, he is thirsty and drinks the stream, his thirst and hunger are appeased, he is satisfied and sleeps; he rises again and is hungry, he is again fed and is at rest. I am hungry and thirsty like him but when thirst and hunger cease I am not at rest; I am, like him, pained with want, but am not, like him, satisfied with fullness. The intermediate hours are tedious and gloomy. . . . Man has surely some latent sense for which this place affords no gratification, or he has some desires distinct from sense which must be satisfied before he can be happy."

—JOHNSON, "RASSELAS"

The quotation was copied onto the first page in his father's tiny, neat quill script. The rest of the diary was blank, except for a heading every two or three pages in his father's hand—"Death Valley," "Primary Gold," "Secondary Gold" and more—as if he had planned formal essays on each subject and then was waiting until he knew more, or less. At the end of the diary was a page of Greek and Latin vocabulary. His father had the largest library in Panamint City, probably in Nevada territory—over four hundred books—but it had not helped. Shorty had thumbed through the diary only once, right after his father's death, and those blank pages had filled him with horror; they seemed a vacuum that had claimed his father and could suck him in too. He had looked up quickly only to face Emerson—"Self Reliance" and "Fate"— staring from the shelf.

And now, nine years after his father's death, he had been opening the diary again, every day. What did he expect to find? Hicks and his scams were sucking him down the more he struggled to break free, and now this money . . . His marriage was a rising whine in his ears. And why was he turning to his father, dead and unmourned, the least likely source of comfort on earth? His mother, Catherine, was still living in Panamint City, but he hardly spoke to her. Each consultation of his father's diary only angered him more. And he found himself wondering, for the first time, with a sympathetic curiosity, just what his father had been thinking about, the weeks before he died. About *his* wife and partners, his children . . . *his* life in this desert canyon . . .

Back in Providence, his father and Shorty had once argued over a passage in the *Iliad*, when Achilles is angry at Agamemnon and is about to draw his sword. Suddenly Athena appears, visible only to Achilles, and says she has come to stop his anger, "ai ke pithai": if you will obey, or be persuaded, or in the hope that you might calm down. No one, from Liddell and Scott to his father, seemed to know what the phrase meant, and so no one could resolve in this crisis the relation of man to God, that is, how Athena advises us to get a grip on ourselves. Shorty had favored Pope's translation:

Let great Achilles, to the gods resigned,
To reason yield the empire o'er his mind.

His father favored Chapman: "if thy soule will use her sovereigntie in fit reflection." Shorty now remembered the argument with bitterness. Was that what his father was engaged in, "fit reflection," the moment before he blew himself up? Was the fuse lit by sovereignty of soul? The translation was lost. Only the empty diary remained.

There was no need to take the diary out this morning; Shorty knew the first page by heart. But the other pages, he thought, the blank ones . . . How would he know them? And he could smell her. June. His wife's sister. His best friend's wife. That didn't help. He could smell her skin, he could smell if she had been in the room two hours before. He shut the door hard.

At dawn Frank Shorty Harris walked to work through the empty streets of Panamint City. Dust swirled behind his baggy trousers and his boots; short legged and hard armed, he left toe prints in the dirt and hobnail heel marks on the boards. His hands were jammed deep in his trouser pockets; his loose jacket flapped behind. He leaned forward against the air as against a post or a wall or a room; when he paused for a moment he stood his ground, occupying his own body with an air of uneasy triumph, tiny and taut and vigilant as Napoleon in Russia, a man who must push in all directions or be crushed.

But on a deserted street corner in Panamint City, no adversary could be seen. He strode to the assay office and turned the key in the black padlock. As he pushed the heavy door, the iron hinges squealed and groaned in the still air. Inside he raised the shades behind the scales and hung his jacket on a peg below the sign: "A just balance is His delight." He pushed his white sleeves up and secured them with garters as he read an assistant's notes for the day: sample from the prospect near Frenchman's Ridge to be divided and assayed; low grade; probably crucible assay but check for arsenic and sulphides; Mr. Harris would please confirm.

Out back he built a small fire of kindling and charcoal under the muffle furnace, then turned to the sample: a hundred pounds of dirt from the Panamint Range in a dirty burlap sack bearing faint red circles. Shorty knew the design. Pride Flour, from Los Angeles, but the letters had faded. It wasn't the first time this sack had been filled with ore, had bulged on either side of a mule's back, had squatted outside an assay office. Shorty shook his head. Had the sack ever held paydirt, five dollars to the ton? Twenty-five cents to the sack? He turned the tag over: "Buckeye Mine Sample One."

He'd heard about it. Hicks had given Mann and Hern an advance, two cousins from Ohio who had come out the year before. Hern had gone back when word reached him that his wife had died of pneumonia. Back in Ohio he had stashed his six sons with their aunt and returned to the Panamints. The two didn't drink much, lived now and then in a tent down canyon but spent most of their time on a claim near Frenchman's Crest. One night in the Nugget they had told how their savings had dried up in a year. Thirteen children between them. They were farmers whose land had been overmortgaged during the drought in 1870. They needed the money.

Shorty shook his head again as he carried the sack to the weighing room and emptied it into the hand crusher. He picked through the decomposed slate, conglomerate, dust, pebbles, sand. Hicks had said there were tiny filigrees in the slate; it might average out all right. He poured the crushed sample onto a clean tarpaulin and quartered it three times, saving opposite quarters each time and crushing each remnant again. He screened the ten-pound remnant, weighed a ten-gram sample to a tolerance of five milligrams, and recorded it. He stared at the ore. Worthless. He could tell when he opened the sack. He could probably have known from one look at the digs.

He closed the windows and shut the blinds behind the scales to keep direct sunlight off the balance. He mixed the flux—five parts sodium bicarbonate, four parts potassium carbonate, two parts borax, one part flour, and eight parts litharge. He added a nail to balance sulfides, combined the flux with the ten-gram charge in a crucible, and stoked the furnace.

As he cleaned up the quartering room and arranged the cupels he imagined the two men: farmer's overalls, new boots, blue shirts, wide black hats; two men swinging picks at a crumbling ledge, farmers now and then looking to the cloudless sky as they wiped their faces and necks with bandannas, turning back with a shock not to the team and harness and rich black loam but a pick in the hand where a plow should be.

"What the hell do they think they're doing?" He brought the crucible out with tongs and set it to cool. Big slow farmers hanging on his word. Every year he'd seen them coming, their cow eyes full of gold. He separated the gold button, what there was of it, from the gross slag and placed it in the cupel, back in the furnace. He watched the tiny button in the cup. The surface film had gone and the button glowed. He could smell the lead oxide. Feathers of litharge crystals gathered on the sides of the red-hot cupel. The litharge flux was passing off, into the bone ash cupel and the air; the button dwindled, smaller and smaller. Jesus, would there be anything left? Even he knew that farming was better than this. As the thought clarified he drew back his foot to kick the scales. But the transformation had begun. The gold button shrank in the red-hot cupel. Shorty leaned forward, shielding his eyes. Rainbow colors began to play over the surface as the litharge formed the thinnest film over the gold. The button seemed to be spinning—his heart beat faster and faster; he leaned closer; the tiny bead spun, suddenly brightened, and freed of lead glowed brilliantly for just an instant—flared—flashed—then a dull film slowly closed across the surface, and the moment was gone. The cupellation was complete. He leaned back and sighed. His face was flushed, his eyebrows were singed. He lit a cigarette, smiled, and pushed the cupel farther back to heat up for a few minutes and guarantee the purge of dross.

When it was cool he stared at the tiny bead in disgust. With quick, jerky movements he parted the gold and silver, poured off the nitric acid, annealed the gold bead over a low flame, and watched the natural gold color emerge. He leveled the pans on the button balance, picked up the tiny yellow bead with tweezers, and placed it in a pan. For this they had left Ohio bottom land. He weighed the bead at .13 milligrams, marked the figures on a pad, and began the arithmetic. Total: $1.39 per ton. He placed the button in a tube, corked and labeled it, and attached it to the ten-pound sample charge sack. Then he took a large card and recorded the relevant details. He wrote across the card in red crayon, "Nulla Bona," tied it to the sack and slid it to the end of the shelf. On second thought he reached up, turned the tag over, and wrote on the back: "The world owes me a living." With one swipe he could wipe out the rack of test tubes. He could feel the brittle glass, hear the crash, see the flying fragments catch the light like swallows, in the evening, on the wing. That's how June would say it.

He went outside and stood blinking at the yellow light. The dawn had come—flared, flashed—and gone. The wind was moaning on the ridge. He stood near the furnace and lit another cigarette. He looked up at the mountains. Small dark holes, rickety timbers, fantastic lacework trestles with tiny ore carts, dizzying switchbacks, men with lanterns, ropes, tools, dynamite. "A dream come true." He could see every detail of his house in the afternoon, complete with himself facing the other way. An old man was leaving town with nothing but a pick, a pan, a blanket, and a jackass. Shorty snorted, threw away half a cigarette, and stomped inside. There had to be more.

After the assay of the Buckeye sample the boiler was ready. He filled the hopper with ore, started the steam crusher, made himself coffee, and sat, feet on the desk, blinds drawn. He spread the *Panamint News* across his knees:

Truth and the marvellous go hand in hand when America finds a good gold gulch.

The motto was followed by T. S. Smith's original statement of purpose: "To furnish the people of Panamint with the latest news; to give to the 'outside world' accurate information regarding the mines; and to make money." The last wasn't true, Smith claimed, but if he didn't say it no one would trust him. Shorty reached for his coffee. The east wall by the furnace, and the south wall where the dark boards took the sun, were stoking up. He pulled the blinds tighter. He sat back and scanned the front page:

July Fourth. Contestants and nominations for the July Fourth Goddess of Liberty contest may still be registered at the mayor's office. The Goddess of Liberty will ride in la grand pageant de burro with three little ladies in waiting on a float.

We know the hungry and bereaved will have their memory strings plucked when they recognize under the float their old friend the butcher's cart, first vehicle to reach Panamint City and which served us many years as a hearse.

16

The parade will also include trained goats and educated fleas from Resting Spring.

Bishop Randall. We were amused neither by the sparse turnout for Bishop Randall's sermon in the Lotus Dance Hall last night, nor by the behavior of those present. Panamint City was lucky to be graced by the visit of the Episcopal Bishop of Pittsburgh, but as he observed, "unbelief prevails among the multitudes." Rudeness, too, we might add.

Bishop Randall. The lecture committee had paid an old man and a cracked soprano two hundred dollars to declare that though All is Vanity yet His Yoke is Easy and His Burden is Light. Just like that. Shorty had tried to walk out; May had fixed him with a glance. They ought to string him up, he thought: Rustling Religion, Poaching Peace.

About him in the office the light grew strong even though the blinds were shut, the raw raised grain of wood came forth, the splinters shone silver and the walls pushed waves of heat across the room. He pulled his tie off and tossed it on the desk as his eye wandered down to the bottom of the page:

Thank you. Ted and Henrietta Hopefield wish to thank the Panamint City Volunteer Fire Brigade, Lieutenant Virgil, friends, and neighbors, for their efficient help in containing the fire, and removing the remains of Mr. Russell. It is in times like these that friendship is precious. Again, Thanks.

Hopefield. She was head of the Lecture Committee. "A just balance . . ." My mind is not right, he thought.

The rest of the page was filled with articles on "The Biggest Mirror in the World," the mirror for Dexter's bar arriving that day. The articles were all gathered under the headline "A Day for Reflection": when it would arrive (6 P.M. that day), who made it, shipped it, the frame, cost, how it was almost dropped at Le Havre, etc. He turned to the second page and read the biweekly economic summary: the Wonder, Hemlock, and Wyoming mines were yielding $2,500 per ton; eight tons per day of silver ore was going to Senator Jones and Senator Stewart's smelter, two tons of copper ore per day was being freighted out of Surprise Canyon for the long trip to Britain to be smelted. Gold production was one ton per day. Stocks other than gold had risen another 10 percent.

Below the economic news was a small feature on Virginia City's Belcher Mine: its stock had risen from $1.50 a share in late 1870 to $1,525 a share that week of 1872, and "A gentleman visitor from the East, viewing the activity in the vast main shaft, wrote to his home papers: 'A wondrous battle raged, in which the combatants were man and earth.'"

Shorty laughed a bitter laugh. "Man and earth." They have no idea, he thought. Try man against man. Try one man against himself.

The crusher rattled and fell silent. He threw the paper on the floor, set the dirty cup aside and walked to the crushing room. The red "Nulla Bona" crayoned on the dangling Buckeye tag caught his eye. No need to rub it in. He gently tucked the tag under the sack.

At noon Hicks came through the door and shut it behind him. Shorty didn't even look up. He had seen it all, seen the pimply-faced runaway sixteen-year-old boy from West Virginia stagger into town, crawl up a hill and by sheer luck and sudden need squat on the richest vein in Surprise Canyon. Hicks had picked up hundreds of thousands in cash and investments, stocks, buildings, franchises, women, burros, more friends and even more enemies than he could meet in a lifetime—and once he had convinced himself that he was rich it all seemed unreal, so he pinched himself with culture: traded his mule for a horse, got a cane, a new accent, and finally a woman who could read. It worked. He felt so real that he entered politics. First and second generation of himself within ten years: Panamint's mayor. Then came the second wave of strikes that created Panamint City. Hicks was running with the big boys.

"Frank, I need the twelve hundred dollars," Hicks said.

"I haven't got it." Shorty folded the paper and got up from the desk.

"You have properties all over town, Frank, and you owe me three times that much."

"So does everyone else, Brandon. Most of those properties are in May and Abigail's names. The one above the Stewart mine assayed at nothing yesterday. You know that and so does everyone in town."

"But they don't know that in Argus. There's a friend of Gibbons coming in with the mirror this afternoon. I told him the Stewart claim was worth twenty-five hundred dollars."

"The assay report—"

"You do a lot of assays. You could forget a few."

"You're rich, Brandon. Borrow."

"A little cash problem, Shorty. Let's just say I'm twelve hundred short of sixteen thousand cash and somebody is impatient and I don't want the bank to know and the rest is none of your business. You owe me, and you're about the only one I can trust."

"Lucky me. I can't raise it."

"What about Dayton's claim? Don't you have a sample waiting?"

"Yes."

"I hear that ground's good. Tell you what: give it a low report, I'll take it off your hands and turn it over for five or eight hundred. Then I'll let you off the hook."

"I don't fake assay reports, Brandon. You know that."

"You'd be doing your friend Dayton a favor. You know damn well the claim's marginal and he'll bust his butt working it anyway. I'll give him one hundred cash and save him time."

"No."

"Frank, you're not so squeaky clean. I could tell stories."

"They'd all include you, Brandon."

"Look, Frank. Say your formula was doubtful on your Stewart assay. Say maybe you ought to do it over. Then it hasn't really been assayed yet—not properly. That's all you have to do, not really be sure. Not till tomorrow. This Jud Foster will be in from Argus at four. Sell to him. He's loaded. Twenty-five hundred bucks."

"He can't be that stupid."

"I've made sure he is, Frank. He's had lots of inside tips. He's bringing cash. It's that or Dayton's assay report."

"Either one is my decision."

Hicks moved to put a hand on Shorty's shoulder. Shorty stepped back.

"Frank, you're in an excellent position in this town. People respect you, you do a good job, and you're sure as hell the only one here who speaks Greek."

"Reads Greek."

"You'll be mayor, if I say so. Then you won't have to worry about your little girl. Be smart, Frank. Get me the cash today."

Hicks reached out to the doorknob, then turned.

"Frank, if you don't want to be rich, why the hell did you come here?"

"My father brought me, Brandon."

"Jesus, your father." Hicks looked down. "I'd forgotten that." He straightened and started out. "I'll meet you at the Nugget." He poked his head back in. "And after lunch I'd like you to meet the bishop."

Shorty sat down at the desk, then dropped his pen and shoved his chair back. As he ran his fingers through his thick dark hair he remembered one of his mother's friends saying that he looked more like his father every day. Hicks and money weren't the real problem, he knew that. It was something far away. He jerked his hat and coat off the hook and stood by the door, one hand on the knob, as if listening.

◆ ◆ ◆

Many people resented his sharp wit and dull fat baby face puffy in the lips and underneath the eyes, but T. S. Smith wrote the

Panamint News every day and there was nothing else to read. That noon he held court as usual at the corner table of the Nugget: black hair slicked down, pink silk vest with mother-of-pearl buttons, gold watch chain. At night he taught ballroom dance. In his lapel he wore a tin button: "Panamint City, Queen of the Basin."

That particular Fourth of July the queen was humming. On that Fourth of July, Smith had said in yesterday's editorial, "Panamint City will make the coronation celebration of Louis XIV look like Thursday Night Mah-Jong at B'nai B'rith. We can match the Sun King point for point in cash and wit and beat him flat in taste."

Men had set out days before from the Slate and Argus ranges, Searles Lake, the Confidence Hills, and the Grapevines, converging on the Panamints. They filed down every trail from above and up the canyon from the valley. By noon, when the stores and mines had closed, the streets from Chinatown to the mayor's mansion were jammed with milling crowds.

Everyone knew the story. Somebody from Virginia City had been drunk at Dexter's, bragging about how classy they were up there in Virginia City and Gold Hill, the hotels and appointments and such, and the Panamint City boys had begun to match him word for word. It wasn't long before he said that Virginia City had the biggest something or other—Shorty had heard mine, hotel, live bear, organ, rock crusher, whorehouse, or whore—anyway, the biggest. And James Tracy replied, cool as you please, "We got the biggest mirror in the world." "Where?" said the Virginia City man. "It's being made for us in Paris," said James. He took a long drink. "How big?" said Virginia City. "Thirty-two by twelve." They all drank to that. "One piece." Another toast. "In a silver frame."

The next day someone told James what he'd said. But luck was with him; it was July 2, a good time for civic projects. On the evening of July 4, 1870, Panamint City dispatched a messenger to Paris with fifty thousand in cash, one hundred thousand in stock certificates and a draft on the Temple and Workmen Bank in Los Angeles for one million. No sense being caught short.

The honesty of the messenger was an issue. They selected a madam known as Pearly Gates, a woman widely known and respected who had a lot to gain, in publicity and reputation, by honoring the bargain. She was promised fifty thousand dollars, deposited in Los Angeles, to be collected on her successful return. She left with cash, stocks, the draft, and very few clothes. "I'll pick up duds in Paris," she told the girls, who were green with envy.

Nothing was heard for almost two years. Then in April Dexter had received a telegram: HOLD ON I'M COMING STOP PEARL. A letter had followed; she was engaging wagons and would arrive in two months, in time for the Fourth. When a San Francisco newspaper with photographs arrived, it was obvious that Paris had done its stuff: the mirror was flashy and Pearl, never drab, was stunning. Panamint City shares rose 25 percent. If her Parisienne hairdresser had been as smart with paper as he was with scissors he could have made a killing in the stocks. Once the mirror had crossed the Sierra, couriers arrived with news every day. They were feted with French champagne and slipped pinches of Nevada gold dust until generally they found storytelling worth their while. Stories of the mirror's passage through Virginia City were especially rewarded; it seemed to take a long time going through.

For the last two days the two-team, twenty-four-horse caravan had been in sight from the hills above the canyon: first descending the Slate Range, then crossing the ten-mile floor of Panamint Valley. That morning, July 4, the caravan had started up the wash of Surprise Canyon. It would take all day to ascend the canyon and reach Dexter's, where the front wall had been knocked out and a new bulletproof wall built behind the bar. The town had been whetting its thirst for some time. Fast freight wagons loaded with whiskey had been passing the mirror in the Owens Valley, their glinting bottles whizzing like satellites past the greatest glass of all. The story yesterday was that three men looking at it from the Wildrose Canyon Cliffs at sunrise were struck blind. But it was crated.

By noon every saloon was jammed and the whiskey crates, stacked to the rafters, were disappearing like desert rain. That afternoon, drilling contests and burro races, and that night, the hanging and unveiling of the mirror at Dexter's Hotel and Saloon on Main Street. The two hundred tickets to Dexter's, originally ten dollars apiece, were going for fifty at noon. The following day was declared a holiday, and some said the next day too, and the one after that.

When Shorty arrived for lunch, a crowd surrounded the corner table where Hicks had just ordered another round for anyone who could hear or hold out a glass.

"C'mon over, Shorty." Lane made space for him on the bench. Shorty nodded to the men and pushed through to the corner table.

"You look like hell," said Lane.

"I'm hungry," said Shorty.

"For what? You look like hell."

Shorty felt his throat tighten, and looked away.

"Let's hear the editorial!" said someone behind Lane. Shouts of encouragement. The slosh of beer into glasses. T. S. Smith rose from his chair, spread the paper on the table, and leaned forward. The room grew still, a hundred dusty men in white shirts and open jackets, glasses in their hands, ears cocked. Shorty looked out the window, so Lane could not see the tears.

"Panamint City has come of age," Smith began.

"Hear, Hear!"

"Shhh."

"Can you hear me in the back?"

"Go on, go on."

"Panamint City has come of age. With the arrival of the greatest mirror in the world, during this our tenth year of existence, we should all pause and hold up an even greater mirror to our city." T.S. coughed and smirked; Lane shook his head.

"Our city is mature and prosperous. Our mines are still producing at well over two thousand dollars per ton. Our population of five thousand now enjoys hundreds of brick and wooden business establishments where all the necessities of life . . ."

"Necessities of life," thought Shorty. Necessities. "He is hungry and crops the grass. He is thirsty and drinks the stream." He looked out the window at the bare brown hills above town. Lane was watching him.

". . . As an index of our prosperity, I offer a few facts from our latest license tax census: we now have five dry goods stores, sixteen restaurants, five beer halls, forty-eight gambling houses, and sixty saloons." T.S. was interrupted by murmurs of "hear hear" and "I'll drink to that."

"Dance halls and homes for fallen women," he continued, "are not covered in the census because, as you know, they are not legal and contribute to the city's revenue only through fines, when they can be found. But a friend of ours suggests that there may be about twelve of the former and twenty-seven of the latter."

"Twenty-eight"—he was interrupted—"I count twenty-nine." Laughter.

"Now this is a prosperous city," he looked about the room for quiet. "Yet some would argue that this great city has not yet matured."

The hills above town were brown and bare and beautiful.

"They point out that we have as yet no town hall, no jail, no library, no post office, no school, no church, no theater, no bank, no Wells Fargo shipments because of the road agents at the nether end of Surprise Canyon, and our mail is still very erratic, as every reader knows."

The hills were pure and brown and bare and beautiful. Paydirt. Shorty smiled as if in pain. The town was built on paydirt sure enough, but no one knew.

"And it would be nice if we could do a little clean-up of the trash and offal in the alleys, and bury some of the waste even if we can't afford a sewerage system, and we could shoot a few thousand dogs, and perhaps set aside two square feet in the middle of town for a mesquite bush and call it a park, for as a lady friend of ours recently arrived and fined said, 'A fresh blade of grass would bring you down on your knees to worship.'

"Now we think this is a great city, and we have some specific recommendations for the next decade . . ."

The piece was loudly cheered before the crowd began shouting amendments: Don't build a church; they'll close down everything else and monopolize Sunday—"it happened in Austin"—"I don't mind no man's religion long as it don't mind me." Don't build a jail; the government will outlaw the mining camp sentences: banished, flogged, or killed—"git, git beat, or git hung"—"don't need no jail for that."

"I believe we're growing up." A man struck the table, loud and insistent. Shorty started from his revery. "Institutions—legal institutions—will stabilize us." Men at the table agreed, others in back hooted. Hicks tapped his cane on the floor in approval. Someone in back shouted, "Giving Hicks more government is like feeding shit to a dog with worms." Hicks rose red-faced and the room grew quiet.

Shorty looked at the hills and then looked straight at Lane, and Lane looked back as if to say, "If it's not your hand, fold."

A man burst through the doors. "Mirror's halfway up the canyon," he shouted into the room, then saw the quiet crowd facing Hicks at the corner table. "What the hell's going on here?"

"Po-litical discussion," said someone on the fringe.

"Well, it's coming," said another.

"I'll drink to that." The meeting disbanded.

When he had finished his lunch Shorty walked out onto the porch and sat on a bench. He looked down Main Street.

"I'm twenty-three," he said out loud. The dust, the heat, the fresh dung from a twenty-mule freighting team, the unpainted boardwalk, the signs thicker than needles on a pine, the jammed streets, the noise, music, firecrackers all blended into a familiar background as he hung his hat on his knee and leaned back against the wall. The whole town seemed as useless as his father's death. Or his father's life. Or his own.

Lane and T.S. came out and stood on the porch smoking. No one was near. Shorty's throat was dry. He wanted to talk to Lane, and Lane knew it. Shorty tried to speak the words he had already chosen and revised in his head, but they stuck. He could ask little enough of anyone; how was he supposed to ask this of Lane? So the men stood silent, and Shorty could easily imagine that if he should ask Lane how you know if it's your hand, Lane would reply, "That's the secret of a good gambler." You see, Shorty thought to himself, he can't help.

"Lane, have you heard from my mother?" Shorty gazed down the street.

"No, but I'll bet your kid brother's having a helluva time in L.A."

"I hope he stays there. I hate losing in chess."

Lane laughed. "So how are you, Shorty?"

Lane was a professional gambler who looked the part, and rumors stuck to him like burrs: he was a lawyer, a murderer, a pianist back east, a discredited son of an earl. But he had long before told Shorty his true story. He was born in New Orleans, son of a drunkard riverboat engineer and his Cherokee wife. He was fourteen, an odd job boy, when his mother was raped, tarred, and hung for stabbing a Frenchman. The next day he helped his father bury her, bought a ruffled shirt and headed west through Texas, supporting himself with poker. A good poker player, but not good enough, he wound up in Panamint City, established a clean reputation as the house gambler in Murphy's Nugget Saloon, and gradually became closer and closer to Shorty's mother, Catherine, who after Shorty's father's death lived in a spacious apartment over the Nugget. So Lane knew about Shorty the things no one else knew, the bay window of the three-story house in Providence where Shorty had sat to read, his violin lessons and performances, the sudden flight of the family to the West when Shorty was ten and already known as a prodigy in music and school.

Lane, T. S. Smith (with a law degree from Fordham), and the younger Shorty were always reading, talking, meeting visitors, catching news of the outside world. Just a few weeks before, Shorty had found notice of the premiere of *Aida* on December 4, 1871, at Cairo, to celebrate the opening of the Suez Canal, and with his knowledge of Verdi, Shorty had expanded the article for the *Panamint News*. For years the three men had been drawn together, two uncles for the fatherless son.

The two older men remained silent for several minutes, Smith surveying the street, Lane leaning against the post with his coat held back by the hand on his hip. Shorty slouched against the wall, his hat on his knee.

"Shorty," Lane said, "I could help with five hundred or so. Until your mother and Alex get back."

Shorty was silent.

T.S. moved closer and spoke quietly. "I hear a lot in my position, Shorty. Hicks may be close to overplaying his hand, and the whole house of cards—smelter scams, kickbacks, fraud—could come down. Including those who are too close to him."

"Thanks, T.S." Shorty sighed. "You should watch out. This is a rotten camp."

"This is a promising city," said T.S., laughing.

"It's rotten."

"They're all alike, Shorty. This is my fifth camp. You're the only person I've ever known who actually grew up in one."

"I want out."

T.S. put on his jacket. "To more of the same? I've got to go to the office. Just be careful."

"You too."

Lane and Shorty watched the silk suit step over the dung.

"You know you could go to San Francisco, start over." Lane looked up at the sky. "Catherine and I could help."

"Thanks."

"Shorty, don't lose your pride."

But something about the way Lane spoke, or the way he crushed his cigar and started down the steps, something made Shorty certain the ax had not yet struck, and sure enough Lane said without looking back, "Your daddy would never forgive me."

Shorty sat slumped against the wall. Lane passed out of sight in the crowd down the street. Why had everything come to this? Sometimes he saw spots that seemed nothing more than the pressure of his mind against his eyeballs. He closed his eyes and slipped into a reverie. He was Christopher Columbus being rowed toward a green island; an armored Spanish soldier angrily routing natives from a mud village said to be made of gold; a religious leader pointing to the site of a future city in Connecticut; he was an old man with a hammer in one hand and a chunk of rock in the other, rising in wonder and surprise; he dreamed of a quartz crystal: hard, cold, precise; angled where it should be angled, smooth where it should be smooth; natural and perfect. He heard a voice say, "Stone."

It was at this moment that Hicks shook him awake. "Shorty, I'd like you to meet the bishop of Pittsburgh."

Shorty looked up and blinked. There was a sweating Hicks and a gaunt man with cold blue eyes. ("Was that really the bishop of Pittsburgh?" Shorty had asked Lane in the Nugget. "That old goat?" Lane had said, "Since I can remember he's been running around the Basin converting widows and spreading the word like thighs.")

"I told the bishop," Hicks was saying, "that you'd be one to appreciate his sermon." Shorty stared. Then he heard himself say, "I didn't like it."

"Excuse me?" The bishop shifted his feet.

"You mean it was not your favorite text?" Hicks said with an awkward smile.

"No, that isn't what I mean," said Shorty. "I mean Ecclesiastes is the best goddamn book in the Bible except for the last six verses which are lies."

"Look Harris—"

"No, it's all right, please," the old man said. He motioned Hicks away and leaned close to Shorty's ear.

"Listen you smart-ass little son of a bitch," the intense whisper burned into his ear, "you may be right about me but you're still gonna wake up one day saying nothing but Fear the Lord, if y'ain't been struck stone dumb."

The man straightened up. The fire faded from his eyes.

"Stone dumb," thought Shorty, looking down. "Now that's possible."

"Line up, line up!" It was Murphy, pushing people into place. In the street a man was setting a black box on a tripod and shooing the crowd away.

"Hicks, Bishop, here. Shorty, you stay seated."

People were dragged in and placed. Movement, straightening.

"Hold still!"

Flash. There he is in the Briggs photograph, taken after lunch on that amazing Fourth of July, 1872, and now resting in the archives of the University of New Mexico. Shorty is seated on the bench, hat in hand, in the upper left, behind the posed, lounging group: "The Boys with the Bishop of Pittsburgh in Front of the Nugget Awaiting the Arrival of the Great Mirror." Shiny black eyes, dark hair, thick strong wrists and stubby fingers, five foot four. He sits straight, rigid, dignified, as if he shall not be moved. But they always sit like that in the old photographs—like a tree that's planted by the water or a father or a Bible illustration— reinforcing one's sense of loss.

A photograph. Tinted, browned, with the fine resolution of the old eight-by-ten plates. It's very like a memory. One has no right to bring it to life—but that too is an illusion: the belief that the past has died.

CHAPTER 2

Afternoon

"Here it comes." The walls of Surprise Canyon are barely two wagons apart and rise perpendicular for three hundred feet. People flattened against the stone as the first horses appeared, their mouths dripping foam, their chests straining against the harness. Chains clanked, wood groaned and squeaked. Everyone shouted and waved coats, bottles, bandannas. Abigail, sitting on Shorty's shoulders, let go of his thumbs and pulled his hair in wild delight. Two more horses, eyes rolling; more and more of the long gray beam between them kept coming into view. Another pair, another pair. May and Shorty backed up against the wall.

"Here it comes! Get back."

The first team of twelve horses had rounded the corner. The chains pulled taut. Another beam appeared, and the second team of horses. The lead horse reached Shorty and Abigail; she leaned over his head, reached out, touched the lathered flank, shrieked and sniffed the sweet, wet odor on her fingers. The leather groaned, the sand crunched, the chains jingled, and above the din could be heard the long hollow breath of each horse as he struggled wild-eyed by.

"There it is! The mirror!" People shouted. Firecrackers echoed, deafening all in the canyon. The horses didn't blink.

The front of a large freight wagon came into view. A teamster stood with legs apart holding the reins in one hand and waving his hat. On the seat beside him was Pearly Gates in scarlet taffeta dark with sweat and spilled beer. Beside her was a smiling, waving Brandon Hicks. Then it came. The giant crate had been partly torn off, and in the face of the mirror, tilted back on edge, they could watch unknown canyon walls around the bend jerk by in the opposite direction. As it drew abreast the mirror almost filled the canyon with its silver-framed dancing reflection of the stone above their heads. Hats went high in the air, children clung like burrs to the hubs and gray side boards.

The Volunteer Fire Department brass band struck up a tune. The music, shouting, pushing, and screaming swirled upcanyon in the wagon's wake. Shorty ran alongside the wagon, Abigail bouncing on his shoulders, and shouted up to Hicks, "The buyer from Argus?" Hicks yelled back, "Meet me at your office in an hour."

When the crowd reached town Shorty, Abigail, and May walked home by back streets.

"I've got to go to the office. We'll have time to give Abigail a nap, eat, and go to Dexter's for the hanging," he said.

"She'll need the nap. Jim Dayton had to go to Big Pine yesterday with ore samples. He asked if we'd take June to the party tonight. Shorty, what's happening with Hicks?"

"Nothing."

She studied him. "I hope I can get someone to stay with Abigail."

"You mean you haven't arranged that yet?"

"It doesn't matter. I'm tired and not—"

"Tired! And miss the mirror party?"

"Well, we'll see."

"How in the world do you expect to find someone now, for tonight?"

May shrugged. They lapsed into silence. The air was yellow with dust.

Hicks was waiting outside the assay office.

"He's dead," he said as Shorty walked up.

"Who?"

"Killed. Foster was killed yesterday in Argus."

"So what the hell am I supposed to do?"

"Sell something else. I don't care. But I need the full twelve hundred, and I need it by tomorrow noon." Hicks turned away.

Shorty walked home wondering why he felt he was in a dream. The money really was a problem now; Hicks could put his family out in the street. Yet he couldn't take it seriously.

Inside, he took Abigail up to her room for a nap. She sat up on the bed and he sat in the rocker and looked at the shelves of sheet music he had collected for twenty years.

"What will it be today, Abby?"

"Nobeese, Daddy, nobeese."

He smiled. "We don't need music for that, do we?" And the two began to sing, together, the soprano lead from the Mozart Lorettine Litany, "Sancta Maria, ora pro nobis," and then he took the tenor entrance, and they skipped the chorus and went to the final duet, she singing the soprano and he alto. All of her life my mother would know those parts by heart.

Then, as every day, she sat quietly while he sang the lullaby "Greensleeves." He closed his eyes while he sang, and when he had finished he was astonished to find Abigail sitting bolt upright in bed, staring at the opposite wall, or off into space beyond the wall, as if in a trance. She sat silent for perhaps a minute. She didn't move or blink. He remembered sitting hour by hour in the sunshine of the bay window on the stair landing, in Providence before they had left, not thinking or reading or playing the violin.

"Abigail," he said very softly, "what are you looking at?" She neither answered nor turned.

"Abigail, what are you doing?"

Without breaking her stare she replied, "I'm looking out of my face."

Tears welled up in Shorty. It was almost more than he could stand. Without disturbing her or trying to put her to sleep, he left the room, closing the door softly. She was still staring at the wall.

After dinner Shorty walked quickly to the Daytons', head down. Above, the sunset flared. As he knocked on June's door he was nervous. He had not asked for this arrangement. It had never been easy. "I wonder when someone's gonna whack that hive," Lane had said years before. She was trouble, no question: long and lean like a pony, the opposite of twin May. They were part Kiowa, born before and after midnight of the last day of May, and May had always been calm and sweet while June was fast and nervous. The twins and Jim Dayton and Shorty had all come to Panamint City in their teens, the first children in town who weren't Chinese, and had for ten years grown up together. It was no surprise that Shorty and his best friend Jim Dayton had married the twins; the question was which one. They had married their opposites; Shorty first, taking the placid May; then big, calm Jim took June.

Until the last few years, when Jim's money was going, the four had been close. Shorty and June had always taken the lead, planning the parties, drinking too much, arguing, getting in fights. One fight both remembered. They had been teenagers, and June recalled the fight years later to Abigail on her sixteenth birthday.

"All of us was in it but May—she was crying, of course—but Shorty was taking us on, fists, teeth, rocks, you name it. The dust was so thick I couldn't hardly see"—she smiled as if in sweet memory of a mother's embrace—"but I remember I went to the bottom of the pile and he was on me with both hands at my throat so I shoved a handful of sand in his mouth and nose hard as I could. His eyes were wide open and he didn't blink. His hands just got tighter round my throat. Only other thing I remember is a couple of men standing for a while at the opening of the mine, and one was Mr. Harris, and I remember thinking it was funny he didn't break it up. Well, it was the day he died." She looked up and smiled at Abigail, eyes shining. "I told you Shorty was a lot of fun." And Abigail, though only a teenager, knew that her father and June had a past she did not understand.

He knocked at June's door and waited. The lapped boards of the house were splitting, the yard was all mud and discarded lumber. Dayton worked shifts at the mines, in the mills, sold hardware, prospected. Shorty wondered, was that what lay ahead if he crossed Hicks? Suddenly June opened the door.

"I'm not ready," she said. "Just got the kids down. You better come in and have a cup of coffee."

She shut the door behind him and his eyes adjusted to the darkness. The curtains were drawn. She wore a silk dressing gown and moved ahead of him into the kitchen. He stood behind her as she put the pot on the stove. Then she turned and leaned back against the counter, her arms folded below her breasts, and looked at Shorty.

"Thanks for taking me," she said. Then, as if first noticing, "Where's May?"

"She can't come. Not feeling too good."

"Missing the mirror party? Jim and May are the dullest people in the world."

He laughed. "I'm glad I'm exempt."

"Oh, Harris, you're not dull. You're dangerous."

He said nothing.

"Jim's in Lone Pine."

Shorty nodded. She looked at him closely, then her tone abruptly changed.

"Shorty, what's wrong?"

"I'm not going to complain to you about money, June."

June laughed. "Indeed you aren't. It can't be money."

He shifted uneasily. "I owe Hicks a little."

June's laugh had a harsh edge. "Consorting with Mr. Hicks. Reap what you sow, brother." She looked him straight in the eye.

Suddenly he remembered the fight, remembered June beneath him shoving dirt in his mouth while he strangled her and rubbed his arms against her breasts. He backed up a step. She was still leaning against the counter, arms folded. The water had begun to boil. The cups were behind her.

"Should I get the coffee?" he said, stepping forward.

"Sure." She didn't move. They were very close. Her smell filled his head. A clock ticked in the living room. The water was boiling.

"Maybe you should change," he said suddenly.

"A lot of people think so." She licked her lips, and smiled. She still didn't move, and she kept smiling. The clock ticked. Shorty felt pricks of heat in his palms.

Then a baby cried a loud, sharp, frightened cry.

"You'd better get the baby," he said.

"Appears I have a lot to do," she replied, then slid against and past him into the room. Then she stopped and turned. "You think you can choose your feelings, Harris. Like clothes in the closet." She left. He went to the counter and poured the coffee with shaking hands. "I am not," he thought, "going to make it through this day."

She reappeared in a stunning black velvet dress, her strawberry blond hair on her shoulders, a blue cameo catching the blue of her eyes.

"Come on brother," she said in breezy good humor, taking his arm and pressing close. "I'm thirsty."

She called the baby sitter from next door and they pushed through the crowd in the street, up to the saloon. Hicks had given him tickets, Shorty said. June raised her eyebrows. She really could be a bitch.

Dexter was arranging red velvet drapes along the wall behind the bar. At ten o'clock, people said, the mirror would be unveiled. Shorty and June pushed in behind a man with a tuba.

Men were telling stories of Great Nuggets—Galler's from the spring south—"I was in San Bernardino when he stumbled in"— "His name was Goler"—"big as my foot"—"the strike at Austin"— "Yeah, but that was nothing to Breyfogle's ore"—"McCarthy saw that chocolate-colored sample in Austin, a thousand dollars a ton"—"ain't no such place, I been all over the Amargosa and ain't seen no reddish rock with a lone mesquite"—"Well, what the hell was in his pocket"—"Look, I even found his goddamn campfire and the broken arrow"—"I'll take the Gunsight"—"pure silver laying around in lumps . . ."

Hicks was in the corner with Jacobs and Eliphalet Rains.

"We'll go over to Hicks's table and have a drink." He had to lean close to her ear to be heard.

"He's a mule's ass," June said.

"You don't really know him."

"He's an ass." She was looking around at the crowd as she continued. "And you've kissed every part of him that lay along the path of your career."

The day had been too long, the week, the months, and he felt himself snap. Without looking back he left her standing there, walked through the crowd, and came up to the end of the bar. His fists were cramped shut when the drink was placed before him. He drained it, slammed the glass down, and walked out the back door. "That goddamn bitch."

June, meanwhile, was laughing with friends at the bar, carefree and loud. She stood and drank and laughed until suddenly she too slammed her glass down and pushed through the crowd. She flung open the back door, hopped down the steps, and ran right into Shorty, who was coming back mad and ready to say he wasn't, or worse, ready to forgive her. She was angry again just looking at his quiet, rigid form, his lying face.

"I'm sorry," said Shorty. June stepped two steps forward and slapped him as hard as she could across the mouth. His hand shot out almost simultaneously and brought fire to her cheek and temple. She staggered back. He caught her before she fell.

"Bitch," he hissed.

Then it happened, and it cut his life in half. The past was before, the future would be after. And the same was true of her. Their eyes, without a word, mirrored each other's recognition, widening with puzzlement, then fear, then a hard-edged acceptance, clear and decisive. She straightened up, put one hand behind his neck, and gently brought him to her lips. When they separated at the sound of an opening door he could not remember his previous life.

They moved easily together into a shadow and stood silent. Shorty had never seen anything so beautiful. Her eyes were wet, her cheeks flushed. Her pounding heart was audible, counterpointed by quickened breath, and he could feel the air and blood rush to every smooth bulge and folded crevice of her skin. Her neck and shoulders glowed; the pores of her body swelled open, glistening. Her breathing skin, her thick hair, and the musky odor of mysterious damps dissolved into a rich wet scent that diffused her presence beyond the eye's simple outline, and just to draw into his lungs a breath of that sweet air was to lose identity.

The wild blood flushed away appearance and left a single being where there had been two; one person both feeling and felt, certainly knowing and certainly known. Her fingers pulsed lightly on his arm. The aftertaste of her lips; the slightly more acid flavor of her tongue; the bland slick of her teeth and a thousand other sensations passed through and disappeared like shafts of afternoon light.

"It's you," he said.

"It's you," she smiled back. So much seemed so easy, so clear. He remembered the soft stomach of a girl who was poking sand in his mouth.

"You always wanted to strangle me," she said, as if inside his head.

"I should have," said Shorty.

He had a key to his mother's apartment. They walked down the alley past Meyerstein's, went up the back stairs of the Nugget and let themselves in.

Afterward, as he looked at the ceiling, Shorty realized he had been waiting for the single moment when his life would go up in smoke. Poof! Now it had happened.

He thought to himself that what he had missed, what he could not live without, was power. And now it had come in the unexpected and most beautiful form of blood. June had been right. He couldn't choose his feelings. And Lane was right. Shorty knew his hand had been dealt. And everything, everything he had just thought and felt, he knew was true also of June.

But even as they touched each other in simple, mutual wonder, slowly, inexorably, something began to whisper like a rival toad in the other ear. Must all former ties be broken? The enormity of his situation, so innocently sensed, began to filter to his mind. He thought of his family, his friends, the future. But he had been preparing—had been prepared—for this moment all his life, and he was ready. His mind clicked with a precise and irrevocable decisiveness; he knew how to play. "Come with me," he said.

"What?" Her face showed puzzlement and fear. "What do you mean?"

"We'll go away. Tonight, right now. Forever."

"I have a husband and children."

"Leave them or bring the children. This is it."

"What do you mean, this is it?" She knew what he meant.

"Let's go," he said.

"I can't do that, Shorty." She turned away, visibly tensed. He thought he'd better back off for a moment. Perhaps it did seem like a lot to ask.

"Look," he said, "we have to think about this." He didn't mean it. He knew she could see through his ruse.

"OK." She didn't look at him.

"I love you," Shorty said. June reached over, squeezed his hand, and brought it to her hip. He felt his blood surge. Or was it hers?

"I know," she said and let go.

"Well?" he demanded.

"Well what?" She sensed that she was being rearranged into a landscape where nothing was impossible for him, as if he could take her—the right her—and leave the other one. He said:

"You know damn well what."

"Shorty." She moved against him and looked down as she fingered his chest. "This is what we have, right now." Her tone sickened him. He told himself that these seconds, these few words, would be the last whispers of honesty she would ever utter. She had wanted him, damn it. He was furious with himself for relishing even this moment of sweetness with what he knew to be the earliest nostalgia, but he could not push her away. It was disgusting.

"Shorty. I can't." She put her arms around him. "I can't."

"How can you betray yourself?"

"If that's how you want to see it," she said and turned away. Already the bitterness evident in her voice he sensed also in her movement, her color, her smell. She lay a foot away with her back to him. He was desperate. He was her, and she him. Surely they could do something about that.

"Don't you see?" he began, "Our lives have headed for this point—"

"You men are all alike." Her voice was cold. "All you've got is between your ears and legs. Well, all I've got is sleeping in another bed—you see I'm used to it—and they can't be tossed on the back of a burro and hauled off to each new adventure. They're all I've ever had, Shorty. My blood."

He couldn't believe it. Surely this was just some mood, a mistake. Then she turned around with a new face, composed, implacable.

"We're really quite different. We'd be at each other's throats." Suddenly she spun away and cried. He felt hope; they had broken through; he put a hand on her bare shoulder, but she sat up with flashing eyes, pulling the sheet to her chin. Her hesitancy, tenderness, and fear were vanished.

"Get away from me, you snake." She backed off the bed, slightly crouched, pulling the sheet with her. Her fists were clenched, her teeth bared in a sneer.

"Your best friend's wife. Your wife's sister. You little son of a bitch." She backed off further. Shorty couldn't even feel anger.

"June—" He reached for her arm.

"Don't touch me."

"This isn't the way, June."

"You think you're so goddamn smart." She walked over to the table and looked at the vase of flowers. She swept it off with the back of her hand. When it shattered against the wall, the fragments caught the candlelight, like swallows, he thought, at evening, on the wing—she whirled around.

"You think you're so goddamn smart. You're an ass."

"June, I know what you're doing. There'll be time for this later."

"Listen to Shorty Harris. All the answers. Panamint's finest. Just listen to Mr. Harris, our next mayor. You should try betraying yourself sometimes. It would do you a lot of good."

"June . . ." She was right. Even at the moment he admired it.

"You can fool my sister and your stupid buddies, but not me—"

"Look—"

"Shut up. You don't know anything. You're dumber than Jim." She threw her head back and laughed. "You think you're so goddamn smart. He's been taking you for years."

"What the hell do you mean by that?"

She moved closer and sneered in his face.

"I mean the gold in Johnson Canyon. He found the rest of that vein . . ."

Shorty's mind flashed back years, to himself suddenly awake by the fire, asking Jim where he'd been, what he'd seen. The conversation about his tracks up the canyon, Jim's hesitation . . .

". . . and he had a buddy from Big Pine file on it for him after you'd come back. He's been working it for six years, getting good ore. And says there's more."

Shorty couldn't absorb it. Jim? Yet neither could he concentrate, it all seemed so far out at the edges of his world, so far from the center that was in himself and even to this moment so perfectly reflected in June as she vibrated in front of his eyes, trying only to escape intact its field of gravitation.

"June, it doesn't matter—"

"You think you're so smart." Her voice had risen to a scream. "You think you're so smart, but while you're snaking on his wife that big oaf is out there working the claim he stole from under your nose." She waved at him. "You've been cheated for six years, you jerk." She laughed. "It's the best thing Jim's ever done."

He moved toward her for the last time.

"Get away you snake." She crouched, then her expression softened and she straightened up, crying. "You ruined it, you stupid son of a bitch. Why did you marry her? I was the one that could have given you a run for your money." Tears rolled down her cheeks. "Didn't want the sparks to fly, right, Harris? Shorty learns violin. Shorty learns assaying. Shorty learns to think he's happy and every goddamn thing. And now you can't live without the fire."

She spun away. The touch of that strong, soft stomach seemed only yesterday. One dress strap was halfway down her arm. She flicked it up as she left the room.

Shorty sat still for several minutes. He felt nothing; but worst of all, he felt he was no longer alone, and that she knew whatever he knew.

So knowledge is that easy, he thought, as if, like one near death, he had the opportunity of final review.

He cleaned up, dressed, walked to the Nugget, and pushed through the crowd to a seat at the bar. Could she come and go just like that? It was impossible. And was she asking him to live there, carrying on an affair behind Jim and May? Is that "adjustment"? Sovereignty of soul? He saw the cupel glow again in the furnace; the flash gave way to a dull film. He tossed off a shot of whiskey and ordered another. The room was full of cheering and whistling, shouting, laughing, hands on shoulders:

"Leadville's big, but that's cause they ain't found it yet up in Montana."

"Aw you're full of it. I was up there in '66 and it was chicken feed."

"You don't know how to look."

"You! An' you're the one what sold half the Lone Star for two thousand. Jesus Christ!"

Well you kin talk and talk, but fer my money—"

"Y'ain't got no money."

"Had it once."

"He did too. Old Tom here threw a party in Denver for a week in '60 you young fellers wouldn't a survived for two days . . ."

"Aw go on Handy. Think I can't drink?"

"Drink hell, you little shoat. You wouldn't a got a buzz on 'fore those Denver girls woulda scared ya to death."

"Pshaw. I can handle myself."

"Don't doubt it. But would ya let a woman?"

Men sat back on their haunches and howled.

"Well, you can talk all you want about great strikes. But I tell you one thing, strike or no strike, Sid Goshen was the greatest man that ever lived."

"That's the truth." The men at the table grew suddenly quiet. The circle of silence opened like a blossom to the edges of the room.

"They say he was around Pioche the year before it started."

"I saw him there."

"Who?" Someone called from the bar.

"Sid Goshen."

"Struck more paydirt—"

"Hell yes, and gave away more 'n the rest of us seen."

"I'd like to be on his tail."

"Thought he died few years back."

The old man leaning against the piano opened one eye: "He's up in the Ruby Mountains." People looked at the stranger.

"I heard he's near Silver Peak."

"Well, to Sid."

"To Sid."

Then the talk and laughter closed in again and the silence was gone.

Shorty looked again at his wedding ring, a piece of quartz set in a gold band. An old man, in front of Gorman's Watch and Jewelry, an old man with thick hands and a burro had looked over his shoulder and said it was "good rock." The memory warmed him. For a moment the party noise flowed around like a song or a pleasure remembered from childhood, a tune some faceless mother had sung at bedtime night after night, her starched white blouse bent close above the bed. Tears came to Shorty's eyes. The man with the burro had been old, old with a soft voice, black beard, blue eyes. Shorty turned the ring over and over.

"That's serious drinking, Shorty." It was Small O'Keefe, in his stovepipe hat, seated next to him. One of Hicks's goons. The last person, except maybe Hicks, that Shorty wanted to see. Shorty tried to focus on the beady little eyes. At least he could see that Small was alone. Two more shot glasses appeared on the bar before him.

"Where's McDonald?" Shorty shouted.

Small shrugged. "He was supposed to meet me here an hour ago." Then, with a smile. "Where's your wife?"

"Go to hell." Shorty looked into the pockmarked face beneath the high black hat. Small O'Keefe and John McDonald. The worst of the desert rats, who had robbed three stages out of Austin for a total of eighteen dollars, who had stoned and burned Chinatown on New Year's Eve 1867 making jokes about "Chinks in the walls" of the hovels where families were trapped; who had come out from behind the rocks after the first silver strike ("The lizards were going the other way" said Lane) and lately had tried to hold up the Stewart and Jones Smelter shipment, while on the mayor's payroll. But the silver was cast in four-hundred-pound balls ("Sure John, help yourself," the driver had said), so they had to sit on their horses and watch it roll away. All was not lost, however; just by telling the story they had earned free drinks for a week.

"Mr. Hicks hopes you're enjoying the evening," said Small. "He also hopes you won't forget your obligations. There's a gentleman from out of town at his table right now who wants some properties. Hicks has been expecting you for some time."

"I'll be right over."

Small turned away. Shorty could barely follow the talk. He tried to turn his head to Hicks's table, but his stomach flopped. The room was fuzzy. "I've got to get outside," he thought. White shirts pressed on his eyes—ironed, unironed, clean, dirty—then the burnished rub marks on the brass foot rail, the shiny mica windows in the stove, the yellowing of the curtains where by day they caught the sun, and the white clay in the welt of his boots. "White," he thought. "White quartz makes white sand, white sand makes white dust, white dust makes white clay." He looked at the ceiling. "White clay makes white quartz." He yearned to run his hand along the dry rough flakes of the invisible beams; he heard the hewing ax slice and split the soft green wood. The inner bark was wet. When it came off in long strips you could smell the life of the pine. The ceiling—when had Dexter tinned it? The hewed beams, the newspaper insulation, the milled boards had all disappeared. Creamy white recessed squares of tin, with elaborate high relief friezes, covered the wood. He stared, dizzy and amazed. Sweat trickled into his eye. On the ceiling were flaming white torches bound with white vines, sheaves of white wheat, white leaves. Garlands of white laurel and hissing white snakes gracefully looped from torch to torch. Then a continuous arabesque of tiny white swirls.

"White tin." He was talking out loud. Small watched him. "White as skin," Shorty said and laughed. He put his head down on his arms and looked at the ring in front of his nose. Clear white quartz with three dull yellow flecks. Tiny flecks. Gold flecks. Gold. "Lustrous, yellow, malleable, does not tarnish." He had said it out loud. He looked up. June was leaning on the bar not three feet away. She held his eye as she drank.

His head rang with silence. Then he was suddenly aware of the song, of snow in the courtyard of St. Francis Grammar school in

Providence—that's when he had heard it before. Taunts and a fight, a bloody nose, a starched sister with hands stern as his father's. And they were singing it now. Nausea swept over him. Feet and mugs rattled the boards:

Oh, McDonald is dead and his brother don't know it
His brother is dead and McDonald don't know it
They're both of them dead in the very same bed
And yet neither one knows that the other is dead.

Breath. Gasp. A quick swallow. A long rising "oh . . ." with knowing looks and winks; Small, who was sure he had no brother, most amused of all; then the rising voices collapsed into a hundred different entrances:

McDonald is dead and his brother don't know it
His brother is dead and McDonald don't know it
They're both of them dead in the very same bed
And yet neither one knows that the other is dead.

He put his head down again and longed to be outside, to feel the roundness of the earth against his cheek, the white mud of a town searching for the Lost Gunsight.

He was awakened suddenly by quiet. The band had stopped. Dexter was finishing a speech about the mirror, about the wonderful civic spirit of Panamint City, about his bar. Dexter walked to the edge of the giant curtain. The band began to play, and the crowd to sing, "My Country, 'Tis of Thee," and Dexter pulled the rope. The curtain fell. Shorty looked up. There in front of him was the colossal glass and intricate silver frame. All of Panamint City stared into it, and he stared back at an image corresponding to himself eye to eye, mouth to mouth, pore to pore. So familiar, so strange. He could feel the distance widen, as a town grows smaller and smaller from the back of a speeding train. "Land of the pilgrim's pride." There in the mirror was Hicks with his loose jowls, and T.S., and June flanked by men. All of Panamint City, with Shorty Harris in the middle. Suddenly Shorty leaned to Small's ear and shouted over the singing, "May I borrow your pistol?"

Small leaned back and examined him. Shorty was quick and bright-eyed. "No, wait," said Shorty. "I want to buy it. Twenty-five bucks. Here." He held out the money. It was twice too much. Small's slight puzzlement changed to the slightest smirk.

"Sure, Harris." He pulled it out and handed it to Shorty. Shorty spun the chambers. It was loaded.

Shorty raised the pistol slowly, aimed across the bar at his face in the mirror, and fired.

The room fell silent. Mouths stopped open in the middle of words. No one moved, but all heads turned back and forth to find the source of the shot until, following each other, like a school of fish they all pointed in one direction. Toward the pistol in Shorty's hand.

The crowd stepped slowly back, arranged around the smoking gun. One by one they looked up, where Shorty was looking. In front of him was a single hole in the mirror with a thousand lines radiating from its center. No glass had fallen.

Still, no one spoke. Shorty looked to one side and then to the other without expression, unless for a moment the eyes of obsidian seemed to flow, like the coming alive of a panther in glass. Then he raised the pistol and fired again. The shot dislodged the fragments—they flew up into the gaslight; slivers landed in front of him on the bar; he smiled—and then, finally, there was the avalanche of glass. Three seconds of silence.

"My God," a man murmured. Then a man at the other end of the bar laughed. Silence. Someone else laughed. And another. And another. In a few more seconds the room was swept by shouts and hundreds of shots rang out through the legs of dancers up on the bar, weaving to the deafening song.

When the last sliver of glass had been blasted from the frame, shots continued to embellish patterns on the ceiling and in the middle was Dexter—Jason Poindexter III, from Albany, New York—laughing and firing at his silver gilt wall while dancers kept up a tinkling descant on the glass now spread across the floor.

Shorty drained the shot glasses that were slid to him. Within five minutes he was a legend. People were taking bits of glass as souvenirs. Dexter quickly opened his entire liquor stock free to the town and put five men to packing little gold dust pouches full of glass, selling them at ten dollars apiece. The price rose with speculation. Within an hour it was said that the Panamint version of the mirror had already sold for twice the price of the Paris model and was not only the most expensive mirror in the world but by far the largest, being at last a mile wide and still growing. Shorty looked about, finished a drink, picked up three slivers of glass from the counter in front of him, crawled with some difficulty up onto the bar and with more difficulty stood up. Instantly the room was chanting, "Harris, Harris." He waved for quiet.

"I have here," shouted Shorty, "I have here the first three slivers of the original glass, and the pistol that was the miraculous agent of the mirror's destruction and resurrection." He waved the items for all to see.

"And I will sell these relics for a mere twelve hundred dollars. Get yourself a piece of the West."

As he climbed down, he could see the grins of Lane, T.S., and Hicks. The sale took thirty seconds. He walked over to Hicks, put the money in his hand, turned away from the speeches of admiration, and sat at his seat at the bar.

He was suddenly tired. Well-wishers clapped him on the back. He asked for water and sat quietly. As far as he could see ahead, his life was illusion, or farce. He did not like either prospect. "This," he thought to himself as he looked over the shouting crowd, "this is not my fate."

Within an hour of the mirror's transubstantiation a stranger entered and stood at the bar next to Shorty.

"Hello." He was drunk.

"Hello," said Shorty.

"Buy me a drink and I'll make you rich."

"Sure." Shorty gave him one of his free drinks and nursed his own.

"Don't you want to be rich?" The man wavered, regained balance, and stared at Shorty.

"Sorry, I forgot. Make me rich."

"Well sir, I know about a strike."

"That so."

"Yup. Seen the ore myself."

"Don't say. Where?"

"Well sir, right on the claim. See, I was heading east from Big Pine over the Panamints, and early this very morning in this canyon on the Death Valley side—I was a bit lost—but I was sober, cold sober—happened on this fellow by surprise. He was nervous to see me, you know, and a big fellow too . . ."

Shorty looked up.

"Had some of the richest ore I ever seen. In a yellow streaked quartz vein under loose dirt. Long. Wide. He'd just found it. Today."

"What canyon?"

"Dunno a name."

"Was he dark haired, large arms, slow moving? Black mule? Black boots?"

"That's him. Hey, you know him? He was near to shooting me till he found out I was traveling east, 'cross the Amargosa."

"Then what are you doing here?"

"Met a man near Eagle Springs who told me my buddy had left our claim and gone back to Austin, so I came here to hole up 'fore going back to Big Pine."

Shorty looked into his drink. Jim had struck something new that day, something big near the claim June said he'd stolen from Shorty, and was nervous enough to threaten a man till he found he was traveling east. So he hadn't yet filed. But this man knew he'd found it and where it was. Shorty looked at his weathered, grizzled face and ordered another drink for him. The man licked his lips.

"Have you told anyone else?" said Shorty.

"Nope."

Shorty's eyes crouched. The man stopped drinking and froze.

"Well," the man looked way and wiped his mouth. "Come to think of it, I told one feller. Was just coming into town when I met this man with a bottle—said he was coming over here to see the mirror—say, where is this mirror I been hearing about?" He looked around, mostly at the ceiling.

"Go on," said Shorty.

"So I told him for the bottle. Laid up in the shed next door, drank it and come right in here. You're number two." He held up four fingers.

"Was this man wearing a brown leather vest and guns?"

"Say, you know 'bout everybody, don't you?"

Shorty looked around. Small was still in the corner. McDonald was not there. So an hour or two before, McDonald had heard the same story and had taken off. It was possible that Jim hadn't left that day to file in Big Pine, but had taken all day to stake and gather samples and would leave in the morning. Four or five hours up the Panamints, another two down into the canyon. The old geezer had sure traveled that day. A man could just about make it by dawn. And that's what McDonald had figured.

Well, hell. Why not. Maybe he was going in that direction anyway. Shorty called the bartender over and asked him to give his friend one bottle of whiskey every hour for three hours if he didn't leave the stool and didn't speak to anyone. The old man understood. "But how . . . ?" "Piss in your pants," said Shorty. He drank three glasses of water, paid, and walked out.

At home he searched the dark closet for the old rifle and cartridges, a pick, shovel, hammer, canteen, two pots, and a blanket. Most of the equipment had belonged to his father. He'd steal the jackass.

"Is that you, Shorty?" May sounded alarmed. Shorty looked up. "Yes." He was cold sober. He put on his high-laced boots and baggy wool pants, his old white shirt and brown tweed jacket. May sat up in bed. He wrapped the rifle in the blanket and picked up the tools.

"Shorty, where are you going? What's happened?"

Shorty looked at her. He looked at his daughter asleep on her back, one arm flopped across his pillow, the other holding a doll near her open mouth.

"I'll send money," he said and walked out.

May sat upright a minute, waking up. Then she leaped out of bed and ran to the front door. At the upper end of the street she saw a man in a coat leading a jackass. It was hard to believe that he was only twenty-three. The man and the beast turned up Frenchman's Canyon, up the trail that led to the top of the Pana-mint range and over to Death Valley. She felt forebodings, but none of them made sense. Was he leaving her? It was impossible. But she knew that Shorty had traits she didn't understand, and in the morning she'd ask Lane what Shorty was doing. He'd know.

◆ ◆ ◆

Panamint City dropped below as the man and the jackass moved back and forth up the headwall of the canyon. The lights and noise from Dexter's became faint and brittle. When he reached the level of the spur ridges, the entire crest of the Panamints, north and south, rose into view and the moonlight flared on the alkaline flats of the valley. Step by step Panamint City became a place in a canyon somewhere below. The pass gained, he continued north along the rocky ridge. Ahead of him, the summit of Telescope Peak rose another two thousand feet. The jackass stumbled on the bad footing. Shorty jerked him forward. To his right the huge salt flats of Death Valley glistened. To his left, the lights of Panamint City twinkled out one by one as the spur ridge intervened. Now the lights were gone. He would be above Wonder Canyon, almost directly above the soft spot in the stomach of the earth that marked the site of his father's Sardine Mine. What had his father known? But he had fifty-five years left to chew on that and at the moment, as he ascended the ridge at ten thousand feet, the air was clear and stars shone in the face of a moon three-quarters full. His mind flashed to the town, the bar, the narrow deep canyon, the press of people on all sides, the noise and stone above his head. Bang. The glass splintered into glints of light across the sky and froze. The silent stars were shaped to the bowl of his head, reflecting nothing from earth unless it was the white quartz crystals scattered across the desert, natural and perfect and still. He heard a line of music that he sometimes hummed to Abigail, that—he suddenly remembered vividly—he had played on the violin the night his father died. The thought struck like a hammer. Was he leaving his child as his father had left him? He pulled down his coat. The searing, fading flash of a meteor made the night more still.

He passed the summit without pausing. It was cold. He continued along the gentle ridge, now wide and open. There were snow patches on the north side. One day, as kids, he and June had climbed to this peak. Why had he been so shy, so scared? But her memory was painful and he knew that if left out it would rot; so he buried it.

Hour by hour passed. He came off the ridge to the north of Johnson Canyon, his and Jim's old prospecting grounds, and descended a spur to the east. Below him Death Valley lay more vast than he remembered. He could see the southern half, stretching forever, still far below. An hour later, in the belt of piñon pine at six thousand feet, he tied the jackass to a tree. There was a saltbush for feed. He should be directly above Jim's old claim now, about two thousand feet up.

He sat on the ridge, absolutely still, and listened. Within five minutes he heard a stone rattle no more than a mile away down canyon. That was all he needed to know. He took the rifle from the jackass, loaded it, descended the spur ridge until he was sure he was past the noise, and then dropped off the ridge on a traverse angling upcanyon. When he was almost to the canyon floor, which was sloping up as steeply as he was descending, he saw a light flicker around the bend. He climbed to stay above the wash, and soon the coals of a campfire came into view behind greasewood bushes a quarter of a mile away. He stepped down to the wash without a sound and moved behind the shoulder-high greasewood. The sky was gray in the east.

He heard voices. They had both made good time. He slipped across the wash toward the sound. There were more words spoken that he couldn't quite hear. When he rose from the bushes he was twenty yards away, directly behind McDonald, who in his right hand held a pistol aimed at Jim. Jim stood beside the fire, sleepy and scared, barely visible to Shorty past McDonald's shoulder. Ore samples glinted on the ground. He had once seen McDonald in a gunfight in Nagle's bar. McDonald had shot one fellow and then dropped spinning to his left and shot the one behind him. Shorty aimed at a point two feet to the left of McDonald and waist high. He spoke quietly and evenly so as not to jar his aim.

"McDonald."

Then he fired. At his name McDonald dropped and spun to his left and he was hit in the chest before he'd even seen the gun. He stared wildly as he lay on his side long enough to see who it was, murmured "Harris" in disbelief, curled up, and died. With McDonald down, Shorty found his loosely held rifle pointing at Jim.

"Shorty, is that you?" Jim shaded his eyes from the fire. The figure in the dark didn't move. Jim could see the moon glint on a barrel.

"Thanks, Shorty."

Slowly it dawned on Shorty, the answer. He could kill Jim with McDonald's pistol. Shorty could have come late and killed McDonald. Then he could have June, who would inherit the gold. Of course June would figure it out with one glance.

When there was no reply, Jim began to sweat again. He clutched his hands.

"Shorty, I'm sorry." Jim stared into the night. "I just want to say one thing." Jim wiped his nose. "I'm not apologizing." He looked up. Shorty could see his eyes glisten. "I'm crazy about gold, Shorty, and there's nothing I can do about it. I know you won't understand, you're not like that. But I can't help it. It just happened."

A minute of silence. Jim peered into the night. Then he saw glints run up the barrel; it was lowered. Shorty stepped forward into the light.

"Shorty I didn't want to . . ."

Shorty silenced Jim with a wave of the hand. He couldn't think how to say anything about the pain they shared. Maybe June would tell. Shorty remembered his campfire with Jim, somewhere near in this canyon, eight years before, when Death Valley was, as now, a lake of predawn white. Jim had known about the gold then, had worked part of it for eight years. He looked across the fire at his friend heating a can of beans. Jim Dayton obsessed. It was wonderful. He had never felt closer, really.

"Shorty, Hicks will find out you killed McDonald."

"Not unless you tell him."

"He'll guess."

They ate in silence. When the red dawn, the yellow dawn, and the purple dawn had passed, the sun itself appeared. Shorty got up.

"Going back so soon, Shorty?"

"Going east." The words just popped out. "The Rockies."

"East?"

Shorty could see his family in his friend's puzzled eyes, and could think of nothing better to say: "I'm gonna strike it rich." Jim looked down at the ore, in dismay. He was stumped. It was half Shorty's.

"Call it even," Shorty said.

"How the hell can it be even?" Jim waited for an explanation.

Now it was Shorty's turn to look down in dismay.

Finally he said, "Maybe you could help May and Abigail a bit, till I have some luck."

"Sure, sure, Shorty, I'll be glad to, you bet. And I'm sorry it came out this way."

"There's a while yet, I guess."

The two men shook hands. Shorty felt hopelessly confused, blessed by an ignorant thief he had tricked.

High above, on the ridge, a man in a stovepipe hat watched Shorty work through loose rock and sand up the slope to his jackass, lash the rifle, and head down toward Death Valley and the rising sun.

It had been a long day since that walk downtown at dawn, and a long night. Panamint City. Already it seemed improbable as a story in the Boston papers. He'd never even walked out on a job before, much less fallen in love, left a family, and killed a man. It was going to be a scorcher. Even a blind man new to the desert would have known not a shadow would be left by noon.

Yet even as he stopped and pulled the rope tight to keep the rifle off the mule's flank, he knew that he had needed something more, and still needed it, something far away. As he walked leading the patient jackass, the words rang in his head: "I am, like him, pained with want, but am not, like him, satisfied with fullness."

Man and beast suddenly emerged from the canyon and stood at the top of the alluvial fan, looking down at the vast open alkaline floor two thousand feet below. "I'm in it," he thought, in Death Valley, the first chapter of his father's diary, the first blank page.

CHAPTER 3

Death Valley

Shorty walked down, down, out onto the valley floor, and his apprenticeship began.

Once there was water, though now it sounds like a myth of Paradise: after the last ice age Death Valley was a huge lake rippling in the sun, six hundred feet deep, banks thick with vegetation, at the end of three rivers: one from the Owens, Searles, and Panamint valleys to the west, one from the Amargosa Basin to the east, and one from the Mohave to the south. All three flowed into the south end of Death Valley where now the little Amargosa River runs here and there, a few hundred yards at a time until it disappears—whether up or down, by evaporation or by soaking in, no one knows. But the flaming swords at the gates are crossed behind us; the water is gone and the valley is dry, although a few springs like Tule and Mesquite or wells like Bennett's and Shorty's or pools like Badwater remain. Some of this water is seasonal; some can support no life; some has vegetation; some is suitable for mammals. There is usually groundwater six feet below the valley floor, too alkaline to drink.

Like the rest of the earth the region is still drying out, still falling farther and farther from its ancient paradise. Some forms of life, such as the pup fish in a few Death Valley pools, are hold-overs from the Pleistocene lake. Archaeologists tell us that the land once supported a large population of Indians; they are now shrunk and scattered, like the fish, at occasional oases. All this means that for life accustomed to the temperate zone, Death Valley is getting worse: hotter, drier, saltier, more dead. The mountains fall back on themselves—the Basin has no outlet to the sea. Hardly the answer to our fathers' prayers; hardly the place to satisfy desire. "It's not what he did. It's what he loved."

The valley he loved. The valley would stretch more than half-way from New York to Boston, is the lowest place on the continent, is surrounded by mountains twice as high as anything east of the Mississippi, is filled with—or empty with—mud, salt flats, silt, gigantic fans of alluvia spreading down from canyon mouths, sand dunes, pools, wells, springs, sparse and brittle vegetation, sage, greasewood—all surrounded by a welter of colors: red, brown, yellow, purple, white. The skin of a stripped naked old earth blackened, blistered, cracked by wind and heat. The ground temperature of Death Valley has reached the boiling point. Like a head full of facts, a bucket of water left in the sun can evaporate in an hour.

♦ ♦ ♦

Europeans did not quickly place their heads at the mercy of the southwest deserts. In 1849 white men walked in, looking for gold. They dreamed the dreams of Columbus, Cabeza de Vaca, and Coronado—dreams not of farms and families but of sudden and staggering plunder, dreams that took form, matured, bore fruit: in the booms of 1870 and 1900, the busts of World War I, Shorty's grave of 1934. Shorty grew up with the Great Basin, and he saw it graduate to paved roads, Ranger slide shows, and clean rest rooms.

The dream had been a long time coming; the desert was its last frontier. So forbidding was the central Basin that after hundreds of years in South American jungles, in Mexico, California, and the Rio Grande, the Spanish still had not explored Nevada. In 1849 there were only two proved routes across the Basin: one north, from Salt Lake to Sacramento, and one south, from Salt Lake to

Las Vegas and then just under Death Valley on the old Spanish trail to Los Angeles. Those two routes and the Sierra formed a huge triangle.

Until 1849 little more was known of this triangle than the English had known two hundred years before. A map of 1690 labeled the empty space above the missions of Mexico: "New Granada. Discovered about 1540, of a barren soil and little known." The discoverer of 1540 was Coronado, but he did not push north of the Colorado River into the heart of the Basin. Only one of his subordinates, Cardenas, headed in that direction. What he found remains a mystery, for he never returned. In 1536 Cabeza de Vaca was quick to believe that he stood at the edge of the promised land. The Pueblo Indians kept pointing north. "Mas alla," they said, you will find what you want.

We ate not more than two handfuls of prickly pears a day, and they were still so green and milky they burned our mouths. In our lack of water, eating brought great thirst. . . . I have already said that we went naked through all this country; not being accustomed to going so, we shed our skin twice a year like snakes. The sun and air raised great, painful sores on our chests and shoulders, and our heavy loads caused the cords to cut our arms . . . when we gathered wood, blood flowed from us in many places where the thorns and shrubs tore our flesh. At times, when my turn came to get wood and I had collected it at heavy cost in blood, I could neither drag nor bear it out. My only solace in these labors was to think of our Redeemer, Jesus Christ, and the blood He shed for me. How much worse must have been His torment from the thorns than mine here!

—CABEZA DE VACA

Cabeza de Vaca turned back. Later Spanish explorers stopped where he had (they had read his journals) and peered north into the Basin, searching the sage flats and barren ranges, the white playas, studying each shimmering mirage—the mountains floating upside down in the sky—for some trace of the Seven Cities of Cibola, made of silver and paved with gold.

Silver and gold. It was not a simple dream that brought the first men to the Basin, not the bankers but the zealots, the strong, crazed passionate men with visions of empire and paradise—gold and souls—forts near ore and missions near the damned. Priests, prospectors, colonizers and con artists, Mormons and Mafiosi: Salt Lake and Las Vegas. Joseph Smith from upstate talking with the Lord, heading west; no other Christians could stand him. Bugsy Seagal from Chicago, his violin case stuffed with cash; his own Mafioso brothers turned thumbs down. The New World. Smith and Seagal, looking for a fresh start. Smith was hung in Ohio, Seagal was gunned down in Beverly Hills. The Basin attracted the blessed and the damned.

A fresh start. On April 1, 1849, Shorty Harris was born Frank Rutherford Harris in Providence, Rhode Island. While fifty thousand rushed to San Francisco the infant was cradled in a fourth-generation rocker on the second story of an eighteen-room house, out of town. Hides from the two family tanneries were shipped to Liverpool on the schooner *Catherine B. Harris*. Death Valley was not on the map.

Item: In September 1849 in Salt Lake gold seekers joined Mormon farmers going to a new colony near Los Angeles. The goldseekers hoped to beat the crowds to the mother lode by way of the new southern route pioneered by their guide, Mormon elder Jefferson Hunt. Talk of history repeating: the Latter Day Saints coveted mission wealth. From Salt Lake the company traveled southwest toward the region that had stopped Coronado three hundred years before. Ten miles a day. Impatience, anger. Why not strike due west and be done? A man from New York produced a pen-and-ink map that he had bought in a Salt Lake dry goods store for a dollar. The way west, across the triangle, looked short and clear. Arguments, fights, warnings from Hunt. Near Mountain

Meadows the wagon train split up; some headed straight into the setting sun.

They got in on the ground floor, but it was a little different from what they had imagined. Nerves became raw. In one argument, two partners sawed their wagon in half and walked away, one to the east, one west. Most parties turned back to Hunt's trail. Pinney's group of eleven men set off on foot; nine would die. Perhaps bolder than even the Spanish and certainly more anarchic, three wagon groups continued to pick their individual ways west through the unexplored ranges and long dry valleys; the thirty men from Illinois who called themselves Jayhawkers, the Brier family—a man, a woman, three sons—and the Bennett-Arcane party of thirteen men, two women, and four children. At first morale was high: they were on the route of their choice, walking across a new land.

The Nevada ranges run north–south. West they traveled, up and down, crossing the ranges together or apart. The valleys became larger. They had to watch their grain and water. At the end of summer the high desert was dry; the water table was low; the autumn rains were late. The bunchgrass was brown, the cattle each morning were slower to come to the yoke. They had expected to reach California in two weeks. October passed, November. Bunchgrass gave way to sage. They captured a Paiute as guide, but he slipped away at the first waterhole. Each pass revealed more of the same. Weakened and scared they stood amid the stunted juniper at the top of ridge after ridge and looked down the dry hills to yet another dusty valley floor. And another range beyond. When would it end? They burned the man's map and went on, sullen and tired, knowing that Hunt had long before reached the sea, had watched slow combers rolling through morning fog.

Camping together one night in December the families heard young Manly report on the land he had scouted ahead: "There's a wide, waterless plain. Then there's a low, black, rocky range, and beyond that the mountains with snow."

"The Sierra," a man said. "California."

On the plain the sage and greasewood brushes melted into the distance. No sign of water. The young Jayhawkers pushed ahead. But the plain was the Amargosa—"the bitter one"—and the mountains were the Funeral Range. For five days the Jayhawkers crossed the dry plain; on the fifth day they ran to the Amargosa River, broke the salt crust with their heels, lay down, and drank. Sick and crazed by the salts they struggled up the Funeral Mountains and looked over. A man sank to his knees and cried. Below was a vast, bare white valley lower than any they had crossed, surrounded by mountains higher than any they had seen. North and south the valley stretched to the limit of vision and beyond. California? "It looked like Hell," Turner said. They stared at each other. They had to get out fast, faster than sick oxen could haul. They were weakening day by day. They slaughtered the oxen and cooked them over the burning wagons. The firelight glittered in a circle of hollow, hopeless eyes.

The Bennett-Arcane party limped slowly behind. On Christmas Day they found the Brier family camped in Furnace Creek wash. They too had burned their wagons. "It was a mistake," Mrs. Brier later wrote, "as we were about five hundred miles from Los Angeles and had only our feet to take us there." The children sat in the sand sucking bacon rinds while their father, a minister remembered with hate in every diary, lectured his family on the joys of education. The next day Mrs. Brier put a child on her back and crawled across Death Valley.

The young Jayhawkers divided their food evenly and broke camp, every man for himself. One by one they hurried on, meeting strangely now and then on barren flats and in uncharted ranges farther west.

The Bennett-Arcane party, which had kept its wagons, tried to find a route out. To the south, breakable salt crust brought the sick oxen to a halt. Up a canyon of the Panamints they came to a cliff. They retreated to a brackish well on the valley floor, Bennett's Long Camp, and there sank to the ground in misery a few miles from the spot where Shorty's grave now lies "in the valley we loved." Bennett and Arcane must have seen the same dusty mesquites that Shorty saw; their animals must have nosed the same brittle arrow weed at the edge of the bare salt flat. Little George, a Shoshone from Ohyu, crawled close to the Bennett camp night after night, and later recalled: "They killed cows and burned the wagons and made big council talk in loud voices like squaws when mad."

Two young men, Manly and Rogers, left the Bennett camp on foot, pledging to return with help. Other single men deserted. Two families with four children remained, weak, sick, delirious, exposed to the bone dry winds and freezing nights of the valley in January. Suddenly, after twenty-five days, Manly and Rogers appeared with one gaunt mule and supplies. They had made it out of Death Valley and across the Mohave to a farm. Then they had turned around, though none of their kin were left behind. They had almost died walking out; they almost died walking back in. But their heroism aroused the company. There was hope now, a cache or two, and a route.

"Good-bye Death Valley," said a tearful Mrs. Bennett as they crossed the Panamints. The name stuck. Little Marcia Bennett, bloated and gray, slumped in a saddlebag slung across Old Crump, the Arcanes' ox, slow but sure. Ahead lay Panamint Valley, the Slate Range, the Argus Range, the Mohave, the ranches of San Bernardino, and the surf washing the Pacific Coast. They sang together as they walked:

Oh, Lord
I am a pilgrim
And a stranger
Traveling through
This wearisome land.

These first Europeans had learned little about the desert and had wanted to learn less. When they reached California they told harrowing tales. The land, though now famous, was still unknown, but among the stories they told in the California gold fields that spring of Shorty's first birthday was one destined to change the map.

Item: Midafternoon of New Year's Day 1850. They had long since stopped dreaming of gold; their only hope was to live. The ox meat was gone. One by one some of the Jayhawkers were picking their ways up the dry slopes of the Panamints. No food; rubber knees; swollen tongues; and no end in sight. Suddenly Bennett—a Jayhawker, not the Bennett with a family—raised his eyes. Was that a deer behind a greasewood? He jerked his rifle to his shoulder and squinted—no sight!—the front bead was gone. Still looking at the shape behind the brush, he stooped. As if by magic a thin flake of rock was in his fingers. He wedged it in the slot, aimed, and fired. A deer bounded away. Sick at heart he wandered on. The ground was full of gunsights.

The Jayhawkers straggled to White Sage Flats. No food, no water. They sat. Others arrived. Bennett took out his knife and began to whittle his sight. It was solid silver. The men wearily passed it around. "Where did you get it?" "On a mesa below. The ground was black with the stuff." He hung his head. "I missed a deer." "What luck," someone said. No one moved.

The story might have died with the men had the younger Turner not shot a deer that night. Then, as the amazed group watched the meat brown over the fire, thinking of water, a second miracle: snow began to fall. The men sprang to their feet and scooped it up in hats, whooping with joy at the luck of the New Year. It is impossible to know how that night affected their minds, memories, hopes; but the legend of the lost gunsight had been born. In the morning they hurried west.

Once safely in California the Jayhawkers remembered the tiny bead passed around the fire. Each man knew just where the mesa "black with silver" must be and after a few drinks was likely to talk about it, for they weren't getting rich—and some day, they vowed, after just a few months had exposed certain memories and washed others away . . . All California knew of "The Lost Gunsight" find.

Item: Turner was first, six months later. He and his party were lost from their first step in and barely made it back to Fort Tejon alive. He quit. "I seen the elephant," he said.

Item: Dr. E. Darwin French, one of Turner's party, returned right away with four others. Their Shoshone guide said that the spring at the west edge of Panamint Valley was the last water. He refused to continue. Dr. E. Darwin French named it Darwin Springs and retreated. What the Shoshone called it is forgotten.

Item: In 1853 Ashmael Bennett went back in. He couldn't find the mountains or the silver. In 1855 Manly reached the Panamints and returned empty handed. In 1856 the Reverend Brier—perhaps the education business was slow or the children retarded—came in alone. No one knows where. During these years California was staked and worked. The Sierra was full.

Item: In 1856 a second son, Alexander, was born to Mr. and Mrs. Harris. He was named after his grandfather, a Boston tea merchant.

Item: On the 1852 "Map of the United States and the Territories between the Mississippi and Pacific Ocean, Compiled from the Survey Made under the Order of W. H. Emory, Major First Cavalry U.S. Commissioner, and from the Maps of the Pacific Rail Road, General Land Office, and the Coast Survey," the Death Valley region was still a blank marked "Unexplored Territory."

Item: In 1857, when Shorty was eight, he crossed from Boston to England on the family freighter and spent three months with relatives in a stone farmhouse on the fogged green waste of Northern Ireland, continuing his studies in Latin, Greek, mathematics, and the violin.

Item: In 1858, after Shorty's return, Mr. Harris's tannery business suddenly folded. They sold their house. Shorty, age nine, who had already given two violin recitals, left parochial school to work in a shoe factory fifteen hours a day. Mr. Harris often stayed away from home at night. The family moved to at least three different apartments within eight months.

Item: In 1859 gold was struck in Colorado. For the second time in a decade the plug was pulled on Boston and New York and everything loose drained west. One hundred years to the day after his Ulster grandfather had set out to try his luck in the Colonies, Mr. Harris put his family on the night train. They traveled straight through to Independence, Missouri, then crossed the plains by wagon to Denver. They spent two months in Gold Canyon. Nothing. They kept going west. In the fall they crossed the divide into Utah with four oxen, a wagon, and two horses. It happened so fast— what could they have thought, the Providence merchant, his charming wife, the two boys, as they stood at the west edge of the Gunnison plateau and gazed at the red and white treeless waste ahead?

Item: In 1859 the Comstock Lode was discovered near Reno. The first desert gold. With the Sierra and the Rockies already staked, out-of-luck prospectors turned to the Basin. Stories of the Lost Gunsight revived. That winter Mr. Harris crossed central Utah without going north to Salt Lake. No one knows by what route he did it or how, with a wife and boys ages ten and three.

Item: In the spring of 1860, while Harris was approaching from the east, Dr. French became the first man to reach Death Valley from the west. With thirteen men he rode from his ranch in Northern California down the central valley to the Kern River, up over the Sierra, past Owens Lake, Darwin Springs, and Panamint Valley, over the Panamints, and finally down to the floor of Death Valley and all the way across to Furnace Creek. April 1860. The first white men to cross Death Valley on purpose. But they saw no mesa black with silver. French, disgusted, refused to stake the rich deposits he had found in Wildrose Canyon and the Coso Range. They returned. In May the word spread that they had made it, with the loss of only one horse, in and out of the dead heart of the continent.

Item: On May 14 the Harris family reached Pipe Spring, a Mormon settlement near the Utah-Nevada line.

Item: In late May Charles Alvord left the saloon at Lone Pine and followed French's tracks back in as far as Panamint Valley. He turned south and entered a narrow canyon on the west side of the Panamints. Five thousand feet higher and six miles back the canyon opened into a big basin: Surprise Canyon. At the back were cliffs rich in silver. He came out to the south and followed the Spanish Trail east, below Death Valley, to Resting Spring.

Item: On June 17, 1860, Harris and his family checked in at the Stagecoach Inn in Resting Spring, following the old Spanish Trail. The men in the dark, cool bar were talking of French and the Lost Gunsight.

"He didn't go far enough south," one said.

"I think Bennett was crazy from the first."

Alvord walked in the door straight from the desert, took a shot of whiskey and said, "It doesn't matter."

"What don't matter?"

"French and Bennett don't matter cause I found it."

"Found what?"

"Silver," said Alvord, "in the Panamints."

Harris grabbed him by the sleeve of his jacket and spun him around hard. Alvord said he already had a partner, thanks. Harris let him go. ("No kidding?" Yarborough said. "That was Shorty's dad? The one who broke Charlie's arm in Resting Spring?")

Item: Before dawn the next morning, June 18, Alvord left with a man named Jackson and crossed the southern end of Death Valley. That was June 18 and it was ninety-six degrees at dawn. Not a good time for desert travel. The others watched from the shade of the porch.

Item: The next morning, June 19, Harris checked out and packed his animals. Mrs. Harris rode a horse and held Alex. Shorty rode a burro and strung two mules. Mr. Harris walked, stringing a mule. That was all they owned on earth. They dogged Alvord's tracks for three days. Alvord crossed the Panamints, hurried up Surprise Canyon, and staked the Gunsight. That night, June 21, the Harris family stumbled in and found, instead of a mesa littered with silver for the picking, a series of hard quartz veins with rich intrusions on steep slopes far above the canyon floor.

In only two years Mrs. Harris had lost her house in Providence, yanked her boy from school, and dragged two children in her husband's tracks across Death Valley on the summer solstice to an empty canyon in the Panamints. Tired she must have been, and she and Mr. Harris had words that night. He walked away. She and the children were asleep on the ground when Mr. Harris came down the slope after midnight with rock samples. He put up the tent beside them and began crushing ore. Later that night Shorty was awakened by gunfire. Jackson ran down the canyon screaming. He was never found. Alvord had been shot through the head as he slept. In the morning Mr. Harris hauled the body out by the wrists— Shorty remembered that one arm was awry—stripped it of boots and clothes, buried it, annexed the tent, and jumped the claim. Three hundred years after Coronado Mr. and Mrs. Harris, Shorty, and Alex were the first whites to come to the desert to stay. There can be no doubt about Shorty's background: "pioneer."

And in ways it was indeed the promised land. At six thousand feet the air was cool, the ore was rich, the water of three springs clear and cold. The juniper and piñon were thick on the north-facing slopes. There were deer and mountain sheep. Mr. Harris built a stone cabin roofed with piñon branches and tent canvas. Mrs. Harris started a garden. She had few seeds and the soil was poor, but water was abundant, the climate was mild, and their cabin on the north side of the basin caught the afternoon sun. It could be done.

With news of the strike the dam burst and prospectors poured into the Basin. More came and staked every month. In 1861 Indians killed six miners in the next canyon. Mr. Harris was the first one over to stake their claims. In 1862 twelve men called a meeting to form the legal district of Surprise, which in ten years would become Panamint City. Notices placed on bushes or under rocks brought men in from the hills to be charter members, for the Panamints were becoming a refuge for men hiding from the law.

Next to Harris's tent, Nagle set a board across two barrels and sold whiskey. By 1863 there were three thousand people, thirty saloons, a red light district, a Chinatown, fights and shots and huge teams of horses and mules chained to clinking freight wagons where six years before had been "Unexplored Territory." A fresh start, but not quite: merchandise stores sold everything Boston could package or crate and ship around the Horn: pickled herrings, caviar, glass chandeliers, champagne, cherries, a love seat upholstered in red velvet "Made in England by Chemwick and Sons, Upholsterers by Appointment to Her Royal Majesty, the Queen Victoria."

Milled lumber appeared—ponderosa pine freighted all the way from Carson City at exorbitant prices—and the Harris family built a clapboard frame house at the head of Main Street. Mrs. Harris supervised the work. The porch had a railing and columns and gingerbread corners, the bay windows copied the house in Providence, and on the roof was a small widow's walk. The Harrises ate at an oak table from good china, and later, the men took port in a paneled den. A woman with a past, a woman born in Richmond, Virginia, could hold her head up, if she were rich and stayed on the boardwalk and didn't walk through the dung of the dirt streets or between the filthy tents or the flattened tin can and newspaper shanties of Chinatown, or through the red light district where the hurdy-gurdy houses whooped and hollered and sang day and night; and if she didn't try to leave and therefore discover where she lived, if she didn't try to go too far: the six miles out Surprise Canyon, across the empty, dry, white Panamint Valley, a thank god drink at Darwin Springs, through the silent Slate range and across the dry Joshua tree plateau to Owens Valley, then north for three days to Virginia City, across the Sierra, the central valley, and the coast range to San Francisco. Money could bring anything in, but getting a live body out was still an inconvenience. And if she did escape, where would she be?

To California, San Francisco was the hub; to New York, it was an outlet; to Boston, a fable; to Europe, a joke. One invested in Surprise, perhaps, but good God, live there?

Thousands lived in the Panamints, in the only desert city north of the Hopi mesas. Half had come to rape the land and the others had come to rape them. Plus a small minority, the wives—just as visionary and zealous as their husbands, they believed that there they could make homes.

Mrs. Harris knew that it could not last, that they would take what they could and run, yet like everyone else she nourished the hope that this would be it, the vein that would never end. There would be a railroad, a park, an opera . . . it would be marriage, not rape. But they could never quite decide on their relation to the land. So every day the thud of blasting rattled windows shaded by lace curtains, and Mr. and Mrs. Harris tutored Shorty, Mrs. Harris in Latin and Bible, Mr. Harris in Greek, English literature, chemistry, and mathematics. Outside, lyceums, concerts, and the Ladies Auxiliary; drilling contests, burro races, murders, and random shots. Then in 1863 Mr. Harris died in a mine explosion—the Sardine mine in the Panamint Mountains. Shorty's carefree frontier days came to an end. The town's growth slacked off at the same time, sending fears of bust up Main Street.

The explosion was not heard in Providence; there was no obituary in Boston. To relatives back east, the tall, stern, silent, and many said brilliant and dishonest man had long since been lost to the aliens and darkness of Western space. At times Shorty would say he killed him, though most people thought that an idle boast. In one day, in six hours really, it happened.

CHAPTER 4

Mr. Harris

The night before Mr. Harris died, that night nine years before, that night as every night a bar closed in a mining camp; a rag dropped in a sink; a last lamp went out. A troubled man in Colorado walked home alone in the dark, humming, leaned on a corner, vomited, felt for a knob, and yearned for the sag of his bed. But it did not enter his mind that half an hour later the same scene would be performed by another man in Utah; then another in Nevada, then California; and in his soundest sleep he never dreamed—and would have thought it silly if he did—of the small pigtailed man just then burping high above the Yangtze on his straw. Yet that night, as every night, locked in his mind a man lowered his body to his bed and without knowing what he did, in dreams within his strangest dreams tried only to forget he was unique.

That morning, as though not every morning, that morning alone again the turning globe of earth rolled the Himalayas up into the sight of sun. First the wind-picked tips of rock and glaring ice rose into light, then molded cornices, high ridges, delicately fluted corridors descending to the blinding mass of glaciers, and as soon as these high valleys turned to light another range had swelled east to the dawn: the Karakorum, Hindu Kush, Afghanistan, the Caucasus, Mount Ararat, Parnassus, each in their turn arose again this day; the Alps, Pyrenees, Dover cliffs, whitecap after whitecap until the

Appalachians shadowed hollows splotched in West Virginia; eastern Kentucky; Cumberland County, Tennessee. East to west before the coming sun the tide of darkness drained, rushing across Ohio and the plains, hiding long in deep trenches, leaving behind little pools of darkness here and there—behind the Rocky Mountain Front Range and the Tetons, the Wind River Range of Wyoming, in the canyon of the Gunnison, the Green, the Colorado—pools of darkness cut off from the retreating sea of night and left behind to dry up in the sun. Wheeler Peak on the Utah line, the mid-Nevada ranges one by one— Shell Creek, White Pine, Worthington, Tempahute, Pahranagat, Pahute—the rocky Funeral Range, snow-covered Panamints—light pressed down from the summits one by one and squeezed the darkness westward to the great Sierra wall, from there, to yet another sea. The sun moved on darkness, and earth again was born.

A mine at an elevation of seven thousand feet on the west side of the Panamints, having its being in the earth, had also to awake, though that day would be its last. After the red dawn, the yellow dawn, and the purple dawn had passed like premonitions, the sun itself appeared and went to work so early and so hard that even a blind man new to the desert would have known not a shadow would be left by noon. And so equally illumined was each upward-struggling thing, so perfectly did each sage branch, grass blade, rock, rabbit turd, so perfectly did the rounded massifs and tapering ridges of a sandy beetle track receive the horizontal rays that even the oldest observer of the desert could have sworn that the far-off sun, in its tangent touch, burned all alone and only for each high place of the earth.

Folsom thought of the heat. It would be a scorcher. And five hours later, when he stepped out from the Sardine Mine shaft squinting and blinking like a cow at swarming eye flies of light, the only color was yellow above in a disk and yellow below in spots, as if the barren valley were a rippled lake reflecting fragments of the sun. "White goddamn hot," he said and lit a cigarette, backing like a lizard into the shade of the mine.

In front of him, past the rubbish heap of sand, rocks, tin cans, and bottles, the hills sloped down in blinding bare rolling undulations to the valley floor. As Folsom peered he heard playful shouts and in a few seconds saw their source: children came running, stumbling up into view—the twins, Jim Dayton, the little Harris boy, and George Somebody—laughed themselves around the far side of the ore heap and pushed each other onto the sharp rocks, kicking up and breathing dust with a noise and animation that in the midst of that stillness seemed strange as a dust devil spinning over the still land, its impetus invisible.

"How do they do it?" Folsom said aloud to himself, thinking of the heat, but suddenly he was aware that someone was standing a foot behind him and a little to his left. He turned and looked at the elder Harris. "How do they do it?" Folsom said again, this time in direct address. Harris seemed not to hear. He stood immobile, as he always did, fresh shaved as he always was, neither young nor old, tan, tall, handsome with eyes of obsidian. He looked unblinking out of the mouth of the mine until it dawned on Folsom that he wasn't looking at the light or the mountains or the valley or the children or even at his own child being pushed into the dust any more than he was listening to idle talk. Folsom gave up and answered his own question—"Must be someone raised a pack a desert rats"—still watching Harris's eyes for some twitch of recognition. Several seconds after he had spoken, Harris turned toward him and looked straight into his face. Harris showed no expression at all—no relaxation to hug, no hardening to punch—unless for a moment the eyes of obsidian seemed to flow again, like the coming alive of a panther in glass. Then it faded, and there were just black eyes in a brown face. Harris turned away, spat once against the far wall, and walked back into the mine. When he was invisible Folsom turned again to the churning kids. "Must be rats," he said out loud, grimaced, muttered "son of a bitch," and chewed his cigarette. Then he went back into the darkness.

The fight took a serious turn. Shorty jumped up and pushed George. Dayton intervened. Shorty pushed him too. Dayton grabbed Shorty's sleeve; he spun loose and hit George on the chin with his elbow. George swung, Shorty ducked and tackled him; then all three went down.

The girls wandered over and were laughing when someone's foot hit June's ankle. She swore and kicked into the thigh as hard as she could. But she'd stepped too close, and while she was still kicking, the other ankle was grabbed and down she went.

Shorty was on the bottom of the pile, but he knew when he had June, and as he delivered an elbow he was aware of her soft upper stomach underneath his right hand. He spun her over to her back as she squirmed and then he pressed on top, his body on her body, his eyes on her eyes. He felt her thighs struggling against him and ran his forearm back and forth over her breast as he strangled her.

But the numbers were too many. Shorty could vaguely sense the point when they lost all patience and no longer tried occasionally to stop but simply beat his staggering body until he lay senseless in the sand.

He raised up once, half conscious, and they were sitting down a few feet away. No one noticed him. Jim's back was turned. For a few seconds he hated Jim purely—he felt that all other feelings were illusions—he hated this big boy who was so dumb but sometimes seemed to know more, who had been the one to tell him that his parents had sex and then had held him at arm's length, laughing at his impotent anger.

Jim strolled over, leaned down and grinned. "Howarya feelin' old buddy? We were hoping you'd wake up cause it's too hot to carry a corpse to town."

"I'm OK, thanks."

"The twins gotta get home for lunch." Dayton paused. Shorty sat up slowly. "You coming, Shorty?"

"I'll stay here. I'll eat with my father."

"You sure?"

"I said it, didn't I?"

The others started down. June looked back and stopped: "You all right, Shorty?"

"Yeah. Sure."

"Bye."

Short watched her go, wondering how she could walk away like that, with her soft strong stomach, her long thighs. Did girls know? How could they withhold so much? When she had disappeared he walked stiffly to the north side of the shaft entrance, sat in the sand, and settled his raw shoulders against the splintering timbers of the mine.

He must have dozed. When he awoke he thought a long time had passed, and he felt as if something were present. At first he thought it was the desert, which sometimes brought silence so close that it seemed like a friend. He looked across the valley. Nothing. Only the heat waves moved, and the waves themselves were a kind of shimmering stillness—stillness of the air, stillness of the land mirrored by dancing reflections, stillness of the sun, which seemed to stop at noon and soak the valley in its heat.

Suddenly Shorty realized that the presence he sensed was closer than he thought. His father was sitting thirty feet away on a box, holding a full lunch bag in his hand and staring out at the same valley. Shorty wondered if they were looking at the same mirage— if two people in different places can see the same mirage—and if so did their gazes meet, or were they looking parallel off into space so that even on the farthest planet in the other corner of the universe their looks would fall on barren places thirty feet apart.

The boy shifted to draw his father's attention. Mr. Harris kept looking to the west. Shorty got up with a grunt, moved closer to his father, sat, and dragged his finger through the sand. Suddenly he was amazed by a deep voice.

"Been in a fight boy?"

Shorty jumped and answered as the other voice trailed off, "Yes sir."

Then he waited. He knew his father was going to speak. It didn't happen often, and it wasn't pleasant, but he knew.

Mr. Harris lowered his head, raised his bag and peered in. He drew out a piece of biscuit, put it in his mouth and looked up to the valley again, but though his jaw moved on the biscuit, the man remained silent.

After a while Shorty noticed the box on which his father sat. Shorty drew a deep breath, waved quickly at the box and said, "What's that?"

It seemed that most of the afternoon had passed before his father said, "Dynamite."

"What for?"

The father turned his head toward his son and gave him the look to which the son had learned to expect no sequel—in looks or words—and if there ever was a sequel in action, no one he knew had made the connection. Talking to his father or just plain looking at him, he always ran into dead ends.

He'd had a dream, several times, of trying to get to the center of a town; every turn he took ended against blank adobe walls, yet he could see the tops of more buildings, and he knew that his various tries from east or west had ended a long way apart. If he got out of the wagon and walked in he would have to find his way out—or worse, knock on the door of one of those still, dark mud buildings. He could see himself poised, hand raised, in front of the old wood and rusted iron. No. He was too young, too scared. He sat forward on the faded buckboard seat, resting his elbows on his knees and holding the patient reins loose, looking at the tops of the surrounding buildings and wondering what lay past the dust brown walls, at the center.

His father stopped staring at him, turned to his lunch bag and pulled out another biscuit with chicken. He opened it, peered in, pulled out a small bone and sticking it in between his lips drew the meat off with a sucking sound, chewed, swallowed, then flicked the cleaned bone away with his forefinger. He sucked his thumb and forefinger, wiped them on his pants, then mashed the biscuit firmly together with both hands.

"Blasting," he said, as he pushed the bread into his mouth and looked over the valley, erect, munching, still.

"He looks like a king," the boy thought, remembering a bright illustration in his parochial school Bible of some gaunt Old Testament figure—Moses or Daniel or Abraham or Ahab—sitting on a rock in the desert, staring at the facing page of the text. The boy could remember sitting in the overheated room in the bedlam of winter recess, stricken by the illustration. It was the first time he had imagined that someone might know things he would never guess. Nothing had ever pained him so much as the presence of that superior understanding.

The rest of the lunch was silent. The boy guessed that whatever it was wouldn't come. He chucked rocks at a greasewood bush and tried to hit a lizard wedged still and blinking under a ledge while his father finished his lunch and picked up the remains, wiped his hands clean and seemed about to rise and return to the mine. Suddenly the man spoke.

"Know what that is, boy?" he said, squatting, one lean finger pointing at a rock the size of a fist three feet in front of him. The boy stared. It looked like pretty ordinary rock, probably rolled from higher up, soft, reddish brown, a few flakes. The boy licked his lips.

"Metamorphic. Some iron, manganese, a little mica?" His voice cracked and he coughed. "Mica?"

The finger was still pointing. The boy wondered that the eye and finger together didn't blow the rock apart.

"Stone," his father said and straightened up, grasping the lunch bag in one hand and the dynamite in the other. "Remember that. Stone."

Was that it? The boy sat sullen while his father walked without a backward glance around the first timbers of the mine.

Shorty looked at the rock. Something was going to happen. Slowly his eyes lifted to one beyond it, then to another, and another, and where the rocks were indistinguishable he focused on a sage, then greasewood bushes here and there dotting the next knoll down, and the next. On the third knoll he could see only dots; past that was just a slightly greenish bare brown hill sloping down the miles of alluvial fan to a lighter tan and then to patches of white salt on the flat valley floor. Beyond, another range of rock rose up, and above that was only the sun long since burned past yellow, hung still in the middle of a whitened sky. "Stone."

He felt the anger grow. He remembered another picture, not the illustration from the Bible but a picture in his history book of the giant stone figure in the desert with a lion's body and the head of a man, a man-beast that would someday start to move, his teacher said. Hairs tingled along the back of Shorty's neck. Suddenly he jumped up and wanted to shout "Dad"—he'd never even used the word—but he didn't. He stood by the mine with clenched teeth and clenched fists drawn up tight and hard and silent as everything else for as far as he could sense or see. "Stone." The son of a bitch.

It was the last time that he saw his father.

When he raised his head and started down he knew that something had passed, like Christmas or a birthday.

Around the bend he came upon Shoshone Tommy, the crazy Indian of Wonder Canyon and the alleys of Panamint City, sitting cross-legged in front of his circle of rocks. Shorty tried to sneak around; he'd heard it all before.

Without even looking up, Tommy pointed to a stone in the circumference, at the end of one radiating line, and said:

"You come from the north, the place of wisdom. The home of the buffalo. Your color is white."

Shorty fingered the rip in his pants.

"But you were born toward the east, the yellow place of illumination. Home of the eagle, who sees far." Tommy paused, looked up, and smiled. "Your name is White Eagle."

Shorty nodded. Last Sunday he'd heard the same speech. Tommy's eyes were bloodshot, his feather was broken and tied with a twig splint, and his braids were full of straw.

"Thanks, Tommy," Shorty said, "but I've got to go." Tommy was paying no attention to him, just studying the rocks.

"You must go south, White Eagle, to the place of the mouse, who sees nothing far off but lives close to the ground and feels things with his whiskers. That will be difficult for you. He has the gift of touch. His color is green."

That was a new one. Shorty wondered why he should have a new one today. "Real good idea. Thanks again," he said, and was several strides down the path when he realized that he was running south, toward Panamint City. "Good luck," he heard behind him. His skin crawled.

As he slowed to a walk, his father's face beat on him like the sun. "Stone." He felt the roundness of the rocks beneath his foot, the roundness of the hill, the roundness of the earth. If he walked straight ahead he'd come out in the same place. Round and round like the sun. He stopped. His black eyes stared unblinking at the land. The sun had moved a little west; the first shadows were splotching the mountains on the western rim of the valley. Soon that range would pass from tan and red to purple, purple to blue, blue to black as the sun sat on the ridge and its rays entered the Sardine shaft and struck the farthest back wall as they did every day in summer, going deepest into the earth just before sundown, over and over, round and round, touching the deep, tired stone. Shorty stood still and looked toward the moving sun, looked back at the Sardine shaft with premonitions flitting through his head like bats, aimless and confused in the mine at dusk before they all detach and rise in one great spiral to the evening sky. In his mind he saw his father at the back of the shaft, standing in full sunlight, in the middle of the stone. The box was at his feet.

He ran most of the way home. "Mom . . ." he almost shouted, but he didn't know what to say and she did.

"Good lord, look at you! Who did that? Shorty! What's happened?"

While his wounds were one by one opened and cleansed he lay back with closed mouth.

Clean and dressed an hour later, as they stepped out into the street he looked at the sun, just above the freighting building. Three o'clock. Four hours till sundown. He looked back to the north, at the zigzag trail where it disappeared over the ridge toward the Sardine.

They went into the dry goods store. Shorty fingered the soap in the barrel, turned each piece over. No stamp, No name, no picture. Lousy soap. He rattled a bead curtain and grabbed a pick, handled it, felt the balance, and threw it back into the keg.

"Ma." He said it low and looked over his shoulder. She seemed not to hear. He leaned up toward her ear. Even at thirteen. "Ma I want to talk to you."

"Sure boy sure." She turned away. "Mr. Johnston, how much is this chair please?"

"Ten dollars ma'am." Johnston watched her raise her eyebrows. "Eighty percent of that's freight." Shorty walked out and stood under the portico. Three freighting teams were standing in the dust, their wagons emptied that morning. Tagged bags of ore were stacked near the assayer's office, waiting to go out. The teamsters would wait till the sun went down a bit. There was plenty to do in the meantime: bars and women. Three teamsters were sleeping in the shade of the porch.

Shorty looked past the buildings up the ridge at the Sardine trail, then up Main Street to where it dead-ended at the upper end of the canyon and the rubble rose steeply to white rock. It was funny, he thought, how different it always seemed down here. Inside a room, it was hard to imagine Panamint City, and in town it was hard to believe the desert, and standing on Johnston's porch, he thought, you don't see the town either the way someone does above, up at the Stewart-Wonder or Wyoming mines, or when you come around the ridge from the Sardine and the canyon opens up below to a city of four thousand people, and a person coming home can look down and pick out his home. Tears came to his eyes. He remembered the campfire in the desert, coming out four years before, how every night he'd relax with his father and mother and their mules and packs around the glowing coals that pressed back night and filled in the space with family. After dinner and a smoke his father would get up and walk away from the fire, out of sight into the night, and the boy got in the habit of going out too, in the opposite direction. Ten paces did it. Something was stretched. Suddenly the fire was so small, the bent woman so frail, and the next few steps when he could just barely see the flickering firelight on the sage beneath his feet, the next few steps he had always counted.

Always, beyond the camp at night, no matter where he went, at any instant he could have shut his eyes and pointed within three degrees of the fire. Something kept bearings on that base, something deeper than mind or emotions. Something made that little star-sized fire the center of his universe. So he knew that he had never left home. When he returned his father was usually seated again, staring into the coals. Shorty wondered if his father had felt the same pull, had ever gone beyond the circle, lost his bearings—and whether he'd returned by instinct or by choice.

And right now, what was his father doing? Could his father in the dark shaft point within three degrees of their house or was he gone, loosed, free? Did he come back home each night by instinct or by choice?

The light hurt his eyes as he squatted in the porch shade and stared up at the zigzag trail. The mine was out of sight.

"Ma I gotta talk to you." His mother was hardly out of the door when light and dust and her son assaulted her at once. Then Shorty lowered his voice and calmed himself. "Ma I want to talk." He looked at the sun as they walked into the street. Four o'clock. Sundown at seven.

"I'm going to buy the chair, son. It will look nice in the dining room."

"Ma!" Shorty stopped in the middle of the street and looked around. He took his mother's arm and turned her up the middle of the deserted street.

"Did you see father leave this morning?"

"Of course. I cooked him breakfast."

"No, I mean did you see him actually go?"

"Yes, dear."

"Was he carrying a small wooden box, like so?" Shorty indicated a box about a foot long and six inches square.

"No. I don't think so."

"You sure?"

"I think so."

Shorty looked at her sharply. "So he wasn't carrying anything?"

"I didn't say that, son. He had his lunch bag."

Shorty looked down as they walked. "Ma, do you remember seeing a box like that around the house?"

"No dear, but why the questions? What box?"

"Oh just a box I lost, Ma. I had some ore samples in it. I thought Dad—Father—might have picked it up by mistake."

"I hope you find it. Now we need groceries. Coming in with me?"

"No Ma, I'll just wait outside."

"I'll need help carrying home. Alex is at Gorman's."

"I'll be here."

"If you want to go someplace special, your father can help when he comes home."

Shorty looked up sharply.

His mother thought he was angry with her. She saw his knuckles white around the wounds.

"Son, what's wrong? Did something happen up there you haven't told me about?" She paused and studied his flashing black eyes, then she suddenly softened. She moved forward and, putting a hand on his shoulder, squeezed gently. "You saw your father, didn't you?" Shorty looked at her in the eye and relaxed. He felt a natural smile grace his face. He breathed again. "No Ma. I didn't see him." Then still looking her full in the face he lowered his head and said, "I'm big enough to help."

"Oh!" She laughed and hugged him, turned and went into the store.

Shorty stood with his head down until she had passed through the door. Then he turned abruptly and walked down the street to Dobb's Hardware and Mining Supplies. When he was sure no one was watching he moved inside.

"Can I help the young Mr. Harris?"

Shorty's throat was dry.

"Ah, yes sir. Do you have any dynamite?"

"Why yes we do."

Shorty paused and felt his mind stammer. He didn't know if it showed.

"Does anyone else in town carry dynamite?"

"No they don't. I've got you."

"Oh. Well, I was thinking I might want some . . ."

"What in hell for, Shorty?"

"Well, Jim Dayton and I were thinking of prospecting . . ."

"You ain't even found it yet! I'd have to speak to your father, if that's possible." Mr. Walsh gave a snort. Shorty ignored him.

"That's just it. He said he would maybe pick some up for us, just a little. Could you tell me if he has? Lately?"

Mr. Walsh leaned over the counter and looked at him. Shorty looked quietly back. "Please, sir?"

"Your father hasn't bought anything here for at least a year."

"No?"

"No. And don't ask me if I'm sure. His partners buy. It's my goddamn business."

"Did he ever, I mean a year ago . . ."

Walsh sighed. "As a matter of fact he did. More than a year and a half ago. I used to get sent a fool box about so"—he shaped in the air a box one foot by six inches square—"but it was too small for mining. Haven't seen those little boxes for a while."

Shorty was looking down. "Well thanks, Mr. Walsh." Then he drew up and gave his best straightforward look as he extended his hand. "I guess he didn't get it for us."

Shorty turned in the door and looked back. He spoke very distinctly.

"Excuse me again, sir. But could you tell me the time?"

"Why yes Shorty. It's ten past five."

Shorty walked out. The shadows had already flowed out from Surprise Canyon to engulf the shanties of Chinatown. "Too small for mining." Just one box. And hidden. In half an hour the town would be dark. He watched the shadow advance. The sheen faded from the back of a black mule, from the tips of his ears.

The trail on the ridge and the mountains behind him were still dazzling bright but already there was just a touch of yellow again, as at dawn, softening the light and making the greasewood leaves look strange. He didn't wonder anymore what was going on up there. In his mind he saw the first few bats drop off the ceiling as if to test the air. It would happen at sundown.

He walked to the grocery. His mother hemmed and hawed. As soon as she brought an item to the counter Shorty called out the price and crammed it into the bag. Beans, rice, potatoes, salt pork. Outside the shadow crept up the street; went past. Finally she finished, and Shorty stood outside with both bags while she paid. The street was dark and the line of light was moving up the slope. An hour till the sun would enter the mine and touch its farthest wall.

They walked home. He sat down beneath the clock as it struck six. Suddenly his mother brightened up.

"I've got an idea, Shorty. Let's take a walk. We can start up toward the mine. If we don't make it, we'll meet your father coming down."

Shorty stared in disbelief, then shook his head. "No Ma. I don't think that would be a good idea." He felt his forehead. "I'm pretty sore."

She held one curtain aside and looked down Main Street.

"Well maybe I'll go alone then. I've been restless in town all day."

"No Ma!" Shorty wasn't sure if he had shouted or not. "No. I mean, father said he might spend the night up there."

"Spend the night! Well I declare. Who ever heard of such a thing?" She stood in front of Shorty with her arms crossed, rocking on one heel, and watched her boy run his fingers through his hair. "Shorty, you told me you hadn't seen your father."

The clock was ticking. From where he sat he could look out and see the third switchback swallowed by darkness.

"Dayton saw him. Or maybe he saw Folsom. Said something about maybe working late, a rich strike or something."

"Are you sure?" Her voice was stern.

"My head's pounding so I can't think straight."

"Well, I guess I oughta stay then."

Shorty leaned back. She ran her fingers through his hair. He dozed. Suddenly he looked up, found the spur ridge in shadow and almost jumped from his chair. The sun would be entering the mine now, foot by foot. His mother wiped the sweat from his brow. Shorty forced himself to settle back and watch: this would be the real shadow now, the shadow of the Slate Range, the shadow that had come ten miles across the flat, up the fan and the foothills, that had engulfed the local canyon and now was creeping up the Panamints, the shadow of the western edge of earth.

The clock ticked, ticked, ticked. He was aware of a washcloth on his forehead. As he looked up at the yellowing sage, the greasewood and mesquite, at the sand again turning a rich gold all over the ridge, as his father's steady eyes and the heat and the silent knowing figures and the roundness of the earth came back to him, he knew he wasn't crazy and he was hardly startled by the sound of rushing wings, the unmistakable rush of millions of bats churning, getting ready to rise in vast circles, bats aroused by the approach of night and by the slow, sure movement of the stone, round and round, above their heads. His mind emptied. Then with absolute clarity he saw his father standing against the back wall of the mine in yellow sunlight. He was standing erect, looking at the sun. At his feet was the box. Folsom stopped gathering tools; the others too. They looked at the strange, silent, unblinking man as if wondering how he got there or who he was. Because of the blinding light they didn't even notice the fuse until it sputtered into the box.

"My God," said Folsom.

From his chair Shorty saw the dust spurt from a thousand points at the head of the next canyon. He didn't blink. The bats would be gone now.

A second later the echoes rumbled through. Mrs. Harris paused in her wiping of his forehead. "Who's blasting so late?" she said and moved lazily to the window. "That's funny. It's in Wonder Canyon. No other mines that way are there son?" He didn't answer. She thought the poor boy was fevered. Several people were out in the street, looking at the dust. They spoke to each other and pointed. Someone got a horse. Mrs. Harris stepped out on her porch and watched. In fifteen minutes someone had reached the ridge, looked across the gulf, and shouted what they could back to the town.

She couldn't believe it. Her hands gripped the railing of their Main Street home. But she should have known, she thought, something like this. Already one man had come back from the ridge. He spoke to her from the street, holding his hat in two hands. The mine was gone. There was no one in sight on the trail or in the canyon. He shrugged. What could they do? Didn't seem to be much chance, not much at all. She went inside. Her boy was still in the chair. She went to his side.

"Shorty. There's been an accident."

He looked out the window at the sage and sand. A scrap of conversation from the year before came into his head. The family had gathered for dinner. He and his mother had just finished a lesson in St. Mark. Alex had reached for the butter before grace and gotten his fingers whacked. Shorty could feel the blue china cold beneath his palm. Suddenly he heard himself say, "Don't you think it would be terrible, Father, to be crucified, to be hanging on the cross?"

Why had he said it? His father blew on his soup. Then again: "Wouldn't it be terrible? What would you do?"

And his father, spoon held level halfway to his mouth: "Watch the nails rust."

Shorty sat by the window. His mother stood beside him. They watched the mountains cover themselves in darkness. Stars winked. She looked so weary, as if she had seen it all before. Then she left to fetch Alex.

Later Shorty heard him sobbing in his room. Then his mother was by him again. "There is nothing else to do," she said.

"Do." The boy spoke out loud. "Do. Do!" He slammed the arm of his chair and cried. His mother stood in the doorway. After a while she went to her room. "Do! Do! Do!" She heard the screams, and later, the violin, the opening solo from the third movement of Bach's *Wachet Auf.* He had performed the piece in Old North Church, in Boston, six years before. And Catherine began to weep for all she had lost—for losing Mr. Harris and so much more.

PART 2

Montana, 1872–1876

Gold is a disease of the heart.

—CORTEZ

CHAPTER 5

Launched

When he left Jim Dayton's campfire and walked out of Hanaupah Canyon that morning, seeping like the last trickle of freshet between vast vertical banks of sand and gravel, inching like a finger of wet silt down the six-mile alluvial fan to the floor of Death Valley, to the spot where now his grave is marked, he had no intention of sinking like the Amargosa River into the sand. He knew only that he had to get away for a while. He pulled his hat down and lowered his head to shade his lips. Miles passed. Heat. Like paint, glue, clay, he was drying to shape and color, hardening to form, and every step made the change of state more firm. But though his will could tell him to go, it could not tell him where to go, and hour after hour he was forced to refine his pace, relax his limbs, and relinquish direction to the guiding land. Marching gave way to wandering. In that trackless waste, his steps, which were the very signs of his will—of his intensity, his agony—his faltering steps gave hints of that grace which is a special blessing of the damned.

The first day was bad. The second, out of Death Valley, over the Funerals, across Ash Meadows and into the Spectre Range, was worse. Delirious, for he had not stopped to eat what little food he had, he missed Indian Springs. Beyond his knowledge and beyond any map on earth he wandered through mid-Nevada ranges

illusorily name-captured, now as always, only by "Pintwater";
"Desert"; "Sheep Range"; walked up dead-end canyons and across
alkaline flats named in hope by those who have seen them: Spring
Valley (dry); Three Lakes Valley (dry); in hope and prayer seen
and in reverence named that it might come to pass, precarious
names in a precarious land so that the map becomes a Bible, a
record of vision, a testament of hope while the bitter truth is put in
parenthesis by scholar-geographers back home: Greenwater Valley
(dry); then steered by an old prospector who gave him a biscuit
fried in bacon grease, who asked him kindly where the fire was and
then watched him for a hundred yards, making no judgment and
drawing no conclusions, Shorty crossed the Sheep Range to Hidden
Forest, drank at Wire Grass Spring, and slowly descended—man
and jackass dwarfed by the giant Yuccas—to Mormon Well.

The man behind the counter gradually emerged from the darkness, came forward, took the rope, and tied the jackass outside
before leading Shorty in to a seat. He looked young, but Shorty
knew he wasn't. Fit, clean, he brought food and drink unasked;
Shorty knew he would not have to pay; that he was this Mormon's
brother; he hated the food. There were other men at the next table.
One tried to sell him a map of the country he had just crossed.
"Look," he said, and laid a legend length of his giant finger across
the paper, "You've come a hunnert miles." There was nothing on
the map except "Dry Lake" written twice somewhere near the
Amargosa.

But someone else had another map, not for sale, which unfolded
the country to the east, and his partner had tales of gold in Colorado. "Pulled up stakes have ya young feller?" Shorty listened.
"Clear Creek's the place to be. A man can't miss."

Shorty peered across the table at the ruddy freckled face above
the stubby finger. "Can't miss." Shorty pulled the lamp over, above
the map. The cracked, dirty sheet showed a maze of mountains
covered with crossed picks and shovels. Shorty looked up at the
door, the rectangle of blinding light. He could see the towns, the

camps, one after another. The hustling crowds, shafts, trestles, rocky outcrops. He saw McDonald go down, spinning, to the dust, his child lying asleep. His heart pounded. The two men smiled and nodded, and one took a dollar for the map. Shorty folded it into his pocket.

On the way to Colorado he explained himself to his mule, over and over, his voice rising to a shout on the empty Gunnison Plateau; then he stroked the silken ears. Gone was the assayer's eye, the red crayon, the just balance. He'd show the bastards. One big strike. A real strike. Just one. The mule held his pace beneath the creaking ropes.

Like the greenhorns coming from the East he turned up Clear Creek and stumbled on packed stones past miles of buildings strung out along the narrow winding canyon—derelict hotels named Florence, Victoria, Regents Park, Cote d'Azur; saloons, beer halls, bakeries, shacks, deserted houses made of log, lumber, with porch railings, drop cornices, and gingerbread lace. Empty windows and open doors. Rusted machines, wheels, cables, mounds of tailing and refuse and rotted timbers strewn across stripped slopes: the deadfall of the last flush times in '64. Prospect holes pocked the mountains. Anyone could see that the country had been used up and thrown away.

But up the canyon past Black Hawk and Central City large stamp mills pounded, ore cars waited, and the dusty street was full. He went into the Mint Lounge and found what he needed to know. The time of self-worked claims, "retail mining," had passed. At less than a hundred feet the rich, weathered rock had given way to pyritic ores containing sulfides that kept the gold from combining with mercury. The middle-aged man speaking to Shorty looked into his whiskey as he turned the glass in his big hand. The bartender listened.

"Refractory," he said indignantly. "Son-of-a-bitching ore refused to be worked. Least by me. Oh, yes, there's others, of course. Mr. Stallings of St. Louis, or Mr. Work of Chicago, they've worked their ore down to fifteen hundred feet in Gully. By eatin' up the little fish claim after claim, and building smelters and mills with millions, that's how, and hiring college boys from that German school and giving them a couple of thoroughbreds in Denver and a small stable for the missus, that's how, and employing a couple thousand like me and you still hanging around to get down in their mines and dig for three dollars a day. That's how. Oh yes, they can work it. Here's to 'em, sons of bitches. And their money. Now the railroads comin' up. Gonna be right smart little company town here." He drained his glass. "Hope they get butchered by Utes."

Shorty went to the assay office. He had twenty dollars left. They had no openings and said that the two other offices along Clear Creek were also fully staffed. "Try the mines," they said.

As he came out of the office he caught a glimpse of a stovepipe hat ducking into the saloon next door. He went to the back door and peered into the room, but found nothing. Would Hicks really do that? He thought a moment. It didn't make sense.

He went up canyon to Pyrhite, the last outpost. There were no boardwalks. Twenty wooden buildings: each porch had a different slant. Tar paper and tin roofs and one small sign: "Hotel." No work. The mines were small and few were paying. Shorty looked up at the cut-over, treeless hills, the black holes and yellow tailings. He'd have to stake himself, then get out. To the north. He'd heard things about Montana.

He went down the canyon to Gully, glancing now and then over his shoulder and down side streets. On twelve dollars he could last two weeks if he slept up on the hill. Something had to give.

The afternoon thunderstorm drove him into the Teller House. He ordered beer at the bar. A voice said, "You're in from California, are you not?" The tall man next to him had a neatly trimmed white beard and twinkling blue eyes. In his hand he held a beaver hat. His boots and high canvas gaiters were muddy; his wool shirt was patched and darned.

"Yes I am," said Shorty.

"So I have heard. I've heard also that you know something of assaying."

"Yes I do."

"I'm Josiah Graham. I represent myself and my brother. We own several mines in Clear Creek Canyon. This week we are outfitting a prospecting expedition of approximately twenty men in hopes of exploring the Elk Range before first snow. In addition to expenses and the opportunity for secondary claims on promising ground, you of course, if selected, would receive a handsome daily wage in your status as professional assayer."

"Oh."

"Are you interested in being interviewed? You're not engaged at present?"

"Yes. Yes indeed. I'm interested." Shorty thought he had never seen such kindly blue eyes. The man smiled warmly.

"Good. You are stopping here, at the Teller House, I suppose?"

"Oh. Yes, I suppose I am." Shorty looked at his beer.

"What is your room number?"

"I don't remember."

"Quite all right. I can ask at the desk, Mr, uh . . ."

"Harris. Frank Harris."

"Very good. I'll call for you in the morning at seven o'clock sharp and we'll talk further. Breakfast is on me."

"That's very kind. Thank you."

They shook hands. Shorty watched the impressive figure stride to the door. Through the window he saw Mr. Graham put his hat onto his head and glide off, swinging a cane from his fingertips.

The room came with board: eight dollars. Well, what did it matter now? The bed was too soft, the room was hot; he couldn't sleep. At 6:30 A.M. he was in the lobby, waiting. He wanted to intercept Mr. Graham before he caught sight of the room, the dirty blanket roll, the two blackened pots, the pick and old flintlock. "In from California." At ten after seven he jumped from his chair with a start and bounded upstairs to number seven. No one was there.

He waited inside until 7:20. Was there another entrance? Could he have come and left? Shorty went to the desk. No messages, no inquiries. No, they did not know Mr. Graham. He went to the bar. The same bartender was there.

"Graham? Sure I know him. Naw, he ain't been in."

Shorty bit his nails and looked at the lobby.

"Say, friend, did Mr. Graham offer you a partnership in the Ophir Mine?"

"What?"

"I say, did he offer you half the Ophir?" The bartender laughed. "Figured you was worth it, didn't you? That's what he usually does. Nice old man, but head looser'n a hoot owl's. Lives in a cave up on Sheep Knoll."

Shorty repeated in a hollow voice, "Sheep Knoll."

"That's right. They say he's a half-wit from a family with money in Kentucky who sent him to Denver for his health, but he skedaddled." The bartender paused. "Don't depend on him," he said kindly.

Three-forty was left, subtracting the beers and hotel bill. He bought a sixth of a pound of flour for two dollars, two pounds of potatoes for twenty cents, and two eggs for twenty cents. There was no wood on the hill; at night he slipped down and stole scraps from the backyard of the Temple of Fashion.

He could find no work. He was down to one potato. Two days later he was walking toward the grocery, holding his last silver dollar, when he slipped in the muddy street. Catching his balance he saw the flash of silver disappear into fresh dung, beneath a horse. His last dollar.

He straightened up and looked about. The street was filled with people who boldly returned his gaze. Miners, teamsters, well-dressed men of business, clerks in white shirtsleeves and garters. Everyone bustling with business. People with things to do. He looked at the pile. It was steaming. As he watched, the horse continued to empty itself. He straightened his back, pulled at his shirtfront, and buttoned his coat. The bastards. Bastards.

Montana. Rich quartz. Nothing could stop him now. Just a matter of steps, one after another. A matter of steps. Without a backward glance he walked to the office of the Paradise Mine, stepped over the threshold, and entered the dark room.

For three-fifty a day he worked at the one-thousand-foot level, naked to the waist, wearing loose cotton pajama bottoms and boots. Every thirty minutes he withdrew his candle from the wall, leaned his pick against the ore cart, and walked out of the side tunnel to the ice water barrel. There in the company of other glistening men he stood silent and sipped cold water from the chipped enamel ladle. Though his head was bound with a turban, the salt sweat filled his eyes. His arms and hands were too gritty to wipe his face. The rock was hot around him, the seeping water steamed. Boots fell apart in two weeks. Some days the giant blower worked, some days it didn't. They ran it from above. One day a man got his sleeve caught in the fan. He had a second to choose: have his arm hacked off instantly or take the chance of going through whole. He grinned, took the long shot and came out in six pieces. They said his name was Galloway, come from Iowa with a wife and two children to seek his fortune. They said luckily he was insured by the Chosen Friends Benevolent Fund.

Shorty didn't speak to them. He would stand small and silent in the corner of the elevator while others complained of the company's profit, the low pay, the stupid milling practices. He lived on fifty cents a day in a tent with a German who spoke no English. In two months he had saved one hundred fifty dollars. He quit, collected his pay to the hour, bought the mule he had kept his eye on for a week, packed his equipment, and left toemarks up the north wall of the canyon, heading for Montana. Others had done it. It could be done.

Through a succession of districts, rocks, camps, towns, and silent independent partners he worked up the crest through the Wind Rivers and into the Madison Valley of Montana. Silver interest had died down in Butte, and they said that Crab City to the north—renamed Helena at the insistence of the mayor's wife and in her honor—had lost its bite. He didn't laugh.

He found himself pushing through November snows across the Whitefish Range then up the valley of the Stillwater. December along the Kootenay. The snow became too deep, the days too short, the air too thin in his lungs, and when the trees began to pop he realized that he was no longer prospecting but just walking, so he turned his pine-branch snowshoes around and went back to winter at Eureka, on the Stillwater. Once stopped he thought of home. He sent a letter to his wife and child: "I am in Montana, looking for gold. Love, Shorty."

In the earliest valley thaws of 1873 he was gone with two other men from the woodstoves of Eureka into the rugged Lewis Range to the east. They ascended the Flathead River into Canada and worked up a promising tributary into the Rockies, a stream now called April Creek. While they worked upstream their concern was color: how much showed and where would be its richest concentration. They stopped to pan every pool. Shorty stamped, muttered, and looked to the hills, dreaming of a good thick vein—he could feel the dry, weathered, rotten quartz crumble in his hands—he had held it in the office, he had heard about it all his life, and now, finally, he knew that he needed it. Gold. It was no longer an excuse to get away; it was where he had to go.

As he sat by the fire that night he took his father's diary out of the packsaddle for the first time since Panamint City. The empty pages stared back under their headings, and near the end was the page of translations. Now in the midst of huge ponderosa pines glowing by firelight, deep in the woods on the border of Canada, he studied the neat lettering in his father's hand:

χρυσός	gold
χρυσήλατος	beaten of gold
χρυσοδαίδαλτος	richly wrought of gold
χρυσοκάρηνος	with head of gold

χρυσόπαστος	sprinkled with gold
χρυσοπλόκαμος	with tresses of gold
χρυσόρρυτος	flowing with gold, in a stream of gold
χρυσομάνης	mad after gold
χρυσοχόος	one who gilds the horns of a victim
χρυσόχειρ	with gold on one's fingers
χρυσόφιλος	gold loving
χρυσίον	piece of gold, money; term of endearment
χρυσομηλολόνθιον	little gold-beetle; term of endearment
χρυσανθής	with flower of gold
χρυσωπός	beaming like gold, with golden eyes
χρυσόπτερος	wings of gold
χρυσολεγείν	to speak of gold
χρυσογραφείν	to write in gold
χρυσανταυγής	reflecting a golden light

aurum	gold
aurarius	golden
aurifer	gold bearing
aurigena	begotten of gold
aurora	dawn

CHAPTER 6

April Creek

Shorty knelt by the stream running fast with snowmelt and milky glacier silt; knelt on the cold, wet gravel of the north bank where the April sun had already melted the snow; on a gravel bar deposited thousands of years ago and only touched briefly by the floods in June; just downstream of a large slate bed that cut across the river and, being hard and having eroded slowly, formed a cascade that made talk impossible; a slate bed laced with veins of quartz.

At the first slack water, fifty yards below the white-veined slate, Shorty knelt and worked the gravel in his pan. Downstream, at the next eddy, was Tom Wood; out of sight below the bend Jasper panned the bank where they had found good color. For two days they had scouted this stream; damn good slate; new country, never worked; anything could happen. They laid out four-foot strips across the first three exposed gravel bars below the falls and divided up; each dug to a depth of four feet, panning every shovel as he went. Shorty's first pan turned up enough flakes to cover his fingernail: fifty cents. He looked at the deep spring snow on the upper ridge. The cornices were iced and glistening in the sun. He dug once more, dumped the load into his pan and let out a long sigh.

Shorty dropped his shovel, knelt, dipped the broad pan into the stream, swished it about, agitated the gravel, then began spilling water over the flared lip in little waves that washed the lightest particles away. He dipped in more, stopping to pick out larger pebbles. In a few minutes, only a thimblefull of sand was left. There were flashes of dull yellow. He held the pan at the water's edge, tilting it until the lip was almost horizontal, and ran tiny waves of water quickly in and out. With each receding wave some lighter particles washed away, and a thin trail of yellow ran out almost to the edge of the lip before he raised it imperceptibly and stopped the flow. One last swish and careful tilt: the quartzite sand drained, revealing ten or twelve tiny flakes of gold. He placed one finger on the deposit and poured the water out, then pressed his finger down. When he turned it over, he had thirty cents' worth. Chicken feed. He looked around to see if anyone was watching. He threw the gold away.

He looked again at the gravel bar. The quartzite pebbles were dark and glassy; that corresponded to the visible quartz veins in the slate. Some of the pebbles were pyroxene. He looked up at the left bank of the slate: the veins seemed irregular; one was lenticular.

There was less in the next pan; nothing in the one after that, or in the sixty pans that he proved out through the afternoon.

They came together at dusk. Shorty shook his head; Tom shrugged. Jaspar opened his pouch. He had at least an ounce, a hundred dollars. Jaspar and Tom were jubilant. Shorty hesitated; he asked about the sand. Jaspar wasn't sure; he thought the quartzite was light; the mica certainly was. Why? Shorty shook a sample from Jaspar's pouch and peered at it. The nuggets were very smooth. He said it wasn't from the slate bed; those veins looked lenticular and were probably formed at greater heat, had glassy quartz and brown mica, were not the source of Jaspar's gold, which should be more hackly if it had only come that far. They said he was nuts; why argue? It was there; maybe a younger intrusion in the same series of primary deposits had already weathered away and left this placer; anything could have happened. Shorty was excited, said then it should show up closer to the slate. Tom said maybe the stream used to run harder, or straight through.

Shorty said it used to be slower, obviously; he thought a seasonal tributary entered where Jaspar was; it looked like it to him although no one could be sure till the snow melted. Maybe the gold came down from the side.

Jaspar said if Shorty just wanted to talk he could have stayed in Eureka. He said Shorty seemed to know an awful lot about a district he hadn't seen before. Jaspar ripped the ax from the trunk of the tree; if it wasn't too much to ask perhaps they could build a long tom and sluices and work the gold. Someone could at least start a goddamn fire, he said.

"Who appointed you boss?" said Shorty.

"Me boss? Shoulda known not to take a famous partner."

"What?"

"Famous. When I went back to Eureka for supplies there was someone asking all over town for you."

"Who?"

"I dunno."

"Did you say—"

"I didn't say everything I know. Not like some."

Shorty looked at Jaspar's back, his broad back in the big sheepskin coat, hulking near the food cache in the dark firs.

The next morning Shorty sat up in his blankets, pulled up the heavy canvas flap, and looked out of the tent. Wet blanket, muddy ground. The first spring night without frost. The giant fir and spruce trunks faded upward; occasional drops fell from bough to bough above. There seemed no light at all, no sign of dawn, yet snowbanks gleamed in the forest and their damp, cold breath laid a mist about the camp; a horse stomped; the cataract was muffled in the quiet air. He rose from his blankets and stood on them in his socks and woolen underwear. He felt for his trousers, pulled them on, then sat and jimmied his feet into boots wetter and stiffer and colder than he had left them. He recalled some other time, pulling boots on in a bedroom. There was a woman, and a child. His child. Abigail. He listened a second to Tom breathing in his sleep.

He rose without lacing, took a heavy shirt off the nail driven into the tent's center post—"Watch it rust"—and stepped outside. He stood within the circle of trunks and mist, buttoned his shirt with fingers still warm from sleep, tucked it in, and pulled up suspenders. Spruce twigs, shavings, match, ironwood; a trip to the stream; cold water in the eyes, cold fingers, a pot full; coffee swung from the bar; lower the meat bag; bacon; raise the bag. He ran a finger inside the dark iron skillet: it felt clean; he wiped it with his shirt elbow, moved the coffeepot over, set the skillet on the three large rocks in the coals, carefully spread the fire under the pot and placed more wood. He laid in six thick strips of bacon. The fresh wood began to crackle; the pot murmured; hard to tell which was the stream; the ghost white slices lay like strips of snow melting into the iron dark until they shriveled and then they sounded like the fire, the sizzling followed by pops. One layer of mist was filled with bacon smell. Drowsy, he sat back on a saddlebag. Smoke rose from the rumbling river in slow curls; the white strips sizzled and popped; flames shriveled in the ironwood and the pot rumbled in slow curls of smoke rising, gathering light; everything on edge, about to be seen, poised; then the murmurs and crackles parted for an instant around the first clear note of a bird. Somewhere in the darkness a horse pissed its long, noisy, puddly piss. The ammoniac odor of warm urine drifted past. His boots were too close to the fire, and he could smell the leather. The bacon smoke swirled to his nose. All three smells were warm. April. He felt his father's diary pressing into his ribs, thought "Aurora," "Dawn," and smiled. The snowbanks would soon be gone.

"Jesus Christ, he's a goddamn go-getter today!" Jaspar was awake. Shorty blinked, then stretched, yawned, and began to lace his boots.

"Rich rich rich!" he said.

"Smells good," said Jaspar, quietly, and threw his blankets to one side.

They worked hard with whipsaw, axes, and adze. First came the rocker, with a canvas bottom and whittled riffles. But even though they worked quickly, by early afternoon they knew that they were losing a race. The mist and low clouds had burned off to the warmest morning of the spring, and by noon the runoff was raising the river an inch an hour. By early afternoon the bar had shrunk to half its original size, and long streamers high in the western sky had blended to a milky white, thickening toward gray.

Tom stopped and leaned on his ax. "We're early," he said. Jaspar looked around at the equipment and supplies they had packed in, then at the shrinking bar.

He straightened up, laid his shovel aside and said they would have to stow the camp on higher ground, go back, and file on the claim. Wait for high water to pass. Where to stake? Jaspar and Tom assumed they would stake three joint claims covering each of the bars. Shorty fidgeted. They looked at him. Well? Shorty said he'd like to have a look at the back of the terrace across the river, where the tributary entered. The first drops of rain fell. Jaspar looked at the gathering sky, the river rising toward the camp yet to be moved. They already had three workable claims. Three paying gravel bars in a canyon of the upper Lewis Range, somewhere in mile upon mile of snow-drifted wilderness. In their hands. Jaspar spat. "Why?" he said.

Shorty squatted and looked in the pans as he spoke.

"The upper sample comes from the slate. It's the weakest. Your rich sand is much lighter. Now, you may be right about this being an older deposit, but either way that upper claim will likely be wasted."

He stood up. "But here," he waved back into the woods, "that's a tributary from up high. In a month when the snow melts it'll come a-roaring, and I think that terrace is its delta."

He peered across the river into the flat woods. "It's a delta, and at the back of this terrace'll be another little delta, where it used to enter, and if there's another terrace there'll be another. That little

stream over there has the gold. That's the source. Not the slate. If I
had two more claims I'd put 'em both right back there—"

"Wait a minute!" Jaspar almost shouted. There wasn't even a
stream in sight. Dark firs and snow.

Tom shook his head. "A bird—"

"—in the hand is dead," said Shorty.

A long silence. Shorty studied the woods and steep hillsides
above. Drops fell. Jaspar spoke wearily:

"It's true, if you're right, the source oughta be rich as hell. If
you're right. Tom and I will move camp and stake the lower bars.
Shorty, look at your damn terrace."

Shorty came back in two hours with a few lumps of frozen
gravel in a pan. It was raining hard and the gravel bars had gone
under. "It's a tributary, all right, but there's just this one terrace. I
couldn't dig deep."

They poured boiling water from the coffeepot on the frozen
lumps and went down to the stream to work it out. They kneeled in
muddy boots and wet coats; rain dripped off their hats; they kept
moving back from the rising river. They had to admit the sand
looked like Jaspar's sand all right, but there wasn't much color. "I
couldn't dig down," said Shorty. They waited, thinking he would
give in. He looked up, smiling and expectant above the worthless
sample.

Jaspar straightened. It must have been a hard decision: three
separate claims would cut Tom out of the good bar; or he and Tom
could go joint and let Shorty chase his wild goose alone; or they
could preserve the family. "Guess a third of it's yours," he said.

"I don't mind separate claims," said Shorty.

Tom looked at Jaspar.

"Well," said Jaspar, "Stake it joint and let's get packing."

They had to move that night. The river entered the tent while
they were asleep. With no trail and high water they led the horses
through pitch blackness, walking into trees and water and rocks
without warning.

Shorty started laughing. "I just wish," he said, "I just wish I could tell some boys back in Providence that this is a creek." Shorty kept looking back over his shoulder as if in the middle of the night in the trees in the flood he would catch sight of his gold.

They spent two months in Eureka. No one asked for Frank Harris and no one could describe the man who had. In June they returned to work the gravel bars and Shorty's terrace. Three companions: Jaspar, thirty-six, six foot two, from Independence, Missouri, big hands, who when they returned in early June took silent charge: felled spruce one on top of another along the imagined lines of the cabin walls; almost stacked spruce up from the stumps, working out from the site in four lines, so that Shorty and Tom had only to trim, notch, and raise. The steel rang, needles fell, white chips ringed the bare stumps, the negatives of winter, dark circles in the snow beneath the heavy boughs.

Jaspar hardly spoke or unhandled the ax till it was done. Then he unbuttoned his dripping woolen underwear for the first time in five days, took a chunk of smoked ham to the river and floated out of sight. When he came back, naked and dripping, ham fat congealed in his beard, he said it was a great job, clapped them on the back, picked his wet underwear out of the sand and dust, pulled it on, called the tributary Harris River, laughed, and drank for three days; on the third day he lay delirious in one corner of the unroofed cabin, seeing Indians; he kept his pistol under his blanket and screamed from time to time as Shorty and Tom walked in and out with pails of caulking mud; on the fourth day he leapt up as Tom entered, began crying, pressed back into the corner with both hands on his .44 and fired two shots. Tom stood still. His mud pail began to drip. Shorty threw his bucket at the corner and dove through a window hole; Tom ran out the door. When Jaspar fell asleep they took the whiskey and gun. Later they nursed him on coffee. He laughed to hear what he had done, ran a thumb across the edge, and said, "Jesus Christ, what did you guys do to the ax?" At fifteen he had fought in the Civil War, usually for the North, he said. He shot a cow elk in June, their first fresh meat.

Tom: five ten, twenty-two, from Lexington, Kentucky, blue eyes, genial and open. He spoke pleasantly and was ignored. He talked about getting rich and going back to Lexington, where he had a little girl waiting. For weeks Shorty and Jaspar thought he had a daughter. He was four years older than his wife; he had not heard from her in two years. Tom slowed down after two weeks of shoveling. He gradually took over the lighter chores and the cooking. Tom was easy enough to be around.

Shorty Harris: barely five feet four, twenty-four, black eyes and dark brown hair. Quick, tight movements. Once Jaspar, watching Shorty shovel, could almost see things passing through his head like gravel through the sluice: the quick glance at the trough—now, who had braced it wrong—at Tom—why doesn't he turn partway around and save his energy—the long tom—should have built the rockers of a harder wood—the location—and the quick glances up—what bird was that?—and finally a long look at the windswept cornice high above. Now what the hell could he want up there? Could he have done that better too? Shorty caught Jaspar watching and looked back straight into his eyes.

In Providence Shorty's favorite game had been rolling marbles down a track. His grandfather had given him sections of slightly hollowed blocks that he would put together in long inclines and banked curves. The marble would jump off at a fast curve or a bumpy joint. By releasing two marbles two fingerwidths apart he could have a race of sorts. The second marble he considered the underdog, although starting higher and being the fastest it usually won. He would play for hours, running through the collection until he had the best for that course, then taking all comers. Teeth clenched, palms wet, his nose almost touching the outside edge of the fastest curve, he would watch his yellow marble gain down the big ramp, fall behind over the first hill; then the two marbles would flash past his nose a quarter-inch apart, rocking high up on the edge of the trough, and in the last straightaway his yellow under-dog would move up and bump the leader. Beneath the freckles his slow smile pulled the lips from his teeth.

When he went to work at the shoe factory he stopped playing.

"He's too good for us," Jaspar said to Tom. "A hard-rock man."

In one month he quit. He did not know why. Perhaps he did not like the work, the work of water in the dark, rich forests, and he from a light, dry land. The water washed the vein, washed the gold, sorted and placed. The men rewashed the gravel in the long tom pans. The work of the ocean, of waves made by wind and moon, the work of tides that washed incessantly back and forth, back and forth upon a beach of gold as the long tom rocked and squeaked like a moored ship and the glacial water rose and fell with the rhythms of day and night, day and night, continuous, steady, sure; plow gravel and water it: plow more, water more, slow and sure: a crop, a harvest: reap what you sow. He needed more.

Shorty sold out his interest for half their supplies, a pack mule, and two hundred dollars in gold. Tom wanted to accompany him for just a few weeks, as a lark. Shorty didn't care; Jaspar didn't care. The two young men left that afternoon.

The evening after they left, a man in a stovepipe hat walked up to Jaspar's fire and said he was Shorty's friend. Jaspar said he didn't know any Shorty Harris and had no partners, but any fool could see it was more than a one man set-up, and Jaspar figured it wouldn't be hard for the man to pick up their tracks. The strange little fellow took his horse and moved upstream before dark.

CHAPTER 7

Search, 1874

April Creek flows west, into the north fork of the Flathead River. The outcrop of slate cut across the tributary from the northwest, and it was from the north that the secondary tributary, "Harris River," a cascading mountain creek, came with its gold.

Shorty thought it likely that the slate formation cut by April Creek outcropped somewhere to the north with richer veins cut by the Harris River. He planned to follow the watercourse, study its drainage, and trace the line of the slate.

Shorty and Tom crossed the terrace and began pushing up the steep slope beside Harris River in long switchbacks, leading two mules. Tom fell silent. Shorty held his pace. He left the creek and angled for higher ground. On a flat, Shorty unrolled his blanket and gathered wood. Tom stumbled in and lay by the fire while Shorty cooked. The trees were stunted, twenty feet high. When the moon rose, Shorty could see snow on the ridge across April Creek and icy summits not that far above.

At first light Shorty started up the ridge. The snow was frozen solid, the walking fast. By dawn he had gained the tree line and a view of the country ahead: fold upon fold of ridges rising to iced peaks and dark rock. His map said only "Rocky Mountains" and showed no tributaries of the Flathead. He folded it into his pocket. Far to the east, in the gray light, snow banners trailed from white summits. He became conscious of the wind roaring up steep snow slopes below. His ears and hands were cold.

To work: He looked down on April Creek. There was the slate bed, cutting diagonally across just above the bend. He projected its line up the ridge, past the camp, into the unknown land behind him. Where would it come up again? He traced an imaginary line north into the basin drained by Harris Creek. Somewhere in that basin, creeks must cross the bed of slate. No outcrops were visible. He stared again at the strike of the visible slate and traced a line up the ridge with his thumb. Where in hell did it go?

His thumb was frozen. He suddenly remembered crossing the cold snow of Telescope Peak at night, just one year before. The high snow ridges were the color of dawn, the dawn on the salt flats of Death Valley floor. The desert pecked at his memory like a beak inside a thin shell.

"I'll find the son of a bitch," he said and drew his cold thumb into his fist.

Tom was still asleep. Shorty made coffee, packed, and waited. He heard a twig snap in the woods, from a heavy animal, like a bear. He brought his rifle close.

Tom's lids fluttered open.

"Let's go," said Shorty. He began to pack the mule. "There's your coffee."

They angled off the ridge back into the mountains and emerged onto the soft alpine meadows of a high basin. It was an old glacial cirque, kept clean of trees by avalanches, green with alpine grass and moss, tinted with lupine. The Harris River headed in a trickle from a small glacier a thousand feet above. Shorty panned the first rivulet as it crossed the meadow, and as he knelt he waved Tom ahead to the next. When they reached the stream below the glacier they panned with special care, then descended along the other bank, testing each tiny tributary and the main stream. No color.

They worked the basin for two days. Shorty was sure that the vein would cross this valley. On the third day, he saw slate high on the eastern rim. He ascended the snow gully in their old tracks, then clambered up to the rock. It was folded and severely weathered, rotten rock, shale and sandstone, with a small coal seam. He stood on talus so steep it slid with every step; he stood above the steep snow, far above the valley, and cursed. The strike was all wrong, southwest, the rock wrong; it was all too far east anyway; he should have figured that out from the valley. Besides, if it was rich there'd be some placer below.

The sun was going down. He looked up, found a short, steep chimney, and wriggled up past the slate cliff. He gained the top of the ridge at twilight and studied the land again. If the slate in April Creek dipped just a little more than he had figured it was possible that the bed passed downhill of this entire valley, running a little more west perhaps, crossed Harris River somewhere down in the steep woods, and crossed the range west of this basin. Son of a bitch. They'd have to backtrack all the way to Harris River and pick up the slate somewhere below. He scanned the basin, looking for movement. He had the feeling that a bear was following him, and neither one of them would want to be surprised.

He and Tom camped the next night at the first tributary of Harris River, a six-inch stream from the east ridge, at dusk. Shorty panned in the dark, after supper, and proved it out by firelight. No color.

The first waterfall up Harris River was a granite intrusion with no mineralization. These were evenly banded mountains, and his slate bed ran with the bands. As they went up the next day he started recognizing formations, and soon he knew the slate bed should cut across . . . They panned a pool and found some color.

When he saw the second waterfall, there it was: the edge of a slate bed, angling at about thirty degrees and pointing straight at the bed on April Creek. Laced with light quartz veins highly mineralized. The sand in the pool was light. He walked into the spray and ran his fingers on the vein. Quartz, copper, pyrite? Just because the gold wasn't visible . . .

They panned, good color, one pan after another. The sand got richer to a depth of one foot, then went barren. At dark Shorty quit.

After dinner, fire nearly dead, they smoked.

"Well?" said Tom.

"Well what?"

"Well, I guess this is it," Tom said.

No answer from the glowing pipe.

"I mean, I guess you were right. This was the source for those placers, all right." Tom peered at the glow, trying to find a place to fill in the silence. Then he swallowed and went on, "But I guess it's most gone now."

The other pipe was tapped on a boot. It was the only sound in the woods. Five or six glowing red flakes lay scattered on the ground. Tom watched them disappear one by one, and heard the grinding of a heel.

"Yup," came from the darkness.

"Well?"

"Well what?"

"What are you gonna do now?"

There was a silence, then rustling. Shorty must be crawling under his blanket. Was he sleeping in his boots?

"I'm gonna quit, Shorty." Tom peered at the blanket in the dark. "Do you mind being alone?"

The next day Shorty helped Tom take the mule down to April Creek. He sat within sight of the cascade, looking at the slate bed and the mountains, trying to figure where the quartz-bearing formation might appear above. Then he slowly made his way alone up by the waterfalls of Harris Creek, panning again as he went. Jaspar sent Tom back to warn Shorty that a man had been looking for him, but Shorty was already gone, and a tired Tom looked back up the steep slopes with resignation.

Shorty's camp that evening was quiet and cold. A cloudless pink sunset had flared off into bright stars and a hard frost. He sat smoking while his mind viewed, as in an eagle's dream, the country beneath him, searching for the little rabbit hole of gold. "A fresh start." He didn't smile now at the familiar words. "Go back rich." The fire crackled, then he suddenly looked up. Something else had cracked. Thinking bear, he took his rifle, left the dinner remains by the fire, and backed off into the woods behind him, circling in the dark below the sound, for the cold night air had begun to flow downslope.

Within half an hour he was seated again at the campfire, warming his hands and the remains of his dried elk stew, his gun leaning against the tree ten feet away. Small O'Keefe walked silently into the camp behind him and picked up his rifle. Shorty kept looking at the fire and said, calmly, "I know a hundred bad Irish jokes."

Small stepped around in front of him.

"Hello, Harris."

Shorty looked up at the runt in the stovepipe hat, holding a pistol and Shorty's rifle.

"I said I know a hundred—"

"Maybe you don't see this gun, Harris, or who this is."

"Maybe you don't know I saw you coming and found your horse and rubbed fresh grizzly shit on his bridle. Then I turned him loose and he headed out like Eureka would suit him fine. And maybe you don't know my mule won't let anyone on her and I doubt you want to see my friends at April Creek again. So you can plug me, or we can both go, but you sure as hell are walking out."

Small fidgeted. This is too easy, thought Shorty, but then, what smart guy ever worked for Hicks? You, he thought.

"Anyway," said Shorty, "Brandon Hicks is a long way away. You may as well sit and have some stew. Look," Shorty stood up and turned around, pulling his shirttails out. "I'm not armed." He sat down again. "And I've got a pint." He opened the bottle. Small eyed the bubbling stew, unloaded Shorty's rifle, and sat opposite Shorty, pistol in his lap. After eating awhile, he said, "MacDonald was my friend."

"He was killing Dayton. I had no choice."

Small's pig eyes had a hard glint, then he went back to eating. Shorty let him eat, then asked, "Why are you here?"

"Hicks was very angry at you."

"What does he want?"

"T.S. was about to publish a special edition of the paper, all about Hicks's dealings."

"What happened?"

"T.S. disappeared."

Shorty looked down. "Jesus Christ. Dead?"

"Maybe not. Hicks thinks T.S. told you most everything."

"You mean you're supposed to kill me?"

Small shrugged.

"What's to gain?" said Shorty. "You've gone a year, a thousand miles, after me? I don't know any more than everyone in Panamint City."

Small smiled. "Hicks had business in Colorado, and I have relatives in Butte." He ate awhile.

Shorty's curiosity was oddly distant.

"What are you going to do?"

Small shrugged again. "Tell me one of your jokes, Harris."

Shorty poked the fire, threw on some fir branches and stretched out.

"Father O'Malley was missing his bicycle, you know, and he went to the bishop and said his bike had been stolen and what could he do about it. 'The Lord will help you,' said the bishop. 'Just recite the Ten Commandments, and when you get to "Thou shalt not steal," mention the bike a bit in passing, and the Lord will give you a sign.' A few weeks later they met in the village. 'Did the Lord help you, Father?' 'Ah, sure He did, your excellency, and He didn't wait for theft, for when I got to "adultery" I remembered where I'd left my bike.' "

Small laughed. "I know that joke. My father used to tell it."

"Really? It's a Kildare joke."

"My family's from Kildare."

"O'Keefe?"

"Mother's side. Donelly."

Shorty sat up. "My mother's brother married a Donelly in Carlow. I was over there for the wedding, in 1858 I think."

"You were in Carlow? Jesus Christ. It must have been Colleen Donelly."

"That's right!"

"Oh, she was a beauty. I grew up with her, you know. We came over in '49, when I was ten. Sorry bunch of us it was, too, when we landed in Boston."

"I was born that year. Left Providence in '59."

"I heard your old man had money."

Shorty's eyes misted. "I guess he did, once."

"My family ain't never had shit."

"Ah," said Shorty, "the O'Keefes have had their proud moments."

"Not in this country. You hear about Mike and Denny O'Keefe," Small began, "goin' the rounds in Boston, and soon they were feelin' no pain and wandered into the rich folks' neighborhood and Mike says, "Let's have one for the road.' So they go into this pub that's got the longest bar they've ever seen and behind it is this huge mirror all the way down to the end. . ."

Shorty looked up but Small didn't notice.

". . . floor to ceiling. And Mike says, 'Hey Denny, look at that guy way down the bar there, he looks like me, an' the fellow beside him looks like you. Maybe they're cousins. Let's buy 'em a drink.'"

Shorty didn't laugh, and as he finished another pull Small suddenly remembered the mirror in Dexter's and held the bottle in midair.

"Gosh, Shorty, I'm sorry. I didn't think—"

"It's nothing."

"I'm sorry. Hell," Small grinned, "I don't know what got into you that night, but it was my pistol."

They fell silent.

"How's my family?" said Shorty.

"Fair, I suppose. Dayton is helping out, but he's not got as much as he thought. And June helps, and your mother and Lane."

Shorty swallowed and looked away.

"I suppose you could go back, if that's what you mean."

Shorty didn't reply.

"But it'd be best to go back rich." Small took a drink. "I guess Hicks told May he'd give her money for some of your worthless properties. She told him off good."

Shorty laughed.

"And I guess June was there. She told him off really good. Beat him with her bonnet in the middle of Main Street and kicked him in the nuts."

They both laughed.

"I got the property papers for you to sign," Small was still laughing, "to buy me off, you know . . ."

"Under duress," said Shorty.

"Yeah, and guess where they are?"

"Saddlebags." Shorty was laughing.

"To hell and gone I guess, behind that grizzly shit."

They laughed long and hard now, and Small rolled over to reach for the pint and the pistol rolled out of his lap and Shorty's hand that had held out the bottle to Small went smoothly down and came up with the pistol without Small even seeing it done. He finished his pull on the bottle, lowered it, and saw the pistol in Shorty's hand. They looked at each other in mutual surprise.

"It just happened," Shorty said. "I didn't plan it." Small's crinkled face looked hurt. "Here," Shorty said, handing back the loaded gun. "I'm sorry."

O'Keefe's eyes were moist. He took the gun and laid it behind him, on the ground.

They smoked awhile. The pint was finished.

"What'll you tell Hicks?" said Shorty.

"What do you want me to tell him? And the others?"

"That I'm on to something big."

"Twenty percent to Hicks?"

"That'll cover you?"

"I guess."

"But it's stupid. How would he know . . ."

Small looked hurt again. "It's stupid, and he'll yell, but he'll believe me." Small smiled. "I'm not the brains of the outfit, Shorty."

"The luck of the O'Keefes?" They laughed. Small peered about the camp in the darkness.

"You're not on to anything here."

"I will be."

"Where?"

"I don't know. Somewhere around here. Within a few miles."

"Want a partner?"

Shorty hesitated. "This is something I'd better do alone."

"Well, I guess tomorrow I'll head back." Then they were both laughing again. "How the hell am I going to do that?"

"I'll take you down," said Shorty, "to Tom and Jaspar. They'll give you a horse. There's a fellow in Whitefish that brings in supplies. Send the horse back to camp with him. You'll probably find yours on the way out. It's one drainage the whole way. You have money?"

Small patted his vest and nodded.

"Well," said Shorty. "I'm tired."

Again, the next day, Shorty made the trip down to April Creek. Tom and Jaspar could not understand his leaving right away. He hiked straight back up to his camp.

◆　◆　◆

Just himself now, and well into August. There would be mist in the lower valleys. He rolled on his side, the frost crunching under his elbow, and looked across the clearing. The grass was so yellow before dawn. Or was it the time of year? He looked for aspen, and found some a mile away upslope. Yes, they were yellower too. He hadn't noticed. He wondered if his daughter knew that leaves turn yellow, or that deer drink at the small times of the day. He sat up in his blankets.

He had a good line on the vein. Two points of reference for the strike, and two different angles for guessing its dip. The words rang hollow in his head: "I'll go back rich." He stood for a moment in his underwear, on top of his two blankets, wondering which was the lie: rich, or go back. Or both.

The vein crossed Harris Creek on so low and so forested a slope that Shorty figured it would be buried until it went over the bare ridges above treeline. It might be cut here or there by streams, but all fed into April Creek, which they'd already panned. So, he thought as he dressed, I'll find the vein where it crosses the ridgetop. Oughta be visible there.

He could see three peaks on the ridge, all high, nine or ten thousand feet, steep, rotten, banded, intruded sedimentary-metamorphic peaks. Small glaciers. He poked sticks into the fire. He knew he couldn't stay up there long, not at this time of year, and supplies would run short, but maybe he could locate a high outcrop before the first big snow and come back in the spring. It occurred to him that he was not acting very reasonably. He watched the fire and slid cold fingers about his coffee cup. Suddenly the flame went out on the uppermost stick. Thick curls of smoke circled from its tip; then, charred and gray, it broke in half and fell, breaking again and again into red coals, to the ground. The sun hit the ridge above. He watched the fire die.

He climbed out of Harris Basin over to the next cirque west and swung his heavy supplies from a stunted hemlock at the lower end of the meadow, near treeline. He looked around. No sign of the vein. He had a month. It had to be within ten miles west.

♦ ♦ ♦

The mountain was steeper and bigger than he had thought. It took him several days to prospect up to the summit above, and then he saw an awesome peak rising to the west and realized that he had only climbed a bump on the ridge. No trace of the vein. But it could easily be on the other side of the big peak.

He went down to camp. Evening: a snow flurry. The next day it stuck till noon. He took a light pack and approached the ridge again. It must be September, he thought. Powder snow dusted the rocks. Overcast, no wind. On top of the ridge he was caught in another storm. He sat down to wait it out. He sat for two days in a blanket, eating cold hardtack and snow. When the storm was spent he rose, dizzy and weak, to go down, for the year if not for good, but the sky deepened to a bowl so blue that he tumbled into it, up and up into the brilliant light. He walked the ridge, light-headed and graceful, without knowing that he was fifty feet above the vein, which was running along the rock below, parallel to the ridgetop. As he climbed he could not see it, and it was buried beneath rubble at the ridgetop. At the summit he stared to the north and west. Nothing. He was weak and giddy. He knew he should return to camp. With the next storm for sure the summer would be gone. Tom and Jaspar were probably at the cabin. He could drop in for a rest and they could pack out together. He could use a mule. He turned to go. When he turned he saw the western face of the spur ridge for the first time. There it was—the dark slate band running the entire length of the ridge almost in a line with the April Creek camp miles in the background, angling underneath his feet out of sight, and—he turned again—it would cross there and cut east again down the north slope—he ran down steep talus on the north side, blocks rolling beneath his feet—an unknown basin and a green glacial lake twinkled far below—and in ten minutes he stood on an outcrop of slate laced with veins of quartz. It angled northeast, visible down to tree line, where it disappeared beneath the soil. He slung off his pack and grabbed his hammer; pounded away at quartz veins right and left and smashed rocks in his hands. No color. But he'd found it, by God, he had a line on the vein and it couldn't get away. It was just a matter of time. He could almost feel the yellow lacings now in the barren rock he crumbled in his fist. There's some right here in my hand, he thought, but it's too dark to see.

He raised his head suddenly. The sun was gone. Flame-colored mare's tails were sweeping across the sky from the west, and the shadowed sides of the icy peaks were blue. He felt so light he thought the spinning earth might flick him off.

♦ ♦ ♦

He wintered in Butte, "the richest hill on earth," a huge wind-swept rise of copper, nickel, tin, gold, and silver, in a semiarid, frozen valley of Montana Territory.

It's never far to a bar in Butte. Across a mud lane, between the horse piles, down a boardwalk. Shorty walked into a dark room. Two kerosene lamps hung from the ceiling; a wooden counter with a glass front along one wall: "Sundries": apothecary jars, clothing, candies; along the other wall, a wooden counter with a brass foot rail, three men drinking; a rack of liquor bottles; glasses; drawings of pretty girls with high collars, hair up, holding a bottle in slender fingers, head turned slightly; behind both counters, dimly lit implements: harness and bit, ax, scythe, a long selection of shovels, pans, drill bits, augers, all with wooden handles and dull steel; light only from the two lamps and a roaring coal stove four feet high; red flashes from the mica windows and peephole joints, from the grate-shaker hole. All surfaces wood, blued tin or steel, glass, ceiling white tin; flames gave light.

As men talked and the stove roared, in a corner of the room sat Shorty. He swept out, tended bar, and sat against the wall, feet propped up. On the floor beside him lay the books he always carried—the Bible and his father's diary—and now, in addition, every geology and prospecting text he could find. When done with the textbooks for the day, again and again he returned to his father's blank diary chapters: "Primary Gold," "Secondary Gold," "Free Gold," "Strikes, Dips, and Displacements," "Free Water," as if those empty pages must have the final word.

In the spring of 1874 he read of Verdi's Requiem Mass for Mazoni at St. Mark's in Milan. News from another planet—he roused himself to write for the score, through a friendly Italian bookstore in Butte, directly to Giuseppe Verdi, care of St. Mark's Cathedral, Milano. But he knew that he and Butte and the Rockies if not the whole country could not exist for Milan, and he suddenly felt scruffy and poor and small.

He told his bookseller friend, Alfredo Cippolato, that he was onto a big lead that would soon cash in and he'd make it to Bayreuth, Germany, for the Ring Cycle premiere the next year, and take Alfredo and anyone else in Butte for that matter, and they talked of Wagner's performance of Beethoven's Ninth in 1872. Shorty had sent five dollars to the Wagner Society to help build the theater. They talked a lot, for both men knew they were lucky—Germany aside—just to be able to buy each other drinks.

Through the dark, long winter, Shorty poured his energy into the blank chapters of the diary, seeking there his Jubilato, Requiem, and Agnus Dei. The other men in the bar hardly noticed anymore when Shorty raised his eyes from the geology books to stare blankly at the walls, looking out of his face. "Primary Gold."

CHAPTER 8

Primary Gold

I have before me on the table a small vial of gold. Perhaps fifty little flakes and nuggets, surprisingly colorful—dull orange and yellow earth tones, muted—and smooth; they would all fit on my thumbnail. One pan's worth—ten minutes' work once the deposit is found—thirty cents, about a dollar in Shorty's day. I panned it in April Creek last year, not two miles from where Shorty's search began. This is secondary, "placer" gold.

Beside the vial is a chunk of white quartz the size of my fist. In the quartz are tiny dark brown veins or filigrees slightly sprinkled with yellow specks. The quartz is very rich and rotten, from Wonder Canyon. I could smash it with a hammer, grind it, pulverize it, separate the elements by water or a centrifugal drum, and I would have some iron, copper, a little silver, and perhaps the same amount—thirty cents' worth—of gold. Primary gold. The Source. Kneeling by a stream in the Canadian Rockies in 1873, Shorty Harris, assayer and child of a mining camp, was familiar with gold both as an element and as the absolute center of a centuries-old European and racial if not universal myth and obsession that was largely responsible for the discovery, exploration, theft, and settling of this continent and that now, for the first time, he knew he needed. Gold: that strange and rare mineral which, far beyond its value on the exchange, has moved the hearts of men.

Although knowledge of gold's formation in primary deposits and disintegration into secondary deposits, and of techniques appropriate to the recovery of it in either case, was disseminated in the mining communities by texts such as Dana's mineralogies, along with countless treatises on prospecting, this is not really a matter of geology. And though this knowledge was mastered and modified by those thousands who between 1849 and 1914 patiently walked over every mile—it must be, for the blankest map is sprinkled with the crossed pick and shovel that signifies a mine— every mile of ground between the Rockies and the coast, from Mexico to Canada, this is not really a matter of experience.

If I could chronicle the development of Shorty Harris's understanding of gold, every other event in his life would be superfluous. Gold and the search for it lay behind and around him, and ahead. Gold was his prospect, and though it might seem an unusual or exotic or colorful perspective, he would have said by the end of his life— indeed did say to me though not in so many words—that all prospects are contained in that formidable beginning and possible end to which his father had pointed with a steady and suicidal hand: "stone."

The Formation of Mineral Deposits in Igneous Rock

Primary, or original, mineral deposits are produced during the cooling and crystallization of fluid rock. This is the "time of mineralization":

When fluid rock of average composition cools and crystallizes, minerals of definite chemical composition form in an orderly sequence, commencing with the olivines, pyroxenes, amphibols, and plagioclase feldspars, and ending with biotite mica and orthoclase feldspar, muscovite mica and quartz.

The "orderly sequence" of formation is accomplished by the gradually lowering temperatures of the cooling rock; one by one, each at its proper time, the minerals form. Thus quartz, at the end of the sequence, remains fluid or vaporized the longest, and crystallizes last.

Conversely, when the rock is warmed—as someday it will be, whether by the dipping of the continental plate, as has happened often, or by the enlargement of our sun, as will happen once—the same orderly sequence will be followed in reverse and the quartz will return soonest to its fluid state; the last shall be first. Quartz thus occupies a special, extreme position in the "orderly sequence" of minerals, and it is this extreme position in a system of perfect symmetry that causes it to be associated with that most extreme element, gold.

Even after the quartz has cooled and the last "rock-forming mineral" has set, most of the "metallic minerals," such as gold, silver, copper, lead, zinc, and tin, are still in a fluid or vaporized state; because they do not "enter into the composition" of the rock-forming minerals, because they have "an affinity or attraction for" sulfur, oxygen, and some of the rarer elements, and because their temperature of crystallization is so low, especially in the presence of water vapor:

It therefore happens that during the crystallization of a fluid rock-mass the minute quantities of these valuable mineral-forming elements are separated, segregated, and concentrated.

During a period of cooling, gold becomes concentrated as it awaits crystallization. This is true to some degree of every mineral; true to the highest degree of gold. It waits longest, crystallizes last. Strangely enough, one could say in geological terms that gold "desires" most to be "pure": separated, segregated and concentrated. Gold is no mere bauble, its place in our eyes and hearts, no accident.

In an ideal situation, that is, an abstracted and therefore simplified and unnatural one, mineral deposits would be found as pure concentrations within the igneous rocks and one might, like a skillful surgeon, simply open the granite and remove the balls of gold: Alas, this is not a matter of fact.

Instead, an infinite number of variables intervene between cause and effect, between the hot fluid rock at the core of this earth and the tiny tip of gold at the surface. These variables, naturally, make gold's actual origin and placement obscure and complex. A few of the known variables are:

First: Fluid rock that simply comes to the surface, that is, extrusive or volcanic rock, cools too quickly to allow a useful separation of minerals, and thus in practice gold is rarely found in the simplest case of rock cooling—volcanic extrusions—except in minute, scattered traces.

Second: The fluid rock in which we are interested cools more slowly inside of or under other rock, where it has forced itself in what are called igneous intrusions. The character of this other rock, said to be "intruded," its joints, fissures and faults, its general permeability, its own minerals, melting and combining, will affect where the intrusions go, and how they cool; that is, how thoroughly the gold is separated, segregated and concentrated; how pure the gold becomes before it sets.

Third: The cooling rock is generally moving upward, forced from below. The higher the fluid rock is forced, the farther it is from its source of heat, and the closer to the surface of the earth; therefore the faster it cools. So along the vertical length of a vein of intrusive rock many rates of cooling may exist; the rate of cooling is also affected by the thickness of the vein, the insulating value of the intruded rock, the presence of water vapor, all of which factors may change often within a single vein, always affecting the cooling rate and therefore affecting the concentration of the gold.

Fourth: These intrusions and crystallizations occur not once but repeatedly through geologic eras, sometimes along one vein, sometimes taking different courses, sometimes differing in mineral content.

Fifth: In its constant contortions the earth's crust bends itself, buries, heaves, recompresses and reheats, severs, fractures in new directions, and freshly intrudes, so that a single vein is rarely the product of a single "time of mineralization"; or if it is, not for long.

Where, then, to look for gold? Earth's precious sweat and purest mineral, last to concentrate and cool in tiny filigrees perched like perfect blossoms atop vast upheavals from the earth; near igneous intrusions; not at their center, but at points of greatest travel from the hot core; near the last rock to cool, often quartz; in formations where the last vapors come to rest: little fissures and veins; high in veins at the time of their intrusion, farthest from the source; nearest the surface; veins drawn out long and fine, veins of quartz that experienced one delicate temperature change out of millions and now lie momentarily exposed, blossoming veins breaking through the crust—earth to air, one element meeting another naked to the eye—but the bloom no sooner opens than it begins to weather, fade, fall, and wash away.

So then it is a thin slice of time and space, the top of a vertical line, a point really, a vanishing point—a moment only and the delicate flower is gone—where and when one finds primary gold.

CHAPTER 9

Secondary Gold

To find primary gold one must, like an apprentice, move through the lower stages of knowledge and desire, approach through traces that wash away. Those lower traces are secondary gold.

A mineral six to nine times the weight of water, such as copper, is considered heavy, and silver, eleven times the weight of water, very heavy; gold, depending on its purity, has a specific gravity of 15.6 to 19.3. Even in highly impure field situations, when gold is sometimes alloyed with silver, one knows that the gold in a stream will be at least eleven times heavier than water. One of the heaviest elements, in practical situations gold is the heaviest mineral or rock likely to be found in its environs. Magnetite, for instance, 72.4 percent iron, has a specific gravity of 5. Agitate a pan of water and gravel; below the magnetite will be copper, below the copper will be silver, below the silver will be gold— gold that has been removed from its primary deposit.

Whereas the placement of primary gold depends upon temperature, the placement of secondary gold always depends, in one way or another, upon weight. This is reasonable, for the secondary gold is sinking back toward the center of the earth, and gravity, not rising heat, is now its law; and it is appropriate that all weight is measured by the standard of water, for water is the greatest agent of downward movement on the surface of the earth.

It is a fine paradox that the lightest particles reach the sea first, while the heaviest particles remain high up nearest their source, at every moment sinking so effectively that the stream can hardly carry them along. The earth is top heavy. Are the weighty, the powerful so impatient to find their place, so loath to go along for the ride? Gold has such extraordinary weight that water carries off everything else first, leaving gold further "separated, segregated and concentrated" into little pockets or "placers" of water-worn nuggets close to their source.

In a primary deposit, fused by heat and pressure, fresh from the core and then cooled, the elements are imperfectly separated, unevenly distributed, and sometimes complexly alloyed; a primary deposit is in its origin, nature and general situation somewhat obscure. There is a saying: "The more hackly, the closer to the source."

A secondary deposit is more refined, the result not of creation but of something more like dispassionate analysis: in a secondary deposit, water judges size and weight, separates and sorts, makes clear distinctions. When all is sand the gold will be pure at the bottom. But even so, the secondary is not primary, for without heat, what would water sort? One shudders: all clarity, and no matter; the mind without passion; a bottomless sea.

The balance of the universe requires deposits of both kinds; hot rock and cold water. Though the search for it has driven men to madness, the contemplation of gold, which tends toward all extremes, brings one to a halt; and therefore, in some cases, to rest.

The Formation of Mineral Deposits by Weathering, Transportation, and Concentration

Secondary mineral deposits are formed by the weathering of primary deposits, followed by the transportation and concentration of freed minerals. The prospector must know how this weathering works. The following agents weather rock, turn back the upthrust of the earth until it falls of its own weight upon itself:

Air: Chemical weathering: Oxygen and other gases interact with chemicals in the rock:

Ore deposits . . . are sometimes greatly changed in the zone of oxidation, certain or all minerals being removed, some entirely, some only to be redeposited a little deeper to form zones of enrichment.

Because of this enriching drainage, in the Southwest there is another saying: "The deeper the richer." Mechanical weathering occurs when temperature changes cause the rock to expand and contract, and when windborne particles abrade. Other air-related weathering is caused by a combination of air and water.

Water: Moisture dissolves certain air-borne gases, some of which then form acids: moisture will penetrate cracks, freeze and expand.

Running water: Falling as rain or draining off, water will have the impact of its weight and speed and carry abrasive particles and acids; falling as snow may accumulate and drain off in avalanches with tremendous impact or compact for eons into glaciers with abrasive particles the size of a house—and finally run off as water.

Groundwater: Acids leach the rock. The zone of weathering extends from the air to the permanent water table: rarely deeper than one half mile; one sixtieth of the earth's crust; one eight-thousandth of the distance to the center of the earth.

Organic life:

Growing plants take carbon dioxide from the air, store up the carbon, and release the oxygen. When they die and decay, part of the carbon is converted back to carbon dioxide, which, being taken into solution, forms carbonic acid, a solvent of rock material. Decaying vegetation also forms the dark matter, or humus, in the soil, and this, too, forms acids that attack and destroy rocks, converting them into soil. Roots of trees penetrate small fractures in the rocks and, growing, split them apart.

Such organic destruction may be important in areas of high rainfall; but in such areas the same plants and the same roots that use water to dissolve or fracture also prevent water erosion by covering the rock with a mat of soil. It follows that in a cold, wet country such as British Columbia, only near steep slopes or in fast streams are the minerals likely to be on the move; but there, where the rock is naked, weathering will be fast and thorough.

Organic life: Animals that burrow and loosen or appropriate the rock to their own purposes may be said in the broadest sense to "weather" the land. In this case the geologist speaks from the point of view of the rock, from which point of view the rest of the universe looks "natural": most notable of the weathering animals are worms and man.

These are the weathering agents, impalpable or soft—gas, fluid, plants, flesh—that destroy rock. They attack the primary deposits that have crystallized at or near the surface of the earth between the water table and the highest ground, a thin margin only five miles deep in which the rock has no rest, for no sooner has it cooled than the moisture condenses and decomposition begins; in which heat and cold fight never to a standstill, although neither wins; a thin margin of interpenetrated earth and sky in which everything being pushed up is also being broken down, in which growth is simultaneous with decay and the same agents, air and water, serve both; a thin margin in which we live our lives and which shapes all that our unaided senses know.

CHAPTER 10

Free Gold

All gold, then, primary or secondary, is on the move. The prospector, like the hunter, must know where it will pause.

When rocks and mineral deposits are attacked by the agencies of weathering some minerals are destroyed to produce new ones, and others, more resistant, are set free.

Like other free agents, gold at first can do nothing with its freedom but go with the flow: the story of free gold is the story of water.

When we know gold's properties—it is extraordinarily heavy, it is not destroyed, it does not easily combine or alloy, and therefore we know that it will be segregated from lighter elements in suspension and will sink at the very first opportunity downstream of its primary deposit, will indeed remain on bedrock swept clean of almost all other particles—then we realize that to trace the movement of free gold is to know not only how water flows—the properties of a stream at a given time, its current, force, slack spots—but also how water has flowed in the past in a given area—where streams and their slacks spots were.

The factors that affect the ability of gold to sink or "place" are the velocity, direction, and bed of the stream. These variables affect current and therefore determine where free gold will come to rest. The combination of these factors with the geological history of the river can guide the prospector to ancient placers now buried or dry.

Any irregularities in the stream's velocity, direction, or bed will cause slack spots of weaker current—pools, eddies, riffles—where particles will concentrate; larger, hackly gold particles might be found quite purely segregated at the least slack of these spots just downstream of an outcrop; the smaller particles farther downstream will be mixed with the heavier sands; the gold embedded in still lighter particles such as quartz may travel well downstream and "place" only after it is freed. The finest particles will enrich the silt and mud of sandbars for miles: "The result will be a pay streak extending downstream from near the outcrop." Words to warm the heart.

The variables affecting these placements are countless. Outcrops and their ores come and go; their rate of destruction varies; so too the gold's "freedom" from other attached minerals as it enters running water; the water's velocity varies during the year, and near glaciers each day; and most important to the prospector, streams themselves alter course, entire drainage systems—mountain ranges—rise, sink, and disappear.

If a mountain range is being tilted to the west, the western streams will be cutting deeper and straightening their old channels; the eastern streams will be building and meandering, depositing new silt on top of their old beds. On the west side the prospector will look for old "bench" deposits up in the banks and old placers up on neighboring terraces, all above the present water level, the deposits of a higher, slower, meandering stream. Shorty recognized such a situation at their camp on the west side of the Rockies. On the east, a pay streak hit at a depth of four feet, "a deep lead," may continue in a line beneath the present meandering stream along the straight course of a lower, faster ancient stream. A stream may slow down, wander, and raise its bed, then speed up, straighten and cut more deeply many times in its history, affecting both placement and richness of deposits. Given a history of rock and erosion in a certain area, the prospector may be able to focus his search, trying to determine, say, the course of a stream at the time of the last ice age runoff, when erosion was severe and rich placer deposits were formed. In British Columbia there is evidence of deepening valleys during Tertiary time when land already weathered was raised—thus severely weathered minerals already free were suddenly transported and concentrated—"and it is possible that the deep deposits in the Caribou were formed at that time."

So movements of the land up and down, intrusions, tiltings, the varying configurations and types of rock over which a stream is flowing; changes of climate by epoch, season, day, as well as the complex evolution of a stream in a static environment—erosion at one end, deposits at the other, natural dykes, deltas, alluvial fans— and hydrodynamics—how a doubled velocity will transport sixty-four times the material, or how a water flow is shaped—these changes remind us how thoroughly fluid is gold's environment, that thin margin where earth and sky meet.

Whorf's statement that the Hopis' verbs have only a present tense has been a touchstone for those who assert that the present is more real than other times, and Thoreau was pleased to say that for the Puri Indians past, present and future are one. But even a present verb is too slow for the world of gold. "The river meanders" implies a static condition, at least during the instant of observation, and to indicate the possibility of change we would add some ironic fillip such as "now." An idea is unnaturally static. Only the present participle is really accurate: "the river is meandering," for while the river exists only its existence is predictable—predicate-able— it indeed "is," while all other qualities are on the move. Where today it is meandering, tomorrow it will be running straight. Even during the instant of observation it "is meandering increasingly" or "decreasingly," depending on which side of the range we occupy, and no one becomes more conversant with change than the prospector who asks of each valley the same question and receives from each its shifting replies. The more he knows, the more the earth seems drifting about beneath his feet and one day he may well wonder whether he does not know anything, but is only knowing, and even be only wondering that, until he is watching his steps lest the Rockies sinking and the Great Basin rising and California drowning he is into the ocean and gone.

How this flux quickens the search for gold, which out of the rock's flux is concentrated, which out of the water's flux is concentrated, which in all phases of its movement tends to gather to one place; gold gathering as it rises from rock to air, gathering as it sinks from air to rock and never broken down, an element, gold gathered and concentrated and pounded into one gigantic three-hundred-pound nugget in a stream bed of Australia while all around the rock runs, the water runs—let it: gold will be amassing and will find its place for gold longs ever to be pure, sets itself apart, holds few companions, is measured by no other standard than its own which is so high that all the world looks up to it— austere, ascetic, purified, "separated, segregated, concentrated"— and yet so perfectly and grossly there, when found, like a bullfrog in the grass: "yellow, lustrous, heavy, hackly, malleable, does not tarnish."

Free gold? Free of dross. A powerful image, a dangerous one some think for those who live in the thin margin, the zone of weathering and change. Who could love Plato and not quicken at the thought of gold? Gold. Gold! "Here Faustus, try thy brains to gain a deity."

CHAPTER 11

Strikes, Dips, and Displacements

The line of an intermittently exposed vein is not easy to follow, and the convolution of the earth's crust guarantees that it will soon be displaced or disappear for good. But as far as it goes a vein may be followed to the degree that one correctly imagines (a) its shape and situation, (b) the history of crust movement in the vicinity, and (c) the effect of erosion on its placement.

Round or narrow veins, such as those of our body, are not our concern: they follow the cracks, joints and fissures of the rock.

But imagine the situation of a huge, thin sheet of rock tilted, eroded, and covered, so that only an outcropping edge of the sheet appears here or there. This three-dimensional formation—a "bed" with a visible edge—can sometimes be traced.

Example: Layer upon layer of sediment has settled on the ocean floor. One layer of mud becomes shale, then, under heat and pressure, a bed of slate twenty feet thick. This part of the ocean slowly rises and tilts to become a mountain range. Assume a section of ocean bottom containing a slate bed now lies at a forty-five-degree angle, a big tilted slab with a layer of slate. The slate now appears at the earth's surface as a twenty-foot-wide horizontal band running parallel to the top of a ridge and sloping down the ridge's end:

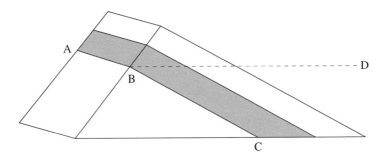

The lower outcrops are far to one side; the higher outcrops far to the other.

The horizontal line of the slate bed, *AB*, is called its strike. The strike is the compass direction in which the edge travels. The tilt of the bed, *BC*, is called its dip, measured by the angle *CBD*. Knowing the dip, one can calculate how far the outcrops will appear to one side or the other as the land rises and falls. For instance, a bed with a dip of only twenty degrees from the horizontal would reappear, one mile higher, about five miles away; while a bed with a dip of seventy degrees would reappear, one mile higher, only about one-fifth of a mile away. The diagram on page 135 shows ideal lines of continuation across typical ground for four beds with a dip of forty-five degrees.

In practice, at least two more factors usually influence the line of continuation.

First, the bed has probably been contorted so that its plane bends complexly. The same principles apply but the application becomes increasingly useless when strike and dip change every mile, or foot. In many parts of the Canadian Rockies, however, the tilted strata are remarkably straight.

Second, entire sections of crust may shift, and a block fault cutting across a stratum may segment and displace the line of

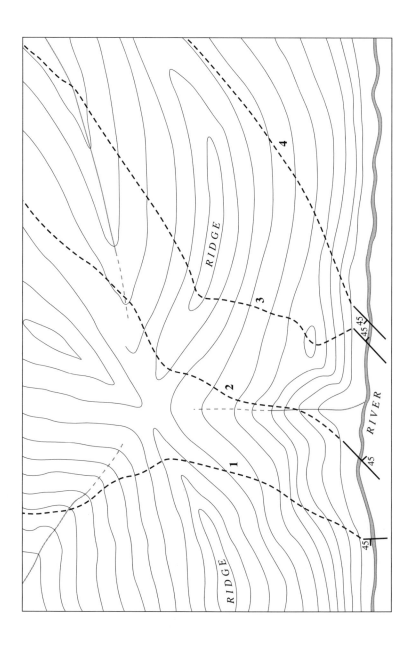

continuation. But if the nature of the block movement is understood, the displaced line may still be traced. If everything along a crack has moved a mile to the east, that's where to look for the continuation of the line. Of course, if the block was also raised, or lowered, or eroded, the relationship between vertical movement and the angle of dip must be considered. The following diagram illustrates how raising and subsequent erosion may have the effect of horizontal displacement:

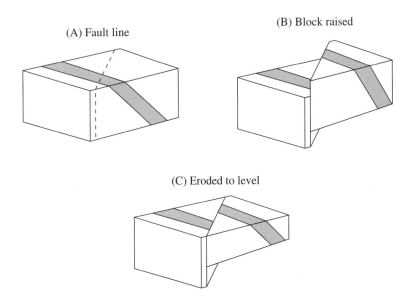

(A) Fault line

(B) Block raised

(C) Eroded to level

Because of these complexities a single formation can rarely be traced for long. On the other hand, the general lay of the land, the observed sequence of strata, and the tendency of one kind of rock to occur near another may provide enough clues for the observant prospector to make an educated search for his vein, while a complete change of formations will warn him that his search should end. But whether this knowledge will make him rich is another question. In the business of seeking there may be a science of knowledge but not of reward, just as in meditative disciplines there is a guarantee of discipline but not of enlightenment. Most of the big strikes were accidents. "Gold is where you find it." The prospector who would grow old gracefully must sooner or later adjust to this truth; and when he does, where are his prospects?

CHAPTER 12

Free Water

What's the birds-eye low-down on
this caper?

The placement of secondary deposits was said to depend upon the weight of gold. Weight in resistance to flow. But when water seems crucial to every phase of decomposition one might wonder if it should not have equal honor in the formula: solids and fluids in balance.

Water, one discovers, does nothing.

Water in its fluid state is the proper image of truth for those hoary old Zen paradox mongers sitting silent in their robes, the sake bottle just an unstrung bow away. Why? The biologist will show that water is central to growth, while the geologist proves that it is central to decay; yet in neither case is water quite the issue, unless indeed the issue be pure agent: the empty center. Water itself does not give life; it bears nutrients, or is used in the process of manufacturing life-supporting substances, and while it is true that nothing grows where there is no water at all, it is equally true that pure water is "stone dead." Conversely there is no weathering unless water changes state to ice and so expands or grinds, no erosion unless it carries harder particles or acids— "clear water flowing over a rock surface cannot erode it"—no transportation unless the earth slants, no concentration but by the force of gravity acting upon the various properties of the substance in solution. All the active verbs predicated upon water lie; water does not nourish, erode, give or take, it does not even in that fine old phrase, "seek its own level," for gravity does the seeking and water just . . . flows; it is at rest; all and nothing; only one verb is left: water waters. So much for language. Beyond is all peace and the bottle. It has often been noticed that prospectors, cowboys, and Indians are extraordinarily self-contained and thirsty men.

As an assayer, Shorty already knew fire. Now in the other elements, earth, water, air, he looked for his place. Yet all this, surely, Shorty's father had known. Why then, were his diary pages blank?

CHAPTER 13

Search, 1875

Shorty swept the floor of the bar in Butte until he met a man he knew from Panamint City, a man his father's age, who gave him work in a silver smelter, weighing and counting bars. At night he read and drank, alone, and thought of home.

In February he bought new boots and clothing, a drill, bits, and a new shovel. Dynamite. A strong, smart mule. Snowshoes. In March he was off, traveling in early morning and evening when the snow was frozen, eight hours a day. At the pass he looked back at Butte. Forty miles away the buildings were dots and dark splotches on the sloping hill; the gashed pit showed red. The men would be in the bars now, as the March moon rose. When they had asked him where he was prospecting he had been vague, "up north," or "Lewis Range"; said he'd found nothing. But he had gathered supplies early. Several had thought he was on to something big, but no one had followed. He thought of the dark band passing over the peak and down the unknown side, and turned north into the blue shadows of the Douglas fir. Crystals gleamed in the snow, and he felt his beard grow heavy with frost. It was tough on the mule, this deep snow at the pass.

Early, early, early. Caught in Goldcreek, Hungry Horse, White-fish by snows and thaws. April. Snow in May on the Flathead, and then the runoff. He haunted their old cabin, waiting for spring, for he had to cross a ten-thousand-foot peak before he could follow the vein to the other side; his mule couldn't go. Jaspar and Tom didn't appear. Had they given up? He took out *A Treatise on Prospecting* and the Bible. Over and over he read "The Structure of Gold Crystals," the Song of Songs, Revelations. In between readings he paced, cooked, and stood at the door. He shot a grizzly.

On the last day of June he took the mule and supplies to the upper basin and camped in a patch of sodden meadow. The bright green line of grass meandered through the snow and widened every day. He slung supplies from three trees and gave the mule his head. Then before dawn, while the snow was crunchy and firm, he shouldered an eighty-pound pack and started up.

The descent on the other side of the peak was treacherous; he was exhausted from the climb, from hauling his pack on a rope up the rocks; it was twilight; fresh, dry, slippery snow covered the slope. But soon, there was his slate bed, angling down into a new basin never explored and showing quartz. He was no longer searching for the source of the April Creek gold, he knew that; once over the divide that pretense was dropped.

He shivered through the night wedged between rocks above tree line. Powder snow blew into his blankets and melted. He had to get moving. Descending slowly before dawn, following the slate when he could, he had his first good view of the basin. Just below was a frozen lake, then a steep headwall; far down lay a blue-green lake flanked on both sides by sharp ridges.

As the slate band went over the steep headwall he could not follow; far below it cropped out again, then disappeared into trees and soil. He worked around the headwall to the right. This north-facing basin had more snow than he liked, and he descended a steep gully backward, kicking footsteps, his pack pulling him out from the slope. Too early. But he made the basin in the late afternoon, skirted the lake, and spread his blankets out to dry on the first stubby tree line hemlocks. He stood beside a popping fire and watched the sun on the ridge: a crack appeared in the snow near the top of the gully he had just descended. It widened, other cracks appeared like lacework, and the white filling of the gully began to move in slow motion, sending up great spurts of cloud as it turned rock corners. Then the sound came, a dull rumble increasing to sharp reports and before he could move the avalanche burst out of the gully onto the open snow slope; the whole slope moved and swept past him a hundred yards away and on across the ice borders of the lake, into the water, through, across to the other shore and up the other slope. A tree was gone. Still. Spindrift in his hair, shoulders, blankets. The fire sizzled. The waves lapped the shore. Green chunks of snow bobbed in the blue water. He rebuilt the fire and shook his bedding.

He moved down from the avalanche basin early the next morning, over the lip to a little gravel bar at the junction of Avalanche Creek and another stream from the east. He spread his blankets again, at noon. He had to rest. The trees were thick. He built a huge fire. While his blankets were drying he tried a pan at the junction of the creeks, in a deep pool. Almost immediately little yellow flakes flickered into sight. He paused, like a dog on a scent. His fingers trembled. He swished the pan more, and with each turn of his wrist the yellow flashed. Richest pan he'd ever seen. Swish. When he was finished he could pinch gold. Fifty dollars? A hundred? He jerked off his undershirt and spread it on the ground, lay down on the wet earth and emptied the gold by his nose. Rough and hackly—close to the source. He looked up quickly as if the source might be charging hard, like a bear. Where the hell was it? He hopped the twenty yards to camp, pulled on his boots, and ran up shirtless to the edge of the lake.

He stared at the headwall he had descended the day before. The slate band slanted across the very top, heading down to the left, and disappeared under snow and soil cover. It would go beneath the avalanche and across the ridge . . . but from there the calculation was impossible. The terrain was too steep. The vein might cross where he was standing—he looked down—it was all loose debris, glacial moraine, no one would even know—and go up the west side—or it might run almost level along the ridge and cross around east into the next basin without ever descending into this one at all. The land unfolded in his head as if seen from above; he drew dotted lines everywhere. Damn, he'd forgotten his pan. He scooped a handful of sand from the lake and proved it out in his cupped hands. Nothing. He tried again. Then he ran back to camp and panned up the river to the lake. Nothing. The water ran fast from the lip to the junction. Free gold might not have placed till then. It was steep, broken ground, with a jumble of rock types. And if the lake was rich, the deposits could be fairly deep. No telling.

He went back to camp and panned a few yards up the other creek; but that too was fast. He followed it for an hour; it stayed fast. No color. He came back and sat by the glittering pool. The junction could possibly be the first slack water for either stream. The vein could cross either valley. He'd just have to find it. It was dark. He was suddenly unable to move. He fell asleep in his underwear and boots by the creek. When he woke up in the middle of the night he felt warm and sleepy and comfortable, and knew he was freezing to death. He willed one leg to stretch, then the other. He rested. He suddenly remembered sitting in the snowstorm for two days, without a fire, the year before. What was he doing? He rose, stumbled to camp, gathered wood, and lit it. He sat near the fire, wrapped in blankets, too tired to eat, and fell asleep again.

He awoke in sunshine, near noon. He made flapjacks, going to the stream twice and coming back with only water in his pan. He sat and ate pancakes with his precious honey, studying the mountains. In late afternoon he gathered more wood and went back to sleep.

When he awoke he felt the forces gathering. July. The snow melted so late and came so soon, but he had plans. For a week he sought a continuation of the vein in the meadows below the headwall. One little patch of slate in the bed of a rivulet at the top of the eastern meadows gave him a line: if that was the same bed, it ought to angle down near the lake, he thought. In the bed of Avalanche Creek itself there was loose slate, but the whole area was so hopelessly roiled by glaciers and buried by debris that he couldn't say the slate debris was part of the vein.

He had to cross the range for more supplies, but as he descended the upper meadows the mule was not in sight. He searched for a day and found the half-eaten carcass crudely buried. One of his food caches was gone. In the meadow silt were bear tracks. He packed as much as he could back over the peak.

Mid-July. He shot a deer and panned the junction for a day. Another hundred dollars. Then he noticed a dark rock outcrop on the western ridge, right above the lip of the lake. Next day he climbed three thousand feet and found a slate vein lying at a familiar angle, with quartz intrusions, though barren. On the way down he came across a veined slab on the talus slope. He picked it up. Color, full of it. Rich color, thick lacings, a primary deposit—well, almost, he was close now—but where had it fallen from? He looked upslope and was surprised to see that he was well to the side of the outcrop, hundreds of yards from its line of fall.

For days he climbed back and forth across the slope. All the way from the creek to the outcrop were pieces of slate, some gold bearing, some barren. Surely they were from the primary lode, and it couldn't be far away.

Most puzzling was the top of the ridge. The outcrop, just twenty feet from the top, had no counterpart on the ridge or over the other side. The slate simply stopped. He sat on top of the ridge.

He thought it was time to check the other creek. Perhaps this line was all wrong; perhaps the hidden valley to the east contained the source. A week later he returned. Little color in the stream, no sign of promising outcrops in the basin, no color in the lake. He panned some more at the junction. He had ten ounces already.

In mid-August he sat in shallow water at the lower end of Avalanche Lake and watched a trout nibble at his thigh. He could feel the skin tighten with each tiny, tickling suck. The sun shone brightly on the white granite rising to the west ridge summit. He sat up; the trout flicked away. From up on the ridge that summit had looked dark. From here it was very light. If the slate ended at the ridge, and the light granite ended too, the ridge could be a fault and a horizontal displacement could have severed both lines. He jumped up and dressed. But it was late afternoon. Another day wasted.

Next morning before first light he was out of camp; by dawn he was sitting on top of the ridge. Which way to go? It was a toss-up in odds, but he figured if the vein had been displaced northward it would be inaccessible anyway, hidden under soil, while south—it might be somewhere along the open ridge.

The ridge was broad and grassy, the sun warm. Another basin came into sight below him, to the west. Meadowlarks sang on the slopes below. Soon the ridge narrowed and steepened. Ahead of him the ridge peak rose, white granite nearly to the top, dark granite on the summit and western side. An impassable pinnacle. He scrambled over broken rocks; the ridge was now twelve feet wide, six, then a line of loose blocks. He was almost to the base of the summit pinnacle when he sat to rest. There, curving around the wall to the right, apparently springing from beneath his feet, was a feeble line of slate. He whooped. But he couldn't downclimb or approach it in any way from the ridge above. It was badly weathered and not easy to trace; it seemed about the same thickness . . . the right angle.

He had just a moment of doubt. Why enter yet another basin? Just how far would this lead? He thought of the rich placer and the teasing fragments. He already had the best placer deposit he'd ever seen. Why cross another divide, into the meadowlark watershed? It couldn't possibly hold the source of the placer gold. He sat and stared. But suppose the higher sections, only above a certain altitude, were mineralized. The rich placer could be from an older part of the same vein. This visible vein was high, close to the altitude of the gold-bearing rubble. And perhaps he'd have a better chance for a lode up high, where severe weathering might bring it into view at any time . . . There had to be a source, somewhere, for the rich showings in his pan.

He went back to camp, packed, and in two days had forced his way through new country into the bottom of Meadowlark Basin. He tested the lake and stream. No colors. He tried to climb up the headwall to the slate ledge, but couldn't make it. He had to retrace his steps. Back in one day. Meadowlark Basin hadn't panned out, the vein was barren and he felt he had used all his options.

In September he sat in the lake, angling with a stick and line. He caught the same trout three times; he was sick of trout and ready to leave. The placer was still good at four feet. Once there had been a tremendously rich deposit in the valley. The source wasn't up Hidden Creek to the east, and it wasn't in Meadowlark Basin to the west. He had combed the hillside below the outcrop and a pattern had emerged: the richer fragments were mostly up basin and up slope. It seemed that the richest part of the primary deposit had been high, and extraordinarily broad, for he had found slate chunks a half a mile from the outcrop and almost level with it. Yet the outcrop was barren, and the slate below it mostly worthless. He couldn't account for that at all. A vein a half-mile thick, with only one edge mineralized? If true, it was gone now.

The continuation: it had been good luck to find the displaced vein so easily curving into Meadowlark Basin; yet it too was barren, like the outcrop. What he needed was that original deposit continued.

He panned. He looked at the mountains. He lazily gathered five thousand dollars' worth of gold with the crudest sluice, cursing as he shoveled the glittering sand into the sluice. He scraped out the gold. He leaned on his shovel and stared upslope. Hidden Creek barren, the outcrop barren, the continuation barren. Why the few gold-bearing fragments across so wide a swath? Everything was obscure except the richness of the secondary gold at hand. He took a sample pouch of sand and a sample fragment. He could always sell. Before the first snow he left.

CHAPTER 14

Deadwood, South Dakota

Shorty looked at his hand, but his mind was not on the cards. Two aces, two eights. He flipped three dollars in. He hated that voice. He was listening to the talk at the next table where two men sat surrounded by a crowd. One had a Boston accent—the real high-class thing—the other Shorty couldn't place. East. He remembered Jack Curtis in Providence—older and richer—who had gone off to college—his senior year everyone in the high schools knew Jack Curtis was going to college—and when he returned he had a new accent. Shorty remembered an older boy in the hall: "I ain't gotta pay two thousand a year to learn how to talk like a rich mick." There was a plaque in Our Lady of the Sea Chapel saying: "Donated by Michael and Sara G. Curtis." Curtis owned a lot of ships, they said. It was the year Shorty had to leave school and later, Providence. The two men at the table were playing some sort of game and fleecing all comers. There was plenty of laughter and interest.

It seemed he could hear nothing but that flat, nasal voice speaking quietly, correctly, precisely. There were big words—big mining words, geological terms. He raised; waited impatiently for the man on his right to fold. What the hell did a rich mick from Boston know about geology? How to lay bricks? He smiled. He'd ask him that. They were asking questions. They'd stumped somebody else and taken his money. They chuckled. Shorty raked in the pot and got up. He was near even. "Later, gentlemen, and thanks," he said, put on his coat, stuffed money in his pocket, and walked stiffly to the Boston table. Men stood three deep around the table. Shorty found an opening and pushed to the front.

Green. Absolutely green. Clean shaven, combed hair, high starched collars, crisp clean clothes. Nice-looking young men; so green. Shorty hunched his shoulders and tugged at his sleeve. He thought of the joke about bricks but felt he'd say it wrong; these two would look at each other and wink. For the first time since leaving Panamint City, for the first time ever, he realized that something was slipping away, something he liked, something that was him. He had read Plato once, in Greek. Who would believe it now? Goddamnit. It was always rich green bastards like this that got your goat.

They were asking the color of basalt, the structure of the gold crystal. They announced the payoff for each problem and people paid a dollar to enter before the question was asked. At first they had been distributing paper for answers, like a goddamn school examination, Shorty thought, but soon they simply waited for answers while the players pitched in coins and occasionally took some out.

Shorty threw in a dollar. The one with the accent looked up at him and smiled. They nodded to each other. It was some question he could hardly hear, much less comprehend. Eight to one. No one got it.

"OK, sorry. This is easy. Two to one." Shorty pitched in again. The one with the accent reached for the pad and pencil. He drew a block diagram with a dislocated vein:

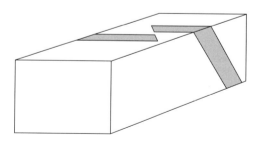

"What's happened here?" he said and turned the picture to the crowd. "Fault slippage," "horizontal displacement," several said right away, and Shorty: "horizontal displacement along a vertical fault." The one with the accent looked up at Shorty, and smiled. "The gentlemen are all right," he said, and four or five men took a pair of coins from the pile.

"Now six to one," he said; everyone crowded around. In a minute he turned the pad. It looked the same, but this time there was a second vein a little different from the first:

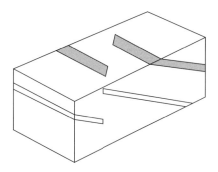

The men fell silent. "Lemme see, I can't see." "John's spine on board that Fargo roan."

"I got it." Shorty spoke. Other men looked at him; they made a little more room. "May I have your pencil?" The Boston one handed him the pencil. Shorty drew the fault line across and down the block. He turned the pad to the easterners and straightened up.

"Same fault as before, but this time the right hand side was raised, then eroded level with the left." Shorty pulled in six dollars and wiped his nose on his sleeve.

"That's really quite good, you know," said the accent, smiling. He looked at Shorty while he bit the eraser. Then he smiled.

"OK. Five bucks to play. Twenty to one." People whistled. He bent to the pad. Shorty threw down five dollars and looked around.

Everyone laughed but no one else chipped in. The two men whispered and drew; erased; drew.

"What's the matter with you guys?" Shorty laughed nervously.

"Ah you jerk. They got ya if they want ya," said the man across the table.

"Let's see, let's see." People crowded around the new diagram. Someone turned it to Shorty. "Sic 'em short man." He leaned on his elbows and stared. There were two blocks, labeled *A* and *B*. "*A* and *B*," he thought. For Chrissake.

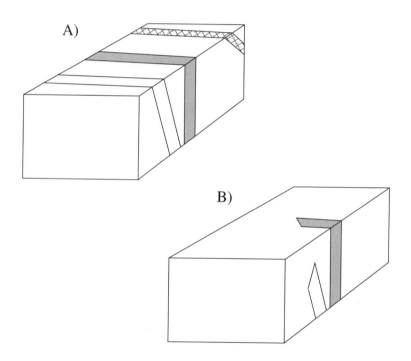

"There's one rule," the man from Boston said: "Nothing can disappear simply through horizontal displacement. We'll honor any other explanation."

Oh you will, thought Shorty. In one glance he knew he could figure it out. It would be complex, but the principles would be the same. Why had the light veins disappeared? At first it seemed the simple opposite of the last problem, but he knew that wasn't likely.

The checkered vein was easy. At some point he'd erode it off. The white vein was cut vertically. So there would have to be an uplift followed by erosion to get rid of it. But the black vein, along a horizontal fault, with no continuation: this was the problem, of course; they wouldn't let him move it off sideways.

"Is the dark vein drawn absolutely vertical?" he asked of the two. They smiled to each other. "Good question," one said. "Absolutely." Shorty no longer noticed their reactions, or the general interest in his question. People crowded over his shoulder. He leaned on the table. How can you get rid of a vertical vein without moving it off the block. It can't erode away.

Start at the beginning: same diagonal fault line, right hand raised and eroded. That would get rid of the checkered vein. No, the right-hand side of the white vein must remain at the bottom. Raise the left side and erode to a level block. That would wipe out the top segment of the white vein. But the checkered and the dark veins were right back at the beginning. Ah, now erode half the entire block. There goes the checkered vein. Now, the black vein. Can't move it off sideways, raising and lowering won't displace it. Of course! Rotate. Tilt and erode.

"Want the pencil?" said the quiet one.

"No thanks. I figured it out." Everyone shouted, joked, clapped, and cheered, then pushed forward to hear the explanation.

"Good for you," said the accent. "Tell us."

"Same fault. Raise the left block until the left white vein is above the surface and erode to level. Now erode the entire block to below the checkered vein. Tilt the left block until the left black segment is all exposed, and erode to level. The right-hand white and black segments remain."

"Very good. Really very good." The two counted out a hundred dollars. People cheered, and Shorty bought a round for the table and said a bit loudly, "Don't prove nothing," as he grinned. Then he heard the flat, precise, genial voice again:

"One more?"

"Oh balls, you sons of bitches," someone yelled. "He got you fair and square."

"Don't do it, Short Man."

Shorty looked down at the smiling face, the black hair plastered to either side of a straight part, the faint shaving rash on a ruddy cheek, the collar, pink knuckles, the gold cuff links: high-graded, washed, smelted, purified, and cast gold cuff links that some poor son of a bitch had dug out of the side of a mountain with his own hands and had loaded on a mule's back and carried down to an assayer's office that he was lucky to leave with a dollar for a bath to wash the last paydirt out from under his filthy fingernails. The cufflinks had a monogram: GRH.

"I'll play," Shorty said. People cheered and groaned and gathered. Side bets mounted. The table fell silent. The quiet one whispered to his partner while he drew and erased.

"Pssst." It was an old grizzled man across the table. He cupped his hand beside his mouth and leaned far over toward Shorty, jerking a thumb at the pair and spilling his drink. "The quiet bastard's been to Yale." The old man closed his eyes and nodded gravely, then straightened again. Shorty suddenly thought, looking at the two, "They're visiting." He thought of his old house in Providence with the cedar wardrobe closets, dining room table, the bay window. They had homes like that. They wouldn't drift around the West for the rest of their lives. They'd have families, homes, businesses. They were just visiting. He saw an old man, alone with a jackass, walking across the barren Amargosa Desert. Was it himself? Impossible. He felt a deep flush of fear and shame.

They had finished. The Boston one looked up, his arm on the pad.

"For your winnings, double or nothing?" He smiled.

Shorty turned aside and spat in the sawdust. He wondered why; he'd never spat indoors before. He pushed the pile of money out and added a few dollars for the drinks.

"That oughta be close," he said.

They passed the pad down and his heart sank. He'd simply never thought of it. "Let's see." He pushed the pad out to the middle of the table so they could have a look. People whistled. A double vein. Never heard of such a thing. How the hell, he thought, do you get a double vein?

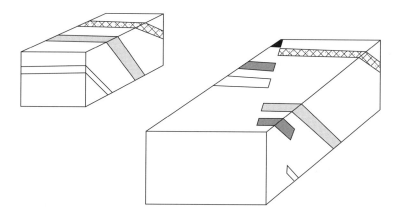

Sure there was uplift and erosion, to expose the white vein, and horizontal displacement. He stared for no more than a minute.

"You got me," he said casually.

"Think about it," smiled the one from Boston.

Shorty flushed, shrugged and pushed him the pad.

"I give up," he said in a voice of ice.

"Go ahead, take a guess." The table became deadly quiet. Shorty's black eyes bored to the back of Boston's head. People looked at the speaker. The easterner smiled. Someone coughed. The easterners looked around. "Hey mister." The voice came from the other side of the table. "Maybe you didn't hear. The short man said you got him." People watched the two faces. Slowly the smiles disappeared. The one from Boston finally cleared his throat and looked down.

"Sure." His voice was husky. "Sure." He took the pad. "It goes like this." Shorty watched the man draw lines. Around him, men were letting out breath, moving and drinking again.

"There's a second fault in this one, parallel to the black vein but slanting across it below. Raise one bloc, erode and"—he brought his pen up with a flourish—"Presto! a double vein." He grinned and turned the pad to Shorty:

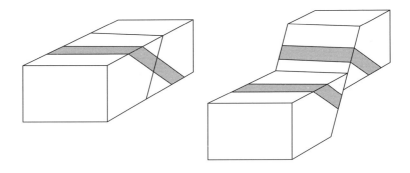

"The rest I'm sure you've figured out."

Shorty looked at the pad. His eyes narrowed. "Lemme see that." He yanked it from the man. He smoothed the sheet with one hand and bent over it. "Goddamn." People stared at him. The easterners looked at each other uncomfortably.

"Jesus Christ. Then both veins were moved horizontally."

"Yes, of course."

Shorty's eyes were wide. He slid the pad at the man from Yale. It hit him in the stomach. He started toward the two, forcing others back from the table.

"Hey easy there."

"Watch out."

Someone tried to grab Shorty but he ripped loose and moved in until he pressed against the shoulder of the quiet one, who leaned as far away as he could into the chest of the other; their heads were turned grotesquely staring up and back; without stopping Shorty leaned over, mashed his elbow past the upturned face, grabbed the pencil and almost shouted:

"So this vein's shallow, disconnected, and this one's deep."

"Yes." They were puzzled.

"Suppose . . ." He stopped and looked into their eyes. Suddenly they realized that he was not after them at all. "Suppose that *after, after* the doubling there was an intrusion and mineralization. It would only come up in the deep vein. The other'd stay barren."

"Of course. They're disconnected."

"And say the surface got all messed up by a glacier. The deposit might be gone and the whole area might look like one tremendous vein,"—he began buttoning his shirt and coat—"but *there*"—he dug the pencil at the displaced double vein—"there, if that was higher, both veins might be intact"—he was shouting; everyone had stopped to listen—he put one boot on the arm of the man's chair and began to tighten the lace—"over there, on one side of that checkered vein could be barren slate, and on the other side would be the original deep slate vein rich as hell." He turned from the table and started for the door. He stopped, turned around and came back to the table. The man from Boston offered his hand. "You can use this to get home," Shorty said, plunked a sack of gold dust on the table and walked out.

CHAPTER 15

Search, 1876

Shorty gathered his belongings, paid his landlord and packed his jackass in the midst of a rush. "Strike" was shouted everywhere: clerks raced from their stores, spoons dropped into soup bowls, bartenders jumped over full counters and the price of mules tripled. Everyone who left town was trailed; only a few hundred knew the right Shorty Harris and where he was.

He paid no attention. It would be a long trip, and April could be cold. Good-bye to the Black Hills, he thought as he led the jackass down Main Street. Then he stopped. It was a long way from the Black Hills to Eureka. He turned to the crowd surging behind him through the main street.

"I'll give," he shouted, and waited for the noise to die, "I'll give directions precise within one mile of my destination in trade for two excellent horses and a saddle."

Men spoke to each other excitedly. Almost immediately three men came forward together with horses. One stepped up: "You can have your pick of these three. Tell any of us," he gestured. Shorty ran his hands over the legs, called for a light and looked at their teeth and hooves. They certainly were fine animals. He spoke to the leader: "Are you sure of the bargain?"

"Sure, sure." Shorty drew the man to one side. Someone sidled up and the man kicked violently backward, catching a knee with his boot. The intruder moved back.

"You're sure?" Shorty looked up at him.

"Sure. Within one mile. Sure."

"All right. I'll take the Appaloosa and ride the bay."

The man turned to his friends: "Saddle Bonanza and pack Jilt."

"Listen carefully." The man nodded and screwed his brows. "It's at an elevation of nine thousand feet"—the man looked up— "four miles northwest of the only abandoned cabin on the third eastern tributary of the Flathead above Kitka Lake."

"The Flathead?"

"That's right."

"Where the hell is that?"

"It flows south between the Whitefish and Lewis ranges, about a hundred fifty miles northwest of Helena."

"You mean it ain't in the Black Hills?"

"No. It's in Montana or British Territories. I'm not sure."

"The Rockies?"

"That's right."

"You mean you're going across Montana Territory and up to nine thousand feet on the west side of the Rockies?"

"That's right."

"Got a sample?"

"Just a placer. Haven't found it yet."

The man looked at his boots. He kept his head bowed. "You know you're plumb crazy. The Black Hills has got the richest deposits on earth, and you're goin' off there."

Shorty looked down at the same boots. "You can keep the jackass," he said. He walked over and mounted Bonanza. A man handed him the stringer for Jilt. The crowd surged around the leader, trying to buy information. He pushed up beside Shorty's leg. Shorty bent over to hear: the man stroked the horse's neck:

"She's a good horse." He looked up. "If there's a bad crust, or something, you know"—he stroked her neck again and wiped his nose.

Shorty nodded. "I'll take care of her." He started out.

"Where's he going?" people shouted at the man; his head was bowed. They waved gold pouches. Finally he looked up and grinned.

"If you wanna get rich, follow him," he shouted. Hundreds yelled and started off down the street. The man motioned to his partners to gather round.

When he left the last pines and oaks of the Black Hills and started west across the open prairie most people stayed at the edge of the woods. It was dawn. Fifty followed him to the Belle Fourche. As they watered their horses he explained that he was heading for Eureka, west of the Rockies on the Canadian line. They thought it a ruse and stayed with him across the naked lava, barren mesas and blind canyons of the eastern Wyoming plateau. He camped alone; they camped a hundred yards away, singing and drinking.

When the party finally reached the Powder River and the green valley of Crazy Woman Creek, some followers stopped with the Indians, others went to the army fort at the foot of the Big Horns. That's where most thought he was going. But when instead of going into the mountains he kept north along the Little Big Horn they began to take him at his word and turned back.

A single man followed a mile behind. One night he came over to Shorty's fire, sat down, and held out his hand.

"I'm Josiah Williams," he said. "I'm going to visit my sister in Butte." They traveled that far together.

♦ ♦ ♦

May: Up the Flathead, pushing through snow. Past April Creek.

June: Up the unknown river to the north. This time he would approach the site from below. He recognized the way to Meadowlark Basin and took the next right, along Avalanche Creek. For two months, it seemed, if not three years, his nerves and energy and will had been held like the clutched legs of a wind-up monkey; now he was set down and he had the feeling that nothing could stop him till he unwound or crashed. He broke trail for the horses without snowshoes: kicked paths through the spruce-shadowed drifts. The creek roared. In the afternoon he heard an avalanche above. Late next morning they were at the junction of Hidden and Avalanche creeks. Parts of the clearing were free of snow. He unpacked quickly, pitched a tent, slung food from trees, then began packing the rucksack. It was near sundown.

He couldn't sleep. He was off in starlight; at the outcrop before sunrise; striding along the broad ridge in frozen snow in the first rays of the sun. He came to the white granite that ended suddenly. The ridgetop was terribly fragmented; it could well be a weathered fault line with an intrusion; to the right was the continuation of the slate above Meadowlark Basin—the wrong continuation, the barren one. Ahead, within a half-mile, must be the original gold-bearing vein.

It didn't appear before the summit pyramid. He retraced his steps to make sure. Then he sat in the warm morning sun and ate while he studied the peak with the thorough leisure of a fanatic, calm and sure of his goal. He would have to cross the summit. He walked back to the broader section of the ridge and tried to look at the sides of the peak: it seemed to be a pyramid of at least three sides, falling steeply away to the avalanche valley, to Meadowlark and probably to a third valley behind Barren Basin that he had not yet seen. But he could see no route. It looked like pictures of the Matterhorn.

No stopping now. He approached the peak again: he would stay on its right to watch for the second vein. He placed a foot and tested; then a hand; he began to move up to the right on increasingly steep blocks of rock away from the ridge. In a few minutes he was in shadow on the west face: he was surprised at the cold. Snow was frozen on the ledges; the drip water had formed slick, dark ice. The rock was steeper. He couldn't ascend. There seemed to be a crack or gully further around so he edged sideways until he reached the gap. It was a snow gully in the rock. He couldn't see how far it went, up to the right. He carefully climbed around the outside corner of rock and reached a foot out to the snow. It was firm. He kicked a toehold, moved into it, placed his palms on the snow and started up.

He found a slab of sharp slate—greenish, weathered, told him nothing—he looked up quickly, then down; it made him dizzy. He picked up the slate and used it to dig footsteps.

When the snow became so steep that he had to push his fingers in he felt scared and looked around. The sight of a basin far below made his stomach turn. He ascended a few more steps, then stopped again. His fingers were cold. His left foot seemed to be slipping out. Perhaps his footholds were melting. He suddenly felt off balance and looked around for a way out of the gully. But how could he move sideways? Couldn't reach far enough down and away to cut a footstep to the side. He'd have to lean out. Cut a handhold. His fingers were numb. He slowly withdrew his right foot from its toe hole and allowed all his weight to settle on the left. The foot was slipping. It wasn't a nice feeling. The slope seemed vertical. Then he kicked his other toe at the snow as far to the right as he could reach, gently at first. Harder. When his boot was buried to the laces he tried to put weight on it, but couldn't move over. Cut a handhold. He leaned his ear against the snow, and breathing hard, above his head he slowly transferred the slate from his left hand to his right, passed the perilous moment in which he had no handhold at all, eased his left hand back into its place and with the right began to chop as far over as he could. When the hold was big enough he pushed in the slate, put his palm on it, and slowly leaned right, transferring weight to the other foot. He held his breath and shut his eyes for the agonizing moment— then he put all his weight on the untested foothold and swung over. Once in balance again he breathed deeply and jammed his free hand and foot into the snow.

But now he had a system. Two more cuts and side steps and he was at the edge of the gully, against the corner of snow and rock walls. There seemed no way out, but he had to get off the snow. The rock loomed above and over him. He stood in the corner. It was still dark and cold. Wasn't it noon? He saw a crack slanting back away from his foot and carefully eased his right toe an inch into it. His boots were wet. Perhaps the rock would be slippery, but he had to get his frozen fingers out of the snow. The wind seemed to be rising. Gusts coming up the gully made his wrists ache. He began to find cracks all over the rock. Good granite, he thought, split by cold. Pray it isn't rotten. He twisted his body and slid his right hand up to a crack above and behind his head. By raising his elbow and pushing hard he jammed his unfeeling fingers in as far as the second joint. The moment again. Holding his breath he transferred his weight. He couldn't even tell if he was holding himself by hand or foot or both, he was so cold. But he was on the rock. It was near vertical. Now he was two feet out from the snow and the gully looked incredibly steep. His cut footsteps disappeared below around a corner. Dizzy and sick, he inched to the right along the crack and finally gained the outside corner of the rock. The angle was not quite as severe as the gully or its walls, so he moved onto a six-inch ledge in the sun, stood leaning against the rock, put both hands into his pants, closed his eyes, and thought to himself, "Don't sleep."

When he came out of his reverie the sun seemed lower and the wind colder. His hands hurt terribly and he had no feeling in his feet, yet he felt refreshed, strong and confident. No stopping him now. Where was he? There was the other ridge, partly in sight. He must be more than halfway around the peak. And below—he pressed himself against the mountain as he looked—was yet another basin—neither his camp basin nor Meadowlark—with a large glacier nestled from headwall to lip. The snow gully pointed down thousands of feet at the blue-green crevasse.

He started up, climbing beside the gully. How far to the top? The gully sloped more gently now. The snow held occasional rocks and seemed to curve to a cliff above—he stopped—the loose rocks looked like slate. He couldn't climb into the gully, so he leaned far out and peered in. Slate. One piece was half quartz. He swore. There were darker grains—if only he had the right light. He kept his eyes on the gully as he climbed. Slate, slate fragments, then slabs of slate on the gully walls; slate everywhere; he pulled himself up a shelf and there, above—he knew it right away—was the source, the vein, overhanging the snow gully—the gully was the vein—of course, the rest of the peak was hard granite—and the overhang above had not been weathered out—it was curving—the strike and dip were all wrong, it was all contorted—he kept climbing until he had one hand on rock, one foot in the snow of the gully underneath a six-foot overhang of rotten slate on edge, rotten slate that broke off in pieces—fragments bounced from his head and shoulders, rattled down the gully and whizzed off into the air above the glacier—half quartz, rotten with minerals, gold, gold alloyed with silver—lovely lacings of gold—filigrees—concentrations the size of a pencil tip—lines thick as a leather needle, flecks, spots, ropes of gold—he clenched his fist and leaned back—the veins of his neck swelled thick with blood—*eeoow*—the long falling sound bounced off the rock, the basin, the mountains and returned—*eeow*, gold! gold! gold! He licked his lips and stared. He'd done it; he'd struck it rich.

How much, how far did it go? He climbed back out of the gully and up around the overhang, scrambling on all fours. At the summit he ran on top of the vein, now a clear white-etched gash through the granite that curved past the crest and ended. Far below was the lake. So the ridges and summit lay along the line of the block fault, just like the diagram. A hundred yards, that's what he had, a hundred yards of mother lode all to himself, one long hunk of quartz full of gold. The rest of it was broken out and gone, but this was his.

The placer deposits would all be under the glacier, inaccessible. Perfect. He flashed for a second to Jaspar standing by his long tom at the foot of the glacier, scratching his huge head. He laughed.

Rich rich rich; in the center; at the top; the basins he had named, the rivers he had traced, the vein he had followed for three years knelt beneath him, offering their gifts, mere vassals now before his round, smooth, glacier polished throne. "Subdue, and have dominion." He stretched again and yelled. His voice bounced back from every direction; he cocked his head as if . . . he yelled again and listened to the hollow return. Not a reply, really; more like the stone could not absorb the sound, and so gave it back. He looked about; good Lord it was late. A gust of wind. Gone. He turned all around, studying the still, silent peaks. North, east, south, west. The sun was going down. Well he'd found it, he'd found the son of a bitch. What he had wanted to do he had done. Sundown. He still had to get off the goddam peak. It was cold.

◆ ◆ ◆

Not quite all he had wanted; not yet. Shorty mined the lode. Burrowed in and blew it out. Even the few who have seen the small, splintered timbers a hundred yards from the summit find it hard to believe.

He found an easier approach from the Slate Peak ridge and brought up his tools. He picked and shoveled for two days, hacking away at the rotted top of the vein, before he discovered that the lower layers, eight feet down near the base of the overhang, were richest. He crawled over and blasted in. He shored the tunnel with tiny alpine fir cut at tree line and carried, shoved, rope-hauled up the vertical granite to the mouth of the tiny mine. Pound, quarter turn, pound, quarter turn. Split fuse. "Fire in the hole!" he would shout to no one and scramble for cover. Drill, blast, clean. Drill, blast, clean.

He crammed the richest rubble into saddlebags, dragged it up to the summit, sorted, stuffed the bag with high grade and flung it off the peak onto a snowfield. It slid down to rest in the talus near the lake. The bag always came apart. Every other day, when he climbed down to the lake for supplies, he stomped across the talus looking for the sack and gold. At camp, he piled ore high as the tent. Back up for more.

When he had driven a tiny adit in about six feet he forgot to notch the cap beam holding the fourth set of posts apart; a week later, ten feet in, as he crawled out of the tunnel toward a driving rain he had a vivid image of the unnotched cap; he crawled back. The roof was dripping. The posts seemed to be inching inward. He got in back of them to have the benefit of the feeble sky light and began to drill a peg hole in the beam overhead. Water fell on his head. The fir shoring sagged. He stopped. Had the post just slipped another quarter inch?

Suddenly and for the first time in three years he stayed his hand—the king in disguise now, came back to his own shores—and looked about with strange surprise. The crumbling gray slate, the angular quartz chunks, facets slick with rain, the glistening drops on the ceiling, the rough-hewn fresh white scented fir posts, the dirty wrists with tiny beads of water on the hairs, the stubby fingers black grained holding the drill still above his head in gray half light, the post inching, inching—"Him and me both," he thought, and closed his eyes. Was that what he had been doing? Just like his father? A chaos of thoughts, feelings, memories began to revolve majestically, a nascent galaxy slowly rotating, gathering stars—hard glints of light from the shattered glass of his past—spinning faster and faster until it condensed, collapsed, contracted to a single banded blue-green ball and he felt as he had the day he walked away from his father's mine, he felt the roundness of the earth completed beneath his feet, the roundness that came to nothing but himself. "Fire in the hole." He opened his eyes and waited for the opposite post to cave inward and fall flat, followed by showering rocks. When it was too late he withdrew the drill and started forward. The other post hit him in the back of the neck. He felt his head wobble. A crush of stone pinned him down. He struggled for a second, then relaxed. The spinning stopped and in the silence one more rock bounced off his cheek and rolled away.

He lay still, tasting blood. The pool of water forming by his nose was black and red. Water soaked through his shirt. One hand seemed to be under his chest; the other was against his face. His chest was cold. He saw his father walk without a backward glance around the first timbers of the mine, and again he saw the flash. "Him and me both," he thought, linked closer to his father in that moment than he had ever been in life; his heart pounded with fear; he felt his face flush with the heat of a desert noon in front of the old Sardine shaft, the weight of the sun pressing down like a giant hand driving his father back into the sheltering cave, back into the tightened ball of earth, driving them both back together to a single point, united now, wedged into the stone, both of them one like some precious essence in the blood of a common mother separated, segregated and concentrated to delicate filigrees veining dark uterine walls. A grandmother he had never known, connections as strange as double veins, sources as rich and barren and hopelessly distant—the thoughts, too, crystallized: "stone." Well. He had finally done what he had set out to do, and now he knew what that was, and he could relax. His father had failed at a life without illusions. How would he do? Now he would either be as dead as his father or, if he ever lived again, by blind luck delivered from the tomb of his own making—round, round, everything was round—he would for the first time be no better and no worse.

◆　◆　◆

Consciousness: wiggled fingers, exposed face. The cave-in had barely reached from head to toe; crushed ribs; crawling, falling, a broken leg; snow; horse; past hunger day after night after day. He slid off Bonanza near the boarding house in Eureka. They carried him in. Meek and dazed he lay in bed through the long winter, mumbling, nursed by a woman who had lost her only son in the Civil War.

In the spring when he got up he knew something had gone, as if a yell had been absorbed by stone. Gone. Quietly he sold the directions to both sites—he'd never staked a claim—for seven hundred dollars, on the basis of a placer sample tied to his saddle and a rock fragment found in his trouser pocket. He gave most of the money to the woman. Bonanza too. He bought a jackass and started south, slowly, deliberately, on weak legs and tender feet, picking up work now and then and moving softly on. In a sawmill at the head of the Salmon he stood for a few weeks dreaming by the clanking green chain, bathed in the odors of spruce and Douglas fir and the inviolable innocence of the red cedar that smelled when fresh cut like the virgin tree still standing and yet impossibly too like the suddenly opened door of an old clothes closet in Providence, a closet that he had always opened thinking only of mother and her secret places, yet entering, had always found full of the freshness of youth; the scent of something still growing or still to grow, though old; driven back into the dark corner, curled into a ball, wrapped in curtains of long wool coats he would press his wet cheek to the cedar boards and smell green fields with lambs, ripe fruit that never falls, sweet high-breasted Mary bending young above her child crying, crying, crying against the ancient cedar slats of his crib. One day he looked up from the sliced trees thinking that the scent of cedar was the scent of paradise and he quit, wandering south out of Idaho into upper Nevada, back toward home. A boom camp high in the Ruby Mountains was his last stop. No one had heard of Sid Goshen. He shoveled dung from the streets and slept in the livery stable, then one evening in August, after work, without drawing pay he walked out, slowly, tugging and talking to a lame mule, headed for Death Valley.

Behind him the bars roared, the picks rang, the cabins mushroomed beneath yellowing trees—aspen, willow, cottonwood, and late in October, golden larch—until the first wind of winter came like the last trumpet, calling dry leaves from branches that no longer cared, and laying them on the ground.

CHAPTER 16

Atlantis

From the floor of Death Valley he looked up again at the Panamints, but this time he was not leaving. He felt strange, coming home. He stopped suddenly at the foot of Starvation Canyon wash. It didn't look the same. A dark line cut across, a half-mile above. An embankment. New. The line continued to both sides across Johnson and Hanaupah fans.

He walked up. The bank was eight or ten feet high and ran for miles in each direction straight across the fans. It had to be a fault. The Panamints had risen, or Death Valley had sunk, eight feet. He remembered someone in Butte saying there'd been a big earthquake during the summer of 1872, right after he'd left.

The more he looked at the new embankment the more uncomfortable he felt. He rubbed the nose of his jackass. Not here. Not in his home. He had thought of Death Valley as a place that came before, before everything, a place untouched, untroubled by life and change. The question was no longer what the land hid, but the land itself. He thought, after the cave-in, that he was at the bottom, but now he had a sinking feeling that the ante had been raised.

He pulled the jackass up the bank and headed for the Johnson Canyon trail. He reached the pass in early afternoon. One of the mines was in view—should be—and wasn't being worked. It wasn't there at all. He hurried the jackass down the trail, around a

bend—Frenchman's Canyon—not a soul—Frenchman's Mine—
deserted, timbers sticking out of dirt—he slipped and looked down.
The trail was wiped out and had not been rebuilt. Sheep tracks
wandered across the little avalanche of debris. He pulled the jackass across the steep slope. Something was terribly wrong. There
was the Prospect Mine, across the canyon, deserted. Then he saw
the floor of Surprise Canyon at its upper end, where Alvord had
first camped, where he and his mother and father had first camped
seventeen years before. It looked the same as then. A dry wash,
mud and gravel banks. Like any other canyon in the Panamints.
He wondered if he was losing his mind. Where were the tents—
houses—thousands of people? He walked down slowly, and the
entire length of Surprise Canyon opened to his astonished eyes.
Timbers stuck randomly out of gravel banks. Broken brick walls
appeared here and there above the cracked mud. The smelter
chimney came into view: the only structure standing, grotesquely
tall above the crumbled smelter walls. Not a soul in sight. He
realized with a shock that even he had never seen it like this—
there had been two men here when he had entered and five
thousand when he had left. He was only twenty-seven years old,
he thought, and Panamint City—the whole damn basin—was only
seventeen. How could so much be gone? He walked through the
town site toward the closed-in stone of Surprise Canyon, his head
full of confused memories drifting like ghosts in and out of the
dust and crumbled walls, looking for their place.

At Ballarat, Murphy told him. His family was alive. It had happened a year before: July 24, 1876: the sunrise faded into a high
overcast. The clouds lowered, and by early morning a light rain
began to fall. Rain in July is always welcome in the Panamints.
Dust settled; roofs, walls, bridles and pick handles were rinsed for
the first time in months; the heat of day held off and the chill of
night stayed all morning in the sand. After an hour of drizzle the
sand was wet and tiny rivulets began to form. Cracks in the mud
disappeared; the drops landed in standing puddles. On and off till

noon a light rain fell. Runoff began: tiny trickles sluiced down the steep hillsides; sand embankments an inch, two inches, three inches high slowly crumbled into the widening streams. All over the Panamints the ground was saturated and water began running from the upper basins, gathering, increasing, flowing toward the narrow canyons. At noon the clouds lowered, darkened, and broke up: the sun shone for several minutes. Then, south of Telescope Peak, above Surprise Canyon, a gray mass boiled upward into an immense thunderhead. The sun disappeared. The canyon and town became dark, darker than anyone could remember the desert at noon. Men came out of dim saloons and stood on porches; some walked home through the puddles of the main street. Horses whinnied and pulled at their ropes. There was a terrific crack of lightning up toward Sentinel Peak; another right away near the Wonder Mine. The canyon walls rumbled, growling back at the sky. Wind was heard high above. The slate gray clouds boiled above the ridges and turned white around each flash. From the porch of the Nugget Murphy watched men come down the switchbacks from the mines, looking up. One dropped his pick and started running as fast as he could. Others followed. In her dark house May swept up the pieces of a cup shaken from the shelf. Then the men on the porches saw the rain coming up from below. It blew up Main Street, bringing the sky to the ground. They could no longer see the hills. The streets, too, became slate gray, dark as the sky. Men backed against the walls, squeezed through doors, and pressed against each other at the windows. People fell silent. May stopped sweeping and looked up. Abigail came into the kitchen and held to her mother's skirt. Drops rattled on tin roofs, then roared; at first they thought it was hail. The other side of the street disappeared. Then the wind stopped and the sound of water falling became the only sound, intense, unbroken; at first rain on tin, and on the ground, and then only on itself, rain on rain, water falling on water. The dog crawled under the kitchen table. For an entire minute the roar filled the town, and the ground already soaked.

"Jesus Christ," someone whispered, and ran down from the Nugget toward his house. Jim Dayton hunched outside and tried to dig a trench around his house. Stirring mud. Others sloshed in quickening sand to pile sinking stones uphill of their homes. People from the tents ran soaking into the bars. But they had only ten minutes to dig or pile or run: ten minutes from the start of the downpour those looking up the street toward Water Canyon saw the first tongue of mud and sand, two feet high, come around the bend, rolling trees and stones. Even as it appeared, oozing rivers of mud rising every second came out of side canyons—Frenchman's, Magazine, Sourdough—toward the town.

The back door flew open; broom in hand, June spun around. In three seconds the mud had crossed the kitchen into the living room and pressed against the far wall; the newspaper and tin collapsed, the roof fell and went under. She and her children jumped out the bedroom window but landed in mud. She could hardly pick up her feet; she felt a tiny hand let go—she turned—her youngest was nowhere to be seen. A second of hesitation. She picked up her eight-year-old and staggered on, running, slipping through the rising ooze.

The crowd grabbed her. Within seconds the town was empty; all ran for high ground, racing between the widening tongues. The slides grew—two, three feet high—met, picked up water and speed. The water was gushing over the mud. When the moving mass of water and earth hit the downtown section it scattered bricks. Jenkins said he watched waves thirty feet high take the smelter. People clawed at the walls of the canyon. When the crest had passed they formed human chains, hand to hand, to reach those marooned. A woman with a clean bonnet and mud-covered petticoats struggled thigh deep through the mud, looking down, parting the slop with her hands and calling out, regularly and in turn, "Matthew! Mark! John!"

Most had reached high ground; fifteen minutes later there they sat, four thousand on the hillsides watching the hot July sun shine from a cloudless sky. In less than an hour the sand was dry. By three o'clock it was a hundred degrees and the fresh white mud began to break into cracks. At first people walked on top of the new canyon floor on tiptoe, but it was already hard enough to hold them all; they walked about, looking for their town, looking down, looking down for anything but the desert they had once made bloom. Whatever they sought was gone.

Murphy was glad to see Shorty, and he knew the fate of most of their friends. His mother was in Bodie, up toward the Comstock. May and Abigail had gone to San Francisco. He'd heard she was married again. Shorty stood in dumb silence. Murphy gave him their address. Jim and June were in Darwin, a new camp in the Argus Range across the valley where most of the folks had gone. He should stop by, said Murphy.

Shorty left. He looked back at the Surprise Canyon wash: the fan was dotted with timbers and bricks. Rain in Death Valley; rain in July. Was it a judgment? "I will not again curse the ground." He turned down toward Panamint Valley. Was this his home? This big land so fragile? For four years, it seemed, he had been fighting water, thinking all the while he had a choice. Were there not different kinds of country, different kinds of deposits, different kinds of men?

He went by way of Sand Springs and west of the Last Chance Range to Owens Valley, then north two days, up past Mono Craters to the high windswept cold plateau beyond, over the rolling plains of stunted juniper where snow lingered under north-facing ledges through June, to Bodie, the latest and loneliest and coldest of the Basin camps: "Good-bye God, I'm going to Bodie," a child had written in her diary. The town was low, squat, barren, lost on the top of the rolling land like a tiny pile of sweepings on a vast brown rug. He got directions to the house.

He stood on the porch. A gingerbread facade again, and lace curtains, though the pattern was different. She always seemed to bounce right back. Footsteps, a hand pulling aside the curtain, and then his mother opened the door.

The hot jasmine and Mormon tea steamed his nose and eyes and brought back youthful memories. He stirred the sugar and told her of Montana, the strike, the cave-in. She paused over the soup.

"You know it's true that your father struck paydirt in the Sardine."

"Really?" He jumped.

"Two days before."

Both were silent.

"Why, Mom?"

She didn't reply. Shorty continued, looking into his tea.

"I knew all day."

She turned, puzzled, ladle in one hand, the other cupped under to catch the drips.

"What do you mean?"

"I knew, that's all."

"How?"

"I saw the dynamite and talked to him and . . ."

"And?"

"I just knew."

"He told you?" Her voice had a harder edge.

"No."

"Why didn't you tell me?" Her voice was shaking. Tomato soup ran from the ladle over her hand. He watched it hit the floor.

"Why didn't you tell me?" He remained silent, blowing on his tea. She stamped her foot, dropped the ladle into the soup and turned about stiffly, wiping her hands on the apron.

"You didn't try to stop him? You know your father killed his father."

Shorty stopped blowing and looked up.

"What?"

"Your father. He murdered your grandfather."

Shorty could think of nothing to say.

"How?"

"Jesus Christ, Shorty . . ." She sat and put her elbows on the table, her head in her hands. She spoke down into the checkered cloth, face hidden:

"That's why we had to leave Providence."

"That's how we lost the money, the factory?"

"Yes."

"He killed his father?"

"Yes. And he killed himself." She looked up and met his eye. She started to speak but he cut her off:

"And I pretty near died."

"I'm disappointed," she said bitterly. "I thought you Harris men did anything you set your mind to."

He sipped his tea. She rushed about the counter and the stove, then left the room. He could hear her crying in back. Silence. Finally she returned, sat, and reached out her hand. He took it. "Did you see Jim and June in Argus?" she said. Why had she asked? "No." "Are you going to?" "No." They had another cup of tea, embraced strangely, and parted. She stood in the door as he untied the two burros.

"Where are you going, Shorty?"

He paused and thought. "Don't know. I guess May left me." His mother stared at him in absolute disbelief. He caught her look. "Or maybe I left her. I'll be back by." He took the road west over the plateau and down—the day warmed up—to Mono Lake. He looked across to the dark, bare craters. There was a mirage. The mountains floated in the distance, detached from earth, grotesquely pulsing shapes in the sky. This was not where he had come from. The desert seemed worse than empty: tricky, not to be trusted. Too much like a father. Too much like himself.

He had known his life would go up in smoke, but would it keep happening, over and over? He felt swept by events beyond his control or knowledge toward what, he could not guess. Free gold. Exactly the situation, he suddenly realized, that he had always feared most. But one thing was sure: he had to get out of the desert. And another thing: once he had needed more, and now he needed less, and that was just as bad.

He looked up at the white sun. Noon. He thought to himself: hole up. The Mono Craters floated, black and ugly, above their fresh debris. "Hard rock." Where had it gone? A line came to him from a book: "It was all sea and islands now. The entire continent had sunk like Atlantis."

PART 3

San Francisco, 1879

Check, *a sudden stop, repulse. Middle
English "chek," a stop; also check! in
playing chess. The word is due to the
game, which is very old. The original
sense of "check" was "king!" i.e., mind
the king, the king is in danger. Old French
"eschec," a check at chess play, from
Persian "shah," a king, king at chess;
whence "shah-mat," check-mate, literally
"the king is dead."*

—REVEREND WALTER W. SKEAT,

ETYMOLOGICAL DICTIONARY, 1882

*And not to have is the beginning of desire.
To have what is not is its ancient cycle.*

—WALLACE STEVENS

CHAPTER 17

The Stranger

San Francisco, May 1879, a decade, according to Frederick Jackson Turner, before the frontier closed: three men sat at an Embarcadero Street bar. Two of them were discussing money; the one with thick fingers and fake rings moaned of his losses in the Comstock bust of '75. The other, in a faintly Swedish accent, said he could find no job. Out from Minnesota for six months, he blamed Washington and the railroads. Said he was about ready to pull up stakes and go north; strike it rich. The ringed man agreed. The bartender snorted and turned away. The ringed man asked the Swede if he favored silver or gold; then he leaned out over the bar and spoke across the Swede's chest to the third man, the stranger, who in tattered coat, patched britches and dirty boots, had the air of one who knows what's happening beyond the last trolley stop:

"I hear there's gold running in the rivers in Montana."

"Yup," the stranger said.

The ringed man and the Swede looked at each other. The stranger was middle-aged, grizzled white; beyond the beard, his cheeks, forehead, and neck were almost covered with dark splotches. The backs of his hands bulged with black veins as he wadded a meatball sandwich and worked it into his mouth; his wrists were dark against the dirty gray sleeves of the coat, a corduroy coat patched at the elbows, open down the back seam between the shoulder blades and missing the left pocket. The front half of the pocket had been ripped to the lining; the outside of the left sleeve and adjoining portions of the back were badly burned. If the stranger noticed the other two staring at him, he didn't seem to mind. He folded his large hands and looked straight ahead while his jaw worked the stuff in his cheeks. The bartender wiped a glass, held it to the light, drew a beer, and set it down. For the shortest second the young bartender looked at the man without expression; then he went back to work. Hanes coughed and, leaning forward again, said loudly, "Been up Montana way?"

The stranger chewed and swallowed, chewed and swallowed. As his cheeks deflated he began to run his tongue around back corners of his teeth; the bristle rose and fell, opened and shut with the motion.

"Yup." He swallowed once more and began to wipe his mouth.

"Do any good?" the Swede asked. Before the stranger could answer Hanes broke in:

"Must be lots of good prospecting up there."

The bartender had been watching the men in the mirror while he washed dishes. Now in a quiet, tense, voice he suddenly spoke to Hanes's image in the glass:

"Bust your bits and balls for nothing, if you call that good."

The stranger looked up quickly at the bartender's reflection and met his eye. Then he turned, reached deep into his baggy trouser jacket and pulled out a roll of hundred-dollar bills one inch thick. He offered one to the bartender, who seemed not to notice as he nodded toward the cash register and the white-haired man near the door. The stranger walked stiffly away, paid, and disappeared into a shaft of bright sunlight.

"Jesus H. Christ," said Hanes. "Gimme another beer, will you, Shorty?"

At three o'clock Shorty hung up his apron, put on his coat and stepped out into the sunshine. He had seen the posters the day before, at the little church around the corner where he had heard a

children's choir practicing three afternoons a week after school.
The posters said Concert, Sunday, 3 P.M., Mozart Litaniae Laure-
tanae, for soloists, chorus, strings, and organ. It was the "nobeese"
he used to sing with Abigail. He slipped into the back of the empty
church as the violins were tuning and the children were taking
their places for rehearsal. The director appeared and spoke about
sharp entrances and breathing and a few trouble spots, the organist
gave the pitch and suddenly the musicians and children leapt into
the Kyrie Eleison. Shorty was gazing into the dim spaces above the
rafters. When he looked down she had stepped out, the soprano, to
take the solo for "Sancta maria, ora pro nobis," a dark little pig-
tailed ten-year-old girl holding the sheet music as if she had no
possible need of it. It was Abigail.

When he had found May's address the year before he had gone
straight to her door, without stopping to think what he'd say.

"Hi. Did you get my letter?"

"No." May had stood in the doorway, arms crossed, speaking quickly and loudly in an ice-cold voice. "What do you
want?"

"I want to see you and Abigail."

"You can't."

"I hear you're married again."

"I'm not."

"Can I see her?"

"She thinks you're dead."

Behind May, a little pig-tailed girl scuttled across the hallway,
not even looking his way.

It was Abigail standing in front of the choir, singing the part she
had known by the age of three. Memories came rushing back to
Shorty, the smell of the house, the lights in her bedroom, on May's
arm in bed that last morning in Panamint City. A nice house. It was
under the mud now. Abigail's pure crystal voice took him back to
all he had had, all he had longed for, all he had lost. And even
from the back of the church he could see the black eyes of the little

girl grow wet with understanding, understanding of Mozart in the way of children who can understand longing even before they have known loss; understand loss even before they have known having— unless indeed they have come at birth from a better world.

After the Sancta Maria he drifted through the Salvus, Regina, and Agnus Dei. Abby had no more solos, but the music dissolved him in a solution of desire and repose. When it was over he felt there must be a way to put his life in order. He brushed lint off his dark pants and rubbed his shoe clean behind his calf. Perhaps if he played his cards right he could really establish himself in this town and have his family back. Not May probably, but at least Abigail. That's what Max's bar could do for him.

After rehearsal he could not help himself. He stood on the street corner until the children came running out the side door. Abigail was walking with a friend. He moved forward.

"Little girl." The two girls stopped and looked. Their brows wrinkled. Suddenly he realized he didn't know what to say, or whether he should speak at all. But as he stood there he thought he saw Abigail's eyes widen. Then she began to cry and her friends grabbed her and they all ran off, giving Shorty nasty and fearful looks. He felt a strong hand on his shoulder and turned.

"Do you live hereabouts?" said the policeman.

"I live and work at Max's bar," said Shorty. "I thought I knew her."

The policeman looked at his clothes, his shined shoes.

"Don't be scaring the children, sir. We need their music."

An hour later Max picked up the rag and wiped the counter.

"Go, Shorty. You're upset. What are you doing tonight?"

"The opera."

"Mein Gott, *Die Meistersinger*?" The old man leaned close and put a hand on Shorty's shoulder. "Walter is a fool and—listen now, boy, a Bavarian knows—Wagner is an evil man."

Shorty put his towel down. "I'll keep an open mind." He started for the door.

"Twenty-nine and so soft-headed. Open mind! Better a wife."

Shorty walked out. A warm evening without fog. He breathed deeply and in shirtsleeves strolled up Pacific toward the Opera House, his coat over his shoulder. His hair was darkened by grease, his eyes naturally dark. He caught a glimpse of himself in a store window. Short, powerful, clean shaven, pale. Bartender. Smart. San Francisco. He thought of the stranger that afternoon. Filthy. Silent. Montana. The old geezer sure had a wad. He wouldn't mind, he thought to himself, a little more of the ready green. Suddenly he realized that someone was standing behind him, watching him look at himself in the glass. He turned around. Brandon Hicks.

"Well well well," Hicks said with a broad smile, holding out his hand as if he had just recognized Shorty, "if it isn't Frank Harris. How are you, Frank?"

Shorty shook the hand nervously but before he could speak or break away Hicks had turned to walk in his direction. Shorty felt a heavy arm across his shoulders.

"Well well well. It's hard to believe." Hicks was walking against Shorty's right side. His plump hand dangled across Shorty's left shoulder. A ruby ring caught the gas lamp lights. "It's hard to believe. The very man I was looking for."

Shorty remembered coming on a nest of rattlers in the Reese River Valley, up on a dry, honeycombed outcrop. He had killed hundreds with a long pole until the stench got to him.

"The very man." Hicks stopped abruptly outside a doorway. "Come in and have a drink with me, Frank."

Shorty smiled and backed out from under the arm. "Thanks, Hicks." He looked up and down the street. "I never got anything from that claim in Canada, and when I got back—"

"Please, please, call me Brandon. You're no longer an assayer's assistant, after all—are you? Good heavens, no. You've age, experience . . ."

"I've got to go," said Shorty.

". . . family." Hicks held his cigar still in midair and looked sharply into Shorty's eyes.

"Fine, Brandon, thanks. Listen I . . . I had no choice with McDonald. I'm going to the opera now."

"How much do you make, Shorty?"

"What?"

"How much does Max pay you?"

"How did you know his name?"

Hicks looked blandly innocent and shrugged.

"I know he owns a bar. Wants to retire. I know you want to buy it."

Shorty looked at his feet. Hicks kept quiet. Finally Shorty looked up.

"I'm going."

"I know more," said Hicks before Shorty's voice had stopped. "Something of his . . . good character. Shame he never had a son. You've lived with him—what is it now—two years? Tell me," Hicks paused and lit his cigar. "Tell me, Shorty, how much does he know about your past?"

"You've got the answers," Shorty said.

Hicks laughed and shifted his stance. With an air of delight he waved his cigar about. "Still the same old Frank." Hicks's face closed around gleaming eyes. He spoke quietly. "Always wanted to go it alone, didn't you? Just like your father." Shorty made no reply. "What you don't know is—listen here"—Hicks leaned close, a large white presence in the night—"You can get what you want." Hicks leaned back again and smiled. "I'm not threatening you, Frank. Forget those little misunderstandings in our past. I have an offer. Temporary employment at four times your present pay. Then back to the bar, with enough capital to buy. Good for business all around. You'll be set for life."

Hicks steered him into a restaurant door.

"Why am I on your charity list?"

"Because you know your rock, boy. No charity at all. Honest work. You know your rock." He watched Shorty's face. "Come have a drink. Hear me out at least. Please?" He paused. "I'll get you to the opera in a cab."

A man in red velvet came from the shadows.

"Good evening, Mr. Hicks. Your table is ready."

Shorty was still stuffing his arm into his jacket when they threaded their way past candlelit couples and through a beaded curtain to a small corner table. Shorty looked about. Some bar. The waiter was looking at him.

"Allow me," said Hicks smiling. Then to the waiter, "Two specials."

Shorty felt his temper rise; what was Hicks holding? Then Hicks echoed him again: "This seems high handed."

Shorty made no reply.

"Who's singing tonight?"

"Cut it."

Hicks smiled and leaned forward. "All right, Frank. I represent the American Consolidated Mining Company. We specialize in making marginal mining properties pay. We need a field agent in Nevada to investigate these properties, recommend them and buy 'em up. This agent has got to know his rock in the field and his chemistry in the office. He's got to be smart and tough enough to bargain. Most of all, we've got to trust him. You can see that you're the perfect man."

"Yeah." Shorty watched some hot frothy whiskey concoction arrive over his shoulder. Hicks hadn't changed. "Perfect. About this company—"

"American Consolidated Mining."

"Who's president?"

Hicks leaned back and smiled. Shorty grunted.

"Who's on the board of directors?"

"I bought out Jonas Osborne at Resting Spring. George Pinney's a director. Caesar Luckhardt. The other four, I believe, are strangers to you."

"I thought Pinney skipped out to Tahiti."

Hicks slammed his fist on the table and leaned across toward Shorty; his loose cheeks shook but his voice was low: "Listen here Harris. This is no frog pond. Forget Panamint City"—his voice sank to a hiss—"and your small-time mayor. You're in San Francisco, Harris, and you're talking to the head of a company worth thirty million and the stakes are high and just because for old times' sake I'm offering to help you doesn't mean I'll let insults go unnoticed."

Hicks sank back and smoothed his hair. After a few seconds he spoke again in relaxed tones. "I've been nice to you, Frank, but don't push me."

"All right." Shorty was stunned by the sudden anger. "Tell me how you do it. Tell me how you make dead mines pay."

"It's perfectly legitimate, Frank, if that's what you mean. Brains and capital. Timing." Hicks leaned back and crossed his legs.

"Look here. These new methods of mining and processing make ores profitable that once were a total loss. But it takes capital. We go to a region that's begun to fail, buy up the claims—and that's a service to those old miners—bring in the big equipment and make the small stuff pay. Bingo. And we create a lot of local jobs in the mills."

"New methods? Large-scale mining, stamp mills, fancy smelters. Anything else?"

"Hydraulic mining if there's water. We can wash away a mountain in a year. Big volume. Narrow profit margin. Strictly legitimate."

"And that's all."

"That's all."

"What if the locals won't sell?"

"Oh, they sell, they sell. Dying to get out. It's a service. Timing. Timing, my boy. That's why we need you. It all depends on smart men in the field who can tell us the moment to move. That and money."

Shorty looked at his glass. Then at the clock on the wall. Hicks reached over and took his wrist.

"One year, Frank. Only one year. There's a camp we're especially interested in. I'd like you to handle it. Desert. Your old territory. It's difficult, delicate—could be big. You can tell us exactly what the ore's like, size up the processing problems and if it's good, tell us when to move. Fifteen thousand dollars, plus expenses."

Shorty looked at the clock. It was a hell of a lot of money. "I've got to go."

"Think it over. I'll pick you up at six tomorrow at Max's and buy you a dinner. C'mon."

CHAPTER 18

Tecopah

Shoshone Tommy had called it Yaga. Now the camp was Tecopah. Shorty stopped at the old bar in Resting Spring, a few miles away, where twenty years before his father had broken Alvord's arm. Squinting into the dim corners, he remembered standing in the same doorway waiting to see where he was, too tired to be scared at the age of ten. Now he was thirty, no longer a mining camp boy or a family man or a crazy prospector. He was a San Franciscan, the past was past, and all he needed was cash to buy the bar. And even though in the set of his jaw as he stood challenging the empty room there was something familiar, still one would have had trouble, looking at the small slick clothes and arrogant countenance, imagining how this could possibly be the man Big Red or anyone else would later call the greatest man who ever lived.

The mines were spread around the little California Valley where the Kingston, Nopah, and Resting Springs ranges meet. There was a small mining camp up near Tecopah Pass and another cluster of buildings, including the Tecopah Resort Hotel, down near the hot springs. Shorty took a suite at the resort, paid in advance through July, and had the assay equipment unpacked from the buckboard. The hotel was pleased to make arrangements to stable his team. Dinner at six thirty. Would he care for a hot mineral bath?

The food was terrible. It had been three years since he'd eaten beans and tinned peas. After dinner he took a stroll. The desert evening was stifling. Why the hell had he left San Francisco for a hot springs in Nevada? For money, he said to himself, and smiled. That's easy. Why had his father come to the same place? He didn't sleep well that night.

At dawn the next day, after breakfast in the dining room, he changed into his old prospecting pants and coat and rode five miles up to the mining camp. The sun was not yet on the trail and beneath a clear, pale blue-white sky he rode lazily in shirtsleeves. It was a confused district, variously mineralized. The three ranges met in a jumble. Formations were inconsistent. Anything could happen in country like that.

Eight saloons, three general merchandise and grocery stores, four blacksmiths full of business. Must be some bit-busting rock nearby, he thought. All day he drank moderately and asked questions. He allowed word to spread that he might be interested in properties.

Hicks's information had been correct. Five years before a number of mines had worked zones of secondary enrichment— where weathered gold and silver had been concentrated without being washed away, so that the first twenty feet of the deposits were ten times richer than the primary veins beneath. Once the zone of enrichment was passed the rock was hard and the mines had ceased to pay. Transportation was difficult. It was a long way to the nearest smelter, and in the primary deposits the silver especially was complexly alloyed and expensive to process. The year before most of the tenters, tinhorns and prostitutes had left. The town was one-fifth its former size. Still, a number of independent miners were squeezing a living from their claims.

"Why don't you go up and talk to Paddy Mack, Mr. Harris, up at Resting Spring Mine. He knows more'n anybody else 'bout this district. Won't lie about nothin' but his age."

Shorty chuckled and sipped his drink. He hated public relations. "What's his age?"

"Says he's seventy-five. Closer to sixty."

♦ ♦ ♦

"Hello, Mr. Harris."

Paddy's claim was at the very back of Resting Spring Canyon, right at the foot of the headwall. The spring emerged on his property. He motioned Shorty to a blasting crate. Shorty dismounted and dusted the sleeves of his jacket. Paddy, less than five feet high, stood watching him, one hand folded across his chest and tucked into a vest that he wore over red wool pajama tops. Napoleon, Shorty thought. A wide-brimmed, tattered soft felt hat shaded his face and half of his long black beard. He stood in the baking sun; there was no wind; the canyon faced south. Shorty tied his horse to a greasewood and pulled the crate into the horse's shadow.

"Sit down, Mr. Harris. Been expecting you." Paddy's dark pants and boots shone white with alkaline dust. He held a dusty pick. Around him was the most backbreaking homemade operation Shorty had ever seen. A tiny adit entered the headwall of the canyon, barely four feet high, and in its mouth was an ore cart made of wood, with wooden and not very round wheels that ran into the tunnel on a rough log track. A rope from the cart was attached to a barrel winch. To the right of the car was a pile of raw ore: to the right of that a clear space where he crushed it, by hand; in front of this space was what looked like a twenty-five-pound sledgehammer with a handle as tall as himself. There was a huge pile of crushed rock and a small screening apparatus. His disassembly line had by then reached all the way to the spring, where a hand-turned wooden water wheel used number ten cans to raise water three feet to a sluice. There he washed the best ore. What he couldn't work he sent by two dusty mules to the camp, thence by freight wagon sixty miles to the mill and smelter near Shoshone.

Shorty could tell most of what he needed to know at a glance. It didn't pay much. The ore pile came from a rotted primary vein. More silver than gold. The same formation outcropped directly above and again high across the canyon. But Paddy had a likely place for enrichment and a water source, and . . . Shorty looked at him again. The man was no more than five feet tall. He couldn't believe the size of the sledgehammer. In this place: the trees gone, an open white canyon facing south. The greasewood and sage were covered with dust. Shorty looked down to avoid the glare. The horse's shadow was pitch black for a second. "Working a claim." He sure was.

Other claims in the canyon were abandoned. At least five adits had been begun, two on the slope above Paddy's, but they were all dead.

Paddy leaned on his pick, one hand in his vest, and let Shorty look his fill. Shorty took his coat off and sat still in his white shirt, cooling down. Finally he turned to the dusty miner.

"Got a drink of water?"

Paddy spat and nodded toward a cedar bucket and ladle by the spring. "Help yourself."

When Shorty had returned to his seat he coughed and looked at his boots, then turned again to the old man.

"Do you have an assay report you'd be willing to show?"

"Yup." Paddy took a dirty folded paper from his hip pocket and handed it over. Shorty studied it. It certainly looked like the silver at least could be profitably smelted.

"You figure you're still in an enriched zone?"

"Nope."

"Really." Shorty didn't believe him.

Paddy spat. He walked over to the far side of the pile, picked out a chunk of ore and brought it to Shorty. It was lighter. Shorty looked at the pile again and noticed for the first time that the far side was a different color. So he'd entered new rock.

"When did you hit the primary vein?"

"Three weeks."

"Any good?"

Paddy shrugged. "Pretty good." Then a strange look passed over Paddy's face. "I figure . . ." He stopped and spat again. Shorty studied him.

"Mind if I take a small sample of each type?"

"Help yourself."

"Well. Thank you very much. And good luck to you." Shorty rose. "Mr. Harris."

"What's that?"

"I won't sell."

Shorty laughed. "Well now I don't know if I want to buy. Besides Paddy," he grinned, "we haven't talked terms yet."

"Mr. Mack," the little man said.

♦ ♦ ♦

"Whaddya think," said Hicks as soon as Shorty had entered the paneled office. Shorty sat down, opened his folder, and laid some papers on Hicks's desk.

"There are nine gold-silver mines within a four-mile radius, marginal or abandoned, that could be worked right away. Here's the rough assay results. A lot of lead, zinc, and tin in the ore that should be recovered. I could get twenty-three properties tomorrow, cheap. The road south to the Santa Fe line is not bad. Sixty miles if you put in a new cutoff south from the town, instead of ninety."

"Lukewarm."

"Not quite. There's one canyon. Here. Resting Springs. It has the best deposits—extensive low-grade silver with lead, zinc, some gold—and a central location. It's compact, the deposits surround the headwall, and there's a strong spring. The mountains in back are eight thousand feet within six miles. They have piñon pine and snow for two or three months, I'm told."

"Hydraulic?"

"The ore is five to ten times richer than marginal hydraulic ore. It's distributed around a natural bowl. The surface is loose. I think you could make a killing for two years in that canyon, and have the rest of the district for a cushion. Put the mill and smelter right outside the mouth, on the road."

"Hm." Hicks looked at the map, at Shorty, and at a page of figures. "No competition?"

"Small time. Town's almost dead."

"I'll check with the directors this afternoon. We've been looking for a small place, small enough to sew up. This might be it."

"There's a hitch."

"What's that?"

"Paddy Mack. Old prospector working a claim there. Won't sell. As a matter of fact," Shorty smiled, "seems after I paid him a visit he bought up most claims in the canyon."

"We can buy and sell a thousand of his kind."

"Well it's true that we can buy the other claims he's bought. But I'm not sure he'll sell his own."

"He'll sell." Hicks reached for a cigar.

"I'm not so sure. He's tough."

"There's tough and there's tough, Harris. You oughta know that." Shorty didn't reply. Hicks sat back and puffed.

"What's his claim worth?"

"To us? Everything. It's at the base of the headwall. Everything hosed out will wash across his property. And," Shorty smiled again, "he's got the spring. Thirty feet away it sinks."

"Ah ha. And what's it worth to him?"

"I don't know. But I doubt he'll sell. I can't tell if he's so smart he sees the whole thing or if he likes his work."

"He'll have his price."

"Or if he's crazy. He thinks he's near a bonanza."

"Oh well. Poor Mr. Mack." Hicks rose and thrust his hand across the desk. "Damn good work, Frank. Damn good. I'll tell the board. Come back at nine tomorrow. We might go for it."

Max Lieber had a slight stroke that night. By early morning he was over it, but the experience left him anxious to go ahead and settle his property. Shorty did not have the cash to buy. Max and Crystal said again that they would very much prefer to sell to him, at a special price, and be allowed to remain in their home on the second floor. However, that special price couldn't be too low; they might live another thirty years and they would need all the money they could get.

The next morning Shorty was tired and worried. The bar could slip through his fingers and all this would be for nothing. Hicks noticed and inquired. Shorty told him the situation. Hicks expressed regret. The board was ready to buy in Tecopah. Shorty would go for the year. They would deposit his salary to his San Francisco account. Hicks excused himself, saying he had a luncheon meeting of the directors and he'd meet Shorty in three hours. When Shorty walked into his office again Hicks leaned back in his chair and smiled.

"I have good news for you, Frank."

"What's that?"

"I spoke to the board of directors and persuaded them that you deserve special reward. We are giving you a bonus: a thousand dollars' worth of American Consolidated Mining stock. That will give you a thousand dollars down on the bar and the directors have agreed to assume a mortgage on the rest at two-thirds of the usual interest rate."

Shorty could only thank him. Max and Crystal were delighted at the news. Hicks got a lawyer and arranged the sale; they signed all the papers the next day.

♦ ♦ ♦

In late August Shorty was not surprised to find his suite again available at the Tecopah Hot Springs. Mr. and Mrs. Land seemed very happy to see him and to hear that he would be in and out for most of the year. He spent a day bathing and unpacking; then he went to work.

The first five purchases were easy, but by afternoon word had spread that the man was back with big money. No more easy buys.

He settled down to the long process of bluffing and waiting, squeezing and snatching. He could talk down the ore, the location, his interest, and finally he could feign impatience and angrily force the issue: now or never, take it or leave it. He represented the company honestly enough: they were a big concern and would use expensive equipment to process the ore by volume. High overhead. Who else could manage it? But he was successful simply because a price that looked low to Hicks in San Francisco looked high to the dusty, lonely men in the canyons.

The prices looked high enough to most, but a handful of owners held out: the smarter ones, the less needy, the ones with key locations regardless of their ore, and Paddy Mack, who now owned most of his canyon. In mid-September Shorty sent a report to Hicks. Much of the town and property was now owned by American Consolidated Mining, but no moves could be made until a few tough customers were bought out, and that could take all winter. While he bargained he would perform more sophisticated assays and send back ore samples so the stamp mill and smelter could be designed and ready by spring. Hicks said keep up the good work, and don't worry.

When he returned to the resort one evening Mr. Land said with an enigmatic smile that he had a visitor in his room. Puzzled, Shorty walked upstairs and opened the door. There was a girl sitting on his bed. She was plump, with clear blue eyes and a pink complexion, cherub lips. She wore a low-cut red gown. The room stank of perfume. She said the Lands had invited her from Austin for a stay. She hoped she and Shorty might get to know each other, although she knew it was mighty bold for a young lady to wait in a gentleman's room like this. There was no telling what might happen.

She was a Mormon with three children, twenty years old, who had left her husband and kids just a few months before. She ordered chocolates from San Bernardino. The boxes came on the stage with the mail, through the Mohave Desert, every week. They arrived as soup. Overnight the box cooled to a stratum of chocolate laced with veins of brown paper. She cooed and rolled her eyes as she licked her fingers. Shorty could hear his mother wondering how she could keep her complexion. When he told Mr. Land he needn't have bothered, Land said that American Consolidated had arranged it.

In October Shorty's troubles began: Paddy Mack's claim was jumped. A man ripped up his stakes and posted new notices. Paddy, shaking with rage, came into a camp saloon and waved an old flintlock at Shorty. The men in town were with Paddy; they knew that claim jumping, even if illegitimate, could involve long and expensive litigation, and they figured that Shorty was behind it to force the sale or lower the price of a property. Somehow Shorty convinced him that he knew nothing. The claim jumper was well armed, and even though everyone in camp knew that Paddy had staked and worked his claim far beyond the requirements of the law, Paddy still had to make a trip to Shoshone to clear the trouble up and ask for help. He lost two weeks of work. When he came back the jumper was gone. A week later another jumper appeared, another professional, Paddy said. Paddy lost another week, and when he returned that man too was gone.

Shorty began to feel uncomfortable in the camp bars. To the atmosphere of open love and open hate of his money was added, for the first time, an element of suspicion, distrust, intrigue. He felt he could no longer move freely. When Paddy, now sleeping at the top of the cliff above his claim, shot a man one night in the act of pulling his stakes, the camp buried the corpse with no questions asked. In the street men looked at Shorty defiantly. He didn't know what to do. He himself was not sure what was happening. He fired off a letter of inquiry to Hicks.

Because of these events many were happy when a new bank suddenly appeared in town, the branch office of an L.A. firm. The well-dressed manager seemed quite ready to put himself in the way of American Consolidated, and the miners were happy to see another big gun call the company's bluff. The new Tecopah Bank began extending loans, on easy terms, to those who still owned their mines. Paddy was able to reoccupy his ground and even to work several claims at once. He took a sizable loan at the bank's advice and employed three men. He began to talk about running a sluice from the mountains. He'd sell the town water.

From Shoshone Shorty wired Hicks about the new bank and waited through the day for a reply. Hicks was unruffled: keep up the good work and don't worry.

Shorty returned to San Francisco for Christmas with Max and Crystal. He owed sizable back payments on his loan and was surprised to find that half his salary had been paid in American Consolidated stock, but since the stock had risen 15 percent he could hardly complain. After meeting payments and paying off some principal he treated himself to the city and blew half his cash. He left the stock in his account.

In Hicks's office Shorty gave a detailed report on the rival bank's activities and wondered aloud if American Consolidated should hold off on smelter plans until more property was secured. Hicks was grateful for the information and advice, but said they'd risk it.

Back in Tecopah the mines were more active than ever; loans had doubled. Then, in late January, the roof caved in.

The same Tecopah Bank so graciously making loans had secretly bought the freighting company, and suddenly rates for hauling the ore were doubled. Since the remote little camp did not offer enough business to attract a competing transportation outfit— if indeed, they began to sense, a competitor would be allowed—the miners were stuck. Within a month mine after mine had defaulted on payments, and the bank had foreclosed. Paddy Mack held out by selling his peripheral properties to Shorty in order to meet bank payments on his original claim. But he could make no profit with such high freight rates. His savings were draining. It was only a matter of time.

It was March when Shorty, after picking up an assay report and purchasing supplies, stopped for a drink in Shoshone. In the back room two men sat at a table. Familiar men. Shorty peered the length of the bar, then left his drink and walked to the inner doorway. The second jumper of Paddy's claim sat at a table laughing. Across from him the Tecopah bank manager smiled. They didn't see Shorty. For a second Shorty felt relieved; he thought he had solved the mystery and vindicated himself; then something gave him pause. When the bankers had such excellent legal methods at their disposal, why had they bothered to jump claims? And why only Paddy's? Unless someone had tried claim jumping first and banking second. He backed out of the room quietly.

Two days later he dropped in on the Tecopah bank manager at his office and invited him down to the resort for a drink that evening. The manager was surprised but couldn't help smiling.

Shorty sent the girl to her room. He and the manager had several drinks and exchanged life stories before Shorty stood up and walked to the window.

"I got a letter from Caesar Luckhardt today," he lied, his back to the man. "He told me your bank is owned by American Consolidated."

"Well well well." The bank manager stood up and sighed. "I'm glad the cat is finally out of the bag. I assure you that it wasn't my choice. I was under strict orders. But it's been damn tough not to share drinks"—he put a hand on Shorty's shoulder—"with the only other civilized man in town."

Shorty didn't turn around.

"Mind you," the manager continued, "this can't get out, or those desert rats would pick our bones."

Shorty spoke out the open window, his drink held at waist level: "What will we do with Paddy?"

"Already taken care of. He missed payment last week. We foreclose tomorrow."

"He'll fight."

"We're armed."

"He'll win."

"Oh, not me, not me. Professionals."

The manager turned in the doorway as he left. "You wait," he said. "It's perfect. How they did it in Aurora, once they get the mines and mills they fix prices and skim off the top instead of paying dividends. Company'll go broke but we'll be rich. That's why they wanted a small place. Control it all." He tossed his coat over his shoulder. "You gotta hand it to Hicks."

Shorty waited two hours after he'd left, then saddled and rode halfway up to the camp. In the moonlight he climbed a spur of the Resting Spring Range and worked down toward Spring Canyon from above. He tied the horse and walked carefully toward the headwall. He saw the embers of the old man's fire and boots sticking out from a blanket.

"Psst, Paddy! Paddy Mack! Psst. Wake up."

"Don't move." The voice came from behind. Someone approached, ˙checked him for a gun, then moved around into his view. It was Paddy Mack in bare feet.

"Don't tell me, sonny. You've come as a friend."

"Yes."

Paddy spat, walked to his blankets and sat down, the rifle in his lap. Shorty spoke:

"They're going to foreclose tomorrow. Armed professionals. If you resist they'll kill you."

Paddy squinted at him and picked his toenails.

"Paddy, here's three hundred dollars. I'm sorry I didn't know. I thought it was just a job, buying land. Clear out tonight."

Paddy stood up in his bare feet, a full six inches shorter than Shorty, the gun in the crook of his arm. He coughed and spat.

"Mr. Harris." Paddy looked down at the fire. He was quiet for a while. "I don't want your money."

Shorty felt the words bubble to his lips: "Maybe you'd better compromise."

Paddy looked at him. After a few seconds he spoke: "You know that big sledgehammer by the rockpile?" Shorty nodded. "It ain't the one I use. Can't lift it. There's an eight-pounder hidden in the cart." The old man sat on his blankets, then looked up resentfully: "I just wanted to tell someone. It's been on my mind."

♦ ♦ ♦

"Quit, eh?" said Hicks. He leaned back and laughed. "Quit? You know the ore, and smelting, and the terrain, the people. Not to mention the plans." He laughed, then grew calm, cigar held away from his lips. "Set us back six months, maybe blow the whole thing."

"I want out."

"We'll let you go in June, Shorty."

"Now."

"There's more work to be done."

"Fleecing stockholders isn't my line."

Hicks leaned forward, wagging his heavy jowls. "Look, Harris." Then he leaned back and softened his tone. "Been down to the bank yet, son?"

"No."

"Well, I'm afraid old Consolidated stock took something of a dive this month. Matter of fact, it's pretty worthless."

"Fine."

"Not so fast. It was doing so well in January we gave you a raise."

"Paid me in stock?"

"That's right. And you're four months behind in mortgage payments."

"I told you to take them out of my pay."

Hicks laughed. "Good heavens, no. Never interfere in a fellow's private affairs. What you've got is in the bank. But look here Harris, you've done such good work maybe we won't foreclose on that bar, even though you're four months behind and broke. And your salary will come in cash from now on—I'll put that in writing. And we'll give you—let's say—until July to pay. How's that?"

Shorty looked at his hands folded in his lap.

"Come now, son. You're going to get your bar. Thirty years old, and owner of a bar on the Embarcadero. What's wrong with that? Wish I'd had it so easy. Not such a bad year after all, eh?"

He stood up and walked Shorty to the door. "I know Max and Crystal would want you to see it through now, wouldn't they?"

◆　◆　◆

Max was propped up on cushions. His eyes were closed much of the time as Shorty told his story. Crystal sat across the bed holding Max's hand.

"He's got us, Max. If I quit, the bank has the bar. It won't come back to you. And you sold it to me—to Hicks—at such a low price that you couldn't possibly afford to buy it back."

"That's all right. We kept the apartment. Tell me, Shorty, have you done anything illegal?"

"No, but the company—"

"Forget the company. You're an American, and believe me, a nation does plenty rotten things. So you've done nothing illegal?"

"No."

"is he asking you to now?"

"Probably not."

"Listen to me Shorty. I come over here in '51 from Munich. A long way, a foolish man. Fifty years old. New machines ruined my tailor business, right? I figured to get rich quick in California. But there was no gold, Shorty. No such thing. It's a dream, eine wunderlieben Traum. I learned, work hard, own this bar. You gotta give a little, here and there, but it's all right."

Shorty shifted. Max looked at him and continued.

"Don't be a child. Settle down."

"To what?"

"What do you want, the perfect? Your feelings are not so important. There is a saying my father told me: 'It is your duty as well as your fate to lose your innocence.'"

"Why?"

Max shouted. "Because you are born, because you are born!"

Shorty got up and went to the window. He needed something more. Something far away.

In this mood he entered the back of the church, as he often did, for choir practice. She was not singing that day. As he listened to a read-through of "Jesu, Joy" he noticed, among the scattered heads in the front pews, a familiar set of pigtails. On sudden impulse he pulled out a piece of paper, a receipt, scribbled on the back and walked down the aisle. He sat in the row behind her and handed the note over her shoulder. She opened it without turning around:

"I am your father."

The little hands held still, the head didn't turn. The choir and organ continued and he thought he saw her shoulders shake. Then she reached in her purse, wrote something on the note, folded it, and waited until the music was over. After the organ's last note had faded into the rafters she stood without looking back, held the note out—he took it—and left, by the side door. He opened the paper.

"Thank you for Mozart."

He returned to Tecopah like a man condemned. A telegram had preceded him. The bank manager was taking over all purchasing and management arrangements. Shorty was under him, a chief engineer of sorts. Shorty said he had to go to Shoshone for supplies. When he got there, instead of buying supplies he took his horse toward the south end of Death Valley. He rode along the course of the Amargosa River. All his plans had failed. Job, family, gold—blown away. The bar would be a nice set-up, if only he could see it through and finally settle down. He knew he was depending on the bar for something, and suddenly, as he led the horse across wet sand in a brief spring rain, he saw a pattern emerging, a pattern as clear as the flowers unfolding at his feet.

He'd been so sure—so sure the primary vein would solve it all, before that so sure—if even for an hour—of June, so sure before that of his marriage. Almost within grasp. He could hear the men talking, ". . . up in Idaho . . . over the next range . . . the man who finds that one . . ." He could see the old, creased faces, the heads wagging, everything lost but desire. He saw it all in a flash: the bar too. Where would it end? Round and round. He answered himself: "Stone." He walked on, numbing his legs first, then his mind.

Late in the morning of the second day he sat on the ground. He'd have to stay with Hicks. The bar was all he had. Things would be better once he owned it in the clear. Beside him the Amargosa River was running, filled by the recent rain. "The Amargosa River": a muddy stream two feet wide winding lazily in and out of the mesquite toward the bottom of Death Valley, fifteen miles away.

Suddenly he noticed an iron pipe standing in the stream, behind a mesquite bush. He rose and walked over. Strange. The pipe had a new brass plaque bolted to it: "Sea Level. U.S. Geological Survey. 1875." Sea level. So here he was with his toes poking into the oceans of the world. Then he looked at the river; the water kept going. He stared at the tiny waves streaming out from the pipe, at the little wave on the upstream side, at the bubbles barely visible in the eddy below. Sea level. He could see no difference in the stream. It went past the pipe, past where the sea should be as if nothing had gone wrong. After all those miles, after snaking through the desert in broad daylight, dry air sucking at its back and sand sucking at its belly, after all that struggle it reached the spot where the sea should be—where a river should be able to sink into the arms of the ocean—didn't all rivers run to the sea? Didn't they? But the Amargosa went on as if nothing had happened at all.

So it hadn't run to the sea. He began to walk slowly down the stream. Far ahead the watercourse was dry. It didn't even reach the bottom of the basin. Not even close.

He came to the place where it disappeared, simply sank into the sand a mile past sea level. The running stream had dwindled to a tiny current; where it ended, standing pools of water the size of his thumbnail spotted the sand for several feet, reflecting a clear, white, sunny sky. Beyond the tiny pools the wet sand was dark, then splotched. His eye moved down the last patches of wet sand. As he watched they lightened and dried. The lightness in the sand crept toward him, past his feet, back the way he had come, a river of dryness flowing upstream. The pools were now behind him. The Amargosa not only didn't get anywhere; there wasn't even a place where it quit.

The sand at his feet splotched, dried, and whitened as he watched. The river of alkaline whiteness, the desert, flashed upstream like a fish. Mud cracked in its wake. It would pass the marker soon and keep moving until the Amargosa was gone again.

He sat, took his hat off, and rubbed his head. After a hundred miles there was no ocean. All the same to the Amargosa. Never going anywhere. Yet in every place it behaved like a river, every foot of it a river, perfectly like a river no matter what was ahead or behind. And when it was time it sank. "It is your responsibility as well as your fate to regain your innocence," he said to himself with a smile, "because you will die." He lay back on the sand, beneath a greasewood bush, and pulled his hat over his face. The day was stoking up again. A thought crossed his mind: "I will not go back to San Francisco." Another thought flowed over it: "Maybe I will, maybe I won't." Then the flow of thoughts ceased and he stopped imagining San Francisco, or what he had been thinking about, or what he would think about, or what thinking is—heat shimmered all around. He crossed his ankles, folded his arms on his breast, and beside the straggling line of dull green at the southern end of the vast valley, he slept.

Around him the bones of the desert bleached in the noonday sun. High in the mountains a coyote sought the blue-green shade of a dusty juniper. Close beside him a kangaroo rat crept to the bottom of her burrow. A chuckwalla backed beneath his rock. On the valley floor a thousand blooms, which the April rain had opened, closed up at the onslaught of heat. On the greasewood bushes the leaves turned their edges to the light; life shrank from the sun till it seemed that only the naked crust was left. Midday in the desert; the thin margin between earth and sky.

He had been in the desert three times before: as a boy dragged in by his family, then stomping off from his family in blind passion, and last as a speculator for Mr. Hicks. Now he had come again, and he felt he had come for the last time, and in a sense, for nothing—was that not what one, looking around, would seem to have found?—nothing at all.

Hicks would try to kill him again, the bar and any hope of Abigail would be gone—and who was he? Then he remembered, in the shade of his hat, hot sand growing cool beneath his back, eyes shut, ears ringing with silence, his father's diary, the little book in the saddlebags he'd left back in San Francisco, and he thought, "I've come to it now," the final chapter, "Desert Laws," the last blank page.

PART 4

The Desert, 1880–1934

Oh, He may not come when you
   want Him
but He's right on time.

—MAHALIA JACKSON

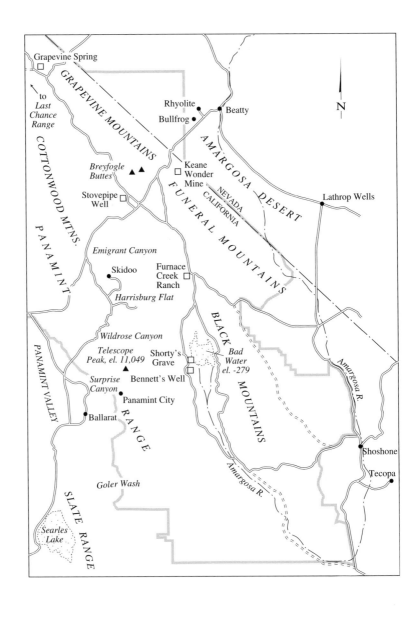

CHAPTER 19

Desert Laws

When the conquistadores first gazed across the red rock mesas and jagged canyons of the Colorado desert they could see no good. Where was the fruitful garden? Where were the shady bowers, the herbs and mallow leaves, the yellow gourds streaked, knobbed and cool to the palm; where was the soft, nourishing vegetable nature conveniently planted for their pleasure in Paradise? The barren land, blasted by sun and wind, was worse than Castile; worse than inhospitable, worse than ugly, wasted or even hostile. Outside the gates. They must have wondered if the loss of a supporting garden implies the loss of a supporting God. "Perhaps He did not intend we should come here"—"it is not prepared for us"—such thoughts rushed through their hearts as two sunburned faces looked at each other in silent disbelief, their aquiline noses repeating the lines of their helmets. The dusty horses stood still, too tired to stir under the long-borne weight of armored men—"Perhaps He has forsaken this place, or . . ." "Do not speak, brother." More than ugly and harsh, more even than damned, the land seemed unaccountable, unimagined by God.

In the desert the adventure was completed that had begun on the boundless but living ocean; they caught a glimpse of a universe apparently uninhabited by their fathering-forth God, who hid behind bright broad-leaved plants and purple blooms as He walked in the cool of the evening; and being beyond His imagination, the scene expanded theirs with the shock of revealed untruth. What they saw was what could not exist. It was not good.

But in that company there must have been some, some Jesuit scholar in a brown woolen robe sagged with heat, trailing in the dust; some bowed being who in facing the barren immense watched the leaves of Genesis fall away one by one until the garden was gone and only the first page was left upon his stark tree of knowledge, and he must have felt that here was the original nakedness from which the rest must be generated; here was the first earthly act of God: "His hands formed the dry land." For a second the others thought that exhaustion and thirst only had forced him to his knees, until they heard his words: "Praise be to God, thy works are beautiful; thou art too good . . ." At a sign from the captain two soldiers dismounted, half-coaxed, half-dragged the mumbling priest into the shade of a horse and while one held his head back by the hair the other forced the comforting water through his prayerful teeth; he lay still, dreaming of the ancient caves of Thessolonika where the monks sat in hollows of the white Mediterranean stone. "Poor fellow." The captain crossed himself and squinted again at nothing. "Sancta Maria, ora pro nobis." "Pray for us, holy mother" intoned the lieutenant in response. But no mother answered, and finding no father in their sight they turned back and headed south toward Indian corn to be had for the picking and Aztec gold for the glory of their king.

Behind them their tracks remained, cleaned of sand by the searching wind as often as they were filled, hoofprints distinct in the desert pavement for centuries, neither altered by erosion nor covered by plants, as if earth and air had agreed that here what was would be what is; for the desert hides nothing.

They were newcomers, the Spanish, and scared, who pushed and propped themselves with bold designs on the people and the land; men who at their bravest—like Cortez trapped in the court of Montezuma—fought. They came to subdue and have dominion, to use what could be cast, hammered or molded to their will. So they searched the desert for workable natives and rock, dreaming of the big bonanza—souls and gold combined in the fabulous Seven Cities of Cibola—but even at the height of their opulence, even in the full flowering of their rich Iberian courage, imagination, and greed, when they found nothing to be bent to their purpose the Spanish found nothing worth possessing, and left.

It is hardly surprising. Why would anyone stay in the desert? Only the Hopis—on Arizona mesas so remote that the priests were content to leave them in their limbo—only the Hopis claim that they live there of their own accord, and that accord began with a divine command. Their Great Spirit, after sending them to the four corners of the Americas, told them to settle on those barren mesas where a harsh existence would end their squabbles and bring the rewards of virtue, wisdom, and kindness. Anthropologists cannot believe it; they search the legends for signs of ancient migrations caused by changing climates and pressures from other tribes; they suspect that the Hopis endure the desert for reasons more tangible than love of virtue. But since the Hopis never expected creation to be the well-stocked larder of man—their Genesis is more humble— perhaps the land never seemed to them so bare. At least they say they love the region that looks as if the two halves of the Christian universe had been superimposed: the now and the hereafter combined in a land of living death. Could it be true, what Whorf said, that for them past, present and future are one?

The Spanish horse, the one that stomped his foot and rattled the lieutenant's armor—he knew. Given his head, he might have found a spring or brackish pool. Of Moorish stock, he had ancestral memories of barren stretches of North Africa and before that, Arabia Deserta, where an Islamic fate—which also plays tricks with the progression of time—held his masters patient as Hopis around the bunched grasses of a waterhole that the horse had known for two days he was approaching and would know for two days he had left. The Indian guide, although a Tewa from the pueblos of the Colorado, knew more than he told of "mas alla," knew of edible succulent roots and lizards beneath the sand, how to line doves and bees to springs; he knew of water and honey and sweet pine nuts and the bulbous cistern of the night-blooming cereus, and even the priest in his spiritual knowledge knew with St. Teresa and Ignatius and Loyola and others of passionate religion from the high, hot, dry plateaus of Castile that the uses to be made of the earth were more various and strange and beautiful than the Inquisition or the children of Adam especially lieutenants assumed, and in a corner of his mind he knew that he had not simply entered a region of lost souls but rather had always lived there, and yet only now did an infinite grace descending allow him to embrace it as home.

Before the prospectors of the 1800s finally scoured the Great Basin, cleaning up behind Coronado like barbers in the boom camps, paid in gold dust, who panned the hair off the floor at the end of the day; before the Spanish missions grew fat off their European agriculture, their imported staples and irrigated gardens; before the first conquistadores toured; before them all the Indians of Shoshone stock lived around the valley the old timers called "Tomesha," Ground on Fire.

Inhabiting is a state of mind that has little to do with years; some men spent a lifetime in desert mining camps without intending to stay, and if they could, they left to die. Nor is inhabiting a condition only of self-sustenance. Even the toughest prospectors rarely lived off the land, but as some became more familiar with the desert they regressed, as we say, to a more ancient or elemental state of mind. Like the Shoshones who pick tough pine nuts and squat to crack them in their teeth or the Australian aborigines who kneel naked, lank, and beautiful as they sip from shallow pools or the Kalahari bushmen who prostrate themselves on the burning ground to suck water from the sand through a reed, some old prospectors became experts in finding and embracing the tiny traces of life that in the barren desert may seem to the seeker like grace to the damned.

The desert hides nothing, though the green eyes of youth and desire can make what is there hard to find.

♦　♦　♦

In the empty space and brightness of the desert the newcomer—conquistodor, Jayhawker, tourist—sees death, and the geologist, like Shorty's father, sees stone.

Perhaps it is the brightness, the exposure, that makes one think what is there is easily seen—a mistake that leads to dismay. Certainly the desert is bright: unmasked by vegetation, with low humidity and clear air, the desert floor receives nine-tenths of the sun's radiation (twice that of a humid clime), and loses that heat each night. The sun comes and goes easily, neither absorbed nor held; variations are extreme. So the impression of essential brightness—the buff color of sand, salt, clay, and silt, which is the ground color of the desert as black is the ground color of space—is not deceptive if one realizes that brightness is not emptiness but light: the brightness is a visible sign that the desert does not dull the force of sun. Nor does it hold on.

Occasionally this brightness is purified to a true white in valley salt flats, or in mountain snowfields, or in the feathers of snowy egrets in the Humbolt sink, but usually the buff color of mud and sand dominates each valley from its central playa up to the light reddish brown of the alluvial fans, where the ground is splattered with stones of every color and sometimes darkened by "desert varnish," the iron and manganese oxide on rocks long exposed to the desert sun.

Above the fans in the canyon walls, the earth shows its full variety: reds and blacks slash the Funeral Range; the Panamints across the valley are topped by light gray slate and sandy granite; the clay hills of Furnace Creek Wash are yellow, white, purple, vermilion. The colors darken in the raw volcanic regions to the deep reds of lava flows and the blue-black of bare cinder cones, while here and there the earth comes to perfect blackness in cliffs of clear obsidian, black volcanic glass, where nothing grows. The desert makes conditions obvious: the interior of the earth is dark, massive, and sterile; spilled out and long exposed to sun and atmosphere it lightens, disintegrates, and supports life, in the thin interface of earth and sky.

Consider how these realities shape desert lives. Being so vulnerable, plants must also be cautious; they must not take too much light. This is one reason the desert seems so bare at first: many of the plants are reflectors, themselves contributing to the dominant and apparently lifeless white. Last year's rabbit brush and matchweed stalks, neither bent by snow nor rotted by rain, stand bright and dry until the next year's green growth has topped the dead stems. In a dry climate decay is slow; the desert does not quickly bury its dead. Moreover, some plants temporarily die back along their stalks in dry periods and later revive. In fact, so many plants meet adversity with brittle, leafless stems that few observers can say which plants are actually dead and which only dormant. In summer, across miles and miles of apparently empty ground the tiny desert plants are a dry-stalk white, matching the ground, temporarily or permanently abandoned by the life processes that would make them green.

Yet even when thriving, the plants of the valley floors grow in clumps and bushes rarely more than waist high, and the color of their scant foliage is usually a light green leaning to yellow. In that climate plants can easily gather sufficient light with a few dull leaves; to use more light they would need more water. Each leaf is a liability, for it loses moisture through evaporation. Some species have no leaves at all: plants ranging in size from greenish twigs to giant cacti and trees manufacture chlorophyll in their trunks or branches. So leaves are scarce and thin; one accustomed to a temperate zone may hardly imagine the growth before him.

In its relation to light the desert is open and vulnerable, but not possessive. Water, however, is another matter. Leaves are not only few and light in color but also surprisingly tough. Their color is dull partly because they are covered with wax or powder or thick skin, which helps slow evaporation. The thick, pendant, soft blue-green leaf of the round buffalo berry proves coarse and brittle to the touch. The leaves of the smallest ground flower may be stiff, serrated, spined. All leaves must defend themselves against the light they gather and must also guard the water they hold.

Its brittleness and the tentative, cautious quality of its green help give the desert the look of a land besieged. With scant, dull foliage, thorns, stiff leaves, and stunted shapes, the growth looks hard pressed, like tree line shrubs. Just what this force is, what presses the growth into low, gnarled, woody stems is not really known; some say drought, others heat, others wind. Whatever the desert is must be the answer, for surely the plants have no ambition but to live. The appearance most of the time is one of uneasy truce: battleground plants, which seem the visible signs of an old stalemate between earth and sky. In the vegetation's form and color one easily senses oppression: the desert—whatever that is— putting checks on life.

But if something lives, then oppression has been met with commensurate vitality. The tough, stubby shapes seem fierce; the slightest relaxation into green, impossibly beautiful. The eye, discouraged by the dullness even of the cottonwoods, willows, tamarisk pines, dry mountain junipers, and piñons, soon adjusts to new standards: then in April the waxed green of the greasewood and of the more favorably watered sages stands out, the mesquites around the Panamint marsh shine at midday, and upslope the little clumps of Mormon tea are bright in clefts of rock. And at the back of some canyons, reeds and grasses wave above watercress in the pool.

And even though most valley plants are scattered, their leaves thin and colors dull, the vast distances available to the eye have a way of amassing color until the subtlest tints, repeated over and over, become vivid. The little reddish twig that grows every ten feet or so in some dry alluvial fans, six inches high, with six or eight dry needlelike leafless branches, can be hard to spot at one's feet. But a mile away it gives the faintest brown tint to the slope, and six miles away the ground appears covered with rust-colored flowers. Approach, of course, and color fades. So also the little yellow poppies growing every twenty feet in May make Panamint Valley, at eye level, solid yellow. If the sage is sparse nearby, a few miles distant the desert looks green. No matter where you stand, you seem to stand in nothing, while all around is more. "Mas alla!" The distant mountains look close. A land where hope, too, is visible. El Dorado is always an hour away.

Not always illusion. The desert dweller learns that sooner or later, that promise is made good. Blooms in the desert, which answer so perfectly to one's needs that by bitter analogy they seem unreal and indeed are as miraculous and ephemeral as the mirage, are not just tricks of the eye. At least the whole body is taken in; when approached they please the senses one by one. Though the buffalo berry leaf is surprisingly tough, the thin magenta bloom of the prickly pear cactus is velvet soft and even at midday is found flopped open, exposed without defense to sun and wind. Until one touches the petals, such delicacy issuing from such a fortress of a plant is hard to believe. One after another: the red and scarlet blooms of paintbrush, the fragrant violet locoweed flower, the wispy purple of the blooming tamarisk bush, the yellow flower of mesquite, the white cotton puffs of the greasewood, the huge thin white jimson weed trumpet and the infinitely various blooms of the tiny ground flowers are all as soft as their enduring leaves are harsh. So life is not always callused: there is respite at springs, and even for the prickly cactus, the occasional celebration of a bloom.

The occasion is rain, but this all-saints holiday has no date. On a global map of rainfall the areas of greatest fluctuation are the deserts. The rain is so fickle that annual measurements are meaningless: Baghdad may receive five years' allowance in a night while ten miles away the drought continues for years. Almost every day in summer you can see rain somewhere, fifty, a hundred and fifty miles away. But it may never fall on your head. At any time there is always a famine in at least one of the world's deserts, for always some place is waiting, and waiting, and waiting, year after impossible year, for rain. The averages are meaningless. Wait or die.

The plant species that have adapted to these demanding conditions are, in a strictly botanical sense, precious. For instance, denude an acre of eastern woodland and kill all roots. Many different plants will invade the naked plot in succession. Birches will replace the meadow grasses and blackberries, maples will replace the birches, and so on. Grasses and trees from Europe and Asia abound. Almost anything that can stand hard frost will root in the rich humus. Trees, shrubs, grasses, flowers, vegetables. The result is an evolving layered forest in which thousands of species come and go and share the available light.

But so difficult are conditions in the desert that if an acre of Death Valley were razed, the first and only species to appear would be those species that were there before. They, and only they, can flourish in that spot.

At the edge of the barren salt flat of Death Valley life begins to take hold, bush by bush. Only the little pickle bush grows every thirty yards or so in playa up to 6 percent salt. In between, nothing. A few hundred yards up the imperceptible slope, where the salt is only 3 percent, a few jagged arrow weeds appear. A hundred yards further, near the subtle but naked line where the playa ends and the huge sloping alluvial fan begins, are greasewood, saltbush, low desert holly, and near wells, here or there, stubby mesquite trees that send roots a hundred feet down to water. On the alluvial fan the sages and cacti begin and continue far up the canyons and upper slopes to the high dwarf forests of piñon pine and juniper.

These are the dominant plants. They stand visible in the heat and light and drought, always exposed. But they are by no means the only plants. Kneel—in April—in the barely discernible dry watercourses at the very bottom of the Hanapah fan, near Shorty's grave in the valley he loved, in the shallow depressions where every year or two the water may for a few minutes take its course across the gravel and sand, and there you will find even in a dry year one, two, three, four species of ground flowers a quarter of an inch to three inches high, yellow and violet; some have purple blooms no bigger than the head of a pin. A few yards further up are reddish twigs and dried trumpet flower stalks. Look to the side. Ten feet away is another nearly invisible watercourse. Crawl over. It has the same flowers and two more species, and a white verbena. Now that your eye, in the middle of this vast basin, has adjusted to the scale, you move slowly up the hard-packed gravel of the fan, crouched, peering at the ground in front of your feet. Lizards skitter and beetles crawl across your path. There is a purple five-spot, and a yellow coreopsis. You turn. There are yellow flowers behind that you hadn't noticed, and to the sides—they stretch for miles, yellowing the fan—and up higher are purple verbena, buttercups, yellow frost mats, giant pin cushions, small-stemmed yucca (soap, needles, sandals to the Indians) and wild heliotropes, and as many more species that you cannot find in your books. You may as well get off your knees; there is no end of life.

And even kneeling you have not seen the desert, for some seeds do not germinate, and some plants do not send up fresh shoots, for years. They are living and invisible under your nose. Each species has a way to wait for rain: the big, visible plants are drought survivors, meeting hard times by drawing stored water from their roots or from their thick succulent trunks and stems. Other plants go dormant in hard times—estivate—while others, especially flowers, disperse seeds that will germinate only in the best conditions: after a sufficient rain, or in the case of the indigestible mesquite seed, only when eaten and defecated; then, finally, its wax covering dissolved by stomach acids, and embedded in fresh wet manure, it sprouts. So even in spring, or in two springs, or three, or twenty, one cannot be sure that the desert has shown its hand. This is a land "exposed"?

In 1925 rain fell on a dry lake in the Mohave for the first time in twenty years. Millions of tiny freshwater shrimp appeared wriggling three inches deep across miles of mud flat. No one had known that the baked mud held such eggs. In a few weeks the shrimp lived, reproduced, and died. Presumably another generation of eggs waits for rain. Who knows the desert? It reveals itself on a scale too grand for the individual eye. The shrimp had learned to wait; they remained from the time of the Pleistocene lakes and before that, the ocean. Like most desert life they know well how to bide their time.

But they also know how to flourish. After years of waiting a dry, prickly cactus will suddenly put forth a sodden, crimson bloom as big as itself; in a day the seeds are dispersed and it is gone. Done. The model is so poignantly innocent that it is hard to imagine a human analogue; if there was patience and purpose, why not retention? Waiting, and waiting, and waiting—without coveting the prize. It is simply done.

The desert is not like a temperate zone with its regular seasons, where if winter comes, spring is not far behind. No, the desert rains are infrequent and unpredictable, and hence instead of encouraging regulation, the desert forces life into ecstatic patterns: long periods of waiting are punctuated by moments of the most intense vitality. All the plants and animals—all true inhabitants of the desert—must learn this law, must be relaxed but alert, indefinitely stable yet open to the most sudden and dramatic change; passive, submissive to the will of the desert for the longest time yet capable of undertaking the full cycle of vitality—birth, reproduction, death— in little more than a moment. The Zen schedule—nonschedule—of spontaneous enlightenment is not more mysterious or dramatic than the desert's cycles of boom and bust. Is this what made Whorf think that the Hopis needed no tenses for their verbs? Surely they knew the rhythms of the land; perhaps they spoke to him from within the no-time of perfect waiting, or the all-time of perfect bloom.

Plants, reptiles, animals, man—all must adapt to drought and midday sun. The surface temperature in Death Valley can fry an egg, while two feet down the ground is cool. Each day the silent force of light descends like a giant hand to press on the valley floor, squeezing the lizards, snakes, mice and rabbits up into the hills or driving them underground where they lie invisible beside the waiting seeds.

At evening they emerge: mountain sheep and deer at high elevations in the Panamints, and black bear in the ranges to the north, and now and then in piñon forests a badger or mountain lion. But these big mammals avoid the valley floor.

Around Shorty's grave the life on the desert floor is small and skinny and hard like the plants, and buff-colored, tapering off to red-brown or dusty green, like the land: white-brown little civet cats, light squirrels, chipmunks, jackrabbits, tan mice, pack rats, kangaroo rats; white-and-brown sparrows, quails, doves, hawks; sidewinders the color of the mice they eat and the sand they hunt them in, rust-marked Panamint rattlers, dusty tarantulas; lizards—brown to green—translucent pale green scorpions and at the edges of the color range matching the bright varied color of the blooms: little pearlescent beetles shining like flakes of black abalone, quick blue jays, yellow bumblebees and bright green flies, iridescent hummingbirds come and gone in dance and matching the obsidian: wasps, ants, black and blacker, brittle and hard.

Here, where the hills lie wrinkled, weathered and sere as an old squaw's face, the temperate conditions of life are reversed. The desert dies in summer, buried under sun. Also at noon. When most of the world is opening up shops, or lounging about, or going to the beach, desert life slinks away to the pine and juniper forests or to the springs and waterholes, or under bushes, or underground, to wait for night, evening, winter, rain. To escape the source of life, the sun. In midsummer and harvest time when lusher climes are fat with growth and seed, the desert seems lifeless. But it is not. It is not. Plants, seeds, insects, reptiles and animals are there, hidden, biding their time, waiting, small or invisible though not unknown to the desert inhabitant who has learned to trust the subtle and ecstatic rhythms that are to them necessity.

CHAPTER 20

Chasing Rainbows

When Shorty Harris went to sleep beside the Amargosa River in 1880 he had come to the desert to stay.

Throughout the eighties he wandered over Nevada, from the Sierras to the Reese River and occasionally east to Pioche and from Virginia City in the north down to the Mohave, traveling from camp to camp, working here and there for wages, learning the lay of the Basin and the look of its rock, cautiously increasing the days of his journeys like a young sailor venturing out of sight of land. He staked many claims, worked some and sold most, but never made more than a few hundred dollars from a single site.

It was a dry time for everyone, and as always in hard times those holed up fared best: the big mines, the stable towns, continued to produce, but new strikes were few, money was tight, and the days of speculation gone. Claims no longer sold. So those out on the fringe—the prospectors—those living at the edge, in the thin margin, without deep roots and no place to hide had to get through as best they could. Shorty was becoming one of them—"Desert Prospector" was a proud term once—one of those who never worked a claim more than a few weeks—skim and sell—and never fell back, having nothing to fall back on and no fat to feed on and so never stopped or rooted, and like the others he could be found at any time drifting alone or with a partner through one range or another of the Great Basin or gathered at midday with dusty men—their numbers dwindling—fetched up like tumbleweeds against dark potbellied stoves or on shaded porches in Lathrop Wells, Indian Springs, Stovepipe Walls, talking of their prospects: of good ground and promising color, of famous regions and unexplored territory, of lost mines and big bonanzas and always of the old days and the old men, the great men, the men like Sid Goshen who had been there and back, the men who "knew their rock."

Like the others he had his favorite claims and could always squeeze another twelve or thirteen dollars from the dust, and now and then he worked a day or two for wages at Searles Lake. Food was cheap enough, the burros grew wild. Like the others he was waiting, shifting, making do until—they talked always of the past and of the future as they sat, relaxed, garrulous, still, feet up on the cold iron stove in Lathrop Wells. The time passed. Year after year Shorty slipped deeper into a reverie of walking, eating, talking, spitting, holding rocks and splitting: fracture, cleavage, hardness, streak—no color. Move on.

In the mid-eighties he traveled for a while with Hot Steam Boyd and spent six months at his alchemical laboratory near Carson City. Hot Steam was a teacher, one of the great old Basin prospectors and the first to realize that gold was formed at the zenith of rising vapors, though he had his own theory about cooling rates and talked a good deal of giant crystals embedded in volcanic vents. Hot Steam first appeared one night at Shorty's fire in the White Mountains, tugging a packless pregnant burro. He squatted, asked to share a blanket, and told Shorty he should always carry lemon for his omelettes. Hot Steam explained that he had not meant to be out overnight but had gotten a whiff of sulfur and had just spent two days beating upwind to find the source, and what with his burro about to foal—so he couldn't leave her—and holding her front legs stiff the whole way he was near done in so he thought he'd skip the omelette which he preferred with onions and go straight to bed, thanks. He looked at the sky and pointed Shorty's blanket at the Pole Star, explaining that he should always sleep with his head to the north to keep the iron in his body aligned with the earth's magnetic field; he went to sleep. Shorty stared at his pan. He was cooking hash.

In the morning Hot Steam's burro had given birth, but there was no feed so Hot Steam and Shorty carried the foal west for two days to Hot Steam's laboratory on the Carson River where there was plenty of grass for mother's milk. After feedings, Hot Steam would lie down beside the mother and the two—man and beast— would rub and kiss the foal's ears until it fell asleep. Shorty stayed six months, trying to turn lead into gold. Hot Steam said they nearly had it. Shorty agreed as he packed. The men met every few years for trips into the Pahute Mesa and the Belted Range.

Eight, nine, ten years slid by. There were no more than twenty of them now—Shorty, Hot Steam, Driscoll, Clair, Corcoran, Aguere- berry, Jake—and Shorty was always going to quit after one more trip. Then in 1890 Jim Dayton returned. He drove a twenty-mule team for the borax works until 1894, when he became caretaker of the ranch at Furnace Creek. Shorty heard for the first time that in 1883 June had taken her life.

June and Jim had been living in Darwin at the time. Afterward Jim had moved to San Francisco, left his eighteen-year-old daugh- ter with an aunt and taken work as cook on a Sacramento riverboat. When the boat sank, he and his cocker spaniel walked ashore. He could find no decent work in San Francisco, and when his daughter married, a friend got him the job of "Captain," mate, and crew of the borax wagons in Death Valley. It paid well.

Apparently all of his gold fever was gone; as soon as he arrived in Death Valley Jim made it known that he hated the desert and first chance he had he would leave. While he was waiting for the chance he fixed himself up a nice little cabin in the shade of the date palms at Furnace Creek and planted a garden beside the irrigation ditch. Year round he raised tomatoes, lettuce, beans, beets, carrots, onions, basil, parsley, radishes, and watermelons.

His cabin quickly became a popular stopping place; silent, dusty prospectors would follow him around the shaded garden while he complained of life and filled the salad bowl. He kept oil, vinegar, and walnuts at home, and in the company icebox were several cheeses that he made himself from his two goats and a cow. Whiskey from L.A. When all the fixings were fixed and the bowls were washed and the two rockers arranged just right on the north side porch, rimmed on two sides by roses and wisteria, Jim would take a chair, motion his visitor to do the same, peer through the dense date palms to the livid desert, crunch crisp salad greens and say after ten years here it would be a relief to go to hell.

He put up with every kind of tramp, impostor, tourist, administered to every kind of emergency and never stopped moaning about the desert and its helpless kind though he had managed to become the only person who lived year round on the Death Valley floor. Like an old general he seemed to crave close contact with the enemy.

He had what Shorty needed: "shelter," Jim called it from the depths of his bunker, while for his part Jim hung like an old salt on Shorty's yarns of desert voyages and buried treasure. Shorty would place a foot on a kitchen chair and wave his arms to show how this time he would strike it rich while Jim would shake his head over the mixing bowl and tell Shorty to pour himself another drink. Without words they somehow arranged an acceptance and rejection—perhaps a purging—of their intertwined pasts; then they created a kind of adaptive symbiosis: Shorty rained visions while Jim fretted out the drought.

During the nineties Shorty narrowed his circle. He stayed in the southwest Basin, rarely more than a week from Death Valley and his friend. In and out, back and forth; his life was full of repetition. But even in the midst of his routines and reveries he was again becoming uncomfortable, for no matter where he turned he kept bumping his head on the notion that a prospector is supposed to find gold. He had waited a long time. Another eight years had slid by. He was already an aging and somewhat disappointed man in 1898 when a rapid series of deaths and changes in the Basin forced him to reconsider his situation; as if a suddenly swollen current had bumped him a few more yards downstream.

"It's a hard-luck spot," said Shorty when they found the body at the foot of Hanaupah Fan. Jim must have sought shelter at the last: he lay on his back, his head and shoulders in the meager shade of a greasewood, a hundred yards from a wagon with two full canteens and three barrels of water. The brakes were set. Much to everyone's surprise he held a piece of gold float, with fair showing, in one sun-blackened hand. The six mules, still in their traces, had died, swollen, popped and dried, but Mate, the cocker spaniel, was still able to drag himself around the corpse and growl. July 15, 1898. It had been 126 degrees at Furnace Creek when The Captain had left, in late morning, for Daggett, 140 miles south, with an umbrella and a basket of fresh fruit. He must have been delirious in the heat. No one knew more.

Shorty and two friends dug as deeply as they could and piled the horse bones on the grave. They built a fire of greasewood—the flames were invisible in the sun—and with a red-hot poker wrote on a wagon board; "Jim Dayton perished 1898." It seemed somehow slapped together and hopeless, a burial at sea. Frank Tilton gave the eulogy. "Well, Jimmie, you lived in the heat and you died in the heat, and after what you been through I guess you ought to be comfortable in hell." Shorty said "Mercy on his soul" and they started immediately for the shade of the ranch where they sat on the porch and drank. The tomato plants were as baffling as children: the men despaired of raising them right. During the next few years, while the garden went to seed and burned out, occasional gold seekers would comb the ledges above Hanaupah Fan looking for the lost Dayton mine.

A hard-luck spot, Shorty thought. Within four miles was Bennett's long camp, where the forty-niner families had lost hope as they waited for Manly and Rogers to return. Within a mile was the ill-fated Eagle Borax Works: In 1875 Daunet and six other men had run out of water, gone mad in the heat, slashed the throats of their burros and wallowed in the blood. Daunet and one other had backtracked to a marshy spring where Indians were camped. The Shoshone had saved them, retrieved two more alive, and buried the others. Daunet, when he reached civilization, filed a mineral claim to the marsh and 260 acres around it. He returned in 1880: a dot at first, dust, horses, wagons hauling a huge iron vat and several thousand-gallon pans. The Indians left. Daunet dug up most of the marsh, but the borax was low grade. They carted out a few tons, made no money, and two years later quit, bequeathing to the marsh the yellow mounds and clumps of rusted iron that still remain beside the Tamarisk pines at the site called "The Eagle Borax Works." Dayton's grave, the wheel ruts at Bennett's camp, and the rusted, abandoned mounds at the borax works: all lie together, baked by the sun and picked clean by the wind at the foot of Hanaupah Fan. Shorty shook his head and spat over the rail of the porch. Jim had believed he would go, when dead, to a better place. It wouldn't be hard, Shorty thought. He could go in any direction once he left his grave.

Two days after Dayton's burial Shorty went east up the wash. He turned left at the line of willows, let the burros go, and lay down in the grass of Furnace Creek spring, the spring where the Reverend Brier had told his sullen, starving brats that knowledge is happiness while beside him Furnace Creek rose only five miles from its annihilation in the burning sand, right there where the Jayhawkers and then the Bennett-Arcane party had spent their last easy unknowing nights before following the water down to the living hell of the valley floor; there by the source of the water for Dayton's garden Shorty stopped for two days and considered.

He had been a prospector for twenty years and had never made a strike worth more than seven hundred dollars. He was fifty years old. He had lost touch with all family—he had not seen his daughter Abigail since she was ten—Abigail—she would be nearly thirty now, a woman, married with children, his grandchildren. He had once looked forward to sharing something with grandchildren, though he'd never known what. He poked at the fire. Tears dropped on his sleeve. He'd had a letter from Crystal after Max's death but had never replied. His only friend lay beneath horse bones and a wagon board in the middle of Death Valley. Would he be buried like that? The thought was unbearable. What would he do the rest—the phrase suddenly struck home—the rest of his life? Was this it?

His life. As he came closer his life evaporated before his eyes. Not many were out in the desert now; there seemed to be no more gold. The Jayhawkers had come through this very spot half a century before, in the year of his birth. All the towns and camps were dwindling; California was a settled state; the West was full of railroads; the country was a nation that went to war. Had he been asleep? It was no time for a fifty-year-old man to be tramping about the desert tapping stone. Half a century since the great gold rush and his birth; a new century about to be born: the twentieth century, and he a desert prospector shuffling about with his burros looking for something he would never find. "Chasing rainbows," as the papers said. It was pathetic, sentimental. And he, who had once been an educated man. In the light of history he found himself ridiculous.

In this mood he realized that he would like to see his mother again. She had married Lane in Bodie in 1895. She was then seventy-two, Lane was sixty-one. They had moved immediately to the central valley of California where they had bought a small ranch near Merced. Shorty suddenly realized that his mother's life could end even sooner than his own. He decided to cross the Sierra and visit them. Perhaps they knew of work. Perhaps he would not come back. Burned out, wasted, dry, brittle—as good, he thought, as dead.

He descended from Walker Pass to the green valley of California: grass, trees, cattle, flowers. He tied his burro to the porch railing and hugged his mother and stepfather. They were in fine fat shape, like barrel cacti in the spring. They had taken well to the long winter rains and the hot, dry summers of the foothills, to the speckled shade of the huge valley oaks around their porch. Chickens pecked, pigs squealed, dogs barked—just like a real farm. Beyond a brand-new fence some fancy beef cattle ranged. They were business smart. Soon they would be rich.

CHAPTER 21

Lane and Catherine

Lane laughed and leaned back in his porch rocker. His hair was long and silver. "Rich," he said, though in fact they hired only enough labor to keep their afternoons free for sitting on the porch, drinking at a subsistence level. Soon neighbors began to arrive for dinner. Lane and Catherine were well dressed and in command. Lane ran a crooked roulette table; everyone knew, but couldn't figure out how he did it. The rich neighbors lost, the poor neighbors won. Lane lent Shorty a suit he had outgrown, "so he wouldn't feel uncomfortable." Food appeared magically, conjured without effort from the kitchen. Shorty kept looking at the furniture, the pictures, the utensils. His collar itched, just like parochial school. A woman stared at his sunburned hands.

After dinner Lane passed cigars and wine to men and women alike.

"Yankees be damned," Lane said in response to a neighbor's remark. "Yankees be damned." He poured Shorty more wine. Catherine turned to her dinner partner, a large-necked, red-faced German:

"The Yankees have never understood the tradition of graceful agriculture," she said in her soft Richmond accent.

Lane brought the bottle up with a twist. "Read Fremont's report to Congress, Mr. Hess"—Lane turned to the man—"describing his arrival at the Mission Santa Barbara in 1842. After four days of hot riding, with very little water, he and his men reached the crest of the Santa Barbara Mountains. Below they saw red tile roofs, adobe buildings and perfectly kept vineyards stretching down to the sea. Within two hours, bathed and changed, he found himself in paradise walking through grape arbors in the cool of the evening, smelling lemon and jasmine—better than paradise, for the priest was a sensible man who put his cigar out before entering the rose garden and who liked Carlyle for his humor." Lane paused and smiled. "The blessed fathers served their own wine." Lane looked at the ceiling, fingering his glass, his cigar. The reverie hovered over the table like smoke in candlelight. "Ah, the old missions." He turned toward Hess again. "For dinner? Snails, trout in lemon sauce." He sat back and drained his glass. "Then the Yankees came along, with a liberal mixture of you Krauts and other attractive Northern Europeans, raised—appropriately enough—the Bear Flag, and the missions were crushed. Goddamn Protestants can't stand anything but rock."

Others at the table protested; they knew Mexicans, a dirty, lazy lecherous lot. Someone told a story of a Mexican vendor in San Francisco who was too proud to do something or other and so was undersold and ruined by the first Yankee peddler who came along, but Shorty could see through their vulgarity and he hung on Lane's replies: his conjured visions of life on the great ranchero of Don Juan Ignatius de Valle in San Bernardino, where the four hundred farm hands and their women danced and drank and sang all night in between seasons of sweating labor; danced with the rhythms of the land, and talk about mining!—Lane turned to Shorty—"They worked ore with a style—none of your goddamn smelters—arrastras an acre across where hundreds of horses and mules trampled a mixture of ore and quicksilver. The animals were lashed to a frenzy while the poisons worked into their hooves. Their bones whitened the grasslands for miles around. And what did they do with their Mexican silver? Banks? Vaults? Oh no, the horses died for good cause, señor—for wrought brooches that swung from the ears and lay heavy on the breasts of their voluptuous wives." One of the women at the table murmured and turned away. Lane leaned toward her and whispered intensely: "Voluptuous!" Then to Shorty, suddenly, "What's that from?" and Shorty heard himself say without a second's thought: "Voluptas, pleasure, gratification of the flesh." Lane laughed out loud. "That's a frontier, that's how to take advantage of a land."

It wasn't until the guests had left and he sat with Lane and Catherine on the veranda that he learned of his brother.

"You haven't heard?" said Catherine.

"No. Is he all right?"

"All right!" Lane choked on his cognac.

"He's in the legislature in Massachusetts," Catherine said.

"Alex?" Shorty tried to remember when he last saw his younger brother. And now in Massachusetts, right above Rhode Island.

"Honestly Shorty, where have you been?" His mother seemed vexed. "Your brother is a legislator. In Boston."

A legislator in Boston? He tried to respond.

"I knew he went east . . ."

"Oh Shorty I told you that he put himself through Brown."

"Oh yes."

"And I wrote you in San Francisco that Uncle Edward was sending him to law school. But he gave up his practice when he was elected."

"I guess it's been a while."

"If you'd come to our wedding . . ."

"Well how is he? Do you hear—"

"He writes regularly, Shorty."

"Oh."

"I guess he's all right," said Lane quietly. "Except that he'll be in Washington someday."

When Shorty rose to go down to the guest house Lane pulled him aside.

"Listen here bud," Lane said. "I always thought Alex was a smart-ass."

Shorty stayed for a week, then made preparations to leave. Back to the Panamints, he said. His mother thought him stubborn. He said there was one canyon he knew on the west side might bear looking into. He declined Lane's offer of a family partnership in the ranch. During his last night the three sat on the veranda, listening to an owl.

"There's a Spanish proverb, Shorty," said Lane as he raised his glass and looked through it to a wine-red moon. Lane's voice was dry. "Living well is the best revenge."

That night the cat knocked over a kerosene lamp. It splashed on embers of the fire and the ranch house burned to the ground. Shorty was awakened by the horses; he ran up from the guest cottage; neighbors came, but it was no use. Lane and Catherine never appeared. It was late the next day before he could pick his way between black timbers to the bodies in bed, disposed in positions of sleep. An empty decanter and two glasses were half melted on the floor. He had a flash of Jim's body in the whitening valley—death by fire— and he remembered a Russian miner in Idaho talking of a Siberian winter so cold that the calves froze in their mother's wombs.

He spent several days making arrangements for the funeral and seeing it through. He wired Alex; condolences returned. Then he took Lane's riding horse and stringing his burro, headed into the foothills toward Walker Pass and the desert.

As he crossed the low divide between Searles Basin and Panamint Valley he tried to remember when he had felt so alone. Not since his father's death, perhaps; certainly not since going to San Francisco. But then at least he'd had youth and time, time before him. Now he was fifty years old. "Fear the Lord." He heard the hoarse whisper in his ear. "Before you're done you'll say nothin' but Fear the Lord."

He stopped at Ballarat for a drink. Jake was there, and laid up. His burro had stepped on his foot and broken two toes. They pulled chairs around the cold stove and propped their feet on the rail. Outside, sand blew against the south window. "Lucky," Jake said, "you were going with the wind." They talked. Jake said he had lost his parents to cholera in Missouri. He had shut his father's eyes and buried both parents with his own hands. He wept a bit to tell it. Shorty looked at his boots. They had another drink to break the spell. Jake patted Shorty on the knee and said he'd give him a little tip: he'd found some mighty good float a few months before on the east side of the Grapevines. First wash north of Spring Canyon. Real fine ledge country. Soon as his foot got better . . . Shorty said he was free for a while. Jake said not to wait: "A word to the wise." Shorty thanked him and sat another hour. Then he rose, said "Guess I'll be going," and left money at the bar for another bottle.

"Save me some," said Jake.

CHAPTER 22

Father Dismay

In the cool upper reaches of Wildrose Canyon he ran into Shoshone Tommy, camped with one horse. They hadn't seen each
other in eighteen years. Tommy had to be eighty. The old man sat
cross-legged by his fire, laughing and talking—why sure, he was
going prospecting. He didn't seem a bit crazy, Shorty thought.
Shorty stopped for dinner and they fell in together to the Grapevines. Tommy had an endless appetite for cacti, mesquite beans,
piñon and juniper nuts, flower stems and leaves. Shorty laughed
at him for traveling like a burro, munching this way and that,
going five miles up a blind canyon to browse on milkweed,
watercress and cattails. They came into the Grapevines through a
back door Shorty had never seen and spent a week in the cool
heights tracing ledge formations. They saw plenty of mineralization, but neither had any interest in low-grade copper or
anything else for that matter other than a lode of silver or gold.
Meanwhile they ate chuckwallas rolled in willow leaves and
smoked in juniper coals.

They'd been together almost two weeks when Shorty, returning
to camp, pulled up short. Tommy was sitting in front of his circle
of rocks again. Shorty had almost forgotten about the rocks, and
the crazy old Indian. He unpacked the burro, let it go and walked

into camp. Tommy had not looked up. He sat and stared at the ground, dressed in patched, faded blue overalls and a cotton shirt printed with cowboys and bucking broncos. His pigtails hung down from his black felt hat.

"Well, where am I now?" Shorty laughed.

Tommy looked up with an expression of surprise, then looked back at the rocks.

"Short Man, you were born in the east, the place of illumination. Your color is—"

"Hey wait a minute," said Shorty. "You told me I was born in the north. My color is white."

"What?"

"Forty years ago."

Tommy laughed. "I miss that one a lot. Especially with Hopis. Look like they got wisdom, but what they really got is illumination." He shook his head.

"Yeah," said Shorty. "It's tough to tell the difference between an eagle and a buffalo."

Tommy laughed hard. "That's right, that's right." He stretched. "They speak very much alike. But you were an eagle."

Shorty paused in his fire building and looked up. Tommy's face was impassive again as he bent above the stones.

"Actually you weren't so far off," said Shorty. "You said northeast."

Tommy didn't reply. Shorty started the fire and began to mix dough. Tommy spoke as if in a trance:

"You have been to the south, the place of the mouse. You have learned the gift of touch. That was difficult for you my son. And you have visited the west, the place of introspection. The color is black."

Tommy fell into a long silence. He was absolutely serious. Shorty stared.

"You have visited all points on the circle, White Eagle."

Shorty could tell from his tone that something was wrong, and he knew that it must concern him. Inside he cringed like a child watching his father slip the belt from its loops.

"You have been to the north, you have been to the south . . ."

Shorty kneaded the dough hard.

"You have been to the east, you have been to the west. You have been to all points of the circle, and the circle is the universe."

"So?" The word came out sharply while he squeezed.

"So you have been everywhere, but you are not at rest. Perhaps you are not the circle."

Shorty didn't reply. Tommy spoke again.

"It is not the Indian way. You do not let go, you do not leave yourself behind, so when you have been everywhere you are not the circle, you are the center. You know all things but you are not all things, and you are alone."

Shorty glared at him. Tommy, bent over the stones, spoke again casually:

"It seems to me you are initiated into your tribe when you die. We initiate boys when they are twelve or so."

Tommy looked up and saw the pain. His face softened, and he spoke gently: "I do not understand the white man's courage. It is more than I could bear."

Shorty gritted his teeth and thought, "Fear the Lord. That's how we live."

The next morning news of Tonopah broke. Shorty had gone down to the three shacks called Leadfield to buy salt. Everyone was packing.

"Haven't you heard?"

"Biggest strike in the history of the Basin!"

"Silver up north by Tonopah, Shorty. Four hundred dollars to the ton."

Shorty raced back to camp, but Tommy said it was too far too fast for him. Shorty slid the pick and shovel under the ropes and pulled the load tight.

"This is it, Tommy. I know it."

Tommy laughed loud and hard. "White Eagle," he said, and held out his hand. "White Eagle, good luck."

♦ ♦ ♦

Tonopah, Goldfield, Rhyolite—from 1900 to 1908 the Basin, like a catus in sudden rain, came alive again with extraordinary strikes and unimagined booms: towns mushroomed and collapsed and thousands poured into the desert while developers and speculators—"paper miners"—proved that they could grow cities by sowing gullibility in barren soil.

The strikes were all accidents, the booms all the same. Tonopah was no exception: a man followed his strayed burro up an unknown canyon, found a likely piece of silver float and an outcropping, then came down the hill with a sample. Butler, who had found it, was tied up on his ranch; Mrs. Butler sent the sample to Attorney Oddie for an interest; Oddie sent it to Assayer Gayhart for an interest. Five hundred dollars to the ton. Third richest ore in history. The Butlers, Oddie, and Brougher—who had a wagon and mules— teamed up and staked the region. When the first ore to reach Austin in October 1900 assayed at eight hundred dollars to the ton, the word got out and the rush was on.

Shorty arrived a week later. The blossoming tent city was in a frenzy. The first hot prospect, the first boom in decades. He leased his choice of Butler's 112 claims (agreeing to pay 25 percent of the proceeds) and went right to work, straining his eyes for the point where his trench would cut the glistening vein of argentite.

Within a month five thousand people were there; within a year twenty thousand. The town, laid out and sold lot by lot by Gayhart, spread across miles of bare volcanic soil and ash. Water was imported in kegs. Goods were bought up as fast as the wagons could be unloaded; the merchants had no stores.

Shorty took a partner, Jack Taylor. Drill, blast, clean; drill, blast, clean—but they could find no vein. On the next claim a threesome from Ely did the same thing, and all around for miles the bare volcanic slopes were dotted by tents and blast holes and houses walled by empty bottles set in mud and roofed by oil cans pounded flat. The fresh tin glared. Saloons and dance halls went up. In spring the weather became still and hot while the blasting, like a continuous eruption, laid a cloud of black volcanic dust over the town. Huge mule teams and power machinery rumbled by, and a little beetlelike automobile appeared, coughing in the dust. The sweating diggers stopped and stared, leaned on their picks. Fancy that. Tonopah, 1901.

Shorty stuck to his claim, working fifteen hours a day into the heat of summer. He and Jack were going bust and ready to quit when the threesome next door, setting off their last four sticks, exposed a three-foot-wide silver vein worth half a million dollars. The dip took it away from Shorty's property; he was eight feet shy at the nearest point. As a friend and neighbor he was included in the spree, but when he regained consciousness a week later there was nothing he could do but sell out for a hundred dollars. He deposited twenty-five to Butler's account and left. The veins were already beginning to pinch, and companies were buying up claims and building stamp mills. He went down to the Crystal Water Company, treated himself to first shot at a fresh bath for a buck, spent the afternoon with a girl, then headed south with a new burro.

Two weeks later "Gold! Gold!" was the cry. South to Goldfield, where the rush was on. Shorty's three Goldfield claims barely yielded wages. The summer of 1902 he traded his two house lots to the blacksmith for three new drill bits, thinking Goldfield had seen its day. Then a hundred yards away Charles Taylor, who had just tried to sell his claim to Shorty for $150, hit a paystreak and made $1,250,000. A new rush was on. Shorty's house lots alone would have brought $80,000, but they were gone and his claims were sterile and food prices had doubled in a week. He sold out for $800.

He spent three days on women and liquor, then walked out with yet another burro past a steady oncoming stream of wagons, mules, miners, stages, and those damned chugging dust-raising automobiles. In October, at Sweet Springs, he heard that the real gold had been struck just after he had left: the "sandstorm" ore was worth $10,000 a ton, a record by any account, and he'd seen paydirt at two to the ton. Shorty began to think his timing was bad.

During the fall of 1902 he crisscrossed the desert toward Death Valley. Every hill was now a likely prospect, so at a pace that tired his burro he stomped in and out of canyons to the south. His full black beard began to turn white. Standing on the bar rail wearing a big black hat he looked like an elf as he nodded to the others and said his time had just about come. "Sure 'nough old geezer"— they'd look at each other and wink.

On a tip from Fi Lee of Ballarat he crossed the Amargosa Desert into the Greenwater Valley. There, just east of Funeral Peak, Shorty finally had a showing. He sent his partner, Judge Decker, to Independence to file. The Judge got drunk at the first bar in Independence and six days later when he finally dragged himself down from the second floor and two blocks farther to the recording office, he found that the land had been claimed. It became the site of Greenwater, fastest boom camp in the Death Valley region, though the ore was never good; it was backed by eastern money, the posters boasted, including Senator Alexander Harris of Massachusetts. Shorty ripped the fabulous poster from the mill site and while newcomers blasted his ledge he tied the diamond hitch again on boxes and tools, swore to his burro that he'd kill Decker on sight and struck north across Furnace Creek into the Grapevines. In the first canyon he came on three men who told him they had just filed on a gold vein at the head of the next draw; not two miles, Shorty thought, from the spot where he and Tommy had camped. They told him he was welcome to what was left. Shorty took a look: local, they had it all. The site became the Keane Wonder Mine, worth millions. Strikes were popping up like flowers in a rain.

In the morning he again tied blankets, food box, pots, kettle, canteens, and clothes on his burro. April 5, 1904. Four near misses in as many years. The wind was rising from the north, the air was cool, and the sun was yellowed by dust high in the upper air. The men holding the claim told him he might as well stay awhile since it had the look of a three-day blow, but he went ahead up into the Grapevines.

He walked into the rising wind; the bending wind from the tropics, the great globe-encircling wind that makes deserts was descending from the upper air, flattening the Mohave and rushing south; tumbleweeds spun by and low streamers of sand began to snake across the flats. By late afternoon the stubby sages whistled and the greasewoods bent before the blast. He leaned into the wind and watched the sand pluck petals and strip the bushes of their lower leaves. It seemed no time since the fire, the death of his mother and Lane. Just another four years come to nothing. At his feet the sand drifted past ankle high, leveling April flowers. He watched the delicate purple petals of a five-spot tear from the stem in quick succession and flicker off downwind. The desert was tossing off color, stripping down to its skin. He held his hat on with one hand and yanked at the burro with another. The sand began to whirl up in his face; he'd have to get to shelter. He tied his bandanna over his mouth and nose. A mile ahead was a broken, rocky cliff. He labored up the steep sage slope beneath it, eyes almost shut. His burro could hardly be held into the wind. He moved slowly up toward a large cave in the south face. The light was a dull orange; the wind moaned over the jagged rocks. Eddies in the lee of the mountain drove sand at his neck from every direction. Finally he gained the mouth of the cave—it was only a long ledge—and with his burro found some shelter against the back wall knowing he would breathe fine dust and sand for days. With pressed lips and squinting eyes he began to untie the load when a shriek detached itself from the sound of the wind and trailed off into maniacal laughter. He spun around to find a red-bearded man in a long black robe standing at the far end of the cave. The laughter died out and the man shouted: "He that troubleth his own house shall inherit the wind."

Shorty sat down and put his face in his hands. Too much, for too long.

He sat for a while, weary, numb, tearless, disgusted. When he cautiously blinked his eyes open and raised his head he saw the man ten yards away, seated, staring out of the cave. The strange light was a dim gray to the left and orange to the right; the sun going down. From the cave they looked downwind for miles across a high sage basin. Tumbleweeds whipped past, coming around and over the mountain behind them. Sand, dust, leaves, branches, stalks and weeds flew past in a blur, resolved themselves into retreating forms and disappeared from sight across the basin floor; it was like sitting on the rear of a speeding train, watching the world rush by. And no way to get off.

Shorty leaned to each side and tapped his head to clear his ears of sand. Then he took off the bandanna and shook it. His pants were covered with dust. He thought of sandy food and lost his appetite. He got up slowly and unpacked the silent burro resting on three legs, head down, eyes shut. Shorty fixed himself a seat against the rock wall and settled back with two canteens, a blanket and a canvas tarp. He took a drink and turned to the other man. The sitter showed no sign of looking his way. Shorty screwed the cap tight, put the canteen beside him, pulled the bandanna up over his mouth, drew the blankets and canvas over his head, and lay down. He squirmed for a few minutes against the stones and sand and then lay still. There was nothing else to do. It would take two days or so.

Through the blanket he could tell when it was almost dark; then it was pitch black for a long time; he dozed. The sound of the wind increased. He had to keep tucking the tarp under his legs. He slept some more, and the roaring dust cloud was full orange when he awoke and looked out. His back and neck ached; he felt he had been lying still forever.

The wind swirled into the cave. The bearded man sat in the same position; his eyes were open; he was covered with buff-colored dust. Shorty felt fine grit in his mouth. The act of spitting seemed to attract it to his lips, and there was no way to wipe them clean. "Well it's here," he thought, and swallowed. He was thirsty, not just in his mouth. The dust choked his nose and throat and made him feel dry inside, down to his groin. He took a long pull on the canteen. It washed the grit away, but when he breathed, fresh dust poured down his nostrils and stuck to his throat. He sat up, stared out at the receding rush of leaves and sand and tumbleweeds, and again became still. Beside his knee, he noticed a little yellow flower, and a purple locoweed in bloom. It had lost two petals. Some grass and moss grew from a cleft in the back of the cave; there must be seepage. Maybe the man got water there. But watching was an effort in the swirling sand, so he closed his eyes.

Sometime during the day the man started talking again, hurling words downwind: "Dies irae! Rex tremendae majestatis!" He repeated the phrases several times, then began to shake as he rose slowly, still facing out of the cave, shouting and opening his arms. The wind caught his robes and he lurched this way and that on stiff legs. Shorty got up, rolled his blankets and tarp back under a rock, grabbed his canteen and approached. Shorty grabbed his arm. The man steadied himself against the rock wall; with eyes tight shut he began to shout again: "Make straight in the desert a highway for our Lord."

"Have a drink," Shorty shouted in his ear. "Sit down and have a drink."

The man did not look at him. He screamed again. Shorty let go and crawled over to the wild man's possessions. He found clothes but no food. The man's canteen sounded empty. He opened it and sniffed. Not even damp. Another gust swirled viciously. Shorty huddled in the clothes. He had grit on his eyeballs. He tried to relax and wait for the fluid to wash it down. He tugged at the lids without opening them; that helped. Soon his eyes were better and when the man was blown to a sitting position Shorty moved quickly to his side and opened the canteen. He held him down with one hand and while the man shouted "Wrath! Wrath!" Shorty poured water through his grinding teeth. He coughed and looked at Shorty for the first time since the day before. A long silence followed and Shorty had to close his eyes again. Soon Shorty let go of the man, hunched his shoulders around his raw neck and moved a few feet back against the wall. He heard some Latin mumblings, followed by the sound of wind alone. Time passed. A long time. He began to wonder if it was still the same day. He had dozed standing up. The wind howled. Then a shout in his ear:

"Who are you?"

Shorty started.

"Shorty Harris," he screamed back without looking.

"What are you doing here?"

"Prospector."

"Father Joachim Dismay." Shorty peeked. The man crawled to the back wall, turned around and sat by his clothes. "Of the Church of Perpetual Grace."

Shorty squirmed to his side, knelt, and held the canteen near his mouth. "Have some water," he said and began to lift the cap.

"No No!" the man shouted. He turned on Shorty like a cat:

"Dead flies cause the ointment of the apothecary to send forth a stinking savor!" He screamed the end of each phrase on a rising note. Shorty carefully capped the canteen. "Salva me fons pietatis!" The words came and went in gusts: "The wolf shall dwell with the lamb . . . the young lion and the fatling shall lie down together." The man waved out across the basin.

Shorty's eyes were full of sand again. He curled up facing into the wall. White granite with feldspar phenocrysts. Not promising. His blanket and tarp were twenty yards away. He didn't feel like opening his eyes and crawling back. He pulled his shirt over his head. The man seemed to have reached a climax and settled down; at least he was quiet. Shorty heard a little rattle. That would be the chain on the canteen cap. The man's drinking, he thought. Good. The light became deep orange again. He slept.

"You're a prospector?" Shorty jumped at the voice in his ear. Without moving away from the stone or opening his eyes he nodded yes.

"Riches profit—"

"—not in the day of wrath," Shorty yelled back. "Don't worry."

"You aren't rich?"

"That's right."

Silence. Shorty was about to go back to sleep when he felt the man's breath in his ear: "Not much of a prospector, are you?"

Shorty squirmed. "Not much." He opened his eyes and looked at the granite. Another day and a half at most, he thought. He closed his eyes. He jumped at the shout:

"Guess if I couldn't find grace I wouldn't be much of a Christian, would I?"

"Guess not." Shorty snuggled into the wall.

"I found it once."

Shorty kept his eyes shut and made no reply.

"I found it once and I've never let go."

Shorty opened his eyes to the stone. The wind moaned and whistled. He could feel the storm moving across the land, north to south, down, down, dragging leaves and thistles to Mexico.

"You never let go?" Shorty said.

"Never."

Shorty rolled over and looked at the man through narrowed lids. The man's face was dry and creased, the beard matted, lips cracked, eyes bright and wild. The man's fingers were moving across his chest, beard, arms, face, lips, quick and restless. Never let go. Tommy's words. Or was it Ecclesiastes again: "There is no man that hath power over the spirit to retain the spirit." He was about to speak when he saw the canteen lying on its side, cap off, a foot away from a dark circle in the sand. A dark wet circle. A wet circle in the desert. It stirred him deep inside: he could feel it soaking in, past sand and gravel to the thirsty, waiting seeds, soaking into dry shells—the pulp swelling instantly, shells cracking, green shoots . . .

"Hey you son of a bitch," he shouted, sitting up. "You poured my water out."

"All rivers run to the sea," the man said solemnly.

Right before his eyes the circle shrank, drying from the edges in, whitening, until only a tiny spot was left, going, going . . . and he saw again the Amargosa River whitening after the rain, running and drying up, running not to the sea but nowhere, nowhere before it disappeared . . . the dark spot in front of him was gone. But the seed would be soaked now. Tomorrow or the next day it would come up, a blade of bunchgrass or a poppy or a daisy or a cousin to that locoweed. He studied the man for a moment; the black robes, the sandy eyes still impossibly open in everlasting expectation of the end. Perpetual grace! Shorty began to laugh. And he'd been lucky to see one good quartz vein in his life, lucky just to know how it looked, how it felt crumbly and soft and golden in the hand at the top of a peak in Canada—and never let go!—he shook with laughter—here was this old man solemn and dark and crazy sitting right there in the Grapevines above Death Valley and saying all rivers run to the sea—an old dried white cracked Amargosa of a man soaking in, disappearing, evaporating, passing away up into the air and down into the sand, talking of the Last Judgment while already the spilled water would be coming up again because even if there was an end to the canteen, Shorty thought, there'd be something had needed it so bad it would just be another beginning. He laughed until the sand swirling into his mouth reduced him to coughs and sobs. Finally he spat twice and said quietly, "You don't know much about the desert, do you."

Father Dismay did not reply; he stared out over the basin. The light was failing. Dismay began to repeat "Dies Irae" again. Shorty took the empty canteen and crawled back to his goods. He ate a piece of jerked beef, had a drink from the other canteen, and tore off a big chaw of tobacco. "To hell with it," he thought, and sat with his eyes shut, chewing and spitting tobacco and sand. After a while he crawled over and offered his food to Father Dismay, but he couldn't get through to the saint. He came back and settled down for a long, bad night.

Shorty knew he had slept pretty well; the orange had faded into the long black and the black had slipped into gray; he could remember that. His eyes were tight shut, one hand was over his face. Then he suddenly pricked his ears without moving, concentrating on every sense. The back of his hand had stopped burning. He listened. Nothing. His neck—no sand dragging like briars across the nape. Silence. Then a clear note—three notes rising— split his head. A wren. Slowly, carefully, he moved his hand, tilting it to spill the dust away from his face. He felt warmth on his cheek. He hung his head down to drain off sand, shook it, then cautiously blinked his eyes open. The dust and sand at the tip of his nose were still. Each red pebble trailed a shadow. He shook his head again and hunched his back to empty sand from his collar, away from his raw neck. Then he raised his head and looked. The sky was a pale white blue, the air still. He could smell sun on rock. The bare peaks were bright with yellow morning light. The wren bobbed and whistled in a cactus twenty feet away. Shorty stood and shook off. The wren flew away. His legs were stiff. He beat his shirt and pants. Beside him his burro, one leg raised, snorted, sighed and shivered from head to rump. Shorty moved painfully over, brushed the burro's haunch, and patted his neck.

Shorty blew out through his nose and mouth and beat his clothes. His burro replied, snorting again, tossing his head, wriggling his ears in a shower of dust.

Shorty laughed and reached for his canteen. But as he reached he noticed, beside the canteen, his rock hammer, the head pitted, the dirt-grained handle worn smooth. He picked the hammer up and gripped the hard cool wood. The handle was shaped to his hand. "Not much of a prospector." "Everlasting grace." The burning eyes—he remembered the fire in his father's eyes as he broke

Charlie Alvord's arm in Tecopah, 1860—when had it begun? In Providence? They had brought the name with them from the Old World. Long before, he thought, before the first boats pushed off for that hoped-for shore, probably just before the first man died. And as he gripped the handle he thought how his own hold had not been let go but pried loose or he would have died as his father had died hating the roundness of the earth beneath his feet, replying flash for flash to the endless generations of the sun. Luck. He felt a kind of pure detachment, and he remembered the ducks: at a lake in Montana, not Avalanche Lake where he'd found the gold but on the way, somewhere, a nameless huge black still cold woods lake high in the mountains at first light or after, yellow dawn; leaning on his elbow, in his frosted blankets, he had first seen them far out to his left, a pair of ducks gliding silently toward him leaving a wide white V on the water and to his right another pair gliding across, erect, still, silent, their wake a narrow V. The two pairs moved toward each other, the only living things in sight. The wide V coming toward him, the narrow V from the side, converging. Half-mile, quarter-mile, a hundred yards. Would they meet? Greet, change partners, fly away? On they glided, their motionless movement bringing them slowly, surely, closer, closer—would they collide? were they blind?—five feet, four, three, two—flash! a fish broke surface close to his right—he flicked his eyes and it was past: the ducks had crossed—he didn't even know which pair in front, or if they had meshed or even switched for that matter just two pairs of ducks calm, unruffled, the black slick water widening between them and the wakes interwoven, four widening lines.

He put the hammer down and looked about. While he had dreamed the wind had come and gone to Mexico, the dust had settled and the sun once more had risen and built a cloud above the Panamints, promising rain. It would be a hot, still day. In the lee of the cliff and behind every bush the drifted dust lay in graceful swirls. He looked across the cave. Father Dismay was lying down, asleep. His robe was alkaline white. The burro brayed and Father

Dismay jerked awake, stared at his alkaline robe and shouted, "They have washed their robes and made them white in the blood of the lamb!"

Shorty walked toward him with the canteen. "Amen, Father." Dismay was waving his dusty arms and singing: "And we shall be changed—"

"In a moment, in the twinkling of an eye," said Shorty. "But it's not the end, Father." Shorty unscrewed the cap and held it to Dismay's lips. "It's just a nice day."

Desmet took a swallow. "The trumpet shall sound," he said more meekly.

"Attaboy. What the doctor ordered." Shorty took another drink himself and looked over the basin. "Nice day."

"A bonanza," said Father Desmet.

Shorty looked at him. "What?"

"Bonanza," said Father Desmet. "It means clear skies."

Shorty considered him a moment. "You're not so crazy, are you."

Father Dismay looked away. "Grace is where you find it," he said, and walked over to Shorty's food box.

Shorty gathered dry matchweed stalks and sage branches and made dough while the fire died to coals. He baked, cooked the bacon, fried the biscuits in the grease and made flapjacks in the slick pan. Father Desmet drained the gallon canteen.

After breakfast Shorty fetched the burro from a patch of bunchgrass and green rabbitbrush above the cave—seepage, the water trickled into the back of the cave—and packed up; food box on one side; on the other, the utensil box with the drills, books, candles, dynamite and caps; two blankets and clothes; all hitched tight; then on top and tied with a separate rope: pick, shovel, pan. He whistled. And hung on the frame ends, two empty canteens. He quietly dropped a sack of flour behind Dismay's clothes.

Father Dismay leaned against the wall. From the look of him, Shorty thought, the flapjacks must be sitting pretty heavy.

"Guess I'll be on my way, Father," said Shorty. Dismay rose stiffly and stood with both hands behind his back. He stared slightly high over Shorty's shoulder and spoke in a deep voice:

"Every valley shall be exalted—"

"Now you're talking," said Shorty, "and they that dwell in the land of the shadow of death have seen a great light." He took the burro's lead. "That's the spirit." He began to move down the slope, picking his way between fallen rocks, sage, matchweed, and prickly pear. "Take it easy, Father," he said over his shoulder, quietly. The sun was up and already a new crop of yellow poppies was bursting into bloom. He stopped, looked around, and called back, "Father Dismay, look!"

"What is it, my son?"

Shorty swept his arm in a full circle: "Golden vials full of odors, which are the prayers of saints!"

He laughed and resumed his way. As the burro jerked downhill the canteen rang on the handle of the pick. Around him the dusty, still land flared with morning light.

He moved east, prospecting, while the sun rolled over the Grapevines and sank behind the Panamints; then south, prospecting; he dropped by Lathrop Wells and traded three specimens for flour and salt; then east again, prospecting, through a brief rain and after, through long red shadows in the Calico Hills and Skull Mountains, and up to Hidden Spring, where he met his old friend Ed Cross with a wagon of booze, and they dropped the load at a ranch and traveled drunk west together under leaden skies—the dawn was a hard line of silver over a hard line of gold, thin bands between black earth and sky—and the weather passed without rain, and two more days went by, and the sun came out, and the cholla bloomed and prickly pear, and the greasewood went from flower to cotton, and a pocket gopher got into the flour sack and a coyote went after the pocket gopher and scared the burro and in the morning Shorty went to look for the burro and he found it nibbling wire grass in a little patch of seepage below a quartz blowout in the Amargosa Hills, full of gold.

Shorty picked up a hunk of rotted quartz and whacked it with the hammer. It crumbled in his hand. Green blotches laced with gold. Filigree gold. Gold blossoms. He whacked it again. More. He picked up another. More. Another. Better. He looked around. The quartz spread for half a mile. Another. Another. Just rotten with gold, every one. He smiled. So his time had come.

He walked back to camp.

"Didn't find him?" said Ed.

"Found him, all right." Ed looked up. "Found this too." He tossed a rock in Ed's lap.

"Jesus Christ." Ed crumbled it carefully. "There's more?"

"Half-mile showing."

Ed smiled. "You serious?"

"Ain't drunk."

Ed started laughing. "This green one's worth fifty bucks."

"Hellfire Eddie, we're rich," said Shorty.

"Rich."

"Rich rich rich!" Ed stood up. They grabbed each other and heaved their hats in the air and two-stepped across the sand—circle your partner—shouting and singing, dancing—shuffle off to Buffalo—in the general direction of the richest quartz blowout in the history of gold.

CHAPTER 23

Rhyolite

Ed knelt by his side. "God that's beautiful rock."

("Looked like a big green bullfrog settin' in my hand," Shorty said later to the press.)

"Look at those traces, Ed. I've never seen anything like it."

("Rhyolite is a highly acidic, compact or porphyritic, variously colored volcanic rock often with marked fluidal, perlitic, and spherulitic structure, having a glassy ground-mass, and consisting of quartz and orthoclase with either mica, horneblende, or rarely pyroxene" he said, laughing, to a well-dressed reporter from the *Boston Globe*. The reporter stopped writing. "Would you repeat that, please?"

"Nope. Have a drink."

The reporter waved him off. "What was your role in founding the town?"

"Walked up and walked away," said Shorty.

"That's all?" The man held his pen above the pad.

"Never wanted to see another eggnog."

"I'm afraid I don't understand."

"That's a story I believe," Shorty said, squatting.)

Ed picked other pieces off the ground. "We better stake right away."

They both looked around and laughed. There was no one in sight, and they could see a hundred miles. The rock was scattered over an open hillslope at the north end of the Amargosa Desert in the hills where the Amargosa River heads, meaning that it first appears—and disappears—a few miles away.

"First thing we better do," said Shorty, "is have a drink, then figure out where the stuff came from. This may have floated a ways."

Even drunk they found the source: an outcrop barely exposed at ground level. Probably recently aired, said Shorty. Something of a debut. They staked four claims along its length. Shorty staked one in Shoshone Tommy's name.

In the evening they moved camp to the nearly invisible outcrop, dug a little level place for a tent and started the fire for dinner. The hillside, and the other hillsides, were almost bare. The desert floor stretched away, tinted spring sage green. Fifty miles off the kerosene lamps at Death Valley Junction winked, and when the moon rose, little silver patches of the Amargosa River gleamed here and there as far as they could see down the vast valley.

"We can start digging tomorrow," said Ed.

"Won't be necessary," said Shorty.

"Why?"

"The situation doesn't require effort." Shorty winked as he lit his pipe. "We'll go to Goldfield and talk, and tomorrow they'll start coming here. This bullfrog strike is a crackerjack. It'll put Tonopah and Goldfield to shame. A lollapaloosa. This is the last night we'll spend alone in these parts, Ed. And they'll come running and riding on mules and pulling carts and pushing wheelbarrows and some driving new automobiles and they'll dig and blast and lay out lots and buildings and organize a volunteer fire company and eastern money will hear about it and toss a few millions around, and down there"—he swept his arm toward the shallow valley at the foot of the slope—"will be women and dancing, and over there, Chinese, and up there will be the big merchant stores and boarding houses and a bank and maybe an opera house and the railroad station and higher up, the fine houses with milled lumber and glass windows and long shady porches, where regular folks will live and raise families." He stopped, apparently finished, and poked at the fire.

Ed waited a few seconds, then asked: "Where do we come in?"

Shorty wiped his mouth and coughed. His eyes were wet. Ed looked down. A minute or two passed. Then Shorty chuckled.

"Oh, we just sit right here in the middle of the whole thing, right on top of the best damn claim in sight. They'll go crazy. Everybody's gonna be our friend. And the more they find beside us, the more they're gonna think is under us, and the less we dig, the more they'll be sure it's there. Can't beat it, Ed. Easy Street, and when you're tired, sell out." Shorty looked up and smiled. "Nothing for us to do. Nature made gold and gold made fools and fools will make us rich. Nothing for us to do but wait."

It happened, just as he said. They went to Goldfield, filed, and talked. He dragged Shoshone Tommy from a Goldfield bar and sent him laughing off. Then Shorty got drunk for six days and woke up to find he had sold half his claim for one thousand dollars, signed, sealed and witnessed. They said it was worth fifty thousand. He blew the money on drinks for the house for two more days. Bullfrogs became a national craze: green and gold rock cut into rings, pins, necklaces. The tent city of Bullfrog became the town of Rhyolite. Rhyolite got its ninety-thousand-dollar bank, its opera house, its railroad station and two railroads, its six thousand people, and even its own stock exchange while in the midst of it Shorty and Ed sat, accepting free meals and drinks until one week Shorty told Ed that he had eaten and drunk enough to last the rest of his life, and there was no sense fetching up against an iron post in the middle of nowhere. He went on a week-long spree, and, legend has it, sold the rest of his claim for eight thousand dollars—he shoulda got a hundred thousand, they said—ordered a boxcar of eggs, a boxcar of milk, and a boxcar of Irish whiskey, treated the town to eggnogs for three days, packed up one burro, saddled another, and left with twenty dollars to his name. People shook their aching heads, gently: too bad a nice man like that had no business sense. Ed Cross married, sold for one hundred twenty-five thousand and got himself a ranch in California. The only person in town to sell out cheaper than Shorty was that crazy Indian Tommy, who gave away the third best claim in the district to Bob Montgomery for a wagon, two mules, and a new pair of overalls. Bob sold to Charles Schwab—that's right, Charles Schwab, president of Bethlehem Steel—for a million. People shook their heads. Ain't that just like an Indian. Sure meet some characters out in the desert.

Shorty was famous for that strike, and the next—for a run of luck is hard to turn. After he had sobered up from the Rhyolite Fourth of July of 1905, he and Pete Aguereberry were hotfooting across the Panamints toward a party in Ballarat when Basque Pete spotted a cropping of free gold. "The Basco" could hardly persuade a thirsty Shorty to stop long enough to collect a sample. They melted out the gold over a greasewood fire. It was rich. Pete staked the Eureka and Shorty staked the Providence, but even though Shorty told everyone they met about the strike—before they had even filed—somehow the two got back up to White Sage Flats soon enough and sober enough to hold their claims—by blind luck the best—and the town was called Harrisburg. Pete spent the rest of his life up there at seven thousand feet in the Panamints, and when Skidoo boomed next door in 1906 and the region attracted some of the Rhyolite freighting business from across Death Valley, the place was pretty lively for a while. But Shorty sold out right away and moved on.

It was then, after Rhyolite and Harrisburg, that Shorty's name became legend. He was already known to all the old prospectors; he had been around all the big strikes and had hit two of his own in two years. And though many of his sometime partners—Hot Steam, Ed Goler (the Goler nuggets and Goler Wash), Ed Cross, Pete Aguerreberry, Tommy—had made names for themselves too, it was Shorty, with his twinkling eyes and way with words, and something else if you met him, it was Shorty who became famous. The man who knew gold. Among the younger prospectors, what few there were, and among the sweating men swinging picks in other people's mines and dreaming of the old days when a man could find his own, his name became a magnet for wonder and hope: he could smell it; he could walk up a canyon with his eyes shut and point; he knew every stone in the Ibex Hills; he'd salted away millions—"he's no fool"—he could map the whole Basin's Silurian deposits—"if he wanted"—"but he won't."

Shorty himself took a little break. With the money from Harrisburg he went to Kansas City, Boston, New York, and Washington, bought his senator brother a drink—Alex was rather uncomfortable—went to the Bahamas, married a twenty-four-year-old girl from Bryn Mawr—it's true, I'm afraid—and was taken back to mainline Philadelphia, where her parents had it annulled. He came back to Ballarat for a while, then went east again. When he had blown his money and couldn't go to Milan, he returned to Death Valley in 1911 with new clothes, new pipe, a leather-bound volume of *Culture and Anarchy*, and no cash. But Harrisburg, 1905, was to be his last strike, and almost the last strike in the Basin. Though he made promising finds here and there, after the financial panic of 1907 the last era of wild speculation ended and even good claims were hard to peddle. At the start of the First World War the slight investment interest still hovering over the basin was wafted away, and Shorty, with the few like him, was left once again not in the vanguard but simply alone. None but friends, at Stovepipe Wells or Indian Springs, were interested in his gold, and their number was dwindling. Hot Steam died in 1910, Ed Goler in 1914. In 1915, at the age of sixty-six, he moved into the one-room abandoned adobe schoolhouse in decaying Ballarat, on the floor of Panamint Valley, to live out the last nineteen years of his life. That simple. It had come and gone: four widening lines.

As if he had a homeowner's obligation to keep up the appearance of the neighborhood he shaved his beard and kept his bushy white mustache trimmed. In pictures taken by the new breed of visitors—mining buffs who came in automobiles and carried cameras—he stands short and slope-shouldered, tan, smiling, with three buttons burst on his white wool long-sleeved undershirt. In one picture he kneels by a homemade stream, wearing a wide-brimmed, round-crowned black hat, and demonstrates panning technique, looking as if he isn't sure just what audience he's playing to in that little black box.

In the late twenties—not long before Bugsy Seagal came to Las Vegas—the region began to awake to its latest phase, but Shorty had been left behind. In 1925 Scotty moved into Johnson's improbable castle north of Death Valley, and L.A. entrepreneur Bob Eichbaum, his eyes full of winter tourists, built a toll road over Emigrant Pass from Panamint Valley to Death Valley. He wanted to develop Stovepipe Wells as a resort. Movie stars began to be photographed at the Furnace Creek Ranch in January. By the early thirties the Furnace Creek Inn had a golf course and swimming pool, and finally a government appeared: "In 1933 Death Valley National Monument was established to preserve the area." That preservation marked the end of Coronado's dream and so brought to a close the four-hundred-year era of which Shorty was, in a sense, the fruit and flowering top, though the casual visitors to Ballarat must have thought he had withered on the vine.

The increased activity and the new automobiles made roads desirable, so Nevada and California began construction in the area. Shorty found himself pretty poor, what with his expeditions shortened by old age and his financial returns negligible, and there were fewer and fewer old friends to take care of each other, so beginning in 1928, at the age of seventy-nine, he worked now and then for the California Department of Highways, spreading gravel and oil on desert roads and finding one day in a state truck, in a newspaper spread under a tar barrel, his brother's obituary: "Massachusetts Senator Alexander B. Harris . . . long and illustrious career . . . colorful past, including a stay in Western mining camps . . . wife and four children." In the distance Shorty could just see the nine squat baked buildings of Ballarat, including his own hut, not nine miles down from Panamint City, where he and Alex had had the run of the town. When he could, he prospected the Panamints for "gold gold gold" as he said (smiling at the camera), pushing one burro and stringing another.

What he did during those last thirty years doesn't matter; what he loved, does. When he was very old, and I was very young, we met. I spent six days with him, the last six days before his stroke, and I was at his bed when he died.

PART 5

The Perfect Knowledge of Shorty Harris

*We gorged on water, burned
willows, shot a deer, cooked. Men
vomited during prayer and prayer
ended. We are the creatures this
desert makes us. . . . The day is
warm and perfect and we are
hopeless.*

—JOURNAL OF JEROME BEDDERLY,

1892

CHAPTER 24

June 30, 1934

Like a distant ship bobbing on lazy billows the figure slowly rose and fell from sight.

"He's coming this way," my father said, and looked at me and Jake.

"It's a man and a burro."

"Jesus, it's hot." I touched the fender and burned my hand.

"He's behind those dunes," said Jake. "Gimme a beer."

Beneath a sun-whitened, pale blue sky the figure approached the two men and the gangly fifteen-year-old and the black model T Ford all huddled, pulled back into the thin shade of the mesquite near Big Dodd Springs north of Panamint Valley. One fender of the car stuck into the sunlight like a lizard's nose. June 30, 1934.

"He's got a burro all packed."

The man was a few hundred yards away, approaching at a slow, steady pace.

"Hey," Jake called, "come get a beer!"

The figure looked up and touched his hat. When he was closer they called again, "Ice cold free beer!" but the old man unpacked his burro and led him to the spring and the shade of the mesquite before he approached, took off his hat, wiped his few white hairs, and reached for the long-held bottle.

"Hot damn," he said and sat down, stretching his stubby legs.

"Where you been old man?"

"North." He waved toward the mountains.

"Where do you live?"

"Ballarat."

Jake laughed and shook his head. "Didn't know anyone still lived there. Je-sus Christ." There was a lull in the conversation. The old man lay back. I can remember his kit: the pick handle shiny with rubbed dirt, the bent shovel blade, the little rock hammer, two dented canteens, two tiny wooden boxes, an old blanket.

"You're a prospector aren't you?" I blurted out.

"Yup."

My father studied him. "A real-life honest-to-God prospector. Hey, I bet I know who you are. You're Shorty Harris!"

"That's right."

"I read about you in *Touring Topics* last year. Look, Shorty," Father leaned forward, "we got a little claim up here in Limerock Canyon. Reckon you could have a look?—give you dinner and all the beer you can drink—and tell us what you think?"

"Is this the geezer you were asking about in Lone Pine?" said Jake. "Is he really . . . ?"

My father shut Jake up with a glance. Shorty was lying still with his hat over his face.

"We got abalone for dinner," my father said. "Brought it straight from L.A. in ten hours."

"Maybe you'd find something else up the canyon," Jake suggested.

"Please come," I said.

Shorty pushed his hat back and looked at me for the first time, then looked harder. I didn't know why. "Well," he said, and paused a long time, "I was going that way."

We introduced ourselves. My dad was a weekend miner. He had a Ford dealership in L.A. Jake sold insurance. It was like fishing, a way to get out. My mother never came. They'd had the claim three months and it looked pretty good. It was only five or six miles from the spring. Shorty walked with his burro, leaving before us, and when he arrived he lay down again and explained that he usually rode nowadays but that his other burro had died two days before and he hadn't had a chance to get another. The wild jacks, he said, had gotten damn hard to catch.

My father showed him around the claim. Jake went to his sleeping roll, pulled out a flask, and followed.

"Well?" Jake said, when the tour was complete.

Shorty looked at Jake and back to my father. He seemed hesitant.

"What do you think?" said Father. "Let's have it."

"I'd sell," he said, "just as it is. Whatever you can get."

"I saw a sign once in a cafe," Jake said. "If you're so damn smart why ain't you rich."

Everyone was silent. "Christ," I said, and turned away.

"Hold your tongue boy," snapped my father. I spun around. Shorty looked at me and smiled.

"I'd sell," said Shorty. "Surface showing's fair but you'll dig past it right away."

"How the hell do you know that?" said Jake.

"Well," said Shorty, taking his pipe out of his mouth and coolly appraising Jake, "from what I've heard of automobiles and insurance this may not bother you, but the truth is you're holding a salted claim."

"Are you accusing . . ." Jake couldn't find his tongue.

"Whoa whoa," the old man said gently. "You're nothing but stuck. Rabbit down a well. Better get a coyote to hop in the other bucket."

"What do you mean, old man," said Jake, poking at the fire. "Don't drag it out." There was a long pause. Jake was worse than my father.

"Far as I know," said Shorty, sighing and leaning back, and I thought I could see him smiling under that big hat, "Hot Steam Boyd first prospected this site in the nineties. Staked a low-grade gold deposit—limestone replacement, marbled quartz—he named the canyon and sold to someone—don't remember who—who sold to A. J. Flack. Now Flack was one of the strangest men I ever knew." Shorty looked about, one eye shut. Jake and my father exchanged impatient looks. "Killed three men cold blooded in between making jams and jellies for the married ladies in Austin. Got shot himself." He chuckled. "Put up, you might say."

My father poked the fire. "Go on," he suggested.

"Well," Shorty cleared his throat, "truth is that before the war Flack got himself some real good ore high-graded from Bill Simpson's mine in the Ibex Hills and loaded it in his shotgun and blasted it all over the head of this canyon—you can still see the sulfur in your ore, and you notice there's no trace of local marble around the high-grade quartz—then he sold out to, ah . . . ."

"Charles Brown."

"That's right, old Charley Brown, for a handsome profit. Well," he said, "Charley dug for four hours and knew he'd been taken. Charley's getting pretty old now, I hear, and needy. Haven't seen him for a while. He still in Lone Pine?"

"Shit," said Jake.

"Goddamn," said my father. "Wait till I find Brown."

"What," said Shorty, laying down his pipe and opening another beer, unasked, "what do you figure to do with it?" A long silence followed.

"What do you suggest?" said my father.

Shorty shrugged, "You're the coyote," he laughed.

Then I said, "Wait for a bear." Shorty looked straight at me in a funny way, and we laughed hard, while my father and Jake sat sulking.

Next morning, after breakfast, Shorty began to pack his kit.

"Guess we owe you a favor, Mr. Harris," said Dad. "Anything we can do? Give you a lift to Ballarat? We're gonna be around here awhile."

Shorty paused as he held tension on the packing rope: "As a matter of fact, you could help me a bit."

"What is it?"

"If you could lend me your young Jimmy there, and if he'd like to take a little trip, maybe he could help catch me a jackass or two. I got a ways to go alone."

I jumped up and started looking for my sleeping bag.

"How long a trip?" said my father.

"Not long. Plan to take the high road"—he nodded toward the Panamints—"back to Ballarat. Got a few things to do. Three or four days"—he looked at me standing a head taller than him—"if the boy's feet hold up. You could pick him up down there."

"Anytime would do. We'll be down at Panamint Springs anyway. We're on vacation through the long weekend."

Shorty stopped chewing and stared at him. I think the idea of "vacation" took a while to get through. My father stared back, then continued:

"We can meet you any time for a week. Say the sixth. But that saddles you with a kid."

"Fine with me. I had a kid of my own once." Shorty looked down at his boots. Dad seemed like he was about to speak, but Shorty didn't notice and went on. "We'll be in Ballarat for a little Oh Be Joyful on the Fourth." Shorty laughed. "For sure."

My father studied the old man a long time. "Well, I guess it's done then."

"What'll I need?" I said.

Shorty turned and surveyed me. Under one arm I carried a huge rolled-up green sleeping bag with a printed cotton liner, and under the other, a lambswool jacket. He looked down to my high, tan, brand-new boots.

"Sure you want to go?" he said. "Lotta walking."

"Oh I'm sure. I'm sure. Is this all I'll need?"

"Extra socks," said Shorty. "Lots."

"Coming up." I dropped the two bundles and bounded to the duffel bag. Shorty bent over, picked up the clothes and started tying them to the motionless burro.

"There you see he's causing you trouble already," I heard my father say. "He's a careless boy."

Shorty didn't reply.

"Can we give you a lift to get you started?"

"That thing can't go where we're going." Shorty snorted and spat.

My father laughed. "Don't care for 'em, eh?"

"Had a flivver once." Shorty paused in the middle of a knot. "Gave it to an Indian who'd stole my burros." He spat again. "To get even."

And so fifty years ago we met, an old man and a boy, the first week of July 1934, at the edge of Death Valley.

CHAPTER 25

July 1: North

Sun. (E.) M.E. sonne. *A.S.* sunne,
fem. sb. + Du. zon, *G.* sonne,
Goth. sunnō, *feminine; Teut. type*
*sunno-n-, *fem. Cf. Icel.* so-l,
Swed. Dan. sol, *L.* so-l, *Goth.* sauil,
Lith. saul-e, *W.* haul, *Gk.* ἥλιος,
Skt. sūra, *the sun.*

—REV. SKEAT

At seven in the morning on July 1 Limestone Canyon was still in shade. Shorty said that they were going north and would have to step along to get up high before midday, and with that single remark he turned and set one foot in front of another in a way that gave the boy an ominous sensation of ignorance. The rope went taut, the burro jerked forward, the full canteens thumped against the handle of the pick, and they were off, into the desert.

A few hundred yards down canyon Shorty doubled back on a faint track, dropped the burro's rope, and began the ascent. They slowly gained altitude over a series of humps and hills that far ahead became mountains.

Shorty had said nothing more about the route; the boy knew only that the sun was on his right. He found the old man's pace uphill a little slow. Soon he was talking—walking behind or beside the silent little man, dodging greasewoods and cacti that forced them apart—talking of his house, his family, his dog, his school—it was private—how he hated math but liked Latin and English—an English teacher, did Shorty like Lindburgh?—his sports—he was a runner, a cross-country runner—he was in pretty good shape, how many miles were they going that day anyway? He ran four every afternoon in season. Would Shorty mind if he jogged ahead at times? His long legs helped of course.

An hour later he had stopped talking. He was surprised to see that the sun was still low in the morning sky. He was a little thirsty. Ahead he saw no promise of shade—they were above the deep canyons, on rolling, treeless hills of stone and gravel. The atmosphere became oppressive: the heat, light, and dryness—or lack of atmosphere, for he felt his body's water was being sucked into a vacuum. The sun climbed, the slow pace continued. The ground became more barren. Fifteen, twenty steps between bushes. The gravel was hard packed, a bright, flinty gray that hurt his eyes if he looked to the east. Ahead, though, the next hump looked greener: perhaps there's a valley on the other side. He wouldn't quite phrase to himself "with water" because he knew that was silly, they had just started; he tried to pretend the thoughts were random, but he knew that already a desire deeper than thirst, something more like an instinctive fear, had begun to direct his eyes and control his mind. The next hump was not greener. Once on it, the sage bushes looked parched and far apart. He wondered when it had last rained. Had Shorty last night said February or March? He counted up: three months, four? The next hill certainly looked greener on top. It took forever to get there. Dry, dry as the others—he looked up and ahead. His father's black hat was a little thin and warm. His feet were getting hot through the soles of his boots. The bare land seemed to stretch forever. A thought tickled the back of his mind: how far back to camp? He looked over his shoulder: it was all gone.

They entered a more barren region. The tiny surface stones were packed into a tight, smooth mosaic, a vast rolling floor of ceramic tiles glazed and fired brownish black. He could smell the heat off the stones; the surface was unyielding, and blisters were beginning on his heels. Within a hundred yards he could see only one plant, a little flat cactus, brown at the edges. His feet were on fire. He caught a whiff of burning rubber and for a hundred yards he kept wrenching himself about trying to sniff his boot soles without breaking stride. The hat fell off; he swooped it up without stopping. He fell behind the burro. He tried walking on his toes, then on his heels, to let the air flow beneath the boots; he tried arching his foot, then curling his toes to let the air flow inside the boots, but his raw feet still burned. His clothes were dry, though he knew he was sweating hard. The moisture seemed sucked from deep in his skin. Heat waves warped everything beyond his feet. The glare of the shiny dark rocks made his head ache.

Soon the ground became soft, loose sand and gravel. It was tiring, but the sand was cooler than the black rocks. They passed little knee-high bushes every ten or fifteen steps, and he began to walk close to them so that now and then he could take one step in the shade. His head was light and his feet heavy. He felt that he was floating and stumbling at once. He began to imagine the coldness of the ground beneath each bush and he delighted in thinking how much heat the tiny patches of shaded sand were drawing from his soles. His mouth was full of cotton. He pictured it, stuffed, like a greasewood in bloom. He spat, but the cotton came back. He retreated, finally, as a last resort, deep into his mind, turned off all pictures, all thoughts, and walked alone.

While following the bushiest route he fell farther behind until he looked up from his trance to see Shorty stopped twenty yards ahead tightening a knot and watching him. When he reached the burro Shorty said: "Don't walk too close to the bushes."

"Why?" He was surprised at the sound of his voice, surprised that it still worked.

"Snakes. Sidewinders. Bury in the shade."

Shorty handed him the canteen, then took it away after a few swallows and looped it over the pack frame.

"How much further?" asked the boy.

"Where to?" said Shorty with a flat expression, apparently puzzled. The boy wondered what he had got into. The sun was directly overhead, pressing down on his hat; head and feet throbbed. Nowhere, nowhere to go. And they'd hardly started. Standing strangely there in the sun in the middle of the endless barren hills, he could only shrug silently and look down. Would the old man do nothing? Had he been brought out there and abandoned? He felt the white force of the sun descend upon him like snow at the Pole. A silent, weightless, all-powerful light. He stood in one spot, crying silently, thinking only of the dark shadow beneath his shoes and hoping that if he stayed still his feet would begin to cool.

When they started again the crunch of boots on gravel was deafening. They moved slowly and individually, for hours, up to and finally across a low divide, then descended to a high, bare red-rimmed basin with a dry mudflat in the center. Crossing the flat they passed between four or five stones, knee to waist high, lying here and there on top of the hard, cracked mud. Behind each stone was a whitish line, stretching straight for hundreds of yards. There was no other scar on the flat. The parallel lines tailed the stones like meteor tracks.

Ascending the long, gentle slope to the east of the flat Shorty angled toward a low rise; a stone appeared—a dot set in a ledge—which as they interminably approached loomed higher and higher—as big as a house, then bigger. The sun had passed the zenith and beside the huge rock and towering ledge was a four-foot strip of shade. Then Shorty and the burro disappeared—the boy blinked—

they had entered the shadow of the rock. The boy strained his eyes at the other world of darkness. When he entered, relief was immediate. He sank to the ground and looked for the canteen.

"Wait," Shorty said softly. The boy took his boots off without looking at his blisters. He lay back and stayed still, for he was about to vomit. Soon he closed his eyes. He heard a sharp, hollow metallic sound, then another, and another. He opened his eyes. Away from the rock the light was blinding, and he could see nothing out of the shade. Near him Shorty was holding a white enameled cup under a ledge of rock. Above the cup was dark moss-green earth that brought his heart to his throat. *Ping. Ping.* He started at the clear cold sound, and licked his lips. The sound changed: the drops were splashing in water. Shorty brought the cup over, half full.

"This is colder," he said. While the boy sipped, Shorty took the two canteens to the spring, set them in the wet moss, scooped water out of a shallow basin with his hand, and drenched their cloth covers. Then he came back and unpacked the burro. The boy watched with dumb amazement. He had not dared to imagine, to ask himself, to consider . . . more, again . . . the pulling on of boots, the walking, the pain. Had not even feared it. Were they really stopping? The walking or the stopping could have gone on forever.

He spoke: "Are we—"

"Done for today."

The boy sank back with a "Hail Mary, Mother of God" and went to sleep. The three formed a line on the east side of the rock: the sleeping boy, Shorty leaning back, arms folded, smoking as he looked out over the basin of strange rocks, and the little mouse gray burro, his back bare, rope dangling, standing on three legs with long lashes closed over his eyes.

When the boy awoke the colors of a sunset were lingering in the east—a delicate alpenglow above the peaks—and he felt terrible. Headache, nausea, thirst. His socks were off and his blisters had been treated with some kind of salve. He heard voices and sat up.

A few feet away two men sat by a fire. One man looked his way— big ears, black eyes, white hair, and bushy white mustache—it was Shorty. They looked at each other for a moment. The boy shrugged. "Tenderfoot," he said. The men smiled.

"Try this," said Shorty. "Drink it all." He handed him a cup. The boy drank it. Salt water. Tasted awful. Shorty knelt by his side and put a hand under his armpit.

"C'mon," he said, and led him around the rock. The boy felt sweat ooze through his pores and evaporate into the night, leaving his skin cold. He was dizzy. He sank to his knees and threw up. Immediately he felt better.

Five minutes later he sat by the fire with a tin of sardines packed in brine, guzzling water between every bite. "Pete," the other man said and nodded. "Jimmy," the boy replied. When he was finished he sat back with a sigh.

The men were talking; the evening was soft and warm. He no longer strained to look from shade to light, from light to shade. The hard edges were gone. Blue-green leaves dotted the ground— where had they been before?—like little pools reflecting the evening light. A flower had opened beside the spring, a soft, yellow-white flower that seemed to have nothing to do with the brutal white of the midday sun. Out on the wash, now glowing red, two burros browsed side by side. He had a vivid recollection of midday: stone against stem, leaf against sun, stone against sun, foot against stone. Silence against silence. Now that was gone. He stretched his feet into the soft cool sand. The conversation trickled beside him. To the east, range after range tumbled down to the banks of the sky.

Far back, below and behind them, the rocks on the mudflat, with their long, straight tracks, were barely visible.

"What are those rocks?" the boy asked.

Shorty and Pete smoked and chawed and worked on the dinner.

"Basalt. There are some like 'em on the slope to the northwest," said Pete. He kneaded dough. "Erratics."

"What are the white marks?"

"Seems to be where they've moved," Pete replied.

"What makes them move?"

"I don't know, Jimmy," said Pete.

"I've heard," said Shorty, knocking his pipe on his boot sole, "it's magic. Others say it's wind, when the mud's slick after a rain, though I've been out there in a wet blow. Used to think it was the tilting of the range, but some say they're going uphill."

"And don't they roll into each other?"

"Appears not."

The boy stared at the basin. Long clean bare red slopes on all sides, rounded low mountains, the huge mudflat and five stones at the end of parallel white lines.

"Has anyone seen them move?" he asked.

"Question is how fast they're going," said Pete. The boy looked at him. Pete handed him a plate of beans and fried bacon butts. "Well, hell, the range you're sitting on ain't holding still."

After dinner Shorty lit his pipe again and Pete took another chaw. Jimmy declined. The three sat around the coffeepot and dying coals, watching the basin play with the light of a three-quarter moon.

"So those stones are moving across the flat, one by one, and nobody knows why," Jimmy said without asking. No one replied. Again the oppression of midday flashed back to him, the heat of the flat, the glare, the silence, the utter loneliness as he had followed the white scar of Shorty's feet, moving imperceptibly across the land.

Shorty poured the coffee. Pete leaned on one of his packing boxes and arranged his coat under his back. He too was looking at the flat. Shorty suddenly laughed. "Some know why."

"Who's that?" said Pete.

"T. S. Harris," said Shorty. "Remember, Pete, after Hicks threw him out of Panamint and his papers folded in Darwin and Bodie and he shot his editor in L.A. and went to San Quentin and got out and put a bullet in his head—remember his note?"

Pete shook his head.

"I have had a great time." Shorty laughed again. "That's all he said."

Pete laughed. "That's what old John Lemoigne used to say. Remember when he died and Corcoran took his claim and everybody who bought it died?"

"Boston Brandon."

"That was the guy."

Jimmy began to wonder how many people had died out there, since none were in sight.

"Brandon. Reminds me of that fellow Hicks," Pete said. "How he died. Remember, Shorty, that friend of yours?"

Shorty nodded and heaped sugar in his coffee.

"What happened?" said Jimmy. Shorty looked at Pete and back to the coffee. Pete shifted and settled back. He knocked his pipe and looked at the sky, as if he was checking to see if it was time to begin.

"He was face down in a dry wash at the north end of Death Valley, right up there"—he waved across the flat to ghost peaks in the north—"at the edge of the Last Chance Range. One leg was dead. There were drag marks behind him in the sand. His tongue stuck out like a horned toad's. He wanted help." Pete took a cup from Shorty and passed it on to Jimmy.

"I had water, and I gave it to him. I'd been in the Last Chance with bad luck myself, lost my animal, cached my equipment, and that water was all I had left. When we'd finished it he felt better. I tried to help him walk. It was terrible hot, in the morning, and he was heavy. Dressed in suit pants and city shoes. After a while he sat down again and wouldn't get up. He cried a bit. Finally he sat still and told me what had happened." Shorty sat back. Pete took his own cup, sipped, and continued.

"Seems he'd fallen on hard times: firms bankrupt, bank busted, under investigation by everybody and his brother, kicked out of the stock exchange. Woke up one day flat broke, facing charges on mishandling public funds, and not enough money to bring a lawyer to court.

"He said he'd had lots of associates in his day and there were many men who owed him something, so at first he thought he'd have no trouble getting back on his feet. But one after another they refused to see him, or their secretaries said they weren't in, until he hadn't a contact left.

"He thought of his family. His parents were dead and he'd never been close, but he had relatives in San Antonio so he spent about all his cash getting down there. One by one his relatives closed the door in his face.

"Finally he was walking the streets with his last dollars in the middle of a hot afternoon, numb, drunk and discouraged when he realized that he had wandered to the Mexican quarter and was standing in front of a sign saying, 'Madame Esperanto, Fortunes, Advice, Palms, One Dollar. Second Floor.' He said it was like a flash, even though half of him knew it was crazy. He looked up— the curtains were drawn—he ran up the stairs and knocked— entered, blinked, stopped—the room was dark as a mine, but he slowly made out an old Gypsy woman in a red mantilla seated at a table with a crystal ball, watching him.

"She motioned him to a chair. He took off his hat and sat down. The room was full of smoke. She waited for him to speak, never taking her eyes off his face. He finally told her that he was Bob Bailey, abandoned by his friends, persecuted on false charges, and he needed money for his defense, and—he added—to build his life again. He felt absolutely certain that she knew something, that she could help. She held his palm. She said nothing. She looked into the globe. Finally she pushed his dollar away and sat back.

"'What's wrong?' he said.

"'You lie, I lie,' she said. 'No use.'

"He gave his real name. She smiled and took his dollar. She looked into the globe again, said it was not pleased; he retold his past three or four times under command until he had admitted everything, had cast himself in the worst possible light. She smiled and looked into the globe. 'That's enough,' she said. 'Now you want help.'

"She studied the globe a long time. Hicks watched her: the long sharp ridge of her nose, the black eyes like two adits in her face, the wrinkled lips painted a brilliant red. He found himself a little scared, believing in her power. Finally she rubbed her hands up and down the side of the globe and tickled it with her long crimson fingernails while she spoke, as if in a trance:

"'The globe will make you rich,' she said, 'if you will obey.' She looked up. He nodded. She smiled, and again bent her face to the globe.

"'There is treasure. It belonged to the god Cacamatzin. It was stolen by the Spanish. Cacamatzin has been waiting for an agent, and you have come at the right time. Listen carefully.' She looked up again. Her eyes gleamed like a snake in a mine. Back to the globe. 'Go to Beatty and ask for Raoul. Tell him I said you are the man. He will bring you to an old Indian, who will take the agent of Cacamatzin to the treasure.' Hicks said he began to wonder. 'You must bring half of it here as a tribute,' she said and watched his eyes. He was scared that his growing suspicion would be detected. He nodded assent. She smiled. 'There is one more thing,' she said. 'Raoul and the Indian must be killed.' She looked at him. 'Will you do that?' she said.

"'How much is the treasure worth?' he said.

"She smiled. 'Enough.'"

"Hicks said he felt like a fool for his moment of drunken trust in her and her ball and her god, for seeking help at all. He told me he knew then that only his own wits could help him and he felt sure he could beat her at her game, whatever it was. As he traveled to Beatty he figured she and Raoul probably had a religious hold over the Indian, and they needed a stranger to play 'agent' and pry the secret of the treasure out.

"If that was true, he saw no reason why Raoul shouldn't be ready to kill him once the treasure was located, since that's the way they worked, and he figured he would have to cover Raoul carefully as they approached the site. Perhaps Raoul had orders too. The old fortune-teller seemed ready to gain either way. She obviously wanted to boogie him; he didn't know what she had over Raoul; they could be related; but she had nothing to lose and maybe someone would dump half the treasure in her lap. It was amazing, he thought as the stage bumped into Beatty, what greed would drive people to. Spanish, whites, Mexicans, Gypsies—all alike. Well, he figured, he knew how to play. He'd just have to trust his wits.

"Raoul was found. He was tall, badly scarred, silent. He listened to Hicks's story. He said, 'Speak to no one and meet me outside the Desert Star at midnight.' If he could get the old Indian to come, he said, they would be rich.

"They met. The Indian was deaf and dumb, dressed in trousers and buckskin with an old black shawl wrapped around his head. He drove the wagon. Raoul and Hicks sat in back, under a dirty yellow sheet stretched over the iron hoops. They carried food and water. After a stop at Mesquite Springs the next day, they headed north up into the Last Chance Range. No one had spoken more than a few words since Beatty. The tracks ended. They crossed an alluvial fan and entered a canyon. Hicks could see no sign of traffic. He figured the canyon was dry and blind. There could be only one reason, then, to enter it. Gold. He kept a hand close to his gun and watched Raoul. Raoul glanced at him and smiled, uneasily, Hicks thought.

"The wagon stopped at a limestone ledge, beneath a lluvia d'oro tree. Raoul jumped out first. Hicks stood behind him while they both watched the Indian carry two shovels to the ledge, yellow with fallen leaves. The Indian came back to the wagon behind them and rummaged under the seat for more tools.

"'Is it buried there?' said Raoul. Hicks prepared himself.

"'Yes,' said the Indian. Instantly Hicks drew. 'Hands up, Raoul,' he said. Raoul faced him, hands up, a smile on his face. Hicks suddenly realized the Indian had spoken. He felt sick. Sweat dribbled from his neck down his chest.

"'I think you better drop your gun, Meester Heeks,' said the voice behind him. He looked at Raoul's sneer. He dropped the gun and turned. The hood was thrown off, a rifle held level. Not really pure Indian: mestizo.

"It was simple, ridiculously simple. Hicks wanted to laugh. They had lived in a Mexican area near L.A., a slum of corrugated iron shacks and backyard gardens. His bank had repossessed their land. Hardships followed. Juan's crippled grandmother, turned out of doors, died a slow and painful death. They blamed Hicks. Juan Fernandez—the Indian—had finally come to the main office of the bank and had asked to see Mister Hicks; had been delayed, brushed off, handled—he broke loose and rushed through to the inner office—this Hicks remembered, and the intense, deep-set black eyes—he grabbed Hicks by the lapels and begged—but the guards charged in and subdued him—Hicks adjusted his coat, then told Juan, calmly, that he hoped all spics and especially his whore of a grandmother went to hell. He spat in Juan's face and turned away.

"Juan's family then moved to Phoenix, where he and his cousins, including Raoul, and his mother, Madame Esperanto, had seen Hicks's picture and had read in the newspapers, with great pleasure, of his trouble. Then fortune had delivered him into his mother's hands. Of course, what could she do, a dumb spic like her. Juan smiled. Raoul smiled. Hicks begged. They laughed and said that they did not deal in murder like him, that they were civilized, respectable, as he used to be, more like gringo bankers, that the most they would do—they looked at each other—was innocent enough: turn a cripple out of doors. Hicks showed them money. They spat on it. They shot him just below one knee and left. It was early September, sixty miles into the Last Chance Range.

"Finally he fashioned a crutch from a green limb of the lluvia d'oro. 'Tears of gold,' it means, in Spanish. The leaves turn yellow and drop off. It's a desert tree." Pete poured himself more coffee and sat back.

"He hobbled down the canyon. Three days passed. On the alluvial fan his crutch broke. His leg had grown green as the crutch, swollen with infection. Then the maggots, yellow as leaves. He knew he was delirious. He dragged himself for a while. He lost track of time. That's when I came," Pete said. "He was crying. Still looking for a way out.

"I was to go to Lone Pine. I was to go to Beatty for help. I was to find a spring. I was to catch a jackass. I couldn't get it through his head that I was stuck there too, and if someone else came they'd be stuck too, and that all any of us could do was walk out, and that he couldn't last the three days it would take for me to get to Stovepipe Wells and back with a wagon.

"He wouldn't believe me. He emptied his pockets—he had five, six, seven hundred dollars—the son of a bitch had even lied to me in his story—it was all mine. I emptied my pockets and showed him I had nothing. I told him where we were, how far from the Beatty–Skidoo route. I offered to cut off his leg. All I had was a knife. I told him Mesquite Springs was five hours away and that he could lean on me. He lay back again and cursed. I was a bastard.

"'All right, then,' he said, reached into another pocket, and pulled out a note for a thousand dollars. 'Here,' he said, 'you win. Go get help.'

"I would have left him to rot then but he started crying like a baby. Well, I stood over him through the worst part of the day, shading his head, and when the sun got low enough I knelt. In late afternoon he woke up and cried some more about how he'd die there, and he cursed his luck, and then he kept demanding I do something, and finally he just lay on his back and looked at me without talking, for a long time, maybe two hours, and when the shadows were about half an hour away his tongue swelled way up, he gasped and rattled, his eyes glazed over, and he died. I closed the lids, took his boot off, and started down, pretty weak. I thought about him all the way to Mesquite Springs and all next night to Stovepipe Wells, and often since. I never did know if he finally realized that he was just plain stuck and no one could help, that he was alone and goin' where he was goin', no matter what. Like one of them stones."

Shorty knocked his pipe on his boot. The sound was loud and clear and made Jimmy feel lonely in the empty night. The boy watched a shooting star leave a thin white track across the sky, and fade from sight. The evening chill reached his bones.

"I wouldn't want to be one of those stones," the boy said suddenly.

Shorty looked at him.

"Nobody likes it at first," Shorty said. The rock behind him gave a hollow echo to his words. "When Rhyolite busted—went from six thousand people to a hundred in two months—and the Tonopah and Tidewater pulled up tracks, the ones who were left came together from all over town and moved into vacant buildings around the old railroad station."

Jimmy looked at him and wondered what that stone face was thinking. Then Shorty softened. "We've had a great time. C'mon over here and wash your plate," he said. Afterward they stretched out—sandwiched, Jimmy thought, between cold sand and colder stars—and slept.

CHAPTER 26

July 2: East

And yet what good were yesterday's devotions?
I affirm and then at midnight the great cat
Leaps quickly from the fireside and is gone.

—WALLACE STEVENS

It was still pitch dark when Shorty woke him up, though before he had rolled up his bag Jimmy noticed the first gray light in the east. A fire crackled. He was tired, sore, pained. He breathed the crisp air. A faint red band pushed the gray farther up in the sky. He ate five biscuits with honey and gulped coffee. In the east the red band was spreading upward and dissipating; beneath it a yellow glow had appeared. The men were packing the burros. He pulled his boots on delicately and laced them as tight as he dared. By the time he was finished, the eastern horizon was edged with purple. Above it the pale yellow stretched upward, still tipped with red, and beyond that the faintest gray still whitened the sky overhead.

"It's a spectrum!" he said out loud. The two men looked at him. "It's the spectrum, in order! I never knew that! You can see it, the whole thing." He stood and looked at the eastern sky. The men looked up for a second, then returned to their knots. "The air must be the prism!" He had goose bumps all over. "It's the sun coming through the air, through the edge of air around the whole earth!" The east was growing brighter; the yellow glare was being purged to white. The brightness began to hurt his eyes.

"C'mon," said Shorty. They were off.

"Where are we going today?"

"East. Near Skidoo."

"Are there jacks there?"

"Might be."

They walked southeast over flint gray pebbles. The mountain air was cool. The brightness in the east slowly increased until it was too intense to last, then suddenly the entire flare collapsed and concentrated into the brilliant white edge of the sun. For a moment every bush and stone on the bare ground, every snake track, cast an infinite shadow. The east side of the greasewood bushes glowed a deep yellow green, and tiny traces of quartz and mica glittered in the gravel and sand.

But almost immediately Jimmy felt the rays strike the left side of his face; the color of the greasewood faded, and the spectrum of the sky overhead gave way to the palest blue, sun-washed in the east with an insistent white. The heat began; his fear revived.

They walked—Pete, Shorty, Jimmy, the two burros—along the faint trail that followed up the crest of the wide, rounded ridge. Soon his thoughts were beaten into submission as his tongue had been the day before and he plodded mindlessly on, already tired, receiving with clarity but without excitement the data of his senses: the succession of white, gray, and brown in the ground, the evenly spaced greasewood bushes eight paces apart, the Joshua trees to the right, the little holes beneath some bushes, the gathered sand around the bases of others, the dull, faded green of the foliage, the webfoot shape of the sage leaf, the skittering lizards, the rough, shaggy bark of stunted trunks and twigs and the crunch of his boot and the horsefly's buzz and the smell of sand. As the sun rose higher he found that by focusing on Shorty's shadow he could reduce the glare. That shadow became his world. The ground flowed through the shadow, taking on color and shape as it passed through, then passing out again to a blinding white at which he dared not look. He watched in a trance the movie at his feet: continuously, suddenly, plants, lizards, beetles and tiny unflowering flowers with curled ground leaves and dead stems exploded into his field of view and flowed by. He walked as if floating, eyes glued to the screen.

When they took a break at midmorning on a bare hump in the middle of nowhere and sank with canteens into the shade of the burros, Jimmy, as he rested, suddenly and for the first time—as if emotion were a luxury—felt a deep revulsion at what he had seen. He pointed to a parched, twisted, stunted sage and told the men he felt sorry for it. Silence. Shorty turned to him with the same look he had given him the night before.

"Why?" Shorty said.

Jimmy shrugged. "Looks like a tough life."

Shorty glanced at the sage, then swept the horizon with his eye.

"What do you think it wants?" he said.

Jimmy thought a moment and replied: "Maybe it wants the best life possible."

Shorty looked again around the bare horizon. "Well?" he said. Jimmy was sullen. He felt sorry for the stubby, gnarled plant, and he didn't care to be talked out of his feelings. Shorty watched him, then spoke again:

"When I was young," Shorty said, "it seemed to me that death was the absence of longing."

"Well," said the boy quickly, "you're a prospector, aren't you?"

Shorty and Pete laughed. Suddenly the atmosphere was totally changed. Jimmy watched them in confusion.

"He's got you dead center," Pete said, chuckling.

"Sure does," said Shorty. "Still," he said, as he rose, "there's longing and there's longing, and I feel sorrier for Jimmy than that bush."

"Why do you feel sorry for me?" he demanded.

"It's a tough life," Shorty said, and turned to him. "That's a fact."

"I'll make it," the boy snapped back.

"Pete," said Shorty, cupping his hand to his ear, "do I hear that sage talking?" Pete and Shorty laughed.

They left. The boy was angry—what a cheap shot—and he hated the old man; he dreaded the rest of the trip. But never before had he tried to bear a grudge while walking for hours in the sun at a hundred degrees and he was at first irked, then, giving in a little bit, indifferent to find that his anger had somehow melted and his mind had again retreated to its roots.

He was still in this trance when Shorty and Pete turned left off the ridge and led the way down a series of steep switchbacks. It was nearly noon. Suddenly they rounded a corner of white rock and entered a dark grove—once again he had to blink and wait for the new world to take shape—willows, cottonwoods, aspen, and tamarisk pines towering above, a solid canopy of shade and green. Ahead a little waterfall plunged six feet into a shallow pool. Huge broad-leaved plants hid the ground. He couldn't believe it. He began to see flowers everywhere, of every color. Before he could unlace his boots and rip his shirt off Pete and Shorty had walked out of their clothes and into the water. He whooped for joy, then stopped and stared at Shorty's disappearing back.

"Hey Shorty," he heard himself yell, "what is that on your ass?"

"He got it in Las Vegas," Pete said.

"Betsy made me." Shorty was blushing.

"Show him," said Pete.

The old man turned around again and grinned over his shoulder. On the left buttock, wrinkled and barely legible, was tattooed "Gold Is Where," and on the right, "You Find It."

♦ ♦ ♦

They spent the afternoon holed up beside the shady pool, eating watercress and boiled milkweed greens, drinking and swimming.

Shorty showed him lupine and huge white jimson weed flowers and the leaves of a night-blooming cereus.

He told Jimmy about the sage they had seen on the ridge. It wasn't the bigfoot sage, he said. Had he noticed that the leaves were deeply notched, like tiny oak leaves, not webbed? The boy shook his head. It was a true mint family sage, an herb. The leaves made good tea. But boil a bigfoot and you'll drink turpentine, he said. The seeds, too, could be ground into flour. It looked like the bigfoot because up on that ridge everything got stunted and twisted, but there was probably a limestone shelf underneath—for all he knew it ran right to this waterfall, he said with a smile—that held a little moisture and gave the thirstier mint sage a chance. He'd never noticed one on that ridge before. He thanked Jimmy for pointing it out. Where there's limestone there could be replacement deposits, he said, and gold.

Finally they packed up, ascended to the ridge and resumed their journey to the southeast. The white middle of the day had passed. Soon Jimmy was hot and tired. Ten minutes after drinking he was thirsty again, though now he had some watercress, mint, and clean pebbles in his pocket, and that helped. They walked on through the afternoon and took another break around six o'clock, still in full, strong sunlight. Jimmy pointed to a knee-high, branched cactus and asked its name.

"Cholla," said Pete. He picked up a stick from the ground and handed it to Jimmy. "Here's its wood."

Jimmy held a hollow perforated tube of light gray wood. The lacework openings were shaped like elongated eyes, and the figure eights of wood looping around the eyes were deeply ingrained and delicate. Though dry, the fragile structure was strong and resilient.

"Cholla," said Pete. "The most vile thing on the desert. Spits thorns." Jimmy looked at the fat, squat, fleshy green cholla, covered with spines. "Only thing that likes it is a cholla wren," Pete continued. "Builds in the thorns so nothing can get to it."

"Talk about funny plants," said Shorty, "this one here"—he pointed to a little leafless, budless bare brown twig beside his foot—"has always reminded me of my father."

Shorty didn't seem to have anything else to say. After a pause the boy said, "Do you think my father's going to find any gold?"

Shorty snorted. "Those flivver mahouts find nothing." He said it with an air that didn't encourage further conversation.

"Oh," the boy murmured, and then added half-heartedly, "I don't much like my father anyway."

Shorty and Pete roared with laughter. Jimmy was astonished at what he'd said. He wondered if the desert was frying his brain. They got up.

Toward sundown they reached the ghost towns of Skidoo and Harrisburg, two clumps of stray foundations and abandoned timbers lying at opposite ends of White Sage flat. They walked right up the main street of Harrisburg. "Was this really named for you?" the boy said in wonder. Jackrabbits bolted from underneath the bushes. The day began to soften. Shorty and Pete told him the story of their strike twenty-nine years before, when they were heading, as now, for Ballarat on the Fourth of July. Shorty had made ten thousand dollars—the boy's eyes were wide—and blown it all on two trips east.

"What did you do there?" the boy asked.

"Mostly opera," said Shorty.

"My mother loves opera."

They unpacked at the far end of town. Above them the sunset flared. The light again broke up into colors gently carried on a pale tray of a western sky as if the sun wished to display, at the end as well as at the beginning of each day, in explanation if not in apology, the complex and delicate beauty contained in its white heat. Jimmy watched the same spectrum he had seen at dawn melt down in the west, and he thought of the blinding white ground breaking into color as it flowed through the quick night of Shorty's shadow; then, as he watched, the day, its delicate structure woven around an empty middle like a piece of cholla wood, was gone. Night. The day was mostly white and the night mostly black, he thought, and those colors at each end passed quickly. But his feet at least were no worse. "Now is when I need a bath," he thought, irked that it came instead at midday, then he looked around at the vast, dry sage flat at seven thousand feet and laughed at the futility of his wish. As he turned he saw the alpenglow, a third spectrum in the east like a deliberate imbalance and he thought it wasn't quite as simple as he thought, and he made a note to watch in the morning for pre-dawn color in the west. He hobbled to the fire and helped knead the dough.

"Haven't found jacks or gold, have we?" said Jimmy.

"There's plenty around," said Pete.

"Remember," said Shorty, "when we camped here with Doc Trotter and McAllister?"

He turned to Jimmy. "Went off to prospect above that ledge up there. Doc had a black burro, called him Honest John, who could steal anything. The other four burros were gray. Well sir, when we came back about noon all five burros were white. Honest John had rolled the rocks off the tarp and dragged out our two sacks of flour. They'd eaten half, scattered the rest and rolled in it. Hot damn. They looked ready to fry. We had a hard time scraping up enough flour for one mess of flapjacks."

"At least they didn't get the whiskey," said Pete.

"Not like Swain's goat in Pioche." Shorty laughed and turned to Jimmy. "The critter would pull the cork and drain the bottle. Swain would come home and that goat'd be drunker than a boiled owl on Swain's booze. Swain said it was reincarnation—his old partner Patrick had returned."

After dinner they smoked. Pete gave Jimmy a pipe, but it tasted awful. The night was cool and clear and the stars were vivid in the north. Beside them the remains of Harrisburg stuck up from the flat plain; beyond, moon-whitened sage stretched across a six-mile flat and up the rolling hills. Behind, to the south, the crest of the Panamint Ridge rose more sharply to the moon that gave no hint of color in its face. Far off, one of their burros brayed. Shorty and Pete looked at each other.

"Good sign," said Pete to Jimmy. "Wild jacks."

The flat was laid out; the hills, even the mountains, were far away and low. The land lay open to the night, as it had been to the day. Jimmy drew closer to the little coffeepot singing on the coals. He had a terrible headache. The night would be cold. A breeze stirred.

"It's pretty exposed out here, isn't it?" he said, simply.

A silence, but he felt it was a supporting silence, enveloped him. He stared at the coals; gross shapes and the glow of pipes to either side. Pete spat. The pot came to a rolling boil.

"Yes, it is," said Shorty.

Pete poured the coffee into three cups and added sugar. They sipped in silence. A jackass brayed somewhere on the flat. A shooting star. A sigh of wind came and went.

Shorty pulled a box behind his back and sighed.

"I knew a woman once," he said, "who wanted to be a cholla wren." He paused, rummaged in his breast pocket while he stared at the fire. A match flared, cupped in one hand. The pipe was a few inches from his mouth. The match had almost burned out before its flame flowed downward with each suck. The smoke made a rosy glow.

"Is she safe now?" Jimmy said.

"She's dead," said Shorty with a shrug, as if that answer could go either way. He settled back against the box. The boy stretched out and wriggled in the sand till he was comfortable, then he threw his sleeping bag over his legs. Shorty adjusted one arm behind his head. Pete threw a few sage trunks on the fire and settled down. Finally Shorty turned to Jimmy.

"Once upon a time," Shorty said with a smile, "once upon a time there was a little girl, and she was pretty wild." He turned on his back and blew smoke at the stars. "Pretty wild. Shoulda been too, 'cause her ancestors were Ulster Scotch, like mine. Maybe like yours, too, Jimmy. Her great-grandmother came over to a religious community in New York State, a strict one, but she got pregnant by the founder and the two ran off to North Carolina. Their child was a daughter, and with their eight other children the little girl grew up on a North Carolina farm, and she got married there to a farmer. But when the West opened she persuaded her husband to go to Oklahoma, and in forty-nine she wouldn't have anything more to do with him unless they went to California right away.

"On the way she got pregnant by a Kiowa Indian, and when they reached California she had twin girls. She gave the newborn babies and some money to a childless German Presbyterian minister in Angel's Camp, up in the Mother Lode, who agreed to raise and educate them as part of his good works. The mother then left her husband and ran off to Sacramento with a policeman.

"The twin children were both healthy and smart, but the minister didn't much like them, and he showed them off as examples of sin—heathens and lust—and he beat them both a good deal in front of the other children who boarded at the rectory.

"When the girls were ten years old they were taken by a middle-aged, childless couple from Indiana—rescued—bought, really, for a contribution to the church—and adopted. The couple had moved around the gold camps, and in the sixties they moved to Panamint City, down here a ways, just four or five canyons down this ridge." Shorty puffed, then dabbed at the pipe with a glowing stick. Jimmy thought the story might be over.

"It was the first settled life the girls had seen. One became the sweetest, most gentle woman you've ever met." He paused again. "Her blood seemed to run smooth and calm. The other was a hellion.

"Time went along, and they both got married. The calm one wanted to be wild like her sister so she married someone ambitious and fast. The wild one married a big, calm man and had two babies right away." He lit the already lit pipe a third time. "But no matter how much house and husband she wrapped around her, the wild one never felt safe. She kept hopping this way and that, hoping that time or chance would help. She almost ran off with another man, a fast one like herself. Her sister's husband." Shorty puffed and looked at the weather. There was none. "Then there was a flood. She lost her youngest baby. They had to move. New town, new house, new friends. She tried to nestle down for a few more years, but whatever it was she was running from could still get to her, so one morning she hitched the mule team, chained herself to a fence post, tied the rope around her neck, and gave the mules the word."

No one spoke. A long time passed now. The boy was disturbed. The tale seemed to have no point. The old man's coldness and distance seemed odd, and cruel. Finally, though, Jimmy was too tired to do anything but slip into his bag for the night.

"It's chilly," he said.

"We're in the shade now," Shorty replied, and leaning back Shorty watched the earth's long night shadow stream out away from a blinding sun until its converging sides met in space between the stars and he thought to himself, "Way out there is my absence from light," while the boy was saying, "Shade of what?" and Shorty, seeing himself lean back with the whole spinning earth for his parasol, said "California."

The boy caught the image. It put the prisms of the sunrise and sunset into a new, and distant, perspective. As he lay beneath the moon in the mid-darkness of White Sage Flat he watched, coldly, as from the moon, the turning globe of earth roll the Himalayas up into the sight of sun. And he knew that was what the old man had seen, though from somewhere farther away, where the boy could not yet go.

CHAPTER 27

July 3 and 4: South

Over back where they speak of life as staying
(You couldn't call it living, for it ain't),
There was an old, old house renewed with paint,
And in it a piano loudly playing.

—ROBERT FROST

Jimmy awoke to the braying of an ass, raucous, loud, and near at hand. Pete sat up. Three wild jacks stood at the edge of camp; Shorty snored; one lowered her head, stretching her neck and letting out a bray that rattled the top on the coffeepot. Pete said it was love.

In underwear and hats they chased them for an hour over the dark flat, until Shorty said they should call it quits and head south by the high route. "Gonna wet a whistle in Ballarat before we sleep tonight."

They stepped away from the coals before dawn. Pete stayed behind, saying he might come by way of Wildrose on the Fourth. They crossed the broad flats at the head of Wildrose and Nemo canyons and began the long ascent to the top of the Telescope Ridge.

There, at noon, above the heat, they strolled along the open ridge—valley after valley spread out to east and west—Panamint Valley, Searles, Death Valley, the Amargosa. To one side the Sierra Nevada stretched north for a hundred miles, splotched with snow; to the other side nameless peaks stood one behind another far into the haze of the Great Basin. Mile after mile they strolled ten thousand feet above the flaring floor of Death Valley, where the Amargosa glittered here and there as it snaked around the Confidence Hills and into the sink. Jimmy said it wasn't much of a river. Shorty said it rose one clear day in 1927 and wiped out half of Beatty. The clearest days were trickiest, he said, and pointed south, where peaks floated upside down and distant lava flows lay flat and dark as cloud shadows though there was nothing at all in the porcelain bowl of the sky.

They walked past the last whitened sages and then higher, where the lupine leaves were edged with silver and the ancient twisted bristlecone pines twined strands of living bark around wood burnished by millennia of wind and ice. Only lichen and a few gnarled trees grew on the talus; the bare slabs of rock lay tumbled and broken in a sky that whistled past, sighing through the half-dead trees and across the jagged ridge. There were snow patches north of the summit. The trees were stripped of growth on their west sides; the few stiff needles of the topmost, battered branches pointed straight east, downwind.

"This is the limit," Jimmy thought. He looked down from the whitened wood and rocks to the white salt flat, lower than the ocean, far below. "Here and there, like white bookends. Everything's between." All afternoon they walked the edge of sky.

Late in the day Shorty suddenly turned right off the ridge into a dense thicket of mountain mahogany. Deer droppings everywhere.

"Down we go," said Shorty, with a spring in his step and a laugh.

Jimmy bounded behind. They seemed to fly down the slope, through the thickening forest of piñon and juniper, sliding and stumbling down the steep rock and finally descending the head of the canyon, where he had to hold the burro back by the tail. Down, down, down for hours, finally along a dry watercourse in a canyon—how thirsty he was—choked with huge pine trunks uprooted by God knows what holocaust or when, down, down until he noticed a light green clump of grass here or there in the dry sand and even though he hadn't been fooled by the bright patches of Mormon tea he knew to trust this sign. When he heard a sparrow ahead he said to Shorty, "We're back, aren't we?" The old man turned around and smiled. They came around a bend to a clump of willows and a spring. Jimmy lay down in the grass, ate jerked beef, and listened to the birds.

"Where are we?" he said.

"Panamint City."

Just below the spring they entered a high open basin. Stone foundations stuck up from the gravel, one huge smokestack seventy feet above the rubble at its base. It was evening. Swallows swirled in the pink air. Yellow cliffrose bloomed on the slope above.

The old man stood still, holding the burro's rope. His eyes were wet. Jimmy stood beside him. The burro snorted. Shorty moved on and sat on a broken wall.

"You used to live here, didn't you?" Jimmy said. Silence. "My mother was born in a mining camp. She didn't say which one."

Shorty sat still. Finally the boy said in a fresh tone, "What was this building here?" slapping the wall on which they sat.

"Big saloon. The Nugget," Shorty said, and he looked at the foundation, thinking as he stared at a browned timber in the gravel, not thinking so much as feeling the slow downfall of the wood, of the mountain mahogany and piñon at the top of the ridge, the needles dropping, the cones bouncing down the dry white boulders of the watercourse, the leaning trunks and dead white fallen branches, the soil of the ridge sliding down like a slipped wig bearing with it all the wood of the range; and the choppers—the ring of ax on wood, the squeak of chains moving downhill—the shouts of the boy on the mule—the lowering whine of the big circular saw biting into heartwood—down, down, and out to Panamint City, not to end as a Nugget rafter but only to pass through that stage, then broken and rotted a little more, in roiled mud and water sinking down, down, through Surprise Canyon, perhaps stuck in its throat for a while but finally disgorged into Panamint Valley to be buried in alluvial debris, the waste of the range, to rot some more and sink and disintegrate until turned to whatever variety of stone they would call the unique hard mass and then thrust up again who knows where, thrust up to light and air again, to break down and support life, to be life, to grow up and be used by forces beyond all control in patterns we choose to call ugly or beautiful, and pray are benign.

"Bet you had a few drinks there in your time," said the boy. Then he felt awkward and vulgar.

"Shoulda had more," said Shorty.

They sat silent in the twilight. Then Shorty spoke again, looking at Jimmy this time:

"You know, I spread my blanket one night on the sand, thinking to mind my own business and get some sleep. It had been a long dry spell. Years, right there. That night it rained, rained like hell. In the morning there were beautiful little flowers, thousands, just popped up, everywhere. Only where I had slept it was bare."

Jimmy looked at him; the wrinkled skin was almost black in the dusk. Shorty dropped a rock. It landed on another with a little click.

"I had a daughter, and a wife," he said. "Wife's dead, I hear. Daughter's married, but I don't know who or where." He looked about. "You can't get away. I used to hope you could."

Jimmy picked up stones and rubbed them in his palm. "My grandmother died a few years back."

"I'm sorry to hear that."

In a little while Shorty got up. "Eight miles down to Ballarat, my boy." He put a hand on Jimmy's shoulder. "Let's go."

In the dusk they went straight toward the one light in the middle of the clump of buildings on the vast floor of Panamint Valley. It was an old hardware store, but the lettering was faded and "Saloon" was painted on a nailed board. There was no porch or roof, though there used to be, and Shorty pushed open the weathered wood door. Four or five men stood up in the lantern light, clapped them on the back, brought up chairs and ice cold beers, set Jimmy's boots up against the wall and whistled and laughed at his bleeding feet. As usual, he was dizzy when he stopped. He half heard stories of bowling at full champagne bottles in Goldfield and mobbing the first Rhyolite liquor wagon four miles from town and panning the gold-paved streets of Grass Valley, after the bust. They kept their arms around each other and their voices and mugs raised together so late that Jimmy was barely conscious when he and Shorty stumbled through the predawn air down the dirt street to a tiny adobe square the color and texture of the sand and mud of which it seemed the least and crudest excrescence, entered beneath a sign saying, "Welcome Please Close the Door When Leaving," fell into a single bed, and slept.

Jimmy slept most of the day. By early afternoon it was over a hundred degrees in the house and the wind was pelting the tar paper roof with sand. He was alone. He looked out. Tumbleweeds shot down the street. Dust swirled into the air. July Fourth. He pulled his coat over his head and stumbled across the alkaline street to the saloon. He had a vague impression of the Panamint Valley floor sliding north. His mouth, eyes, and nostrils were full of dust. He burst through the door.

"Give that boy a drink," someone shouted. "Jesus Christ, if he don't root he'll blow away."

The door opened often. In the orange twilight they lit the lamps. Windows rattled and a fine powder settled where it could, but by then twenty or thirty men and three women—and a young reporter named Ted Ballantine from the *Los Angeles Times* who had heard of the Ballarat Fourth and whose angle, he said, was "The Pursuit of Happiness"—were jammed in the room and the rattling of the wind became only a faint descant above the clink of glass on glass.

At first her cheap perfume and the way she pried his mouth open to admire his gold filling made him uncomfortable, but soon Jimmy got used to the way Martha held his neck when they danced or stood with a hand looped casually over his shoulder. "I never had a child of my own," she said, smiling, and kissed him slowly on the mouth. Jimmy flushed and reached back for the counter. Her hands wandered.

When a big man spoke to her, Jimmy managed to escape. He was in a corner, leaning dazed against the wall, when rigid fingers touched his stomach:

"Hi. Name's Ted Ballantine."

"Hello."

Ballantine took out a cigarette. "Smoke?"

"No thanks."

He lit and puffed.

"Hear your feet are pretty bad."

"Who said that?"

"You been traveling with Shorty Harris. What's he like, the old geezer? I mean, what's he really like?" Ballantine shut one eye in the cloud of smoke.

"Oh," Jimmy shrugged, "I like him."

"He show you any prospects?"

"No, not really."

"I hear he's really just . . . well, you know." Ballantine looked around. One eye was still shut, though the smoke had cleared. The cigarette dangled from his lower lip. "Got a good sense of the old show biz, if you know . . ."

"Well, I don't know . . ." Jimmy felt very fuzzy.

"Any evidence, kid," Ballantine leaned close and smiled, "any hard evidence that the old goat can smell gold?"

"Gee, we were looking for jacks mostly."

Ballantine cocked his eye.

"Jacks?"

"Jackasses . . ."

"Oh."

"Hey, Ace Reporter." Martha threw her arm over Jimmy's shoulder and eyed Ballantine. "You're at a goddamn party."

Suddenly the door burst open. The wind howled and dust swirled in.

"Where is this party?" Nute shouted just inside the door and lit a string of firecrackers in his hand.

"Looks like we're late again," said Sam. Sam Johnson and Nute Drake shook sand and dust from their sleeves, slapped their hats on their pants, and reached for the cold glasses. Sam was old—he looked as old as Shorty—white-haired and creased. Nute was a young giant with raw, meaty hands and a red beard.

"Martha!"

"Nute!" Martha ran and jumped into his arms. Jimmy took a sip of beer and wandered away toward the bar.

"Where you been, Sam?"

"North end of the Cottonwoods."

"Any luck?"

"Naw."

The next few hours brought beer and talk, then whiskey and talk. Nute started smashing empty bottles. Martha had both arms around Jimmy's neck as he sat shyly on the stool. She was dancing against him. Jimmy glanced at Nute and away.

"Don't get any ideas kid!" Nute shouted.

"Aw shut up Drake." The other men gestured at him.

"Uh look Martha . . . " Jimmy said.

She blew smoke into his face and pressed against his knee.

"She could be your goddamn mother." Drake pushed Ballantine aside and came up behind Martha. Then he put a hand on Martha's shoulder and yanked her away. Her hands ripped from Jimmy's neck and she fell onto a table. The room grew quiet.

"Hey," Jimmy said. "That's not necessary."

Nute laughed and hit him square in the face. Jimmy was flat on his back across the bar, listening to the fight. Chairs were smashed, tables turned. He felt hands on his arm. Shorty and Sam led him to a corner and wiped his mouth and nose with a wet towel.

They fought until someone's elbow smashed the south window and a terrific gust of wind—louder than the grunts and shouts—blew the front door out, tearing off the top hinge. Sand and dust poured across the room and out the door; a tumbleweed lodged in the window then popped into the room, bounced off a tabletop and jammed between the stove and the wall. The grabbling couples slowed, stopped, and looked.

"Son of a bitch."

Boards appeared from the back room; in two minutes the window was boarded and the door nailed shut. Drake stood in the middle of the room, hammer in hand, laughing. "Nobody gets out now." Then he saw Jimmy.

"Shit, boy, you all right?"

Jimmy nodded slowly.

"Have a drink." Someone put a beer in Jimmy's hand and another in Nute's. Martha appeared and put one arm around Drake.

"You OK, Jimmy?" she said. To Drake: "You dumb ox."

"Here's to the forty-first consecutive annual Ballarat Fourth!"

"I'll drink to that."

"Listen, uh, Martha . . ." Nute Drake was speaking softly. "Do you think Jimmy's OK?" She looked at Nute's knotted forehead and raised an eyebrow. Nute smiled, "You know, first aid? A little rest?"

Martha turned to the men. "Wicht, is that back room clean?" One of the men went to the door and opened it.

"Clean enough."

"Put some salve on his head." Men laughed. Jimmy looked about, a little drunk and confused.

"C'mon kid, you're going to the hospital." Nute Drake bent down, picked him up like a baby, and carried him through the door behind the counter. Jimmy looked wide-eyed back over his shoulder. Martha followed them in. Nute came out. Inside, Martha slipped her straps. "Jimmy," she said, "I'd like to show you something nice."

Hours later men and women sat quiet and mellow around the cold stove. The wind whined and whistled and rattled the windows in their frames; the sand on the tin roof sounded like rain. Jimmy sat at a table in the back of the crowd, head down on his arms. Martha stood behind him, rubbing his neck and shoulders.

Ted Ballantine—who hadn't been heard from since the fight—said quietly, from the shadow of the wall:

"Why did you go into prospecting, Sam?"

Sam and Shorty looked at each other; men stared at Ballantine.

"Throw the son of a bitch out."

The wind howled. Sam shook his head: "No."

Men stared at the cold black stove as if it danced with flames.

"Sam," said Shorty after a while, "remember that dark Chinaman, the East Indian, in Rhyolite? He was in Panamint City when I was growing up."

"Yes," said Sam, laughing. "Yes, I do."

The group sat silent several minutes.

"Way I remember it," said Sam, "is that he was a cook at the Wellington Hotel in Rhyolite—Shorty's big strike—and one time when we were sitting around outside after dinner listening to him sing and tell stories, he said that prospectors reminded him of a man in the village where he was born." Sam paused. Ballantine nodded. The men were silent. Gusts of sand swirled in beneath the door.

"Seems that back where he came from they didn't have no liquor. They used the juice of a root." (Shorty saw him again, the dark, olive skin, the purple lips, the loose dress standing out white in the evening against the Bullfrog Hills, and he heard the high nasal voice singing.) "But the juice was poisonous and couldn't be used till it had passed through a stomach, like a mesquite bean. So the village always had someone, some boy who was selected at the age of twelve, by chance . . ."

(Shorty heard the soft voice in the dusk, the high clipped words telling tales:

It is a place of infinite peace, where the dark and gentle Yamuna flows beside a flowered meadow, where cattle graze; on the river's bank sweet-scented trees blossom and bend their branches to the earth, where peacocks dance and nightingales call softly. Here Krishna, ever young, sits beneath the trees, the sound of his flute echoing the nightingale's call. How can I describe his relentless flute, which pulls virtuous women from their homes? Wise men forget their wisdom, and clinging vines shake loose from the trees, hearing that music. How then shall a simple dairymaid withstand its call?)

". . . and this boy was fed the root, a tiny bit at first, for the rest of his life. Soon he could stand more, and more, and more, and when he was an old man he could take it straight and not die. By then his urine was full of the juice and was safe for the others to drink . . ."

(And Shorty remembering the voice breaking without warning like a quail into quivering song:

Lord of my heart, what have I dreamed . . .
How shall I go home, now that daylight has come?
My musk and sandalwood perfumes are faded,
The kohl smudged from my eyes, the vermilion line
Drawn in the part of my hair, paled.
O put the ornament
Of your body upon me.
Take me with you, down-glancing one.
Dress me in your own yellow robes,
Smooth my disheveled hair,
Wind round my throat your garland of forest flowers.
Thus, beloved, someone in Gokula entreats.
Basa Ramananda says: Such is your love that deer and tiger
are together in your dwelling place.)

". . . so finally the old man sat in the center of the village, all alone, eating the root, while the others drank his piss." Nute laughed.

"I don't get it," said Ballentine.

Sam turned to the reporter: "Someone's gotta do it. Drink it or print it, I don't care."

Sam got up and helped himself to more whiskey from the bar. Suddenly there was knocking, then louder pounding. "Open the door," said Sam. Nute studied it for a moment.

"We nailed it shut." The pounding continued in between gusts of wind.

"Open it, for Chrissakes, Nute." Nute grabbed a pick and ripped off the two crossed boards that held the door to the frame, caught the door as it blew out, reached through and yanked in two men and a woman and pulled the door shut. Jimmy caught sight of a car outside, as Nute nailed the door shut again. The strangers stood there covered with alkaline grit, forlorn as shaved dogs. One man carried a cello case, one a cased violin. They peered at the men, the room; beams of light radiated from the kerosene lantern through the thick, dim dust.

"We're a touring group . . ." the violinist began, but Sam had already risen and motioned the lady to his chair.

"Don't matter what you are, you don't belong out there." Others were fetching chairs to the circle around the cold stove. Men handed the strangers mugs of beer.

"We are going to Los Angeles," the cellist said. "From Salt Lake. We wanted to see Death Valley."

"You got that done," said Shorty.

"You and the Jayhawkers," said Sam.

"Boy, were we glad to see a light in this place. Do you know what it's like out there?" The men smiled. The violinist continued. "You know you're not on the map?"

"We've heard."

"Where are we anyway?"

"Ballarat."

Then the violinist noticed Shorty sitting in the corner.

"I know you—Shorty Harris. You've heard me play. You came just to hear me."

Shorty looked very pleased and a little puzzled. "In New York?"

"No, in Death Valley. 1923. You came with two burros and camped with us a couple of nights."

"Oh my God. You were the violinist with that movie! That donkey do-do German son of a bitch."

"Right. 'Greed.'"

Shorty laughed. "That guy knew nothing. But you sure sounded good, till your fiddle burned up."

The violinist laughed. "It cracked."

"Cracked hell. It fell apart in six pieces. The end ones had strings, if you coulda' just glued the others in between."

"Well," the violinist said quietly, "I've shown my friends Death Valley. Any idea when we can leave?"

"Maybe tomorrow, maybe day after."

"We perform day after tomorrow."

"I don't doubt it—but where?" They all laughed.

It wasn't long before someone asked for a song, and the musicians looked at each other, and the woman went to the upright piano and opened the keyboard and coughed as the men beat it with their shirts to get the dust off.

"I'm afraid we play classical music," the violinist said. "We're part of a chamber orchestra. The others went by Santa Fe."

The pianist was staring at the keys. Most had their ivories. She checked the tuning with a few arpeggios.

"I guess a Memphis gal ought to know some Clarence Williams," the woman said, and launched into Beale Street Blues.

The dust was thick and the pace was slowing when someone said, "Let's sing."

"I don't know any show tunes," said the pianist.

"Let's hear the violin."

"I don't know, with this dust," said the violinist.

"Nothing stops the Ballarat Philharmonic on America's birthday," said Sam.

"I remember something," Jimmy said, "something to sing that you may be able to play on the violin." To the pianist: "It's in C. No, wait, that'll be too high. Give me a B flat."

Shorty looked up. Jimmy had turned to the violinist and cellist, who had taken their instruments out and were tuning.

"Is B flat OK?" They nodded. "It's by Mozart," Jimmy said. He stepped forward as their bows were poised over the strings, and he began to sing quietly but truly, and with control, "Sancta Maria, ora pro nobis." The pianist improvised, but the violinist and cellist knew the score and began to weave in missing parts.

The room was still as they played. At one end of the piano Shorty stood as if he'd seen a ghost. The Mozart litany was not that famous, not at all. As he looked at the boy's eyes and listened to the bell tones perfectly pitched, he felt his stomach turning over. When the soprano phrases ended, Jimmy took the alto part, and as that faded Shorty heard himself croaking the tenor entrance as Jimmy and the musicians stared in amazement. The cellist picked up the bass lines, and when the improvisations ran out of steam, Shorty led them directly to the Cosa Mystica and the beautiful descending phrases at the end of the quartet. There they stopped. No one applauded or moved, although several men silently raised their glasses before they sipped. The pianist arose and the circle broke. Shorty was shaking as he guided Jimmy to the corner.

"Where did you learn that, boy?"

"My mother. She sang it to me as a lullaby, almost every night."

Shorty looked at the ceiling, and at his glass, sighed, then said in the same way that people say "It's raining," said it as a matter of fact: "Abigail."

"Yes." Jimmy jumped. "I never told you her name."

"No."

"How did you know?"

"She never spoke of her father?" he said, looking down.

"He died when she was young. In some mining camp. Her mother wouldn't talk about him."

"I'm her father," Shorty said. He looked down, pained and shy. "I'm your grandfather."

"But that's impossible. Her name wasn't Harris."

"No, of course. She uses your father's . . ."

"No no. My grandmother wasn't a Harris either."

"She was for three years. And so was Abigail."

"But I never heard Harris spoken."

Shorty was still looking down. "Perhaps not."

"But my grandmother's name was—"

"May Winthrop."

"That's right." Jimmy stopped in confusion, knowing now there was no mistake.

"She went back to her maiden name after I left."

"But you died."

Shorty smiled and shrugged. "That's what she told Abigail. But Abigail—your mother—knew better."

"What do you mean?"

"I saw Abigail when she was ten. She sang the soprano solo in this piece, Jimmy, the Sancta Maria from the Lorettine Litany, in San Francisco—"

"She told me."

"And I heard her and introduced myself." He paused. "And she sort of walked away."

Jimmy just watched him. Shorty rubbed his beard, his eyes misty. "She was younger than you are. I came back out here about then. Lost track. Guess she moved to Los Angeles."

Jimmy and Shorty looked at each other, nervous and uncomfortable as captains of opposing teams meeting in the center of the field. Jimmy was three inches taller than the white-haired old man.

"Look," Shorty said, "I didn't want this. I didn't know."

"I was gettin' along OK without a grandfather, too," said Jimmy, and they both began to smile.

"Don't tell them, please," said Shorty. "I . . ." He stopped and looked away.

"Can I get you a beer, Shorty?"

"That would be nice."

Shorty took the beer and moved to a half-boarded window. Jimmy sat at the table with a barely conscious Nute Drake. The wind rattled the roof. Nute leaned back and took a gigantic swallow from his mug. Jimmy watched the big, raw man, not that much older than himself. Suddenly Nute leaned forward across the table. Long red hair fell across his eyes, down to his beard. Jimmy shrank. "Listen," Nute whispered, and brushed his hair aside. His bloodshot eyes narrowed. His voice was tense. "You and me are nothing. Let me tell you there's places where we don't go." Jimmy sat back, as far from the red face as possible. "There's places, places where the light's so strong . . ." His voice trailed off. Jimmy said to himself, "This man's crazy." "But that man," Nute continued, "that man"—he nodded toward Shorty at the window—"has been there and back!" Nute drew himself up, then gazed at his empty mug. He cradled his head in his hands and rocked back and forth. Jimmy remained rigid. From behind, Martha leaned to his ear and whispered, "Don't worry, Jim. They're all crazy."

Drake left. People were laying out places to sleep on the floor. Jimmy put his head on his arms, closed his eyes, and slept. Shorty turned from the window and saw Martha stroking Jimmy's head. She looked up. Their eyes met and for just a second they shared the fantasy, the boy, which each had coveted alone. Shorty came to the table. They kissed.

"How long's he staying?" said Martha.

"Leave tomorrow," said Shorty.

"Where to?"

"I don't know. Guess I'll take him out."

"When are you coming back?"

"Have to work for the road crew soon."

"Shorty," she said, half plea, half remonstrance.

"Gotta," he said. "Need a stake." He smiled.

She laughed and put a hand on his cheek. "I'll keep the beer cold."

Together they carried Jimmy across the street and laid him on the bed. The wind had died, the dust was settling. "I wish I could keep him," she said. "Well," said Shorty. "I know," she said. Shorty heard the flute echo in the forest. She put her arm around his waist and pulled him close. How can a simple dairymaid withstand that call? They walked away.

CHAPTER 28

July 5: West

I sit a moment
by the fire, in the rain, speak
a few words into its warmth—
stone saint smooth stone—*and sing*
one of the songs I used to croak
for my daughter, in her nightmares.

—GALWAY KINNELL

"Get up." Shorty shook the boy's feet. "Get up."

Jimmy blinked at the one window, the broken pane stuffed with long underwear. Full day. He struggled to a sitting position on the edge of the bed. Shorty handed him coffee in an old tomato can. No wind. Through the open door he saw three burros. One packed, and two with saddles.

It was hot. Late morning. A hundred and five degrees. The glare of full sun on the Panamint Valley floor made his head pound, but riding was a joy to his feet. They rode for an hour.

"I like your friends," said Jimmy.

"They're not all my friends," said Shorty and spat. "One Fourth of July I passed out and they nailed me in a coffin."

"They seemed to be your friends last night."

"In a drought I've seen deer and coyotes take turns at a water hole."

Jimmy pounced: "What do you think of Nute Drake?"

"He shot my burro once in spite."

"Well, Martha sure is nice, anyway."

Shorty smiled. "She's a good woman. I asked her to marry me once, but she said I was too small for hard work. She used to go by the name of Shacknasty Nell, pretty as curly ribbon, and she did a colored light dance in Skidoo in 1907 that would stop your heart faster than bad hootch."

"Well, I like her."

"Look," said Shorty. "Where's Ballarat?"

Jimmy turned around. It was gone, invisible, though he could see all of the vast valley floor.

"I can't find it," he said.

"What's the use of opinions then," said Shorty, "We're somewhere else." They rode awhile.

"Nute Drake said you've been there and back."

"Been where?"

"I don't know. Wherever it's worst, I guess. Death Valley."

Shorty snorted. "Death Valley ain't the end of the earth."

"What is then?"

Shorty looked over. "Earth's round." They rode for a while. "Thought you'd been to school," Shorty said. Then, "Your cinch is loose."

They stopped to tighten it.

"What are we going to do today?" said Jimmy.

"Going to do!" said Shorty. "This is it."

"What do you mean?"

"I mean we're prospecting. We're looking for gold."

"Now?"

"Yes, goddamnit, now."

"Where are we going?"

Shorty gave him that blank stare again. "How the hell would I know?"

"I've got to meet my father on the seventh."

"I know."

They rode across the Surprise Canyon alluvial fan, along the west side of the range. Shorty rode without speaking for hours, his eyes on the naked hills. He stopped, studied the rock, passed the canteen, and entered the narrow defile at the mouth of Wonder Canyon. They passed between the close, high walls. The steep grade and soft gravel tired the burros; they got off and walked. Life became agony—again, Jimmy numbly noted—and he retreated to a dormant state. They plodded for an hour up the canyon. Shorty stopped in the shade and sat, with the canteen, against the south wall.

"No spring?" said Jimmy, looking for grass, half kidding and half in genuine surprise.

"Don't know," said Shorty. "No sign of one."

Jimmy stared at him. "You mean you haven't been here before?"

"I've been here," said Shorty. "But I don't remember. Besides, they come and go."

Jimmy looked around. He wasn't much interested in the search anyway, and as soon as he put it to himself where gold might be it seemed so hopeless that he had no interest at all. The canyon walls had diagonal stripes: red, brown, gray, white. Shorty was looking at the rock.

"Well," said Jimmy, "how do we find it?"

Shorty snorted and drank from the canteen.

"Walk backward with your eyes shut."

"What kind of talk is that?" laughed Jimmy. "You're the expert. Where's the gold?"

Shorty smiled. "Jim" he said, "you're going to think I'm kidding, but I'll be damned if I know." Shorty looked up at the walls. "Take here. Generally the Panamints are lifted on the west"—he tilted a hand—"and going up a west canyon you'll find deep igneous rock—like here—and further up metamorphic and sedimentary with igneous intrusions, and near the very top, pure sedimentary, sloping all the way down the east side to the Death Valley floor." He paused. "Now your big strikes have usually been in the intruded sediments about halfway up. Like Panamint City. That's probably because that zone is at the top of the igneous vein, and gold is a little flower that grows at the very top of its stalk."

Shorty seemed to be drifting off. He came back.

"Down here"—he waved across the canyon—"are some fine quartz veins, but we're deep down where they're likely barren." He paused again.

"Sounds like you're doing fine to me," said Jimmy.

"Only trouble is," said Shorty, "it doesn't work. We're as likely to find it here as there."

"I don't understand," said Jimmy.

"Nor do I," said Shorty, rising. "But by sundown we'll be millionaires. Let's go."

"Where?"

Shorty shrugged. "See that big quartz vein opposite? It may top out in the next side canyon."

They climbed up the steep canyon, leaving the burros behind, up the steep boulders of a dry watercourse choked with piñon trunks. They were tired and had to move slowly. Shorty studied the rock above and the gravel at their feet. He said it was becoming better country for a find—more metamorphic—but he saw no sign that the quartz would blossom above. Finally they came around a corner to the very back of the canyon. There Shorty pointed to a reddish rubble.

"Let's take a look," he said.

They went to the rock. Shorty said he couldn't remember its name, or where he'd seen a strike once in some rock like it, though he thought it had been in Nevada somewhere. He broke a rock apart with his hammer, studied it, pecked at it, scratched it with a penny, licked it. Jimmy could see nothing but black and gray splotches in soft red stone.

Finally Shorty ground the rock down with his pick and pulverized a few pieces, swept them into the pan, and added a little water from the canteen. He swished the pan, spilling water over the lip, added more water, removed the bigger pieces, swished, added water, swished. Something glittered at the joint of the pan. He gave another swish, placed a finger on the glitter and held the pan upside down. Then he brought it back and slowly turned his finger over. Two tiny yellow grains, rough and irregular, and several black specks, were stuck to his skin.

"Is that it?" said Jimmy, more than a little excited—maybe this would be a famous strike.

"No."

"What is it?"

Shorty didn't answer for a while. "Not sure. Maybe iron and pyrite."

"How do you know it's not gold?"

"Should be more hackly, and heavy. Didn't separate enough. Just ain't."

They rested for a while. Jimmy asked what would have happened if the specks were gold. Shorty said they'd be ten cents richer and in 1905 they might have lured five hundred men to the canyon and sold lots. The claims could have sold for eight hundred dollars. As it was, he said, it wasn't workable.

"Wouldn't have been the quartz vein anyway, I guess," said Jimmy.

"No. That never showed. This was just luck and feet." Jimmy began to wonder if Shorty was all right. Was it gold or not?

"Maybe we'll come across the quartz again higher up," Jimmy said.

Shorty smiled. Jimmy drank again. Shorty held the canteen. He said they'd have to go easy, that he wasn't sure of water in the canyon. Jimmy stared. They headed down.

That was the end of the day's excitement. They picked their way down, under and over uprooted pines and loose boulders, then turned up the main canyon, on foot and stringing the burros. Shorty knelt several times to look at the gravel in the drywash, and twice they clambered partway up the side walls to investigate outcrops, but Shorty never even put his pick to stone. The long hot afternoon wore on. Jimmy's knees turned to rubber. He began to stumble in the soft and irregular gravel of the wash. His mind drifted from gold to water, and he found himself studying plants instead of stone, searching for a telltale band of green beneath a ledge. He sniffed at the dry breeze. They walked on. Shorty stopped to let a rattler cross the wash. In late afternoon they were still nowhere in particular in a jumble of canyons on the west side of the ridge. It was not terribly hot, for they were high, at the bottom of the belt of piñon and juniper, but it was hot enough and there was no water.

Jimmy thought his tongue had begun to swell. He eyed barrel cacti the size of a canteen and pictured Shorty's knife cutting cactus flesh. He scanned the peaks above for lingering patches of snow. He watched for a sign of dampness in the sand, any glint of a tender green, any touch of delicacy in the foliage on the slopes above, but he found none. Every plant in sight was holed up, its precious water hidden in roots or guarded by fuzz and wax and thorns.

As a last resort he trusted the little old man ahead to lead him to another miracle—surely his agony was again only a set-up for relief—so his heart sank when Shorty pulled over to a flat above the wash, against the canyon wall, and began to unpack Daisy.

"Is this it?" Jimmy said.

"Don't you like it?" said Shorty.

"But . . ." Jimmy was speechless.

Shorty looked at him.

They laid out a camp. The canyon was in shadow, and the hot breeze that had followed them all afternoon began to change to a cool draft from above. Jimmy eyed the canteen. Shorty gave him two swallows. Jimmy gathered firewood while Shorty prepared bread and beans. Jimmy was miserable. His feet were worse than ever, he was exhausted, his headache was terrible, his tongue was wool, they didn't even have company, and it was a dry camp. Besides, the novelty had worn off. Just when he was beginning to get comfortable. The more he thought about it, the more it seemed to have been a rotten day— though "rotten" made him wince, the idea of squishy overripe wet fruit was so tantalizing; the day was much worse than that; "dried," he thought: withered, hard, and likely to last a long time.

Only a slice of the sunset was visible, directly above the canyon walls. They sat silently at their meal and took water in little sips.

"I don't want to be a prospector," Jimmy said.

Shorty didn't reply.

"It's a tough life," Jimmy said. He looked up.

Shorty was picking little rocks from the sand and lobbing them at a plant while the fire burned to coals. Jimmy watched him handle the smooth stones.

"Hey," said Jimmy, "that's the bush that reminds you of your father."

Shorty said nothing. Jimmy continued: "I don't get along too well with my old man. He's a bastard."

"Hold your tongue," Shorty snapped. Jimmy was amazed and hurt. He mumbled.

"Why should I?"

"Because he's your father," was the stern reply. It was just the tone that Jimmy couldn't stand at home.

"I get it," he said sarcastically. "Honor thy father." Then turning on Shorty: "That was never a very convincing argument to me."

"Honor thyself then," Shorty said, meeting his eyes. "Comes to the same thing."

Jimmy didn't speak. Shorty added quietly, "Though it puts it in a different light."

They finished their dinner. Shorty put the coffee on and fished in his pocket for tobacco.

"What did your father do?" Jimmy said.

Shorty seemed not to hear the question, then he said, "Like everyone, he had his reasons. He died at the back of this canyon." Shorty stared at the ground in front of him. "That's his pick."

Jimmy looked at the old tool worn smooth. "Really?"

"Sure." It was a lie. His father's pick—stolen in Denver— Shorty had sold for two dollars in San Francisco in 1879. He had bought another in Lone Pine in 1881, put on a new handle in 1884, a new head in 1887, another handle in 1890 and so on; the pick lying before him was many times removed from its ancestors and had no relation at all to the one he'd once carried from his house in Panamint City. Still, Shorty and the boy sat rapt.

Suddenly Shorty's body straightened as if he were possessed and his eyes grew bright. He pointed at one of the rocks beside Jimmy's leg.

"Know what that is, boy?" he demanded.

Jimmy was a little scared. He shook his head. Shorty sat straight, his arm rigid, while pictures swarmed in his mind—a chicken biscuit wadded into a mouth, a Bible illustration, a great stone beast stirring the desert sand—then he relaxed and dropped his arm. The boy grinned uneasily. Shorty turned to him and said gently:

"Stone." Shorty's eyes were wet. "Just stone. No need to fear it, though it's a hard thing. Nothing at all to fear." The boy felt thick, strong fingers squeeze his leg. The man turned to the fire and fiddled with the pot.

Stars came out. There was no moon. Shorty spoke without warning:

"That's a cereus beside you."

The boy peered at the plant. His thirst came back in a flash. Shorty had told him, back at the waterfall, that its bulb held a quart of water.

"Shall we dig it up?" Jimmy said.

Shorty turned to him with that blank look. After a second Shorty said, "It blooms during the night, once a year. By morning the flower is gone."

"Have you ever seen one bloom?"

"No."

"Have you ever waited up?"

"Once I fell asleep," he laughed to remember it, "and in the morning there were big white petals on the ground."

Shorty made coffee. His white mustache and white shirt stood out in the dusk.

"I lived five days once on the water of a Flora Morada." He laughed. "I'd been delirious. Saw a camel drinking at a pool and I knew I was nuts. I walked until I fell down. A guy found me and said, "You damned fool. That was no mirage. Hi Jolly turned his camel loose and he always finds water."

Shorty fiddled with the fire.

"Why is it so hard to find gold?" Jimmy said. The starlight made the dry wash ghostly white. The junipers were squat black dots here and there on the opposite slope. Jimmy looked around to check for cactus or flowers. There were none visible; he lay back.

"I don't really know," said Shorty. He turned to the bare wall at Jimmy's back. The rock bands were bent into gigantic swirls above their heads.

"I think it's the pressure," he said. "There's too much pressure." Shorty squatted on his heels and surveyed the canyon. "Each rock acts differently. Every canyon's different, every mile. It's a mess, really." Shorty rose and went to the wall. He ran his fingers over the swirls.

"What causes the pressure?" said Jimmy.

"Oh," he shrugged, "what causes the gold? Heat, pushing up, cold, falling down. Can't get away from it. Stone, sky. It's like the breathing of the earth." He held his hand still against the canyon wall. Jimmy heard the ringing in his ears.

They sipped coffee. Shorty lit a pipe, leaned back against a box, and puffed smoke into the blue shadows of the night. Jimmy sipped now and then from the canteen, thinking that if Shorty looked the other way he'd rip that cereus up by the roots. When he had finished his coffee Shorty piled more wood on the fire and began putting dough in a skillet.

"What's that?" said Jimmy.

"Treat. Biscuits."

Jimmy thought of sticky dough in his mouth. "Great," he said.

"The one trick," said Shorty, as he placed a tin plate over the skillet and banked the fire around a flat rock, "is to keep the pan moving."

Shorty built up the fire and arranged fresh sticks near at hand. Jimmy leaned back, away from the smoke. He said, "Tell me what it's like, Shorty, to make a big strike."

Shorty fiddled with the fire for a long time before speaking:

"Biggest strike I ever made wasn't Harrisburg, or Greenwater, or Rhyolite, or any other that you've heard of. It was up in the Last Chance Range."

"Why haven't I heard of it?"

"Well, that's part of the story." Shorty adjusted himself and began moving the pan over the rock. Jimmy settled down.

"The Last Chance Range," Shorty said, "is the worst range on earth. They're the lowest mountains around Death Valley. The driest and most barren. And it happens that they're also out of the way, up north of your Dad's claim, while the Valley is easiest entered from the middle or the south. Even the old prospectors are scared to go in, and there's never been much ore taken out."

"Why do they go in at all?" said Jimmy.

"Well," said Shorty, "where else are they gonna go?" Jimmy looked at him. Shorty resumed:

"The Last Chance isn't much of a mountain range. Not like the Panamints. Mainly low bare hills of mud and clay and sand baked hard and eroded. No trees at all. Hardly any bushes. The hills have a way of looking the same from all angles.

"Well, I'd been in the desert a long time before I went in with Shoshone Tommy, who used to live right over this ridge on a ranch in the next canyon north. Lived alone." Shorty paused. "Died a while back, before you were born."

"He lived on a ranch?"

"Yup. Nice one, too. Willows, grass, cattle, and a big log house."

"Sweet Jesus, in the next canyon? What are we doing here?" Jimmy sat up and looked for his boots.

Shorty stared. "Prospecting. Anyway, Tommy and I had been holed up at Tom Shaw's cave. Now there was a smart man. Found the damndest quartz vein you ever saw, tunneled in and hit a grotto, all hollowed out, size of a room. Walls were solid quartz speckled with gold. So he moved in an armchair and table and stove and poked a hole for the chimney and just sat there. Never mined the son of a bitch at all. That's where we were. You shoulda seen those walls by candlelight, flashing like stars.

Shorty fed the fire and shook the pan a bit.

"You know Tom Shaw had it made but he couldn't stand it. He sold that vein and got a ranch in California, but he still couldn't stay home. He lost everything at poker in Bodie, and went north. Died broke and alone in a cabin up by Disaster Peak, in Oregon."

He settled the pan on the coals.

"Well anyway, Hungry Bill had told Tommy about something in the Cottonwoods, and then we happened across a Paiute boy who'd been snakebit. We nursed him a few days, then took him back to his family in Sand Valley, just west of the Last Chance.

"The family was grateful, and his father said he'd repay us by giving us directions to buried Spanish treasure. It's an old Indian custom. Well, Tommy and I winked and watched him draw a map of the Last Chance on the ground. He drew for a long time—gullies, ravines, side ravines—and finally two pickle bushes and a 'Spanish Lady' in a line. That's all he would say. A 'Spanish Lady.' We didn't really remember the directions but what the hell, we figured. We had burros and had never been up that way. It was May.

"We went in the right gully, but after that I don't know what happened. I saw a streak on a hill one morning and got separated from Tommy. Luckily I had a burro. I couldn't even find my way back to camp. The clay was too hard to hold tracks. I wandered a few days, going by the sun, but I just seemed to get deeper into the range. I spent hours on hills and ridges, thinking I was bound to see Tommy cross somewhere, but nothing. I got low on water. My burro was weak. There wasn't any feed. In one whole day the only plant we saw was a single arrow weed, which we ate. Once we found a water hole with dead rats and slime. I strained it through my hat and drank, but the burro wouldn't touch it.

"Distances were deceptive, it took hours to get anywhere, and the glare would blind you if you looked straight out. It was white hot all day, and the canyons were too shallow to offer shade. I'd never seen anything like it. Chuckwallas were spitting on their toes to stay cool. Damndest place I've ever been, and me almost dead. When I had only a cupful of water left in the canteen, I knew I had to stop and wait."

"For what?" Jimmy said.

"Who knows?" Shorty shrugged. "Wait, not rest." He shifted. "I sat in a corner of a bare white gully that got a little shade in late afternoon. My burro lived one more day on two pickle bushes, then died. I lay still, taking a sip at dawn and at dusk, waiting. During the third day I noticed rusty patches running down the bottom of the ravine, twenty yards away. I hadn't even seen the color before. I waited until sundown and crawled over. Thought it might be a sign of water. Just beneath the mud was a quartz vein rotten with dark minerals. At first I thought it must be iron, but even crumbled in my fingers and dry-sifted in my hat it separated right out. A little spit and there were nuggets so soft I could press a fingernail in. It was a yellow streak, the real thing, just like the books say— 'lustrous, heavy, hackly, malleable, does not tarnish.'" Shorty intoned the words slowly, as if in a dream. "Weathered and enriched, running for two hundred yards inches below the clay, like a garden ripe for the picking." Shorty looked at his pipe. "The one to end your troubles for all time.

"I was so excited that I grabbed my canteen and crawled up to the top of the hill. No sign of Tommy. I went down the other side and I guess I passed out. When I came to, Tommy was beside me, with one burro and a little water and no food. He was in rough shape.

"I told him what I had found, right over the hill behind me. He walked slowly up. Then he went to the next hill, and the next. I was scared he'd get lost too. When he came back he said he had found nothing, not even my burro, except a strange stake: he held an old weathered board roughly carved into the head of a mother and child. The Spanish Lady. Then I remembered: my burro had eaten two pickle bushes the day before he died.

"As soon as I had strength I crawled back up the hill myself. Nothing looked familiar. I was sure of what I had seen, but I hadn't a clue as to where I'd been when I'd seen it. No trail to follow back. Tommy couldn't even find the hole where he'd pulled up the stake. There I was on hands and knees on that goddamn clay knowing we had to get out fast, if we could, while strong enough to crawl. If I was to see it again, if I even wanted to try, I knew I'd have to start all over. Tommy drove the stake into the clay, as a possible sign, in case we came again, or for someone else. We left.

"It was three or four days before we reached the Paiute camp in Sand Valley. The father of the boy wasn't there. An uncle greeted us. He was terribly sorry. He said the boy's father was crazy and hated white men and had made up the story. Too bad he hadn't been around to warn us. It wasn't the first time, he said. But there was no Spanish lady. The uncle chuckled and slapped his knee. He was just happy we had come out all right, he said. It's so terrible in there, he said. Even if you could find it—the old uncle was smiling—you couldn't bring it out."

"Then he fed us and gave us a sweat bath and danced and chanted the Paiute desert song—"

"Paiute desert song?"

"Yeah: 'The land is hungry. The ants are starving.'"

"That's it?"

"That's it. The Last Chance," said Shorty. He sighed. "The old uncle was probably right. You'd never get it out." Shorty shook the skillet. "Doesn't matter."

"What doesn't?"

"A wise man and his gold are soon parted."

Jimmy couldn't tell if Shorty was smiling. The fire crackled. Jimmy thought about the story of the Piss Man the night before. He said without thinking:

"You're not really looking for gold anymore, are you?"

"Not looking for gold!" Shorty leaned toward him like a tiny Nute Drake. "Not looking!" He stopped moving the pan over the fire as the boy, confused—confused by the day, the fruitless search, the dry camp, the changes of mood—searched in the firelight for the smile he hoped was there. "The Spaniards were looking for it, and old Asa Bennett was looking for it, and the Jayhawkers, and Will Alvord when he went back along their tracks was looking for what they'd found and lost, and old John Goler died looking for what he'd lost and my father too and Breyfogle was looking when he died and Hot Steam and even Tommy and old Paddy Mack—" Shorty's voice broke and he sat mute, choking, until he managed to swallow, and then he said:

"But I'll tell you one thing. I know this, boy, there's going to be one hell of a party in Paris before Shorty Harris dies."

Shorty felt dizzy. His eyes gleamed. For just a second a vein of certainty glittered in his mind. But it seemed to fade as he approached; wasn't even promising; he went through the motions saying to himself you never can tell; it crumbled to dust in his hand.

"We need some more wood," he said.

He didn't look up as the boy rose and disappeared into the night. Shorty did not want to be seen crying, and as he bent his head the desert air rushed to his aid, drying his tears as they slithered, here and there, from pore to pore, gathering in tiny pools, shrinking, leaving on his cheeks only faint traces of salt.

The boy came back with wood and sat down. He looked at the man holding the skillet. Jimmy was sure the biscuits had scorched black but he didn't dare speak.

Shorty awoke and withdrew the skillet. He lifted the lid. The six biscuits were golden brown. He set the pan down, lifted the lid of his box and produced strawberry jam.

"And lookee here," he said, whistled, and brought out four bottles of beer. Jimmy stared. Shorty opened two, handed him one and took a long drink. Jimmy guzzled.

"Anyway," said Shorty, leaning back with a biscuit and staring between the blank stone walls at a slice of star-specked sky, "living well is the best revenge."

They lay silent, eating and drinking. An owl glided noiselessly by.

"I wish I were an eagle," Jimmy said.

"But you're glad you're not a sage," laughed Shorty, thinking even if he is my grandson I cannot help him, any more than I can help myself: there is the agony of not feeling, too. Cold and distant, Shorty looked across the darkness at the boy as a monk, rising from his meditation, might look from the temple at one he had once loved, beyond the gates. "You can't get away," he said, and felt himself sliding back again from perfect peace—how tiring the movement had become—to weep for the mouse and the owl.

CHAPTER 29

July 6: The Western Isles

In Iona of my heart, Iona of my love,
Instead of monks' voices shall be lowing of cattle,
But ere the world come to an end
Iona shall be as it was.

—ST. COLUMBA, 521–597

"Get up," Shorty yelled, waving the rock and pointing. Even in the canyon Jimmy could tell that the yellow dawn had begun and the sky would soon be white with day. "Get up. Look here—this is float, good float, found it chasing Daisy upcanyon—" Shorty was so excited that he could hardly stand and soon they were stumbling up the wash—Shorty pointed out the placer—Jimmy pulling on his pants and stooping to tie his boots, when in midstride Shorty gave an inarticulate grunt, held his chest and sat bug-eyed on a rock.

"What's wrong?" said Jimmy, already knowing something was terribly wrong while Shorty sat still, holding his chest and staring unfocused into space. Shorty couldn't speak. Jimmy quickly caught Daisy; the others ran away. "I'll get help," he said. Shorty smiled. "Shouldn't I?" Jimmy said. Shorty nodded and reached for the boy's hand. Jimmy brought their only canteen to Shorty's side. Shorty shook his head. Jimmy considered a moment, then obeyed. "Dad will have his car at Panamint Springs," he said. Just before he passed out of sight with the jackass Jimmy turned, for a second, half a mile away. Neither waved. He left.

Shorty sat still, following him in his thoughts, wishing him luck—what more could he do?—thinking of the steps, the light, the land: now he would be born again out of the dark canyon—out of the immense stone gates of the Panamints—head, shoulders, limbs bursting into the brilliant light of the open valley and now step by step he would take direction, wrest it from the encompassing land, hour by hour placing one foot in front of another across a shimmering landscape that never changed, on and on, across the vast white blank of the valley floor at noon until—his lips and feet and head dry and cracked as the mud and the point of his journey forgotten, and forward become just the long moving wait of his kind—until suddenly a far-off mountain popped close enough to touch and the first yellow flower brought tears to his eyes as he paused, still, and looked. Then he would walk late, reveling in the cool light of stars, and early, dreading the dawn. By afternoon of the second day the last flower springing between two sun-blackened stones packed tight in a mosaic of orange and black rock spreading for miles, the last flower would bring no tears though every detail of its form would be branded into the brain that face to face with his father's brain would have no thoughts or feelings to relate, no stories to tell; the boy would stand mute before the anxious questions, declining water at first, until he uncovered a few words buried deep beneath the days. And by then he would know it was not help he could bring and feelings would begin to flow back, washing over his mind and tongue. And as they went putt-putt in the little black car down the road toward Ballarat, crunching on fresh celery, the boy's heart behind the windshield would be breaking with confusion though he would know that if he had to, he could do it again, for whatever that was worth, and feel nothing worse than pain.

By early afternoon Shorty felt much better. He was in the sun. He decided he would move upcanyon toward the center of the range, very slowly, to find water or at least shade. He left a cairn with a stick.

He knew that he was delirious. His legs were soft, the ground was soft. He walked as if on sponges or on skin. The earth, the light, his feet, his swelling thoughts seemed to be resilient surfaces that touched in mutual give and take. He pressed a foot down here, the earth gave way, the air pressed back into his nostrils, ears, and mouth. The ground rolled beneath him. He dared not stop or change his pace. He kept his rhythm and took whatever path seemed to give way to his feet.

Soon he came to a shaded ledge with moss. Beneath it water dripped. He sat down. The world about seemed chanced upon: sandy, clay, white granite, pebbles, and slate chips from the ledge at his back. Limestone over slate. The water dripped. The Mormon tea, bunchgrass and holly were green on the slope below. Findleria and yellow cliffrose lay against his shoulder. A rockwort bloomed with tiny white flowers. How they like limestone, he thought. He could hear the splatters from each drop within the rock, tinkling on the hollow slate, dripping down, down, down. A horsefly buzzed. A dove came, saw him, and left, confused. A few hours later two hummingbirds danced by. A tiny iridescent beetle, heedless of his foot, moved along its way like a sunset or all the flowers of the Panamints.

In the sunny rubble was a chunk of milky quartz. He stared at it until he felt himself melting in; then he yielded to the stone with weary resignation; he flowed into the glowing facets. Behind the tinkling of the water was a perfect silence in the changing of the light, and the soundless owl shadow of the swooping night unruffled by the moan of wind across the ridge, or the twittering sparrow down slope. A sharp stone pressed his hip but he did not move. He thought he would like to lick his lips but he could not get the message through. "Nobody's home," he thought. Then he felt his head contract and the quartz expand; his eyes glazed to an opaque white and hardened, until the windows of his soul looked like the stone that he no longer saw.

◆   ◆   ◆

Jimmy found his father and Jake at Panamint Springs. He thought that neither would believe that Shorty was Abigail's dad; instead he couldn't believe it—his father had set him up, had deliberately sent him off with his grandfather.

"Your mother wouldn't let me tell you he was still alive," his father said, "and besides, I wasn't sure the old man wanted to know you. How'd he take it?"

Jimmy shrugged. "He's seen worse."

Jimmy told them about the stones and their tracks across the mud flat. His father and Jake had been there a few years before. Jimmy's father chawed hard as a squirrel on a nut he can't crack.

"It sure looked level. Can't see what makes 'em go." He shrugged. "Those little son-of-a-bitchin' stones are weird."

The boy replied immediately: "They are beautiful."

His father laughed and winked at Jake. "Get him. Those stones are beautiful."

The boy whipped around.

"Drop dead," he hissed at his father. He felt his anger peak as a geyser at its topmost point momentarily stops with a stretched shudder—the opened fullest flower of midsummer—each drop poised, a pure translucent world within the sun, the sun within each giddy trembling drop.

The boy's hate reached its height, then—the moment of motionless perfection past—began the long descent that is the fate of all upwelling sources—sulfurous or sweet—until their several qualities mix and rest in the forgiving earth and sea. The boy's feelings seeped slowly into the muddy cracks of his father's face, cracks that widened as he began to chaw again and smile in genuine good humor. His father turned and walked as he spoke to Jake:

"A little panther," he said, smiling as he watched the crouched black eyes relax. "Damned if we ain't cornered a little panther."

Jake moved too. "You'll get over it. Where's your grandpa Harris?"

Without looking up the boy waved toward the Panamints—beyond the dazzling salt flat, beyond the wrinkled red-brown foothills, canyoned ghost towns, abandoned mines, beyond the middle slopes tinted by piñon pine toward the distant snowfields splotching the upper ridges and summit humps with dazzle as bright as the salt drawn, leaked and leached from their heights to the flat far below; sandwiched between two dazzling wastes he waved toward that height where in his mind the body of a man lay like a stone at the end of its upward track. "Up there," he said.

Shorty was not dead, not quite. They carried him out. On the way Jimmy pointed to the pocket with the float and said it was pretty rich. His father was excited.

"Have you staked?" he said.

"Naw," said Jimmy. "It's just a placer. You can have it if you want."

♦ ♦ ♦

They took Shorty to his friend's cabin in the Sierra Nevada above Lone Pine. There between crisp sheets Shorty lay and looked across the varnished floors, out the window, to green grass and pines.

Jimmy, his father, and Jake returned to Los Angeles. Jimmy came back to the Lone Pine cabin three days later with his mother. Abigail stood in the doorway, a white-haired, black-eyed woman of sixty-five. She and Shorty looked a lot alike.

"Why did you leave us?" she said after an hour of sitting beside him.

"Oh Abby," Shorty said, rolling his head to the side to look at her. "I wasn't much good for this world."

She looked out at the desert stretching east, far below. "You didn't leave us for a better one."

He grinned. They were silent awhile. "Do you still sing?" he asked.

"Yes," she smiled, "all my life. But my voice cracks now. They let me stand in back." She laughed and her eyes flashed. "But I can read better than anyone."

"I met Puccini."

"What?" She dropped his hand and sat back as if to reprove an old man for deathbed lies.

"No, it's true. I met Puccini in New York. In 1910. After the opening of *The Girl of the Golden West*."

"The world premiere?"

"You got it."

"You were there?"

"In his box. I was rich after Harrisburg. Went east twice."

"What did you do, run up and shake his hand?"

"No, we had dinner."

"Oh, stop it, Shorty, or Dad, or whoever you are."

"It's true. Balasco and I were friends. He wrote the play, you know. He was there and I looked him up, 'cause I knew he was from San Francisco. He'd acted in the gold camps—Hell, I'd seen him do Othello in Virginia City—so I looked him up. The opera's true. Balasco's father hid a thief from the sheriff in a mining camp, I forget where. Jesus, we drank for three days"—Shorty sat up, waving his hands—"do you know he did a fifteen-minute light show in the middle of *Butterfly*? The man's crazy. Well, Puccini was grateful enough. They hated *Butterfly* in Milan, and loved it over here. So, you know, he did Balasco's play, and opened it in New York, and Balasco got me seats. I guess that little son of a bitch from the gold camps showed Puccini how it's done." Shorty beamed with pride. "And that night Balasco, Puccini and I went out to dinner."

She put her hands together, then up to her face, and rocked back and forth. "What did you say to him?"

"Hell, I told him I *liked* those Jap scales in *Butterfly* and he shouldn't worry and oughta write whatever the hell he wanted.

'Quante stella' may be corny, but it couldn't be worse than elephants onstage."

"Oh, Shorty," she was laughing with tears running down her face. "What did *he* say?"

"He seemed interested, and said, 'What do you do, Mr. Harris?' Balasco had told him I was in investments, so I said, 'I'm in the business of chasing rainbows.' He looked puzzled, so I told him, 'I walk around the damn desert with a damn jackass most of the time. Looking for gold.'"

"I don't believe it."

"We had a lot more pinot noir, and by the end of the evening he put his arm on my shoulder and said he oughta do an opera on me!" Shorty sank back. "He should, too. But it better be fast."

"Oh, Shorty." She took his hand. Jimmy, watching, thought this is the way he plays for tourists; but it's real.

"Anyway," he said, turning toward her, quieter now, "I gave you Mozart. If I'd stayed I couldn't have given more."

She shook her head. "I was sure mad at you, you crusty old bastard."

"My father was worse."

She laughed. "You're incorrigible."

He thought about that awhile. "Cannot be corrected, in the sense of improved. I think you're right."

That afternoon his daughter and grandson had to return to L.A. "Go," he said. "Go go go." He looked away as he held out his hand.

He lay there another day before he died. They found the note folded on his breast:

Bury me beside Jim Dayton in the valley we loved. Above me write, "Here lies Shorty Harris, a single blanket jackass prospector."

His friends buried him according to his wishes, there by Jim Dayton and the borax works and Bennett's long camp on the floor of Death Valley. They placed his pick, hammer, and blanket in his grave and hastened, as he had thirty-five years before, to the shelter of the ranch at Furnace Creek. About the grave, the desert lay silent in the midday stillness of July. On the creosote bush the waxen leaves withdrew and turned their edges to the sun; the mesquite roots strained downward for the wayward Amargosa; seeds and eggs waited—a year, two years, three—for rain, while beneath the sand the fragile mice and reptiles hid, waiting for gracious darkness. For night or rain they waited, for a cloud or the turning away of the earth, for the blessed obscuring of the sun that would bring life to the naked edge of earth and sky.

Epilogue

Several stories about Shorty's burial are blowing around the Basin: That prospectors appeared from canyons all over the region to stand by his grave, some from Utah and beyond, that three women, one in red taffeta, came from Las Vegas in an automobile, and that the heat was so intense the grave could not be properly dug and was never finished, so that he was buried sitting up, or on a slant, or standing. That Sam Johnson's ceremony consisted of three words: "Dust to dust."

But the strangest story is the one told in Goldfield a few months after his death, a story that spread rapidly among he oldest prospectors, that he was never buried at all, or if he was, that now he could not be found.

The tale took several forms, but most agreed that Stump Mallis, a friend of Shorty's from Pioche who had reason to believe that Shorty had made a map of the Lost Last Chance, dug him up, or at least tried, convinced that the map was hidden on his person—hadn't he a pen and paper, at the last, to make a note?—but had found the grave empty. Some say the shallow grave had been robbed by coyotes, and that only a few scraps of clothes and the tools remained; some say the groundwater in Death Valley is so acidic that it would eat up a body in a week; some say the grave connects to the Amargosa, which rose, sucked down the body and swept it away; some say Mallis was so disgusted by what he found, or ashamed, that he invented the tale to take attention off the act. Some say he found the map and just wanted to throw people off his tracks.

Whatever the truth, the story spread across Nevada and found intense audiences in the corners of dark saloons where men gathered to drink and talk of Tonopah and Goldfield, Greenwater, Harrisburg, Shorty and the Bullfrog—he ordered three trainloads of eggs, milk, and Irish whiskey—he sold out for eight hundred dollars—he was behind every major strike, one way or another— he could smell gold—Shorty and the Lost Last Chance—and whether he had found it and if he had made a map; where men gathered to talk forever of what they had almost found or had found and lost or had found and given away up there in Three Lakes Valley (dry) or Green Springs Valley (dry) or Willow Tree Valley (dry) or Deep Springs Paradise Valley (dry) or in the range or valley or canyon just beyond which hasn't got a name but if they ever get just a little bit of time and a stake they're going up to this ledge where the rotted quartz crumbles in your hand, ripe as fruit on the tree, soft and heavy with gold. An old man spits in the bucket. The embers fall in the potbelly stove.

♦ ♦ ♦

Not only the old men. The last time I walked into Panamint City, in 1979, I was surprised to find it inhabited again. As I rounded a rock at the mouth of Water Canyon I met a boy, perhaps eight years old. His dungarees were patched: on one knee, a square of red-checked wool from an old hunting shirt; on the other, a triangular piece of bright yellow fabric, and pasted to it, a plastic butterfly. He had long hair. He was tugging on a rope attached to two long timbers; across the timbers, which served as skids, were two-by-fours, odd sections of pipe, steel cables and a sheet of corrugated tin. He was dragging the load down the path. Upcanyon were the three abandoned cabins he had apparently raided. He looked up and straightened. The rope went slack.

"Can I help you?" I said, for the load must have been three times his weight.

"No," he said, and stood still, watching me.

I turned the corner and entered the ruins of Panamint City.

My husky sniffed; the hairs rose on his spine; he walked on eggshells around three large, silent, bristling dogs. Behind them I noticed clear plastic on the windows of a wooden cabin. A man sat on the porch, looking my way. He rose, came down the steps, and approached, calling softly to the dogs. "Hardrocks, Cancer." Another man appeared from a garden to my right, and another, uphill, was standing by a juniper. They moved slowly. The canyon was quiet, the air still. The man from the porch was young—in his late twenties, very thin, with long hair and extraordinarily deep-set black eyes. He said nothing, though his manner was pleasant. He and the others—they were all young and long-haired—reached up and slipped my pack from my wet shoulders. They walked toward the cabin with my gear.

"The dogs . . ." I said.

He turned—"They'll work it out"—and led the way. He disappeared into the cabin. I blinked and entered. Slowly my eyes adjusted: four rough cut bunk beds, a red throw rug; a potbelly stove, books and candles at one end; at the other end a kitchen, a girl—she turned around—startlingly beautiful; plump, glowing skin. She held a knife in one hand and an onion in the other. Her eyes glistened. Behind her was a "Miraculous" cookstove, old, black, one leg bound with wire, with a yellowed temperature dial and white porcelain handles on the doors. A chipped enamel sink set in two-by-fours barely touched her stomach. Plastic pipes from above. Dirty dishes. Beans, fried vegetables, a sweet sauce—the room was full of scents. An iron pot rattled and bubbled on the stove; the steam disappeared into the thirsty air—my shirt was already dry across the shoulders. They offered me the only chair. I pulled off my boots and put them with the others by the door. The boy I'd seen on the path walked in holding his boots, washed, picked up a thick folder—Verdi Requiem Tenor Score—sat down in the corner, opened the folder and bent over it, as if he were my lost cousin. I wanted to tell him something, but what?

He had come just in time for dinner, which we ate seated on the living room floor. I asked what brought them there. They had been in the canyon two, three years in the case of Bill—Bill Bradford, I had to smile—their leader. I learned that all together about four men and three women and Bradford's son, the musical prodigy—and at times as many as fifteen people—lived in a number of stone and wood cabins scattered through the piñon and juniper that in the ninety years since the flood had taken hold again in the sandy soil of the hillside. Only the one cabin had a full kitchen and running water, and they gathered in the evenings for meals. They shared a large garden. We exchanged notes on the flow of the spring, the cost of plastic pipe, cold frames, and the single question, in this vast democracy, that links coast to coast: when did you bring in the tomatoes?

They finally asked, in turn, what I was doing in the desert. I replied that I was a retired professor of history and the grandson of Shorty Harris. They looked at me in silence, and something more. "Have you heard of him?" I asked. "He used to live here," said Bradford, staring at the wall. Then he suddenly looked right through me, his deep-set eyes on fire: "His packsaddle is in Ballarat."

"Yes," I replied. "I've seen it. I was with him there in 1934." Again, a stunned silence.

I was tired and turned in after dinner. They had made the best bed for me.

♦ ♦ ♦

"Seen the Stewart Wonder Mine?" Bradford was breaking eggs. I handed him one still warm from the belly of the hen.

Hardly had we started up the slope when I saw Big Red, dark khakis, T-shirt, massive red arms crossed on his chest. He was standing upslope in the junipers, watching us. Behind him was a tar paper shack and chimney smoke.

"Do you know that guy?" Bradford said, watching me.

"I met him once in Ballarat," I replied. "Ten years ago. He's the one with Shorty's saddle."

"He says your grandfather is the greatest man that ever lived."

"I know."

"Don't you like that?"

"The need to say it is a stupid need."

"He works a claim," said Bradford. "Rest of the time he sits in that cabin firing a pistol at the wall."

◆ ◆ ◆

Five of us went up to the old mine, there since Shorty's child-hood. Bradford, his son, two friends, and myself. As we walked they talked about the new Panamint City. John and Cathy, the cook, lived together up the hill; Tom was alone at the moment because his wife of the year before was at the University of Washington studying sculpture with my old friend Dupen. Bradford had been married and had two sons: one eight, with him, and one five, with his ex-wife, in Chile with the Peace Corps. Bradford and two others had been in New Mexico and Arizona; there they had moved from commune to commune, searching for a place with "the right feel." They thought for a while that things looked promising near Phoenix, building Zomes, but Baer, whom Bradford knew, "got off on a family trip" and into manufacturing his freon-gas solar-heater venetian blinds, and what Bradford wanted was a little closer to the land, "back to our roots," so after wandering here and there they had found Surprise Canyon. Bradford called it "Atascadero." By working mining claims they could live within the law, on the land.

I was surprised. What could they get from the mines? Bradford turned and looked at me: a long, hollow-eyed look.

We turned a corner in the trail and almost walked into a huge quartz vein, six feet wide and ten feet high. A tunnel led straight into its mouth. The quartz was stunningly pure, an even, dull milky white pricked everywhere with tiny glints of light.

"Stewart-Wonder Mine," he said.

"Can you still get anything out of it?" I asked.

He stepped inside and ran his hand over the wall. Here and there were blue and green and black splotches.

"Azurite, malachite, argentite."

"Silver sulfide," I said.

"Right." His voice was soft. He picked up a black-and-white chunk and touched the open spot of ore.

"Greatest blossom in the southwest."

I watched him study the crevice in the stone, a dark splotch in a mass of white. Sandals, Levis, a white Indian corta open at his hairy chest, chiseled lips and nose, high forehead. But against that white skin his black eyes glowed like coals on ice, sinking into his brain; white and gray frizzled hairs curled up from his head.

I looked at his son. He too was watching his father. The wind had risen. Dust blew up from the trail, filling the air with a silver sheen.

We took shelter deeper in the mine. Bradford's two companions and his son sat against the wall. Bradford started laughing, unaccountably. "Can we get anything?" He laughed and ran his hands over the wall. His voice rose. I had no idea, he said, how much was left in the walls, in the rubble. Picked over—high-graded—a hand operation could net six thousand dollars in this shaft alone, and what's more—he leaned close—he'd been reading books and studying stone—fine spit touched my cheek like the first scent of rain—and he thought it very likely that this same vein would crop up to the north, in Wonder Canyon—I thought of the Sardine and of Shorty's father, my great-grandfather, who blew himself up a century before in Wonder Canyon, not a half-mile away—suddenly Bradford stopped in the middle of a gust of wind and looked to one side. He pulled his face back and straightened up. His friends looked down at the milky stone floor of the tunnel, up at the milky roof. His son did not look away. The wind moaned in gusts. Dust swirled in.

Bradford's lips were tightly pressed. He turned and faced the tunnel mouth. Slowly, deliberately, he raised his arms above his head and leaned over backward until his face, upside down, grotesquely misshapen, wild hair falling, stared past mine without recognition. Then he turned and sank slowly into a full lotus position, facing back into the tunnel. The wind groaned. The light had softened to a diffuse yellow white. Seated full lotus in the pale tunnel, his white shirt ruffled by the wind, in the midst of a quartz glow that smothered all shadows and fine distinctions, he looked like an ashen Sikh or a ghost, some dead ancestor of himself entombed or enlightened or in some way free at last in the glowing tunnel of the mine.

We waited a long time. The wind was rising. When we walked out of the tunnel high streamers of dust were floating above the peaks. In for a blow. We hiked back quickly. No one spoke. Big Red was gone; his door was shut. We stopped to gather cattails at the spring. We were back by midafternoon, the door closed tightly behind us. The sand hit the plastic windows like hail. We arranged our boots against the wall. Bradford sat in the middle of the floor and stared at the stove. In the corner his boy spread the Requiem over the plastic butterfly on his knee. One of the young men lay on a bunk reading, while the other leaned against the wall and played a flute. I wondered if it bothered the boy. He didn't seem to notice.

I slid off the chair, stretched my aching spine on the floor and watched the yellow afternoon light stream through a knot hole, fill with dust, and creep across the rough posts and dark lapped boards of the wall.

After dinner they brought out wine, which we drank from the bottle through cheesecloth tied around the neck. Puffs of dust came through the cracks and settled, turning the red rug gray. When the plastic blew out of the window over the sink we nailed a blanket up. The broken plastic snapped and rattled outside. A little marijuana, which was not my custom; I remembered accepting the curdled milk, oily soup and resinous wine of hospitable Greeks.

Soon my weariness melted into a full stomach and warm glow. Against the storm the flute played, now joined by a soft but very bright steel-stringed guitar, and the evening, passing through the shutter slits and plastic windows and the glasses by the sink, broke into colors, disassembled from a hardened whole into a spectrum, like the rainbow feather edge of tree trunks in a mist.

Later, when another guitar and harmonica appeared, we sang, mostly sweet sad tunes: folk songs of dead love, Baptist hymns of hope and grace amazing and forlorn, cowboy vigils and laments, "Across the Wide Missouri." Finally I crawled into an upper bunk. A guitar and lone voice lingered, the voice soft, the fingers light and sure:

I am a pilgrim
And a stranger
Just traveling through
This wearisome land.
But I got a home in
That yonder city
And it's not—Good Lordy and it's not—
Not made by hand.

It was what they had sung—the Bennetts, the Jayhawkers in 1849, thinking they were passing through, thinking this wasn't their home. The candle went out. A dim, dust-yellowed shaft of moonlight hung between the plastic windows and the floor. The guitar rang as it was placed in the case. The squeak of a bunk, the rustle of a body turning over, a sigh. A gust of wind shook the cabin; plastic rattled and snapped. Another of their songs hung motionless in my head: "There is a town in North Ontario . . . and in my mind I still need a place to go . . . Yellow moon upon the rise . . . leave us helpless, helpless, helpless."

In the morning the storm seemed to let up, and since I had duties, I got ready to leave. It was only four miles downwind to my car;

Shorty had seen the first putt-putts, and now my car was parked in a valley being surveyed for the MX missile system. They gave me a hearty breakfast—though sandy—lifted the pack to my back and tied the bandanna over my nose and mouth.

We shook hands. I remember the boy watching black-eyed from the corner where he sat with the Kyrie Eleison open on his knee. They opened the door and pushed me out.

A tumbleweed bounced off my legs. The little sand verbena at the foot of the steps had lost its white petals. I called my dog. He came around the corner, eyes squinting, fur flattened, going wherever we were going to get out of that wind. He was a good dog.

We started down the narrowing canyon. Stone closed in above our heads. The wind moved on us from behind. Fresh sand was drifting across the road. A tumbleweed bounced off my back, nearly knocking me over. I pitched against the canyon wall, cheek pressed to the stone. It was cold and sharp and crumbling. Another old ocean bed, coming apart. The song swelled inside of its own accord, as if its mournful voice could plug the widening chinks, ears and eyes and nose and mouth, that let in sand.

Blue blue windows behind the stars,
Yellow moon on the rise,
Big birds flying across the sky
Throwing shadows on our eyes
Leave us helpless, helpless, helpless . . .

At my back the wind came down the canyon like breath through a flute, whistling across the broken lips of rock and sucking from each cave its sound.

♦ ♦ ♦

When I got home, I gave the dog water. The books and papers were piled high on my desk—I had been writing an article on early settlers—and Moses Austin's journal was still open on top of the pile:

Ask these Pilgrims what they expect when they git to Kentuckey the Answer is Land. have you any. No, but I expect I can git it. have you any thing to pay for land, No. did you Ever see the Country. No but Every Body says its good land. can any thing be more Absurd than the Conduct of man, here is hundreds Travelling hundred of Miles, they Know not for what Nor Whither, except its to Kentucky, passing land almost as good and easy obtain.d, the Proprietors of which would gladly give on any terms, but it will not do its not Kentuckey its not the Promis.d land its not the goodly inheratence the land of Milk and Honey. and when arriv'd at this Heaven in Idea what do they find? a goodly land I will allow but to them forbiden Land. exausted and worn down with distress and disappointment they are at last Oblig.d to become hewers of wood and Drawers of water.

—MOSES AUSTIN, 1796